J. Pettigre

The Physiology of the Circulation in Plants, in the Lower Animals, and in Man

J. Pettigrew

The Physiology of the Circulation in Plants, in the Lower Animals, and in Man

Reprint of the original, first published in 1874.

1st Edition 2024 | ISBN: 978-3-36884-860-6

Verlag (Publisher): Outlook Verlag GmbH, Zeilweg 44, 60439 Frankfurt, Deutschland
Vertretungsberechtigt (Authorized to represent): E. Roepke, Zeilweg 44, 60439 Frankfurt, Deutschland
Druck (Print): Books on Demand GmbH, In de Tarpen 42, 22848 Norderstedt, Deutschland

THE

PHYSIOLOGY OF THE CIRCULATION

IN PLANTS, IN THE LOWER ANIMALS,

AND IN MAN:

*BEING A COURSE OF LECTURES DELIVERED AT THE SURGEONS' HALL TO THE
PRESIDENT, FELLOWS, ETC., OF THE ROYAL COLLEGE OF SURGEONS
OF EDINBURGH, IN THE SUMMER OF 1872.*

BY

J. BELL PETTIGREW, M.D., F.R.S., F.R.S.E., F.R.C.P.E.

FELLOW OF THE BOTANICAL, MEDICO-CHIRURGICAL, AND OTHER SOCIETIES;
LECTURER ON PHYSIOLOGY AT SURGEONS' HALL, EDINBURGH;
EXAMINER IN PHYSIOLOGY TO THE ROYAL COLLEGE OF PHYSICIANS, EDINBURGH;
PATHOLOGIST TO THE ROYAL INFIRMARY OF EDINBURGH; &c., &c., &c.

Illustrated by One Hundred and Fifty Engravings on Wood.

London

MACMILLAN AND CO.

1874

PREFACE.

In the present volume I have endeavoured to give a comprehensive account of the Circulation and the apparatus by which it is effected in Plants, in the Lower Animals, and in Man. I have discussed the subject in its totality, in the hope that those parts of the circulation which appeared obscure in the higher animals might be simplified by comparing them with similar parts in the lower animals and in plants. This mode of treatment involves details, but these, I trust, will be found also to add additional interest. I have introduced a large number of drawings in place of the diagrams originally employed in illustrating the Course, in order to efface in some measure the traces of lecturing. I have not, however, found time to recast or alter the Lectures in any way, so that, with the exception of a few verbal corrections, they appear in their original form. This circumstance will not, I trust, detract from their usefulness.

My best thanks are due to my friend Mr. Archibald Constable for having relieved me of the labour of reading the proofs for press.

Royal College of Surgeons of Edinburgh,
April, 1874.

CONTENTS.

INTRODUCTION.

CIRCULATION IN PLANTS.

CIRCULATION IN ANIMALS (INVERTEBRATA).

THE VALVES OF THE VASCULAR SYSTEM.

THE GANGLIA AND NERVES OF THE HEART, AND THEIR CONNEXION WITH THE CEREBRO-SPINAL AND SYMPATHETIC SYSTEMS IN MAMMALIA.

THE PHYSIOLOGY OF THE CIRCULATION
IN PLANTS, IN THE LOWER ANIMALS,
AND IN MAN.

INTRODUCTION.

MR. PRESIDENT AND GENTLEMEN,—The circulation of the blood forms such an important factor in the animal economy that I feel I need offer no apology for making it the subject of the present lectures. The heart, its nerves, blood-vessels, and valves, supply a theme of unusual interest not only to the anatomist and physiologist, but also to the practitioner, especially since the introduction of the stethoscope. In order to give an intelligible account of the circulation, and the apparatus by which it is effected in man, it will be necessary to avail myself of whatever collateral information is within reach. This will lead me to speak at more or less length of the so-called circulation in plants—of the circulation in the lower animals, and in the foetus.

By adopting this method I hope to be able to lead up to the complex circulation as it exists in man, by a series of steps, which, when taken together, will form a sort of royal road to the goal at which we would ultimately arrive. The time devoted to the journey will not be lost if I succeed in placing before you the links (fearfully and wonderfully made) of a chain, on the integrity of which life itself may be said to depend. In some cases we shall find only one link of the chain present; in others, two; in others, three; and

B

so on until we arrive at a degree of differentiation and completeness which, while it commands the reverence, must elicit the admiration of every one who reflects. In the human circulation nearly all the links are present, and it is only by a knowledge of these, as they exist in the lower grades of life, that we can hope to put them in their proper places, when we come to generalise. In the plant and medusa there is no trace either of a heart or pulsatile vessel. In the insect the heart is absent, but a pulsatile vessel makes its appearance. In the fish a heart, consisting of two cavities, is found. In the serpent those cavities are increased to three ; and in birds and mammals to four.

The number of the cavities depends to a certain extent on the nature of the respiration, and this in its turn modifies the temperature of the blood. In the fish breathing is effected, and the blood aerated, by the gills; one cavity (the auricle) receiving the blood from the system ; the other (the ventricle) forcing it directly into the gills, and, through them, indirectly into the system. In the serpent breathing is effected, and the blood aerated, by the aid of lungs ; two cavities (the auricles) receiving the blood from the lungs and from the system ; one cavity (the ventricle) forcing it through the lungs and through the system. In the reptile the circulation is of a mixed character, the arterial and venous blood blending in the ventricle of the heart. In the bird and mammal the heart consists of four cavities—two auricles and two ventricles; the auricles receiving the blood from the system and from the lungs ; the ventricles propelling the blood through the lungs and through the system. This object is attained by a cross circulation—the right auricle receiving venous or dark blood, the left auricle arterial or bright red blood ; the right ventricle propelling venous or dark blood, the left one arterial or bright blood. The differentiation observable in the cavities of the heart is preceded by a similar differentiation in the channels and vessels through which the nutritious juices flow ; the elaboration of the heart and vessels necessitating the presence of valves, which vary in number according to the complexity of the circulatory apparatus. ' In the lowest organised plants, such as the fungi, algae, etc., and in the lower classes of animals, as the polypi, actiniae, and a great part of the intestinal worms, the nutritious materials are transmitted through their substance, without any distinct canals or tubes; while in the higher classes of plants, and in the medusae, etc., among animals, vessels are present, but these are unprovided with any pulsatory cavities. In the articulated animals the vessels are still without any pulsatory cavities, but to make up for the deficiency the dorsal vessel itself has a distinct movement of contraction and relaxation [1].'

With regard to the valves, it may be stated that they are only found in well-formed vessels, and at the orifices of canals or cavities having a definite structure. They are so placed that they compel the circulating fluid always to move in the same direction. They are consequently not found in plants, for in these, as will be shown presently, the nutritious saps at one period of the year flow from below upwards, and at another, from above downwards. A cross circulation, *i. e.* a circulation across the stem, and a circulation within the cells of the plant, are likewise to be made out. The valves vary in number and in the complexity of their structure. In the veins they usually consist of from one to four segments. In the arteries, as a rule, they consist of three segments [2]. In the heart they may vary from two to three, and to these as many intermediate segments may be added. The number, however, may greatly exceed this, for in the bulbus arteriosus of the American devil-fish (cephalopterus giorna) we find as many as thirty-six segments. The valves may be placed within comparatively unyielding structures, as the fibrous rings found at the beginning of the pulmonary artery and aorta of the mammal; or they may be placed within yielding and actively moving structures, as the bulbus arteriosus of the fish, and the base of the ventricles of the bird and mammal. In the former case the structure of the segments is comparatively simple, and their action to a great extent mechanical; in the latter case the structure of the segments is more complex, the segments

---

[1] Cyc. of Anat. and Phys., art. ' Heart.' By Dr. John Reid, p. 577.

[2] The valves of the arteries in the mammalian adult are confined to the origins of the pulmonary artery and aorta. They are termed semilunar from their shape. It happens occasionally that only two segments are present, the number increasing at times to four. In such cases a segment may be absorbed or divided into two by disease. It ought to be observed that rudimentary valves are found in the umbilical arteries. These are, strictly speaking, foetal structures.

being provided with tendinous chords which vary in length, strength, and direction. The tendinous chords are necessary to restrain the action of the segments within certain limits, and to co-ordinate the movements of the segments with the movements of the structures within which they are placed—the bulbus arteriosus and ventricle opening and closing alternately. The forces engaged in carrying on the circulation increase in direct proportion to the number and complexity of the hearts, vessels, and valves, and the number and variety of the tissues to be nourished. It is with a view to reducing those structures and forces to their simplest expression, that I propose to treat the subject of the circulation comparatively. What is true of the particular is necessarily true of the general; and if we succeed in comprehending a simple structure, and in following a simple action, the knowledge acquired will greatly assist us in comprehending complex structures and combined actions. It is comparatively an easy matter to understand a purely mechanical act. Here the forces and resistances can be appreciated with something like mathematical accuracy. It is comparatively a very difficult matter to understand a vito-mechanical act, for in this case we are never exactly sure what is vital and what vito-mechanical. This is especially true of the circulation, where we have on some occasions to deal with rigid tubes and cavities, such as exist in plants, and which are incapable of receiving an impulse from without ; while in others, we have to deal with flexible elastic tubes and cavities, such as are found in animals, and which are not only capable of receiving an impulse, but of storing up the impulse or power communicated, and of expending it as required.

If to the foregoing we add that the action of muscles,—which, in animals, are the chief motors in the circulation,—is comparatively unknown, we conclude a list of difficulties which it will require time, patience, and perseverance to overcome. These difficulties were present in force to the ancients, as a brief *résumé* of the history of the circulation will show.

Epitome of the History of the Circulation.—We are in the habit, and very properly, of attributing the discovery of the circulation to the illustrious Harvey. It ought, however, not to be forgotten that there were many pioneers in this field before Harvey. The Chinese, for example, believed that the circulation of the vital heat and radical humours commenced at three o'clock in the morning, reached the lungs in the course of the day, and terminated in the liver at the end of twenty-four hours. This was a very vague and visionary notion of the circulation certainly; still, it embodied the idea of fluids circulating within the body. The first rational attempt at unravelling this great mystery was made in the time of Hippocrates and Aristotle. It consisted of a description, apparently from dissection, of the principal blood-vessels. Galen, towards the end of the second century, described the course of the blood-vessels in many of the lower animals, and appears to have known the structure and uses of the foramen ovale in the foetus, and that the arteries and veins anastomosed. He was also cognizant of the fact that the arteries contained blood, and described them as arising from the heart; the veins, in his opinion, arising from the liver. He thought that the blood passed through the septum of the heart; and this is actually true of the heart of the serpent. Neither Hippocrates, Aristotle, nor Galen, however, was aware that the blood circulated, *i.e.* started from one point and returned to the same point after making the circuit of the body. Galen believed that the blood simply oscillated; and it is a curious circumstance that, in plants and some of the lower animals, this is what actually occurs.

Mr. Herbert Spencer, for instance, states that in plants the saps ascend and descend in the same vessels, and that their movements are interrupted at irregular intervals. Johannes Müller, in like manner, affirms that in the leech the blood-vessels on one side of the body contract and force the blood into those of the other and opposite side, and that these in turn contract and force it back again, the blood being made to oscillate transversely across the animal. The celebrated Vesalius examined the subject of the circulation afresh in 1542. He pointed out the difference between the arteries and veins, and showed that the veins and the heart contained valves. He also explained that the arterial pulse depended upon the systole of the heart. Here was a decided advance. Servetus, that martyr to science,[1] had, as early as 1531, actually

---

[1] Servetus fell a victim to religious persecution, and was cruelly burned alive at Geneva in 1553.

described a pulmonic circulation. He says, Whereas, in the
adult, the vital spirit (blood) cannot pass from the right
auricle into the left, because of the imperforate nature of
the auricular septum, it must go through the lungs, where
it is changed, *i.e.* undergoes a transformation by coming in
contact with the vital spirit which resides in the air, after
which it returns to the heart. Servetus expressed his belief
that the pulmonary artery and vein had some other function
than that of nourishing the lungs—an inference deduced from
their comparatively large size.

Caesalpinus, in 1583, described the pulmonic circulation
more carefully than Servetus had done, and showed that he
had some knowledge of a double circulation. Nor did the
foetal circulation, with its several peculiarities, escape the lynx
eyes of the anatomists of the sixteenth century. Galen, as
has been pointed out, had a knowledge of the foramen ovale.
He had also a partial knowledge of the ductus arteriosus.
The ductus arteriosus was carefully described by Fallopius,
Aranzii, and Vesalius. The last observer likewise discovered
the ductus venosus, which was figured by Fabricius and
Eustachius. It was reserved however for the immortal
Harvey to place the coping-stone on the magnificent edifice
of the circulation, and to this philosopher we owe our knowledge of the circulation in its entirety, and as at present accepted. Harvey was the apt pupil of a celebrated master.
He studied under the famous Fabricius of Padua, for the
protracted period of six years, viz. from 1596 to 1602.
Fabricius, although entirely ignorant of the circulation as
subsequently developed and explained by Harvey, had, for-
tunately for Harvey, an intimate knowledge of the valves of
the veins, of which he published an account in 1603. From
Fabricius then the illustrious Harvey derived much of that
information which enabled him to astonish the world by his
brilliant discovery. Harvey, on his return to England, instituted a series of experiments with a view to determine
the exact nature and uses of the venous valves. The inquiry
was laborious and long ; and it was not till the year 1619, *i.e.*
seventeen years after he left Padua, that he ventured to teach
the doctrine of the double circulation publicly. Other nine
years elapsed before the *Exercitatio Anatomica de Motu*

Cordis et Sanguinis in Animalibus saw the light. This celebrated work was consequently published in 1628, and, curiously enough, not in England but in Frankfort. It therefore took Harvey some twenty-six years to mature and perfect his views.

Harvey left little to be done, but that little fell to the lot of a worthy successor, the renowned Malpighi, who, in 1661, by the aid of the microscope, discovered the capillary circulation, and the presence of blood-globules within the vessels. Harvey's views, thoroughly matured, and sound in warp and woof as they were, met with a determined opposition, and it was only after many an unseemly conflict between really great men, that the blood was allowed to flow quietly in the double channel which he had taken such pains to discover and describe. There is little chance of its changing its course now ; and the task which I set myself in the present lectures is to point out the course which the blood and other nutritious juices pursue, as they meander about in the organic world, now free, now confined ; now checked by the presence of valves, now hurried forward by the pressure of vessels, hearts, and other forces, to which I shall have occasion frequently to allude as the subject becomes more complicated.

Definition of the Circulation.—The term circulation, in the present day, is employed in a double sense. In its wider signification it embraces the course of the nutritious juices through plants and the lower orders of animals ; in its more limited signification, and as applied to man and the higher orders of animated beings, it indicates the course of the blood from the heart to the capillaries, and from these back again to the heart. The word circulation literally means a flowing round—a going and returning ; and it is well to bear the original meaning in mind, as we shall find that a single circle aptly represents the circulation in most of the lower animals ; a circle, with one or more accessory loops, representing the circulation in the higher ones. In man, the chief circle represents the systemic circulation—two accessory loops representing the pulmonic and portal circulation. The accessory loops may be increased indefinitely to meet the requirements of any particular case.

CIRCULATION IN PLANTS.

In plants the circulation is in its most rudimentary form; in fact it is incomplete as a circulation, *i.e.* as a continuous flow of nutritious juices in a circle. My meaning will be obvious when I remind you, that in trees the sap flows steadily upwards in spring, and steadily downwards in autumn. The chain is, as it were, broken at both ends. There is, in addition to the upward and downward currents, a certain amount of transfusion, *i.e.* of cross currents running in the direction of the breadth of the stem; but the transfusion referred to is trifling when compared with the two principal, and, as regards time, interrupted currents[1]. In order to comprehend the true nature of this interrupted and, so to speak, disjointed circulation, it is necessary to remember that trees have a season of activity and a season of repose; that they increase in an upward direction by means of shoots, in a downward direction by means of roots, and laterally by branches[2]. In other words, they increase in every direction; and this holds true of growing animals as well as growing plants. The shoots, by their upward growth, tend to draw up the sap; the roots, by their downward growth, to draw it down; and the branches, by their lateral growth, to draw it transversely. Here, then, are the materials for an interrupted or disjointed circulation with a certain degree of oneness about it. Nutrition is a principal factor in the process. The

---

[1] 'The nutrient fluids in plants follow certain directions according to the structure and arrangement of the tissues, the locality of the sources of nutrition and of growth, or other actions; and as regards the elaborated fluid, the movement may be—(1) from the place of formation to that of consumption; or (2) to the stem, cells, or reservoirs; or (3) from the latter to the place of consumption.'—*Henfrey's Botany*, as edited by Dr. Masters, F.R.S., p. 570.

[2] 'The sap will flow to the several parts according to their respective degrees of activity—to the leaves while light and heat enable them to discharge their functions, and back to the twigs, branches, stem, and roots when these become active and the leaves inactive, or when their activity dominates over that of the leaves. And this distribution of nutriment, varying with the varying activities of the parts, is just such a distribution as we know must be required to keep up the organic balance.'—*Principles of Biology*, by Herbert Spencer, vol. i. p. 557.

idea of a plant or tree increasing in an upward and downward direction and laterally at one and the same time, is consistent with fact. When a seed grows, it extends itself into the ground and into the air; *i.e.* it spreads from a centre in an upward and outward direction, and in a downward and outward direction [1]. (Figs. 1–3.)

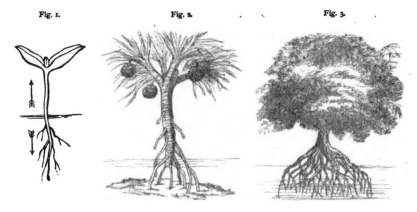

Fig. 1.   Fig. 2.   Fig. 3.

Fig. 1.—'A seedling dicotyledonous plant with an ascending and a descending axis.'—*Henfrey.*
Fig. 2.—'*Pandanus odoratissimus*, the screw-pine, with adventitious roots supporting the trunk.'—*Henfrey.*
Fig. 3.—' Rhizophora mangle, the mangrove-tree, supported as it were upon piles by its numerous roots, which raise up the stem. The plant grows at the muddy mouths of rivers in warm climates.'—*Balfour.*

If, bearing this fact in mind, you imagine that as the tree grows the central point from which it had its being moves upwards (it must do this if it is to maintain its central position with reference to the tree as a whole), then we are forced to conclude that the stem of the tree itself is sending off processes in an upward and downward direction, and likewise laterally. That the central or germinal point recedes in an upward direction as the stem grows is rendered almost certain by the researches of Henfrey, who has shown that the root in growing exercises an upward pressure as well as a downward one; and that if the upper part of the root be relieved from its load of superimposed earth, and the weight of the plant balanced, the root, in virtue of its elongation alone, will cause the whole mass of the plant to rise bodily upwards. This is particularly well seen in the mangrove-tree and screw-pine,

[1] The hydrogastrum, one of the algae, consists of a single cell, but this cell is so differentiated as to simulate a perfect plant, with roots, stem, bud, and fruit.

where the stems are raised completely out of the ground, and supported as it were upon piles. (Figs. 2, 3.)

Two Different Systems in Plants.—The embryo, according to Petit Thouars and Gaudichaud, consists of two portions, a caulinary and radicular; the one having a tendency to ascend, the other to descend. These portions, which may be taken to represent different systems, have different sets of cells and vessels; the ascending system in the dicotyledons being connected with the medullary sheath, and passing into buds and leaves; the descending system, which is situated between the sheath and the bark, being connected with the woody tissue

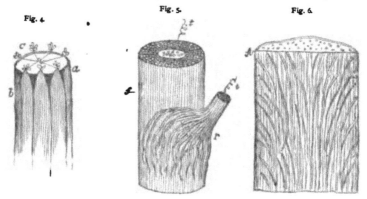

Fig. 4.   Fig. 5.   Fig. 6.

Fig. 4. 'Slip or cutting of root of Maclura, showing a number of buds, *c*, from which proceed radicular fibres, *a*, which are interposed between the bark, *b*, and the fibres of the old wood. The young fibres are traced to the buds, and, in their progress downwards, they remain distinct. This example is brought forward by Gaudichaud as illustrating his vertical theory of wood formation.'—*Balfour.*

Fig. 5. 'Truncated stem of a dracaena after maceration, showing the tracheae, *t. t,* of the ascending system of the stem and branch. The radicular system of the old stem, *f,* is seen in the form of fibres, and the radicular woody bundles, *r,* of the branch are disposed in a grasping manner over those of the old stem. The fibres, according to Petit Thouars and Gaudichaud, come from the bases of the leaves, and belong to the descending system.'—*Balfour.*

Fig. 6.—'Vertical section of the stem of a palm, showing the vascular bundles, *fv,* curving downwards and interlacing. This peculiar arrangement suggests the idea of roots ramifying.'—*Balfour.*

sent down from the leaves. The woody fibres of the leaves, aided by the cambium, are developed from above downwards. This belief in a double system in plants is confirmed by numerous facts, and in especial by the vascular bundles in palms, etc.; these bundles proceeding from the base of the leaves, and interlacing in a curved downward direction, as shown in the accompanying figures.

It is also confirmed by the development of aerial roots, from different parts of the stems of screw-pines, tree-ferns, vellozias, figs, etc.; the stem of the screw-pine actually becoming less in proportion to the number of adventitious roots given off.

(Fig. 2, p. 9.) In some palms, moreover, the descending fibres burst through the stems externally, and appear as roots. If further confirmation of this view were necessary, it is to be found in the fact that occasionally sound wood at a higher level of the stem sends down roots into rotten wood on a lower level. Mr. John Lowe gives a curious example of this in the *Salix viminalis*, a species of willow. The trunk decayed in the centre, and from the sound wood above the decayed part a woody root eighteen inches in circumference descended. It penetrated the rotten mass, and when it reached the sound wood beneath, gave off branches which reached the soil. The radicular stem ultimately produced leaf-buds and leaves. That two distinct, and in some respects opposite, systems exist in plants, is rendered exceedingly probable by the researches of De la Hire, Darwin, Knight, Auber du Petit Thouars, Gaudichaud, and Macaire; the last observer believing that even the roots of plants have a twofold function, the one to extract moisture from the soil, the other to return excess of moisture to it. The presence of two systems in plants, or what is equivalent thereto, is, in a measure, necessary to explain the phenomenon of their general circulation. Without some such arrangement it would be difficult to account for the ascent and descent of the sap, and, at certain periods of the year, the deposit, storage, and subsequent removal of starch corpuscles, the simultaneous increase of a tree by shoots, branches, and leaves in the air, and by roots and spongioles in the ground.

Two Principal Currents in Plants — Proof that the Saps ascend and descend.—The existence of two principal currents can be readily detected, for it is found that if a tree or its branches be cut in the spring, its sap flows in an upward and outward direction; whereas if cut in the autumn, the sap flows in a downward and outward direction. The spring and autumn correspond to the bleeding seasons of trees. Walker [1], Burnett [2], and others have shown that in trees there is no descent of sap until after the development of the leaves. This

[1] Walker's Experiments on the Motion of Sap in Trees.   Trans. Roy. Soc. Edin. i. 3.
[2] Burnett on the Development of the several Organic Systems of Vegetables. Jour. Roy. Instit. vol. i.

was ascertained by making incisions or notches into the bark and wood of trees in spring and· summer. From numerous experiments these investigators came to the conclusion that in all instances the spring sap begins to flow at the root, and that it rises slowly but surely to the very extremity of the tree. This was proved by the tree bleeding at the lowest notch first, and at the under side of the notch before the upper. It was further ascertained that the upward current extends from the stem to the branches. To these interesting experiments Mohl added another of great value. He showed that if a ring of bark be removed, the sap flows up as before the mutilation, but that if a portion of the wood be removed without injury to the bark which covers it, the part of the wood above the wound is no longer supplied with sap, and dries up.

A converse experiment was performed to prove the descent of the sap in summer. When a ring of bark is removed, the girth of the tree increases in volume above the injury, and remains *in statu quo* below the injury. If moreover, as Henfrey states, bark be removed in patches, and the surfaces become gradually grown over by new wood, the greater part of the new growth comes *from the upper side*[1]. This shows not only that the crude sap ascends, but that the elaborated sap descends, and that starch granules and other matters are stored up or converted into wood in the part above the injury. If the tree be cut in summer, the nutritious juices, owing to their greater viscidity and other changes, do not flow outwards; which shows that the nature of the circulation and the material circulated at this period is somewhat different from what it is in spring and autumn. In summer the crude sap, which is absorbed by the roots, rises to the leaves, where, by evaporation and other processes, it is elaborated into the *succus proprius* or proper food of the plant. The

---

[1] 'In dicotyledons the elaborated sap descends in the fibro-vascular bundles of the cambium layer of the wood and in the internal tissue of the bark. It also passes inward by lateral transfusion. In dicotyledons the inner layers of wood generally become converted in course of time into *heart-wood*, the solidity of which obstructs the passage of fluids, which then ascend chiefly in the younger outward layers of the wood which constitute the alburnum or sap-wood.'—*Henfrey's Botany*, pp. 568, 569.

succus proprius, which differs in its constitution from the crude sap, subsequently descends into the stem, through which it diffuses itself by a collateral circulation, to be stored up for future wants. M. A. Gris was convinced that the sap ascends and descends from finding that in winter the medullary rays, wood, and pith, are filled with starch grains, which disappear in a great measure during the spring, and are replaced during the summer. He was led to conclude that there are two special movements of the nutritious juices, as illustrated by the formation of starch granules in summer, and their absorption in spring. That the sap ascends there can be no doubt, for the plant derives its nourishment chiefly from the earth ; and that it descends is proved by the experiments referred to. In spring the circulation is mainly concerned with the elongation of the stem and branches, the development of the buds, and the evolution of the leaves, its course being for the most part upwards[1]. In summer it is chiefly concerned with the functions of the leaf, the elaboration of sap, and the storing up of food for the plant, its course being partly upwards and partly downwards; while in autumn, owing to excess of moisture, a diminution of temperature, and other changes, the course of the circulation is for the most part from above downwards ; the circulation having, so to speak, completed its work for the season[2]. Much more sap is taken up than is given off in spring in order to administer to the growth of the plant. In autumn, when the period of growth is over, this process is reversed, more sap being given off by the roots than is taken up by them. The circulation in a tree, as will be seen, is interrupted or non-continuous, and this is accounted for by the tree having periods of greater and less activity. This holds true also, within certain limits, of animals ; the circulation in animals being most vigorous when the animal is awake, or when excited; and least so when it is in a quiescent state, when sleeping or when hibernating. I have attempted to

---

[1] To the progress of the sap in the direction of the axis in spring Burnett ascribes the early development and vigour of the terminal buds.

[2] It may be well to state, that the ascending current of spring is accompanied by a slight downward current, the descending current of autumn being accompanied by a slight upward current, the spring and autumn currents diffusing themselves as they go. This follows because of the share taken by endosmose and exosmose in the circulation.

convey an idea of the scheme of the circulation in plants by
the aid of the subjoined figures.   (Figs. 7 and 8.)

Fig. 7.

Fig. 8.

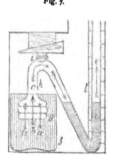

Fig. 7.—Endosmometer, showing endosmotic and exosmotic currents. *f*, Glass vessel containing
water. *g*, Expanded portion of glass tube bent upon itself at *i* and *h*; its under surfaces being covered
by a piece of bladder. *k*, Column of mercury. The space between the column of mercury and the
bladder (*g*) is filled with syrup at aperture *i*. Immediately the water and syrup act upon the bladder or
interposed membrane, opposite currents are induced, the water rising through the bladder and syrup
with great energy, as indicated by the arrows, *b*, *c* (endosmosis), the syrup settling down into the water
more feebly, as indicated by the arrows *a a* (exosmosis). The water sets towards the syrup with such
force as to elevate the column of mercury *k*, in the tube *l*, in the direction *e*. In addition to the principal
currents, indicated by the arrows *a* and *b*, there are minor currents which proceed transversely. These
are best seen when the bladder is made to project beyond *g*, so as to display a certain amount of lateral
surface.

Fig. 8.—Diagram, representing the ascending, descending, and transverse currents in the plant.
a, Ascending or spring current. *b*, Descending or autumn current, *c*. *d*, Ascending and descending
currents of summer ; these being continuous in the direction of the leaves and roots. *a*, *c*, Transverse
currents. The arrows in this diagram represent the endosmotic currents, the darts the exosmotic ones.

In contemplating figure 8 we are at once struck with the
diversity in the direction of the currents ; one ascends, another
descends, or a third runs transversely and at right angles to both.
The ascending and descending currents are most strongly
pronounced.   These currents—and it is a remarkable circumstance—are found in all the higher plants and animals up to
man himself. The object to be attained is manifest. The
circulation is instituted expressly for the purpose of carrying
matters of divers kinds to and from the tissues. But to give
to and take from implies movements in diametrically opposite
directions. In animals with hearts and blood-vessels supplied
with valves, we can readily understand why the circulating
fluids should pursue two directions, the one current setting
from the heart, the other towards it ; but in trees and animals
without hearts the explanation is not so obvious. The descending current could readily be accounted for by gravitation ;
but gravitation can take no part in producing the upward
current.

Endosmose and Exosmose as Adjuncts of the Circulation.—
Without a knowledge of the physical forces, the true nature
of the ascending and descending currents in plants[1] would for
ever have remained a mystery. Dutrochet[2], however, made
the important discovery, that if a watery or tenuous fluid be
placed on one side of a membrane, animal or vegetable, and a
thick or mucilaginous fluid on the other (the fluids having an
affinity for each other, and for the interposed membrane), two
counter or opposite currents are at once established, the thin
fluid setting with a strong current in large quantity towards
the thicker fluid which it penetrates; the thicker fluid setting
with an equally well-marked but more feeble current, and in
smaller quantity, towards the thinner fluid, with which it in
turn intermingles. This mingling or diffusion of the fluids
through each other occasions a multitude of minor, and what
may be regarded as transverse currents. (Fig. 7.)

In endosmose and exosmose we have physical forces which
bear the same relation to each other that the ascending, descending, and transverse currents of plants bear to each other.
In fact we shall not be overstepping the limits of legitimate
inference if we state that the forces of endosmose and exosmose form important factors in the circulation of plants, and
work in the same direction or alongside the vital forces. The
probabilities indeed are that the physical and vital forces
here referred to are separate manifestations of one and the
same force; the vital forces controlling the physical forces
within certain limits to a desired end. From these remarks
it will appear that the living plant takes advantage of existing
forces when it grows or builds itself up; that, in fact, the plant
has its parts arranged expressly with a view to availing itself
of those forces; the living as it were arising out of the dead,
according to fixed laws which govern alike the organic and
inorganic kingdoms. It is this circumstance which enables
the plant to reciprocate with the external world, and which in
some senses fixes its place in nature. Very similar remarks

---

[1] In animals the currents are ascending and descending only when the creatures
assume a vertical position. In animals whose bodies assume a horizontal position,
the terms ascending and descending are obviously inapplicable. The great feature
in the circulation to be kept constantly in view is that one current goes in one
direction, and another in an opposite direction.

[2] Recherches sur l'Endosmose et l'Exosmose. Paris, 1828.

may be made regarding the circulation in animals, inasmuch as in their ultimate tissues the advancing and receding currents referred to invariably exist.

Such being the nature and general course of the circulation in plants, we naturally turn our attention to the channels and forces by which the circulation is inaugurated and maintained.

In the cellular plants, such as the fungi and lichens, and even in the mosses and hepaticæ, there are no distinct channels for the transmission of fluids ; the sap passing from

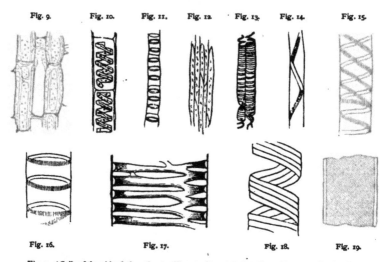

Fig. 9.—'Cells of the pith of *Acanthus mollis*, seen in a vertical section. Magn. 200 diam.'—*Henfrey*.
Fig. 10.—'Cells of a filament of *spirogyra*, with spiral green bands. Magn. 200 diam.'—*Henfrey*.
Fig. 11.—'Cells from the sporangium of *marchantia* polymorpha. Magn. 250 diam.'—*Henfrey*.
Fig. 12.—Woody tissue or pleurenchyma, consisting of fusiform or spindle-shaped tubes overlapping each other. The walls of the tubes are thickened by deposits of lignine.
Fig. 13.—'Spiral vessels, consisting of elongated cells which assume a tubular and fusiform shape, and have a spiral fibre formed on the inside of their walls.'—*Balfour*.
Figs. 14, 15, and 18.—'Spiral vessels from *Sambucus ebulus*. Magn. 400 diam.'—*Henfrey*.
Fig. 16.—'Fragment of a vessel from the stem of a gourd. Magn. 400 diam.'—*Henfrey*.
Fig. 17.—Fragment of the wall of a reticulated vessel of rhubarb. Magn. 400 diam.
Fig. 19.—'Fragment of the wall of a reticulated vessel of rhubarb. Magn. 400 diam.'—*Henfrey*.

cell to cell in a more or less complex series by a process of imbibition, much in the same way that water spreads in a piece of blotting-paper. In such cases the currents set most strongly towards those spots where growth is proceeding most rapidly. Precisely the same thing happens in rapidly growing or secreting tissues. Thus the blood is determined to the stag's horn when growing, to the mamma when suckling, and to the stomach when digesting. This constitutes the *vis a fronte* of modern physiologists.

The Vessels of Plants: their Function.—In plants with well-defined stems and branches there are more or less perfect channels for the circulation of the nutrient material. Thus there are the so-called vascular tissues formed by the fusion of perpendicular rows of variously-constituted cells[1]. The walls of those cells are in many instances furnished with vertical, annular, spiral[2], reticulated, or other fibres[3]; the cells by their union originating the spiral[4], annular, reticulated, scalariform, and other vessels[5]. (Vide Figs. 9–19 inclusive; and Figs. 20–22, on p. 20.

[1] 'A number of cells permanently combined form the tissues of plants. If the cells entering into the composition of a tissue are essentially alike, they form a simple tissue. The simple tissues are divided into the cellular and vascular tissues. In the former (cellular tissues) the cells, however firmly coherent, are only *in contact* by their walls, which form a persistent boundary between them. In the latter (vascular tissues) the cells enter into closer relation, becoming confluent by the absorption of their contiguous surfaces, and thus converted into more or less extensive tubular bodies, which in their various conditions form what are called the *ducts* and *vessels* of plants. The vessels, it will be seen, are in reality compound elementary organs.'—*Henfrey's Botany*, p. 471.

[2] The presence of spiral fibres in cells is most instructive, for in this we see the foundation of a numerous class of structures which were otherwise inexplicable. A series of cells with spiral cell-walls originate a vessel with spiral walls; these vessels may twine in a certain direction and produce a spiral stem—the stem itself may twine around another tree in a spiral manner; leaves, flowers, fruit, may all be arranged in spirals of various orders. The spirals of plant structures may be traced to animal structures. The shell of the nautilus is rolled up in a most graceful spiral; the heart (ventricles) of mammals is a double continuous spiral of exquisite beauty. The wings of birds and the extremities of bipeds and quadrupeds are distinctly spiral in their nature, and their movements are curved spiral movements; nay, more, the vertebral column itself is a spiral of very unusual but delightful curve. The soft cell fibres, equally with the bony skeleton, are twisted upon themselves morphologically. This is a point of great interest. It is important physiologically, as spiral continuous structures give rise to spiral continuous movements, as seen in walking, swimming, and flying, and in the movements of the hollow viscera. Dutrochet (*Braun sur les Torsions normales dans les Plantes*) states that there is a revolving movement in the summits of stems, a spiral rolling of the stems round their supports, a torsion of the stems upon themselves, and a spiral arrangement of leaves—all these being, in each plant, in the same direction. These phenomena, he avers, are owing to an internal vital force which causes a revolution round the central axis of the stem.

[3] 'The annular thickenings are less common than the spiral ones, but sometimes occur in the same cell with reticulated ones.'—*Henfrey's Botany*, p. 484.

[4] The spiral vessels are found in the youngest and most delicate parts of the plant.

[5] 'In the young soft part of the shoot, as in all normal and abnormal growths that have not formed wood, the channels for the passage of sap are the spiral,

C

Doubt has been expressed as to whether the vessels in question are actually engaged in the transmission of saps, but the preponderance of evidence is in favour of this belief. Mr. Herbert Spencer has been able to show by recent experiments that the passage of fluid through the spiral and other vessels is much more rapid than through the cellular tissue. By soaking young shoots which develop little wood in decoctions of logwood and other dyes, he discovered that the only channels stained by the process were those corresponding to the spiral, fenestrated, scalariform, and other vessels of the vascular system. Through these vessels consequently the coloured fluid must have passed. Nor is it wonderful that the fluid should have preferred open capillary channels, such as those formed by the vessels of the vascular system, to interrupted or non-continuous channels such as are supplied by cellular tissue, or any tissue not differentiated into continuous canals. Mr. Spencer took the precaution to immerse whole plants in his dyes, as well as parts of plants. He obtained the same results in both cases, so that it is natural to conclude the coloured fluids traversed the same channels traversed by the crude and other saps when submitted to the action of the plant. The spiral, annular, and other vessels of the vascular system are most engaged as sap-carriers when new wood is being formed in their vicinity, in which case also they are most porous [1].

When new wood is being formed the dye escapes from the vessels of the vascular bundles into the cellular and

annular, fenestrated, or reticulated vessels. . . . The sap-carrying function is at first discharged entirely by the walls of the medullary sheath, and they cease to discharge this function only as fast as they are relatively incapacitated by their mechanical circumstances. . . . It is not the wood itself, but the more or less continuous canals formed in it, which are the subsequent sap distributors.'— *Principles of Biology*, by Herbert Spencer. Lond. and Edinb. 1867 ; p. 549.

[1] According to Mr. Spencer, there is no direct connexion between the age of a vessel and its porosity ; those vessels being always the most porous around which a formation of wood is taking place. Professor Balfour, on the other hand, states, 'that the tubes forming the wood are pervious to fluids in their young state, but that their walls soon become thickened by deposits of lignine, and in the heart-wood of trees their cavities are obliterated. This filling up of the tube takes place often in a concentric manner, and when it is completed the active life of the cell or tube may be considered as having terminated.'—*Class-Book of Botany*, p. 420.

surrounding tissues in such quantity as to lead to the belief that the said tissues and not the vessels transmit the sap. This was the opinion of Hoffmann and Unger, who held that in plants possessed of fibro-vascular bundles, the sap in the first instance passes up from the roots chiefly in the paren-chymatous cellular constituents of the bundles, and that these juices do not pass by the spiral vessels themselves [1]. There are many circumstances which induce me to believe that the vessels and intervascular spaces are both engaged in the circulation.

Mr. Spencer's explanation of the passage of sap through the vascular tissues has been objected to on the ground that the spiral and other vessels of the vascular system frequently contain air. To this he replies, that they only do so during periods of drought, and when they are old—their function as sap-carriers having virtually ceased. The canals which ramify through the stag's horn, he observes, contain air after the horn is fully developed, but it is not thereby rendered doubtful whether it is the function of arteries to convey blood [2].

It ought moreover not to be overlooked, that while the presence of air in the vessels is fatal to the circulation in animals, it does not of necessity follow that it is so in plants. The conditions are not identical. In animals the walls of the larger vessels are not permeable by fluids, so that air admitted into them has no means of escaping therefrom; in plants, on the contrary, the walls of the vessels are especially permeable, a free egress being provided by the pitted and other vessels [3]. The presence of air in the vascular bundles of plants is therefore a natural condition at certain periods —a plant requiring air as well as sap.

---

[1] The difference between the cellular and vascular tissues may be briefly indicated. In cellular tissues the cells firmly cohere, the cell-walls being persistent. In the vascular tissue, the cells run together by the absorption of their contiguous surfaces to form the tubes, ducts, or vessels known as the vascular tissues.

[2] Principles of Biology, vol. ii. p. 357.

[3] Globes of air in a capillary tube with rigid impervious walls require, as Janin has shown, a pressure of three atmospheres to force them on. As however the walls of the vessels of plants are porous a much smaller force suffices, the air escaping in every direction.

Points of Resemblance between the Vessels of Plants and Animals.—Making allowances for difference of opinion as to the function performed by the vessels of plants, there can be no doubt that the vascular tissues of the vegetable kingdom bear a close analogy to those of the animal kingdom. In the vessels of plants we have structures remarkably resembling those of the blood-vessels of animals. In an artery, as you are aware, we have straight, annular, and spiral fibres, these being present in variable proportion, according to the thickness of the vessel and its distance from the heart. Thus

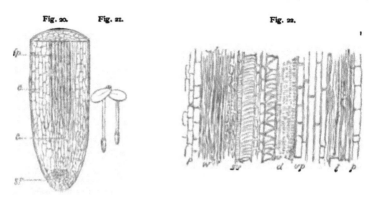

Fig. 20.   Fig. 21.   Fig. 22.

Fig. 20.—'Vertical section of an orchis root, highly magnified. The cells, *c*, gradually pass into dotted cells and vessels, *fp*, the extremity of the root, called a spongiole, *sp*.'—*Balfour*, p. 52.
Fig. 21.—' Magnified representation of two plants of Lemna minor, or lesser duckweed—the green mantle of pools—showing the extremities of the roots covered by a cellular sheath (spongiole).'—*Balfour.*
Fig. 22.—' Monocotyledonous fibro-vascular bundle (from the spadix of Phoenix dactylifera). Vertical section. *p*, Parenchyma, in which the bundles lie ; *w*, wood cells ; *sv*, spiral vessels ; *d*, reticulated ducts ; *vp, vassa propria ; l,* liber cells. Magn. 100 Diam.'—*Henfrey.*

in the aorta the longitudinal, spiral, and annular fibres are all present ; whereas in the capillaries, fragments of the annular fibres alone appear. Very similar remarks may be made regarding the vessels of plants. In these the spiral vessels are found in the youngest and most delicate parts of the plant, the annular vessels being developed a little later in the same bundles, and in similar situations. The reticulated vessels are found in quantity with the spiral and annular kinds in succulent stems, roots, and petioles. The vessels of plants, like those of animals, are usually of a cylindrical form.

While the vessels of plants and animals may be said to be formed upon a common type, there is this great difference between them, and it is important as far as the circulation is concerned:—The vessels of plants, unless when quite young[1], are rigid and have no independent movements; the vessels of animals, on the other hand, are flexible and elastic, and are in many cases endowed with independent motion. This is especially the case in the dorsal vessel of the insect, the veins of the bat's wing, the saphenous veins of the rabbit, the web and mesentery of the frog, the bulbus arteriosus of the fish, and the venae cavae and pulmonic veins of the mammal where they join the heart. There is this further difference, the principal vessels of animals, unless where *rete*

Fig. 23.   Fig. 24.   Fig. 25.

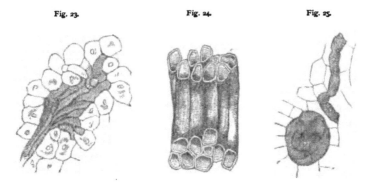

Fig. 23.—'Absorbent organ from the leaf of *Euphorbia neriifolia*. The cluster of fibrous cells form1 1 ʒ one of the terminations of the vascular system is here embedded in a solid parenchyma.'— *Herbert Spencer.*

Fig. 24 —' A longitudinal section through the axis of an absorbent organ from the root of a turnip, showing its annuli of reticulated cells when cut through. The cellular tissue which fills the interior is supposed to be removed.'—*Herbert Spencer.*

Fig. 25.—' A less developed absorbent, showing its approximate connexion with a duct. In their simplest forms these structures consist of only two fenestrated cells, with their ends bent round so as to meet. Such types occur in the central mass of the turnip.'—*Herbert Spencer.*

mirabile[2] is present, are isolated, *i. e.* they occur at intervals, with muscular, bony, and other tissues between. The vessels of plants, on the other hand, are in contiguity, and touch each other. (Figs. 20—25).

[1] The spiral vessels are found in the youngest and most delicate parts of the plant. As these vessels are formed originally by the confluence of cells which are elastic and flexible, a certain degree of movement may reasonably be claimed for them.

[2] In this remarkable arrangement, the blood-vessels sometimes run parallel to each other, and sometimes interweave in a most perplexing and unaccountable manner. The vessels are so numerous and so close, that they form one continuous mass. I have had opportunities of injecting them in the sloth, spider-monkey, and dolphin. They are found in various animals, their precise functions being at present undetermined.

The vessels of animals may be divided into three sets,— the arteries, the veins, and the capillaries; and to these may be added a system of vessels lately discovered, the perivascular canals. The arteries conduct from the heart or centre to the periphery; the veins, from the periphery to the centre; the capillaries uniting the veins and arteries together. Outside, or between the capillaries, so to speak, are the perivascular canals. In like manner plants may be said to have three sets of vessels, an ascending and a descending set, which, as has been shown, radiate in the embryo from a central point. They have also what may fairly be regarded as a capillary system in their leaves, and also in their stems and branches. (Figs. 23–25, p. 21). Whether, therefore, we compare the actual structure, situation, or functions of the vessels of plants and animals, we shall find they have many things in common. The walls of the vessels in plants are flexible and elastic when young, those of animals being permanently so; the vessels of plants and the capillaries of animals are permeable by liquids and gases [1]. The veins of animals convey impure blood; corresponding vessels of plants, crude sap. The arteries of animals convey pure blood; corresponding vessels of plants, elaborated sap. The capillaries of animals expose the impure blood to the influence of the air; the capillaries in the leaves and other parts doing precisely the same thing for the plant. An animal may be said to breathe at every pore [2], and so of the plant—

---

[1] In the young cells of plants the cell-wall consists apparently of a homogeneous membrane which is elastic, flexible, and freely permeable by water. When the cells become older the cell-wall becomes firmer, and opposes a greater obstacle to the entrance of water into its substance. This leads me to conclude that the cell-wall is porous—a point difficult to determine, as the finest microscope fails to detect the pores. The molecular structure of cell-membranes has been investigated by Nägele. From a careful examination of the cell-membrane of starch by polarised light, he came to the conclusion that *all organic substances are composed of crystalline molecules* grouped in a definite manner—that these molecules when dry have no interspaces, but that when moist each molecule is surrounded by a thin film of water. The epidermis of the young leaves of the leek, as Garreau has shown, is freely permeable by fluids; while the epidermis of the older leaves is either not permeable or very sparingly so. Garreau attributed a decided endosmotic property to the cuticle, which is greatest in young parts and least in old ones. When leaves are so old as to have lost the power of absorbing water they can still take up carbonic acid.

[2] Spallanzani was the first to point out that the tissues respired. The subject

a poisonous atmosphere being destructive to both. In animals it is necessary that the vessels extend to the part to be nourished, in order that the growing portions may absorb or imbibe from the blood what is required, while they return to it whatever is superfluous. In the brain and in bone, this absorption or imbibition takes place through considerable spaces. This is especially true of the so-called non-vascular tissues, as the cornea and lens of the eye, and the articular cartilages. The difference between the vascular and non-vascular tissues is only one of degree. In either case the elementary structures lie outside the vessels, and obtain new material from the blood by imbibition. There is therefore an obvious analogy between the nutrition of plants and animals. In both cases the nutritious juices are presented to the growing tissues, immediately or remotely, by vessels or their representatives. In the capillaries of animals and the cells of plants, the limiting membrane is composed of an exceedingly delicate and apparently homogeneous substance, which greatly facilitates imbibition.

Respiration of Plants and Animals.—By means of the capillaries of the lungs, the blood of animals is aerated, carbonic acid and other matters being given off and oxygen taken in. By means of the capillaries of the system, nutritious juices and white blood-corpuscles, also concerned in nutrition, are supplied to the tissues and effete matters taken up. By means of its vessels [1], intervascular spaces and leaves, a tree is nourished, grows and breathes; it gives off oxygen and takes in carbonic acid [2] and other matters. It stores up

has likewise been investigated by G. Liebig. M. Paul Bert (Leçons sur la Physiologie comparée de la Respiration: Paris, 1870) shows that the muscles of cold-blooded vertebrate animals consume, relatively to their weight, less oxygen and evolve less carbonic acid than muscles of warm-blooded animals; also that the muscles of adult animals absorb much more oxygen and evolve more carbonic acid than those of young animals. He proves that all the tissues of the body absorb oxygen and give off carbonic acid.

[1] Some authors are of opinion that the spiral vessels and their allies are receptacles for gaseous matter formed in the course of the movement of the sap within.

[2] 'Leaves have the power of absorbing carbonic acid, ammonia, water, and aqueous solutions. They also inhale a certain amount of water, and they give off gaseous matters, especially oxygen. Thus leaves, in the performance of their functions, absorb and inhale watery and gaseous substances.'—*Class-Book of Botany*, by J. H. Balfour, A.M., M.D., F.R.S., etc. 1871; p. 451.

starch and other compounds, and uses them as occasion demands. The tree, like the animal, may be said to breathe at every pore,—by the stomata of its leaves, by the vessels [1], intercellular passages and cavities of its stem and branches, and by its bark, when this is green. There is yet another point of resemblance between the respiration of plants and animals—the air given off by both is laden with moisture. The oxygen given off by trees and plants communicates to the atmosphere of the forest its peculiarly exhilarating qualities; the carbonic acid given off by the lungs of animals producing, on the contrary, a depressing effect.

Cells of Plants, their Nature and Function.—As the cells of plants play a most important part in the general circulation, and have a circulation of their own, it is necessary to direct attention to them at this stage. ' The cell is the elementary organ of a vegetable structure, but is not the smallest or most simple definite form in which organic matter may exist; it is not to be regarded as the ultimate structural unit, because detached fragments of it are capable of independent existence under certain circumstances,' and a living plant may exist, at least for a time, in the absence of a bounding cell-membrane.

A vegetable cell may be defined as a closed sac, containing fluid or semi-fluid matter. It may represent an entire plant, or only part of a plant [2]. It contains, or may contain, protoplasm, a nucleus, a primordial utricle, starch and chlorophyll corpuscles, etc., etc. Here, then, is a mixture of heterogeneous material, each substance varying in density, and having its own peculiar properties and actions. The cell-

---

[1] In spring the vessels are found gorged with sap, but later on in the season *they usually contain air.* The intercellular passages are also filled with air. Professor Passerini, of Parma, has succeeded in showing that gases are exhaled through the stomata. He obtained his results by causing a plant to absorb a solution of sulphate of sodium, and then placing slips of paper saturated with acetate of lead to its leaves. The parts of the paper corresponding to the stomata were coloured dark, clearly showing that a reaction had taken place.

[2] The red snow plant and oscillatoria consist each of single isolated cells, the cell performing the function of nutrition and reproduction. The fungi and sea-weeds—the so-called cellular plants—are composed of numerous cells, arranged according to a definite order, some of the cells discharging the nutritive and others the reproductive functions. The higher or vascular plants have vessels added to the cells, the organs of nutrition and reproduction being more complicated.

wall is also of uncertain and varied constitution. It is regarded by some as originally consisting of a homogeneous membrane, in which spiral, annular, and other fibres are subsequently developed; others believing that these fibres are present in the cell from the first, and form an integral part of it. Agardh, *e.g.*, is of opinion that the cell-walls are made up of bundles of solid fibres interwoven together. He therefore attributes to the cell-wall a structure resembling that of the blood-vessels and hollow viscera of animals[1]. However this may be, the cell-wall in the young state is elastic, flexible, and freely permeable by water; and this is important, as rendering the cell liable to all kinds of hygroscopic influences.

As the cell-wall becomes older it usually thickens and becomes more rigid; in which case water permeates it with more difficulty. We have therefore in any single cell, or in any combination of cells, the conditions necessary for a great variety of vital, mechanical, and chemical changes; the presence or absence of heat and moisture accelerating or retarding the changes in question. It may happen that the cell-wall, while thickening, remains soft and flexible, and, if so, it swells up the instant it comes in contact with water. If a unicellular plant be placed in a dense liquid, its contents escape, and it becomes shrivelled; if, on the other hand, it is put in a thin fluid, it imbibes the fluid and increases in volume. The red blood-globules do the same. These changes are principally due to endosmose and exosmose. The effect which changes of temperature have upon cells is very remarkable. The stomata of the leaves of plants close in dry weather and open in moist, so that the opening or closing of a part, while due in the first instance to the presence or absence of moisture, is due in the second to structural peculiarities in the cells themselves. Thus in some species of mesembryanthemum the seed-vessel is closed when dry and open when moistened; whereas in the spores or germs of

---

[1] In the cell-walls of Polysiphonia complanata, Conferva melagoniam, and Griffithsia equisetifolia, Agardh has demonstrated numerous bundles of fibres, which cross each other at the joints to form the diaphragm. Between them finer fibres occur, the whole being united by a gelatinous substance.—Agardh, *De Cellula Vegetabili Fibrillis tenuissimis Contextu.* Lundæ, 1852.

horse-tails (equisetum), the cellular club-shaped filaments which form a part of it are widely expanded when the spore is dry, and closed when it is moistened. This would seem to imply the existence of two forces in plants[1], portions of certain plants having the power not only of closing but also of opening. This appears to follow because the presence of moisture in the one case produces the closing, and in the other the opening. The same cause, if I may so phrase it, produces opposite results. A similar phenomenon is witnessed in the action of hollow muscles with sphincters, where, apparently under precisely the same conditions, the sphincter opens or expands when the viscus closes. I am inclined to infer from this that heat or dryness, and moisture or wet, do not act as irritants, and that plants and certain parts of animals move without being irritated. If moisture, for example, acted as an irritant, and caused one plant to close, it could scarcely be regarded as the cause of another opening. Moisture and dryness moreover act upon dead vegetable tissue, where the idea of irritability is inadmissible. Thus a hempen rope shortens when wetted, and elongates when dried. The manner in which cells of wood, liber, etc., swell up on the application of moisture, is deserving of attention. They expand in the direction transverse to their axes, i.e. they shorten in a longitudinal direction as they bulge or swell out laterally[2]. Shortening in one direction is consequently elongation in another. Precisely the same thing takes place in the action of the sarcous elements of a muscle. When a muscle or an elementary muscular fibre contracts, as it is termed, it decreases in the direction of its length, and increases in the direction of its breadth,—in fact the decrease in one direction is accompanied by an increase in another and opposite direction, the volume remaining always the same. It is therefore better, when speaking of the movements of long muscles, to say they shorten and lengthen, and of hollow muscles that they close and open, than that they *contract* and *relax*. The vegetable cell-wall, when dried,

---

[1] In the hygrometer composed of *two pieces* of wood, each having different absorbing powers, a certain amount of moisture in the atmosphere produces a curving to the one side, a certain amount of dryness a curving to the opposite side.

[2] Henfrey's Botany, p. 470.

becomes smaller, so that the mere application or withdrawal of moisture suffices for conferring certain movements upon it [1].

These movements are to be regarded as extraneous, for the presence or absence of moisture may be an accidental circumstance. Cells, however, are living things, and they have living contents endowed in many cases with independent motion. The necessity for such an arrangement is obvious, inasmuch as 'the vital and chemical phenomena exhibited by plants depend in the first instance upon operations which have their seat in the interior of those structures.' Kühne proved the vitality of cell contents by a very remarkable experiment. He collected a quantity of protoplasm from a living plant, and placed it in a cockchafer's intestine. When he applied the stimulus of galvanism to the intestine so distended, it shortened like a muscle. The protoplasm possesses remarkable properties. In some plants it is endowed with distinct movements, rendered apparent by the granules which float in it. The source of these movements is at present a mystery; some authors contending that the protoplasmic mass can change its shape at any moment; others, that the movements are due to increase or decrease in the amount of protoplasm contained within the cell at any given time [2]. Similar remarkable properties are to be attributed to the primordial utricle which has the power of moulding itself into new external forms. The primordial utricle constitutes an envelope for the zoospore of the algae, when it escapes from the parent cell; the vitalised contents of the cell establishing a separate existence. The substance of the primordial utricle greatly resembles that of the amoeba and the soft parts of sponges, all three being endowed with independent movements. The starch granules of cells are developed from the chlorophyll corpuscles, and these last owe their existence to

---

[1] 'There is reason to believe that, in some instances, the cell-wall thickens at certain seasons, and becomes thinner at others; but this appearance may arise from *an alternately swollen and contracted state*, and not from absorption and re-deposition.'—*Henfrey's Botany*, p. 480.

[2] 'During the time when the protoplasmic contents of young cells are becoming gradually hollowed out into spaces filled with watery cell-sap, a regular movement of this protoplasm takes place, which may be observed very readily in young hairs of phanerogamic plants, and which probably takes place in an early stage in all other structures.'—Ibid., p. 551.

the elaboration of protoplasm. There is thus a variety of movements going on within the cell during the period of growth.

The Intracellular Circulation of Plants.—The intracellular circulation, or gyration, as it is called, is most interesting, and in some respects most mysterious. There can be little doubt that it is referable to vital, chemical, and physical changes occuring in the cell-contents; but the precise nature of those changes is unfortunately at present undetermined. Some investigators believe that the circulation is traceable to the nourishment of the cell, and the commotion consequent on its reproduction; others to electrical or galvanic agency; others to the presence of invisible cilia[1]; and others to endosmose and exosmose, depending upon the different densities of the fluids presented from without to the cell-contents. It is therefore referred by one sect to a vital, and by a second to a physical action. Under these circumstances we can only refer to the phenomena as observed; and it is not a little humiliating to think that at the very threshold of the circulation we are confronted with difficulties of such magnitude, and obliged to confess that even in a cell there are hidden powers which neither the microscope, physics, nor chemistry, . can as yet explain. From experiments which I have made recently, and which are fully described further on, it appears to me that the intracellular circulation is due in a principal measure to physical causes, such as absorption and evaporation, endosmose and exosmose, capillarity, chemical affinity, etc.

In many cells a distinct movement of fluids and granules is perceptible; and Schleiden and Mohl are of opinion that these movements take place in all active formative cells at one period or other of their growth. The intracellular circulation is seen to advantage in many aquatic plants. It was discovered by Corti in chara, in 1774[2]. In this plant (chara)

---

[1] Movements analogous to the intracellular ones occur within the mouth, stomach, and rectum of certain polypes. Dr. Grant was of opinion that these movements were due to the lashing of cilia; and Dr. Sharpey subsequently demonstrated that cilia actually did exist in the situations indicated.

[2] 'In chara the axis is composed of elongated cells, placed end to end, surrounded by a number of small secondary cells, which take a spiral course round the primary cells from left to right, and which are often encrusted with carbonate of lime.'

the movements are of a spiral nature, as indicated by the arrows in Fig. 26.

It is not a little remarkable that in the stem of the Tubularia indivisa, a form of polype, precisely analogous movements occur, as was pointed out by Mr Lister [1]. (Fig. 27.)

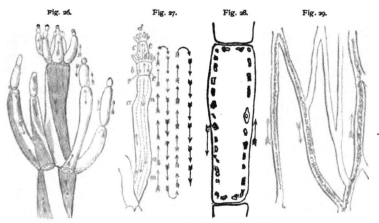

Fig. 26.　　　Fig. 27.　　　Fig. 28.　　　Fig. 29.

Fig. 26.—' A small portion of a chara, magnified to show the intracellular circulation. The arrows mark the direction of the fluid and granules in the different cells. The clear spaces are parts where there is no movement. The circulation in each cell is independent of that in the others.'—*Balfour.*

Fig. 27.—Shows the course of the circulation in the stem of the polype (*Tubularia indivisa*). *a a*, Horny tube, containing a soft substance, continuous with stomach (*b*), and mouth (*c*). *c d*, Tentacula or arms. The ascending and descending currents in the stem of the polype are indicated by the arrows. They pursue a slightly spiral direction, as indicated by the dotted lines in figure—the one setting towards the polype, the other away from it. At *m* and *n* there were vortices in the tube. The arrows to the right of the figure indicate the continuous nature of the currents within the tube.

Fig. 28.—' Large internal cell of vallisneria, showing the direction of the currents in intracellular rotation. There is an occasional nucleus seen in the course of the circulation, along with the chlorophyll grains.'—*Balfour.*

Fig. 29.—' Branching and anastomosing tubes of lactiferous vessels. In them there is an evident movement of granules of latex, as represented in some of the tubes in the figure, the arrows marking the direction of the current.'—*Balfour.*

The movements in chara are made visible by the presence of granules, which rotate on their own axes, travelling in a spiral direction, up one side of the cell and down the other. Observe, up one side of the cell and down the other. The currents in opposite directions, characteristic of the general circulation, reappear. The same currents are perceptible in our own stomachs during digestion. In the case of Alexis St. Martin, who had his stomach perforated by a gunshot wound, the food, when introduced into the stomach, was seen to circulate first along the greater curvature from left to right, and then along the lesser curvature from right to left.

[1] Movements somewhat resembling the above were found by Dr. Sharpey to occur in the tentacula of the actinia.—*Cyc. of Anat. and Phys.* art. ' Cilia,' p. 615.

It may seem far-fetched to trace an analogy between the
gyrating of the contents of the human stomach and the
gyrating of the contents of a vegetable cell; but, in some
of the lower animals, the contents of the alimentary canal
transude through its walls and circulate through the body;
in others (polypes) the gyrating movements occur within the
mouth, stomach, and rectum. I am moreover satisfied, from
dissection and experiment, that the stomach and heart, even
in ourselves, are in some senses identical both in structure
and function; these organs being endowed with a pushing
and pulling power, which enables them to manipulate their
contents and to propel them in given directions. When the
oesophagus is engaged in transmitting food, it pinches on
the bolus by opening before and closing behind it simultaneously—the expanding or pulling and pinching or pushing
action accompanying the bolus from the time it enters the
oesophagus proper until it reaches the stomach. This compound movement can transmit fluids with equal dexterity
and precision, as is well seen when a horse or other large
animal is drinking. Every part of the oesophagus has the
power of opening and closing, so that the part which is
opened the one instant is closed the next, and *vice versa.*
The opening and closing movements which constitute the
oesophageal rhythm, travel, in normal swallowing, in the
direction of the stomach; but the direction of the movement,
in abnormal swallowing or vomiting, is reversed; showing
how perfectly the opening and closing power is possessed by
the oesophagus. Those animals which ruminate swallow in
both directions : first, from the mouth towards the stomach;
second, from the stomach towards the mouth ; and third and
finally, from the mouth back again to the stomach. This
power is possessed by man himself, some individuals being
able to vomit at pleasure, and others confirming the habit
to such an extent as to be actually able to ruminate. The
power possessed by the alimentary canal of opening at one
part, and closing at another, is well seen in invagination ;
the closing portion of gut forcing itself into or within the
opening portion—the act of expansion assisting the movement in virtue of the opening and closing portions travelling
in opposite directions. The act of invagination is produced

by a double movement, similar to what would be produced
in the oesophagus of a ruminating animal if the swallowing
and ruminating movements occurred at the same time.   This
power which the intestine occasionally exerts of shortening
its length by invagination is, I apprehend, a power possessed,
within certain limits, by all muscles—the sarcous elements
of a muscle when the muscle shortens tending towards a
central point, from which they recede when the muscle elongates, very much in the same way as Professor Lister has
shown the pigment-cells in the frog's skin converge towards
a point at one time and diverge at another.   When the
sarcous elements of a muscle converge in one direction—say
in the direction of the length of the muscle—they diverge in
the opposite direction, viz. in the direction of the breadth
of the muscle ; so that, in reality, it is a misnomer to apply
the term contraction to a muscle when it shortens—the act
of shortening in one direction being actual lengthening in an
opposite direction. This follows because the sarcous elements
of a muscle, or the muscle as a whole when it moves or acts,
simply changes shape, the. volume of the muscle and the
sarcous elements composing it always remaining exactly the
same.

I shall have occasion to return to this subject when I come
to speak of the structure and action of the blood-vessels and
heart of animals ; meanwhile I would direct your attention to
the fact that the stomach may be regarded as simply an
expanded and elaborated portion of the alimentary canal ;
and the heart as an expanded and elaborated portion of
the vascular system ; the stomach and heart being constructed
on precisely the same type and performing analogous
functions.   Further, the structure and functions of the bladder
and uterus closely resemble those of the stomach and heart ;
so that the hollow muscles and blood-vessels may be placed
in the same category.   They all receive fluid, semi-fluid, or
solid substances, which they expel at regular intervals.   The
stomach can cause its contents to gyrate like those of a
vegetable cell, and the oesophagus, by the rhythmic movement
of its several parts—*i. e.* by the simultaneous opening or
widening of one part, and the closing or narrowing of another
part (say the part behind that which opens)—can seize and

dismiss the food, and pass it on in successive waves to the stomach; just as a blood-vessel with rhythmic movements, or the heart itself, can manipulate or pass on the blood in successive waves, in a given direction. If however one part of the oesophagus closes or narrows while the part beyond expands or widens, the oesophagus in this way foreshadows the movements which occur in the stomach where the pyloric sphincter opens, when the stomach closes, and *vice versa*. I use the terms ' opens ' and ' closes,' in preference to ' relaxes ' and ' contracts,' because I regard the opening of the sphincter and the closing of the stomach as equally vital acts. This view is borne out by the structure as well as the action of the parts. In man the stomach has two sphincters—a cardiac and a pyloric one. Each of these is composed of two sets of looped symmetrical fibres. The sphincters resemble the valvulae conniventes, and I am disposed to regard them as simply differentiated valvulae ,conniventes, from finding the two halves of the pyloric sphincter of the dog slightly separated from each other —valvulae conniventes, or what is equivalent thereto, being indicated in the oesophagus of the cat. If therefore the stomach be regarded as an expansion of the intestine, and the sphincters as constrictions or partitions which are structurally identical with the other parts of the stomach; and if, further, the oesophagus and intestines have peristaltic movements, *i. e.* the power of simultaneously narrowing and widening in parts, then we are bound to conclude that the closing of the stomach and the opening of its sphincters are equally vital acts. But for this co-ordination the movements would be purposeless. The structure of the intestine remarkably resembles that of many vessels where we have non-striated longitudinal and circular fibres. But many blood-vessels have distinctly rhythmic movements, so that structurally and functionally the intestines and blood-vessels resemble each other. You will therefore, I trust, bear with me, if occasionally, when speaking of the prince of hollow muscles, the heart itself, I refer now and then, for the sake of illustration, to the hollow muscles generally.

The movements in chara, as has been stated, are made visible by the presence of granules, which rotate on their own axis, travelling in a spiral direction up one side of the cell and down the other. The granules vary in size, and are elaborated *in transitu* to befit them ultimately for becoming part of the cell-wall. They may therefore be likened to the white blood-corpuscles of animals, which, as recent researches have shown, are also incorporated directly into the tissues. In Vallisneria similar intracellular movements occur. 'Spiral movements of rotation are also seen in the elongated cells forming the hairs of the nettle, loasa, pentstemon, galeopsis, borage, melon, and other plants; as well as in the separate cells of the staminal hairs of the Virginian spiderwort (*Tradescantia Virginica*)[1].'

The rotations of the protoplasmic contents of cells exhibit a marked resemblance to those of the protozoa; and many observers are of opinion that the moving bodies owe their power of rotation in part to ciliary processes similar to those which render many of the simpler plants locomotive. This view is entitled to favourable consideration, the more especially as ciliary motion has been discovered by Dr. Sharpey and others in the embryos of infusoria and gasteropoda, while inclosed in the ovum[2]; and in the ova of the polype, sponge, mollusc, and actinia. Similar gyrating movements have been observed within the stomach of the polype[3]. In all these cases the presence of cilia has been distinctly made out. If cilia could be proved to exist on the lining membrane of the cell-wall of plants, or on the exterior of the moving particles, much of the mystery of gyration would disappear. Until however these are discovered we must fall back upon other forces, and of these I believe *absorption* on the one hand, resulting in endosmose and exosmose, and *evaporation* on the other, to be the chief[4].

A moderate heat quickens the intracellular circulation, which is arrested if the temperature be elevated above 150°. It is also arrested by prussic acid and alcohol, as well as by solutions of acetate of lead, opium, and corrosive sublimate.

[1] Class-Book of Botany, by J. H. Balfour, A.M., M.D., F.R.S., etc., p. 417.
[2] Abhandl. der Akad. der Wiss. zu Berlin für 1831.
[3] Cyc. of Anat. and Phys., article 'Cilia,' by Dr. Sharpey, p. 610.
[4] Rasconi found that when the embryo of the frog was extracted from the ovum it revolved. He attributed this movement to water entering and issuing from the pores of the skin. *Sur le Développement de la Grenouille Commune.* Milan, 1826.

Prussic acid, alcohol, and the solutions in question, may destroy the intracellular circulation by poisoning and paralysing the tissues, and by inducing an imperfect osmosis; for Dutrochet found that all acids, alkalis, soluble salts, alcohol, etc., because of their susceptibility to enter into combination with the permeable partition of the endosmometer, destroy endosmosis, although they had induced it before their complete combination with the elements of the membrane had taken place; and it is not until this combination is complete that endosmosis ceases. That the intracellular movements are in a great measure due to osmosis, evaporation, and capillarity, is obvious from experiment, as I have succeeded in producing them

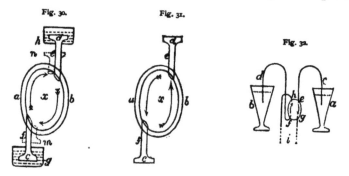

Fig. 30.   Fig. 31.   Fig. 32.

Figs. 30 and 31 show how the gyration of the cell contents may be produced either by absorption and endosmose, or by evaporation, or by all the three. Fig. 30, *a b*, cell containing viscous fluid; *c d*, absorbing surfaces of cell surrounded by water or other thin fluid (*g h*) ; *x*, endosmotic currents, which result in gyration (*vide* arrows), are thus produced. To the absorbing surfaces, evaporating ones, as at *e n, f m*, may be added. Fig. 31 shows how gyration may be effected by evaporation alone. *a b*, cell containing viscous fluid; *c f, d e*, evaporating surfaces. The arrows (*x*) indicate the direction in which the evaporation acts.—*Original.*

Fig. 32 shows how fluids washing the opposite sides of a cell in opposite directions will cause the cell contents to gyrate. *c, d*, Capillary syphon tubes, the extremities of which communicate with water in the vessels *a, b*, and with a viscid fluid in the cell *h e f g*; the one syphon enters the cell at *e*, the other at *f*; capillary tubes being inserted at *g* and *h* to carry off the superfluous fluid (*i*). The fluid within the cell gyrates, as indicated by the arrows. This is ascertained by introducing powdered charcoal into the fluid contained within the cell. In the present diagram the cell has been placed on a lower level than the water contained in the glasses; but it might have been placed as high above the water as it is below it, the gyration within the cell not being produced by the gravitation of the water in the vessels acting through the syphon tubes, but by capillarity alone.—*Original.*

artificially. Thus, if capillary syphon tubes be arranged to act upon opposite points of a glass cell, and supplied with water, they cause the fluid contents of the cell to gyrate (Fig. 32.) Again, if a glass cell be filled with syrup, and endosmotic currents induced on opposite sides of the cell above and below, the syrup begins gradually to rotate (Fig. 30.) The same happens when the syrup is allowed to evaporate from opposite points (Fig. 31).

Endosmosis and evaporation may produce gyration by a conjoined action. When endosmosis and evaporation act separately the gyration is in opposite directions (compare arrows of Figs. 30 and 31). While gyration may be induced mechanically by the operation of physical forces, the life of the plant exercises, or may exercise, an influence in its production.

As a proof that the presence or absence of moisture will not account for all the phenomena witnessed in cells, it may be stated that in the sensitive plant (*Mimosa pudica*), there is a swelling at the base of the petiole, the cells of which constitute, as it were, two springs which act in opposite directions ; so that if from any cause the one be paralysed, the other pushes the leaf in the direction of least resistance. This is exactly what happens in hemiplegia, the tongue when protruded being forced by the healthy muscles towards the paralysed side; muscles, as has been already indicated, having a power of elongating as well as of shortening. If, as universally believed at present, muscles have only the power of shortening, the tongue would be drawn towards the healthy side, which it is not[1]. The springs, if they may so be called, situated at the base of the petiole, are set in motion by the rush of fluid, creating a turgid state of the one set of cells, and an empty state of the other. A kind of rhythmic movement is thus produced. What is it, one naturally inquires, which gorges the one set of cells and empties the other, if it be not a vital power exercised by the plant? The fluid is present to both sets of cells alike. The same fluid certainly cannot stimulate the one set of cells to shorten and the other to lengthen ; and besides, so far as known, there are no contractile tissues present in the plant. Neither can the presence of moisture act as an irritant, moisture being necessary to the life of the plant, and a normal part of it. The only explanation

---

[1] Sir Thomas Watson, in speaking of hemiplegia, says, ' When the tongue is put out beyond the lips, its point is commonly turned to one side. To which side? Why, *towards* the palsied side. For what reason? Clearly because the muscles that protrude the tongue are powerless on that side, and in full vigour on the other. That half of the tongue which corresponds with the sound side *is pushed further out* than the other half, and therefore the tongue bends to the palsied side. Such is the usual fact, and such the explanation of it.'—*Principles and Practice of Physic*, 4th ed. vol. i. p. 503.

that can be given is, that the plant lives, and that it sucks in moisture by the one set of cells, and ejects moisture by the other set, just as one part of the heart sucks in blood while another expels it. The blood is not the stimulus to this act. In the same way the stomach, bladder, rectum, and uterus, close or shorten in one part, and open or lengthen in another, when the proper time arrives for expelling their contents. Here again the contained matters are not to be regarded as irritants, in the ordinary acceptation of the term. If they were, they would be expelled long before they were collected in sufficient quantity.

Movements greatly resembling those of the petiole of the sensitive plant occur in the cilia of the polygastric infusoria. Ehrenberg showed that each of the cilia in question has a bulb at its root, to which minute muscles are attached. Those muscles shorten and lengthen alternately, and so the cilia are lashed about with a flail-like motion. If the body of one of those curious creatures is fixed, the cilia excite currents in the water in which it is immersed; if the body be free, they serve as organs of locomotion. In this case there can of course be no doubt as to the vitality of the movements, and the entire absence of anything in the shape of irritation.

It is most interesting to find in an aggregation of plant-cells movements so obviously analogous to those of muscles. When the one set of cells, Henfrey[1] informs us, is contracted, the other is expanded, and *vice versa*. According to Mohl 'the expansion of the cellular tissue on the upper side of the articulation of a leaf counteracts a similar expansion of the cellular tissue on the under side; but if the upper cellular tissue be removed, so that the under cellular tissue is deprived of its antagonist the equilibrium is destroyed, and *the leaf is pushed upwards.* The reverse of this happens when the under cellular tissue is removed[2].' Here again we have an illustration of what happens in hemiplegia when the tongue is protruded. The tongue is *pushed towards the paralysed side*, and if the paralysed half of the organ were removed, the result would be precisely the same as in the plant. The leaf, it will be observed, is kept in a state of equilibrium by the presence of two forces equally

[1] Henfrey's Botany, p. 628.
[2] Anatomy and Physiology of the Vegetable Cell.

balanced, and the same may be said of the tongue. The leaf and the tongue are free to vibrate on any slight disturbance of the equilibrium. When the leaf is no longer required for the growth of the plant, it is amputated by a vital process, and not by any vicissitude of temperature ; in fact, the process of disjunction begins with the formation of the leaf-stalk, and is completed when the leaf ceases to be useful. Other vital actions might be cited in this connection which go to prove that plants control their own functions—even the roots having a selective power [1]. The remarks made regarding the movements of the hollow muscles and tongue apply equally to the flexors and extensors of the voluntary system ; but, as I shall have occasion to return to this subject, I will merely observe, in passing, that it is not a little remarkable that a mere congeries of cells devoid of nerves and contractile tissue should have the power, so to speak, of acting rhythmically, and of producing motions in definite directions in the absence of an exciting cause—at all events, in the absence of anything which partakes of the nature of irritation. With these facts before our eyes, it is not difficult to understand that voluntary and involuntary muscles have a centripetal and centrifugal action ; and by this I mean a power by which long muscles shorten and lengthen, and hollow muscles close and open.

The intracellular circulation of plants, as a rule, pursues a definite direction. The moving particles, however, occasionally stop, reverse their course, and commence *de novo*. This circumstance inclines me to believe that absorption, evaporation and osmosis play an important part in the gyration of cell contents. That the vitality of the plant is also concerned in the production of the intracellular circulation is rendered all but certain by its occurring only in the active living cells which are engaged in building up the plant, and by its ceasing if the part of the plant in which it occurs is injured [2].

---

[1] Desfontaines carried a sensitive plant with him in a coach. At first the jolting caused the plant to close its leaves. When, however, it became accustomed to the movement, it opened them, thus making itself master of the situation.

[2] When a part of a plant is injured, and the membranous cell-walls ruptured, osmosis may be impaired or altogether destroyed.

That cells are endowed with vitality, and that this of itself is capable of setting inert matter in motion, is proved by the fact that some of them in the lower tribes of plants move about in a liquid medium; the oscillatoria advancing with an undulating motion [1]. Similar moving cells are seen in stephanospharae and other genera of volvocineae; and the cellular spores of many algae are surrounded by cilia or vibratile hairs which, in fluids, move for some time after the spore (zoospore) has been discharged from the plant.

If we accord the power of motion to an entire cell, we shall have difficulty in resisting the conclusion that it also regulates the movements occurring within itself [2]. Further, in some of the lower plants, as has been stated, the living cell contents actually emerge from their temporary prison in the shape of zoospores, which lead an itinerant life until they find a suitable habitat.

The primordial utricle has moreover the power of assuming new shapes; this remarkable structure, when the cell is dividing, constricting itself, in two or more places, *without wrinkling*. But I need not pursue the inquiry further; suffice it to say, that the vital, physical, and chemical phenomena witnessed in plants are due primarily to operations occurring in the interior of cells; the functions of nutrition, reproduction, etc., necessitating movements in certain directions. In connection with the belief that the process of nutrition results in movements of a more or less definite character, I would here cite the name of one revered in physiology and pathology—viz. Sir James Paget—who gave it as his opinion that the contraction and dilatation of the heart itself is due to the nutrition and growth of the organ. He says, 'But there is another thing common to all rhythmically acting organs,—they are all the seats of nutritive processes; and I believe that their movements are rhythmical, because their

---

[1] The ova of polypi and sponges also move freely about before they become fixed. This is necessary to spread the individuals of the original community. To this end they are provided with numerous minute cilia on their exteriors, which serve the purposes of locomotion and respiration.

[2] Some authors attribute the contraction occurring in cells to alternate turgescence and emptying of certain portions of the protoplasm; but, as has been explained when speaking of the movements of the petiole of the sensitive plant, turgescence, and the absence of it, may be equally traced to vital influence.

nutrition is so; and rhythmic nutrition is, I believe, only a peculiar instance or method of manifestation of a general law of time as concerned in all organic processes. In other words, I believe that rhythmic motion is an issue of rhythmic nutrition, *i.e.* of a method of nutrition in which the acting parts are, at certain periods, raised with time-regulated progress to a state of instability of composition, from which they then decline, and in their decline may change their shape and move with a definite velocity, or (as nervous centres) may discharge nerve force [1].'

Certain plants, when vigorous and exposed to a bright light, exhibit rhythmical movements, and notably the Hedysarum (*Desmodium gyrans*), a native of the East Indies. The leaf in this plant is unequally pinnate, consisting of a larger leaflet at the end of the stalk, and two pairs of leaflets placed laterally. The smaller leaflets come towards and recede from each other with a jerking motion, every three minutes or so. The movements of the heart are certainly not more singular than those of the leaves now referred to. It cannot be the light or heat which produces the movements of the leaflets, for they go on in the dark; and as they are most regular when the plant is most healthy, we are not entitled to assume the presence of stimuli in the shape of extraneous irritation. The movements of the leaflets, in some senses, foreshadow a heart, and are no doubt connected with the nutrition of the plant. They teach us one very important fact, viz. that living organs can come and go, contract[2], expand, and perform stated motions at stated intervals, without the presence of nerves, muscles, elastic and other tissues; unless perchance these exist in an undifferentiated form, which is by no means improbable. According to Fee, the fluids drawn to the surface of a plant during light are

---

[1] Croonian Lecture, 'On the Cause of the Rhythmic Motion of the Heart,' by Sir James Paget, Bart.—*Proc. Roy. Soc.* May 28, 1857.

[2] In the wild lettuce (*Lactuca virosa*), and in the stings of nettles, the cells, on being touched, contract and exude their fluid contents. The small leaflets of the sensitive mimosas display cellular swellings at the roots, which, when touched, communicate motion to the leaves. Those swellings apparently consist of two kinds of cells, the one kind having the power of contracting, the other of dilating.—Dutrochet, *Sur la Structure Intime des Animaux et Végétaux,* 1824.

kept in equilibrium by rhythmical evaporation; the rhythmical movements of the leaves being referable to vital changes in the cell contents and vessels.

'Probably the simplest example of rhythmic motions yet known is that detected by the acute researches of Professor Busk in the Volvox globator[1]. At a certain period of the development of this simplest vegetable organism there appear in each zoospore, or in the bands of protoplasm with which the zoospores are connected, vacuoles, spaces, or cavities, of about $\frac{1}{9000}$ of an inch in diameter, which contract with regular rhythm, at intervals of from 38 to 41 seconds, quickly contracting and then more slowly dilating again.' Now, however it may be with the heart, there is no room for doubting that the closing and opening of the vacuoles, spaces, or cavities here spoken of, are equally vital acts; they close quickly and open slowly, just as in the heart; and my impression is that the different parts of the heart close and open alternately and independently, the closing of the auricles taking no part in the opening of the ventricles, and *vice versa:* in other words, the auricles close and open by vital efforts, as do likewise the ventricles; the movements of the auricles and ventricles being simply co-ordinated for a purpose. Indeed the structure and arrangement of the fibres of the heart forbid any other assumption. If we take the fibres of the ventricles, we find they are arranged in spiral figure-of-8 loops, the fibres being continuous upon each other, and crossing, at various degrees of obliquity, with mathematical precision; some being vertical, some slightly oblique, some very oblique, and others transverse or circular. When the fibres shorten they likewise thicken; this shortening and thickening obliterating the ventricular cavities from above downwards, and from without inwards. When the ventricles are closed, all the contained blood is ejected. As the blood, forced on by the closing of the auricles, cannot obtain admission to the closed ventricles, this fluid cannot mechanically distend the ventricles. They are therefore under the necessity of opening just as they closed. During the systole there is a shortening and thick-

---

[1] Transactions of the Microscopical Society of London, May 21, 1852.

ening of all the fibres of the ventricles; during the diastole there is a lengthening and thinning of the fibres. When the fibres of the ventricles shorten and thicken, those of the auricles lengthen and become thinner, and *vice versa ;* and this is precisely what happens in hollow muscles with sphincters. But for the power which muscles possess of shortening and lengthening, it would be impossible to explain how the pyloric valve of the stomach is firmly closed during the first stage of digestion, how it partly opens to allow the chyme to pass during the second stage, and how it opens wide to admit of the passage of undigested masses during the third stage. 'The observations of Cohn [1], published about a year later than those of Mr. Busk, but independent of them, discovered similar phenomena in *Gonium pectorale* and in *Chlamydomonas,* the vacuoles, like water-vesicles, contracting regularly at intervals of 40 to 45 seconds. The contractions and the dilatations occupy equal periods, as do those of our own heart ventricles ; and in *Gonium* he has found this singular fact, that when, as commonly happens, two vacuoles exist in one cell, their rhythms are alike and exactly alternate, each contracting once in about 40 seconds, and the contraction of each occurring at exactly mid-distance between two successive contractions of the other. Here then we have examples of perfect and even compound rhythmic contractions in vegetable organisms, in which we can have no suspicion of muscular structure or nervous, or of stimulus (in any reasonable sense of the term), or, in short, of any of those things which we are prone to regard as the mainsprings of rhythmic action in the heart [2].'

The Lactiferous Circulation in Plants.—Scarcely less interesting and curious than the intracellular circulation, is that occurring within the lactiferous vessels. The lactiferous vessels of plants have been likened by Carpenter to the capillary vessels of animals ; but they may, I think, with greater propriety be compared to the lacteals and lymphatics. The lactiferous vessels differ from the other vessels

---

[1] Untersuchungen über die Entwickelungsgeschichte der Mikroskopischen Algen und Pilze. Breslau, 4to, 1854.
[2] Croonian Lecture, 'On the Cause of the Rhythmic Motion of the Heart,' by Sir James Paget, Bart., F.R.S.—*Proc. Roy. Soc.* May 28, 1857.

of plants by their branching and freely anastomosing with
each other. Some authors regard them as cellular canals
which are lined with a special membrane. However this
may be, they are generally believed to contain the elaborated
sap, which has been exposed to the influence of light and air.
The movements occurring within the lactiferous vessels are
seen to most advantage in plants with milky or coloured
juice, as the india-rubber plant, gutta-percha tree, lettuce, and
dandelion.

To the lactiferous movements the name of cyclosis has
been given ; and Schultz was of opinion that they are vital
in their nature. They are in some cases so rapid as to resemble the circulation in the web of the frog's foot. They
take place in all directions, the currents being usually most
vigorous where the plant is developing most rapidly. They
are quickened by heat, and retarded by cold and the agency
of electricity. It is very difficult to account for them, unless
indeed we refer them directly to nutritive changes occurring in the plant. The difficulty is increased by the fact
that the vessels in which they occur, as far as known at
present, are *non-contractile*. I am disposed to believe that the
lactiferous vessels form a complicated series of interlacing
syphon tubes (see Fig. 29, p. 29) ; the milky and other juices
oscillating in them in obedience to atmospheric and hygro-
metric influences—the oscillations being regulated within
certain limits by vital laws and affinities. I refer at length
to this view a little further on.

The Forces which produce the Circulation in Plants.—In the
winter the tree may be said to be in a dormant condition.
With the early spring comes fresh life, for then the stem
and branches swell and the shoots and young leaves come
forth. The warmth of spring inaugurates the circulation ;
but evaporation cannot as yet be said to take any very
active part in it. The cell tissues of the tree, contracted
and dry in winter, are in the best possible condition for receiving sap in the spring. This the roots supply in quantity.
Through the roots and through the stem and branches a
steady upward stream flows in direct opposition to gravity,
and in the absence of any propelling force. This is a phenomenon which can only be explained by a *vis a fronte*

traceable to nutrition and other changes going on in the cells, and to osmotic [1] and capillary action [2].

In the ferns, according to Hoffmann, there are no channels for the descent of fluid, the sap simply ascending and diffusing itself in the substance of the plant in its progress. These plants grow by additions to their summits (acrogens), and this fact has much to do with determining the upward current, the leaf-action being virtually one of attraction or suction [3].

That nutrition has much to do with the general circulation is proved by the fact that the current always sets most strongly towards those points where growth is proceeding most rapidly : a vine, e.g., which is being forced by artificial heat, drawing the sap with immense force, although its root is placed outside the forcing-house and not participating in the heat. That osmosis also plays an important part is equally certain, from the fact that the juice presented to the cells by the roots is less dense than that contained in

[1] Dutrochet is of opinion 'that endosmose is due to a state of commixtion within the capillary tubes of the septum, and that the two opposed fluids proceed the one towards the other, with cross but unequal motions.'

'M. Poisson and William Power have each in his own way given an analytical explanation of the phenomenon of endosmose, and ascribed it to the action of the capillary canals of the porous septum interposed between the two fluids. In this explanation the phenomenon of the current of exosmosis is set aside, or regarded as occurring merely accidentally. Now this is entirely opposed to the fact; we have constantly evidence of the simultaneous existence *of the two opposite and unequal currents of endosmosis and exosmosis.*'—*Cyc. of Anat. and Phys.* article ' Endosmosis,' by Dutrochet, vol. ii. pp. 101, 102.

[2] ' The height to which different fluids rise in capillary tubes depends on a variety of causes, in appearance very different, but which must have some fundamental analogy. Of all fluids, water is that which rises highest; and substances held dissolved in it which increase its density lessen its power of capillary ascent, which is also diminished by increase of temperature : hot water ascends a less way in a capillary tube than cold water. Combustible fluids, such as alcohol and ether, are like dense fluids in regard to power of capillary ascent, so that combustibility acts in the same manner as density in this respect. The matter of which capillary tubes are formed is also endowed with the power of modifying the capillary ascent of fluids. Thus water at the same temperature will not rise to the same height in a series of equal capillary tubes made of different material.'—Ibid. vol. ii. p. 103.

[3] It ought however to be stated, that inasmuch as the upward current is mainly due to endosmose, a certain proportion of downward current, as has been already explained, is under the circumstances unavoidable. This is necessary for the growth of the stem.

the cells; the free interchange of fluids of different density through the cell-wall and vascular tissues which are freely permeable being unavoidable. The direction and varying rapidity of the endosmotic and exosmotic currents are exactly suited to the requirements of the circulation. The rapid upward rush of the thin crude sap, and the slow percolation downwards of the dense elaborated sap, is just what a *priori* we should expect. The fluid to be elaborated must pass up to the leaves, to be transformed into the *succus proprius* or true food of the tree, and the more rapidly it does so the better. It is otherwise with the elaborated fluid. This is to be carefully distributed to every part of the plant, nourishing the plant and storing up future nourishment as it goes. A rapid downward movement would be unsuitable for the object to be attained. That capillarity contributes its quota is rendered apparent by the fact that the vascular bundles and interspaces are capillary in their nature, and water will travel through them when detached from the tree[1]. The four great factors in the circulation, viz. nutrition, osmosis, capillarity, and evaporation, are intimately associated and may be considered together. The spongioles of the root imbibe watery sap or moisture, and present it to the cells of the root[2], which present it to the cells and vessels of the stem; these in turn presenting it to the branches, shoots, and other growing parts (Fig. 20, p. 20).

Goodsir—philosopher, anatomist, and physiologist in one—drew a parallel between the spongioles of the roots and the

---

[1] 'By far the greater majority of cells in the higher plants originate in forms analogous to those produced by pressure, since they multiply by division, and the septa dividing the newly-formed cells have ordinarily plain surfaces; a spherical cell forms two hemispherical cells, etc. . . , The cylindrical cells of wood are not uncommonly $\frac{1}{80}$ of an inch in length, liber cells $\frac{1}{15}$ to $\frac{1}{4}$ or $\frac{3}{8}$ of an inch (flax). Hairs composed of one or more cylindrical cells, and the cylindrical cells of some of the Confervae, especially Vaucheria, Bryopsis, and Chara, also attain longitudinal dimensions to be measured in inches, while their diameters are measured in hundredths of an inch.'—*Henfrey's Botany*, pp. 475, 477.

[2] In this they exercise a selective power, for Saussure has shown that if the roots of plants be immersed in a liquid containing equal quantities of different salts, they invariably take up more of the one salt than the other; some plants preferring one salt, some another. This only happens when the roots are entire. When the roots are cut the two salts are taken up in equal proportions.— *Recherches Chimiques sur la Végétation*, pp. 247, 261.

external layer of cells situated on the club-shaped extremities of the villi of the placenta. He says, these cells are to the ovum what the spongioles are to plants; they supply it with nourishment from the soil in which it is planted. Thus their action is selective; and they transmit into the interior of the villus the materials necessary for fœtal growth. The nutritive plasma is then taken up by the internal layers of cells, and by them brought into direct contact with the fœtal capillaries. Here a beautiful analogy is established between plants and animals. The processes of nutrition and growth are essentially the same in both cases. The cells of the placental villi, and the spongioles of the plant, exercise a selective power; they absorb what is beneficial, and reject what is prejudicial. They are imbued with a double function;·they can take in or assimilate new nutritious matter, and give off or reject non-nutritious or effete matter. In the plant a thin liquid is drawn from the earth by the spongioles and rootlets, and presented to a thicker liquid of variable constitution found in the cells and vascular tissues. What happens is this:—The walls of the cells and vascular canals being freely permeable, the thin fluids rise rapidly into the thicker fluids — the latter falling slowly through the thinner ones. Here then we have what virtually amounts to a vigorous upward circulation, and a feeble downward one. Precisely the same thing happens in an osmometer (Fig. 7, p. 14). If, e.g., a dense liquid is confined in a bladder, and the bladder be immersed in a thinner fluid, the thinner fluid rises rapidly through the thicker one—the thicker fluid descending slowly into the thinner one. The dense fluid is briskly penetrated by the thinner fluid either from above or from below, according to the position of the latter—gravity having no power in the matter. By adding exosmose as one of the forces of the circulation to endosmose, we are able to explain the reverse currents which we know exist in the circulation of plants; we are also able to explain how the two currents vary in rapidity—how they are more vigorous at certain periods of the year—how they are interrupted and seem to oscillate at times—and how they nearly or altogether cease in winter. In endosmose and exosmose we have two forces which bear a fixed relation to each other[1]. Both operate at the same time. If the one is interrupted, so is the other. It is in virtue of this arrangement that the movements of the sap can be quickened in spring, slowed in autumn, and discontinued or stopped in winter. Moisture, heat, and a living plant supply the conditions. If a part of a plant be forced (the other parts of the plant and roots being outside the forcing-house) endosmose and exosmose are at once called into operation in the part forced —the saps ascending, descending, and transfusing themselves laterally. If the forcing is suddenly discontinued, the circulation is arrested and growth checked. The same thing happens when frost chills a plant in early spring. It is thus that the plant and the circulation of the plant respond to outward influences: the circulation varying at different periods of the year, and of the day and night.

It is difficult to understand how excess of moisture in the ground can be drawn up into the plant and exhaled by the leaves at one period, and excess of moisture in the atmosphere seized by the plant and discharged by the roots at another. The explanation however is obvious, if we call to our aid the forces of endosmose and exosmose. The tree is always full of tenacious dense saps, and it is a matter of indifference whether a thinner watery fluid be presented to its roots or its leaves. If the thinner fluid be presented to its roots, then the endosmotic or principal current sets rapidly in *an upward direction ;* if, on the other hand, the thinner fluid be presented to its leaves, the endosmotic or principal current sets rapidly in *a downward direction.* That two fluids of varying density, such as those situated without and within a plant, will pass through each other in opposite directions,

---

[1] Dutrochet states that we have constantly evidence of the simultaneous existence of the two opposite and unequal currents of endosmosis and exosmosis. It is not to be inferred from this that different fluids having the same density act with the same vigour when placed in an endosmometer and placed in water. All that is meant to be conveyed is, that the same fluids differing in density will produce like results when exposed to similar conditions, endosmose being invariably accompanied by exosmose. Dutrochet, speaking of fluids having the same density but differently constituted, says, ‘Sugar-water and gum-water of the same density being put successively into the same endosmometer, which is plunged into pure water, the former produces the endosmosis with a velocity as 17, and the latter with a velocity as 8 only.’ Dutrochet has made experiments to show that an increase in temperature also increases endosmose.

whatever their position, may be proved by experiment. If, *e.g.*, I take two tubes, one end of each of which is covered by an animal membrane, and place water in the one and syrup in the other, I find that, when the tube containing syrup is immersed in water, the water *rises* rapidly through the syrup; if, on the other hand, the tube containing water is immersed in syrup, the water *descends* into the syrup; from which it follows that the thinner fluid passes through the thicker one, either from above or from below.

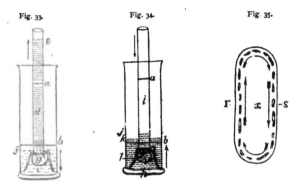

Fig. 33.   Fig. 34.   Fig. 35.

Figs. 33 and 34 explain how endosmose may go on either from *above* or from *below*, according as the more tenuous fluid is placed higher or lower than the thicker fluid. In this experiment two tubes of exactly the same calibre are employed, the ends of the tubes (*l, g*) being covered with an animal or vegetable membrane. The tubes thus prepared are placed in glass vessels also of the same size. The tube *i* is filled with water until the water reaches the line *a*; the tube *d* being filled with syrup until the syrup reaches the line *a*; the vessel *k* (Fig. 34) is filled with syrup until it reaches the line *b*, the vessel *c* (Fig. 33) being filled with water until it reaches the line *b* likewise. When the thick and thin fluids so disposed are left for a short time, the thin fluid in the tube *i* (Fig. 34) descends by endosmose into the thicker fluid contained in the vessel *h*, until the thinner fluid reaches the point *f*, the thicker fluid rising from *b* to *k*; in like manner, the thin fluid contained in the vessel *c* (Fig. 33), ascends by endosmose into the thicker fluid in the tube *d* until the thicker fluid reaches the point *e*, the thinner fluid falling from *b* to *f*. This experiment proves that a thin or watery fluid may be made to pass through the tenacious fluids found in the interior of plants either from above or from below, according as the fluid is absorbed by the leaves or roots. Endosmose, as it were, pushes fluids into the plant; evaporation, as it were, drawing them out.—*Original.*

Fig. 35.—*x* large cell with granular contents (*r, s*) gyrating. This figure shows how two forces may act on opposite sides of a circle or ovoid in opposite directions, and cause the cell or the contents of the cell to gyrate: *vide* arrows.—*Original.*

The force with which osmosis acts is very great, the rush of the thinner fluid into the thicker one being in some cases sufficient to burst the bladder containing the latter. In like manner Hales ascertained that the sap rose with such force in the vine in spring as to counterbalance a column of mercury 38 inches in height, which is equal to 43 feet 3½ inches of water[1].

That endosmose forms an important adjunct to the circulation of plants is obvious from the fact that no plant can

[1] Hales, vol. i. p. 124.

germinate without moisture, and a process of endosmose must take place before water can be transmitted through the cell-wall. 'Water is required for the solution of the nutritive matter of the seed, as well as for exciting the endosmotic action of the cells : and no circulation nor movement of fluids can take place in the seed until water is taken up.' De Candolle states that a French bean weighing 4⅜ grains took up 6½ grains of water during germination. The absorption of this large quantity of fluid is attended with an evolution of force which acts in specific directions according to the structure and condition of the parts at the time.

In artificial osmosis one membrane and two fluids are usually employed. In natural osmosis a variety of membranes and several fluids act and react upon each other [1]. In osmosis there is no visible force at work, gravity being overcome by the thinner fluids nevertheless. In the same way, if a system of dry capillary tubes be arranged vertically in tiers, and have their extreme ends placed in water or other fluid, the fluid will rise more or less quickly into them [2]. Here again, we have a movement of fluids in opposition to gravity, no force being visible. A similar result is obtained if a leash of capillary tubes, or of hair glass or a strip of blotting-paper, be suspended vertically, and their lower extremities placed in water. This result is facilitated if the tubes and hair glass are arranged within a large tube, and if the blotting-paper be placed between slips of glass to prevent lateral evaporation. By keeping down lateral and promoting vertical evaporation, the fluid rises higher. A *vis a tergo* is therefore not necessary to a flow of sap in an upward direction. It suffices if the sap be supplied to a system of cells and vessels fitted to receive it. While the fluid is proceeding in the stem of the plant from below upwards, it is also disseminating itself laterally. This is necessitated by the porosity of the cells and vessels ;

---

[1] 'Liquids are diffused throughout the whole plant by the action of cells and vessels having a different chemical constitution and different functions. One cell takes the juice from another, and acts by diffusion on the others. The cells of the rootlets imbibe by endosmose fluid matters which are carried into the stem, and the cells of the leaves by their exhaling functions aid in promoting a general movement of sap throughout the whole system.'—*Balfour's Botany*, p. 507.

[2] The fluid rises highest in capillary tubes when they are inclosed within a larger tube.

any sap passing along or through them necessarily diffusing itself to a greater or less extent in its passage. It is in this way the transverse or cross circulation is accounted for. Ordinary capillary tubes form vessels with impermeable walls; the capillary tubes of nature, on the contrary, form vessels with permeable walls. The cases, although analogous, are not identical. It is necessary that the crude sap taken up from the earth traverse the plant in its length and breadth; and this, as I have endeavoured to show, can in a great measure be effected by the agency of natural laws, and without effort on the part of the plant or tree itself. From researches just made by Goltz, it would appear that the animal tissues have a similar power of absorbing and spreading a fluid from part to part quite irrespective of the force exercised by the heart in the general circulation. He ascertained this by detaching the heart from the circulation, and presenting strychnia to the tissues. Part of the tissues thus poisoned was administered to healthy frogs as food, and induced in all of them the phenomena characteristic of strychnia-poisoning.

The Vessels of Plants in Summer form Syphons.—When the leaves are fully formed in summer the circulation is more complex, but the same forces are at work. The leaves supply a rich anastomosis or network of vessels and structures, which Mr. Herbert Spencer is inclined to regard as absorbents. Similar absorbents are found in the stem and in the roots (see Figs. 23–25, p. 21). They join the vascular vessels together, and in this way, it appears to me, convert them into a system of syphons, the extremities of which are directed alternately towards the leaves and roots. If a vigorous process of endosmose goes on in one extremity of the syphon in connexion with the root, a similar process may go on in the other extremity of the syphon, in connexion with the leaf: the direction of the currents will be reversed; but opposite forces may act on opposite sides of a circle and yet work in harmony. Fig. 35, p. 47, and Fig. 36, p. 50, will illustrate my meaning.

When the currents are united by loops pointing in opposite directions, and the two systems of syphons thus formed anastomose, a movement of the nutritious juices in a circle similar to what occurs in animals may be established. By placing the two systems of syphons together, we get a circulation which is continuous in the direction of the leaves and roots, and which is at the same time interrupted in both these directions. By this means the circulation may be quickened or slowed, according to circumstances.

This explains how the columns of moving fluids may be made to balance each other—to oscillate, or move on continuously in one direction for a certain period, and in another and opposite direction at another period. It also shows how

Fig. 36.

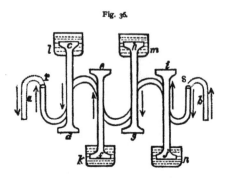

Fig. 36.—Compound syphon, with expanded absorbing and evaporating surfaces covered with animal or vegetable membrane to correspond with the roots and leaves of plants. Through this form of syphon (*a, b*), which essentially resembles that formed by the vessels (Fig. 29, p. 29) and terminal vascular loops (Figs. 23, 24, and 25 p. 21) of plants, fluids may be transmitted in advancing continuous waves (*vide* arrows), or made to oscillate. The peculiarity of this syphon consists in its being composed of a number of simple syphons united in such a manner that their free extremities are alternately directed downwards and upwards. The long legs of the simple syphon correspond to the expanded portions of the figure, and represent the leaves and roots of the plant, or, what is the same thing, its absorbing and evaporating surfaces. Any impulse communicated to the expanded portions, whether by absorption or evaporation, occasions a flow of fluid through the syphon, so that the circulation in plants is directly influenced by the presence or absence of moisture, heat, etc. *f, h, f, c,* Expanded absorbing surfaces covered with vegetable or animal membrane, and surrounded by water (*u, m, k, l*). *i, g, e, d,* Similar evaporating surfaces. The absorbing and evaporating surfaces act together. Thus, at *f, h, f,* and *c,* absorption and endosmose are taking place (these may be regarded as pushing forces) ; whereas, at *i, g, e, d,* evaporation is going on (this may be regarded as a pulling force). The arrows indicate the direction in which absorption and evaporation act. The different columns of fluid by this arrangement may be made to balance each other, as at *s, r,* or to flow in the direction *b, a.* The absorbing surfaces may all become evaporating surfaces, as in seasons of drought, or the evaporating surfaces may all become absorbing surfaces, as in rainy seasons. In the former case the plant is drained of its juices alike by leaves and roots ; in the latter case the plant is gorged with sap through the same sources.—*Original.*

the circulation may be influenced throughout its entire extent by a stimulus applied at any part; how fluids may pervade the plant; how they may enter by the roots and escape by the leaves, or the reverse; how, similarly, cross currents may be established ; and, lastly, how the movements occurring in the lactiferous vessels and within individual cells may be explained.

It is in this way, too, that an excess of moisture in the ground or in the air may be made to pass through the plant in either direction; the excess of moisture in the ground passing up into the leaves, from which it is exhaled; the excess of moisture in the atmosphere entering at the leaves and escaping by the roots. There is nothing antagonistic in this arrangement. If an excess of moisture is absorbed by the root, say at f of Fig. 36, it passes in an upward direction, and escapes at e. If an excess of moisture is absorbed by the leaf, say at c of Fig. 36, it passes directly down to the root, as indicated by the arrow, to d. In either case endosmose is at work. When too much sap ascends from the root, it is endosmose acting in an upward direction; when too much sap descends from the leaf, it is endosmose acting in a downward direction. By placing the dense fluid above a less dense one, we get an upward current; by placing the dense fluid below the less dense one, we get a downward current. But when the currents are once established they may work in harmony; the upward current acting at f and the downward

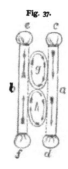

Fig. 37.—Diagram showing how intracellular circulation or gyration may be produced. a, b, Two vessels, the ends of which are covered with a portion of animal or vegetable membrane (c, d, e, f), to represent the absorbing or evaporating surfaces of plants. Between the vessels two vegetable cells (g, h) are placed. If water (say moisture from the earth) is applied at f to the thicker fluid (crude or other vegetable saps) contained in the vessel b, an endosmotic current sets in an upward direction towards e, as indicated by the arrows. If water (say moisture from the air, as rain or dew) is applied at c to the thicker fluid (crude or other vegetable saps) contained in the vessel a, an endosmotic current sets in a downward direction towards d, as indicated by the arrows. Similar currents are produced if evaporation goes on at the points e and d; or if absorption goes on at f and c, and evaporation at d and e. In either case the fluids passing through the vessels a and b wash and penetrate the sides of the cells g h obliquely, and cause their contents to gyrate (*vide* arrows). A similar result is produced if the cells g, h are bathed with a thinner fluid than that which they contain, the endosmose and exosmose induced, aided by the rounded form of the cells, tending to rotation of the cell contents. The porosity of the walls of the cells and vessels favours these results. Absorption may be regarded as a pushing force; evaporation as a pulling force.—*Original.*

Fig. 37.

one at c, giving a continuous circulation of sap through the plant similar to the circulation in the trunk and other parts of animals. Nor is this all. It may even happen that when an endosmotic current, going in a certain direction, falls in with an exosmotic one having a similar direction, the two may blend and travel together. In this case the fluids fuse more or less completely *in transitu*—an arrangement which accounts for every form and variety of movement that can occur in plants.

Intracellular Movements in Plants,—Probable Explanation of.—While the cells inaugurate or commence the general circulation, the general circulation in its turn influences the intracellular circulation. This follows, because when a current of fluid travels up the one side of a thin porous cell-wall, and another and opposite current travels dòwn the other or opposite side, a certain proportion of the currents pass obliquely through the cell-wall, and cause the fluid contents of the cell to gyrate or move in a circle (Fig. 37, p. 51). The cell contents are made to gyrate, even in the absence of opposing currents outside the cell, if endosmotic and exosmotic currents are induced within it; or if evaporation or capillarity be made to act at certain points (Figs. 30-32, p. 34).

The cell and vessel are part of a common stock, and both are influenced by the presence of moisture. The cell and vessel have their long axes running in the same direction, so that fluids entering and escaping from a cell and vessel by endosmose and exosmose produce movements in opposite directions; these movements, seeing the cell is closed and *rounded* at either end, being gradually converted into rotatory ones. The same holds true of the general circulation when the vessels are joined in the leaves and roots to form loops. Certain movements (not necessarily those of gyration) occurring within the cells inaugurate the general circulation, and, when the general circulation is established, it assists the gyration of the cell contents.

As the vessel is a differentiation of the cell, so the general circulation is a differentiation of the intracellular circulation [1]. The intracellular and general circulation are referable to the same causes, and always act in harmony; the gyration of the cell contents within their capsule is equivalent to the gyration of the general circulation, when the vessels are joined by loops in the leaves and roots. The presence of vessels is not necessary to the circulation. This can be carried on in the intervascular spaces, or, indeed, wherever there are cavities or open canals along which fluids can travel [2]. In plants, fluids and air may circulate either

[1] Henfrey is of opinion that intracellular movements take place in all cells at one period or other of their growth.

[2] Rainey was of opinion that the intercellular canals, which are more or less continuous throughout the entire length of the plant, are the channels through which the sap principally ascends; and Tetley was inclined to regard the cells and vessels as secreting organs which operated upon the crude sap in the intercellular canals, from which they separated by vito-chemical actions liquid and gaseous matters. The recent experiments of Hoffmann do not support this view.

separately or in combination. The syphon arrangement, ex- plained here for the first time, accounts for the upward and downward growth of a plant, and for the fact that a stem may send out of its interior ascending shoots and leaves, and de- scending roots and spongioles—the former occasionally assum- ing the function of the latter, and *vice versa*. A single system of vessels or tubes may act by itself and discharge a double duty, or two systems may combine and discharge a single function. This arrangement supplies a circulation equal to the wants of every form and variety of plant. If the plant is simply cellular, the circulation is diffused, *i.e.* the fluids enter the plant in all directions, and escape in all directions ; every part of the plant being provided with nutritious juices, and every part being drained of effete matters. If the plant is provided with spiral and other vessels, with intercellular and other spaces, with lactiferous vessels, and with cells having a circulation of their own, the arrangement is equally simple and equally satisfactory as regards the circulation of nutritious juices in the stem and branches, and the absorption and discharge of fluids by the roots and leaves. The circulating forces in a plant are, so to speak, pitted against each other ; the circulation is *in equilibrio,* and anything that disturbs this state of matters causes motion in one direction or another. Too much evaporation or too much absorption in the leaves, or too much moisture taken in or given off by the roots, or growth in a particular direction, may do this. The cir- culation is universal in its nature, and perfect of its kind. It can be made to slow and stop ; to go on languidly or very vigorously ; one part of it may be active while another is inactive ; it is equal to all the demands made upon it by growth, by reproduction, by heat, by cold, light and dark- ness ; it is equally suited to the simple cellular plant, and the complex fibro-vascular one.

Rainey was further of opinion that the descent of the elaborated sap was through the vessels, and not through the cells or intercellular spaces. Schultz maintained that the sap descended through the lactiferous vessels, these being compared by Carpenter to the capillaries of animals. Spencer states from experiment that the spiral, annular, scalariform, and other vessels, form the channels not only for the ascent, but also for the descent of the sap, the same vessels sufficing for both. There is thus much difference of opinion as to the precise course pursued by the ascending and descending saps.

As the season advances, and the leaves become fully developed, the heat of summer comes into play. Evaporation now begins to take an active part in the circulation [1]. As the sap rises to the leaves, it is evaporated in quantity from the stomata and other parts; these, when taken together, constituting a vast drying surface. The process which is now inaugurated can be exactly imitated by placing a glass tube in water, the upper end of which is slightly expanded, funnel-fashion, and covered with a layer of moist bladder. As evaporation goes on in the bladder, a continuous upward stream of fluid is furnished. The common spray-producer affords another illustration. In this very useful contrivance a capillary tube, or a tube with a capillary point, is placed in fluid, a corresponding tube being arranged to meet its upper end at right angles. A current of air forced through the second tube causes the fluid to rise in the first tube, an effect favoured by capillary attraction when the tube is small [2]. The sap in summer, from evaporation and the elaboration it undergoes in the leaves, is rendered more tenacious, and

[1] 'In the leaves (and green portions of plants generally) the very important phenomenon of evaporation or transpiration of watery vapours occurs, and constitutes probably the most important agent of all in causing the supply and diffusion of food in plants. . . . . In the spring, before the expansion of the buds, absorption is necessarily greater than transpiration; the water in such a case is stored in the stem, where it is made available for the expanding buds and growing tissues generally. In the summer, the transpiration is greater than the absorption; and then the leaves depend for their supply on the stores in the stem, or, failing that, they wither. Even in winter, provided the stem be not absolutely frozen, there is a motion of the juices dependent to a great extent on the temperature of the soil, which is always in that season higher than the air, and it increases in amount from the surface downwards. . . . . The crude sap becomes more and more condensed as it ascends in the stem and other organs. In the leaves and other green parts it undergoes a most important transformation, loses by transpiration much of its water, and receives a new element in its composition, of the highest importance to it as material for development, viz. carbon, derived from the carbonic acid absorbed by the leaves, and decomposed there in sunlight, with the liberation of oxygen.'—*Henfrey's Botany*, pp. 567–569.

[2] In Professor Lister's spray-producer, the second tube is made to bifurcate—one portion descending into the bottle containing the fluid, which it is not allowed to touch; the other ascending and meeting the point of the first tube at right angles, as before. In this case the current of air introduced into the second tube forces the fluid through the first tube, and breaks it up into spray simultaneously. The cloud of spray produced by this most ingenious instrument is remarkable alike for its great size and the extreme state of division to which its component particles are reduced.

adheres with greater force to the vessels and channels through which it passes. As a consequence, there is a slight increase in the amount of capillary action, and a slight diminution of the osmotic action. The vital capillary and osmotic forces vary in intensity, the one being weaker when the other is stronger, and *vice versa*[1].

The *succus proprius*, when elaborated, descends into the growing parts of the tree according to demand, and at a varying speed. It goes from a higher to a lower level; not, however, in obedience to the law of gravity, for it is found that if a branch is bent to the ground, the *succus proprius* actually ascends prior to descending. Gravity may, under certain circumstances, arrest, instead of cause, the flow of a fluid; and atmospheric pressure will cause water to flow into an exhausted receiver[2]. Petit Thouars and Gaudichaud, as I have explained, believe that the embryo of plants consists of two systems—a caulinary and radicular system; the former having an ascending circulation, and tending to develop buds and leaves; the latter having a descending circulation, and tending to develop the stem and roots—each system having cells and vessels peculiar to itself[3]. Many are of opinion that the two systems persist throughout the entire life of the plant. This view is favoured by the growth of plants in an upward direction, and by the presence in screw-pines of adventitious and other roots which grow downwards into the soil (Figs. 2 and 3, p. 9). This growth in opposite directions implies two systems, and a reverse circulation. Mr. Herbert Spencer takes an opposite view. He maintains that the two sets of vessels cannot be demonstrated to exist, and that in reality there is only one set, the fluids oscillating therein in such a manner as at one period to occasion an upward circulation to the leaves, and at another, a downward circulation to the roots; the vessels, according to him, terminating in the leaves and roots in a series of club-

---

[1] 'The entrance of fluid into a plant may be explained by endosmose and certain vital affinities; the escape by exosmose and certain vital repulsions.'—Gyde, *On Radical Excretions*, Trans. High. and Agric. Soc., Oct. 1843, p. 273.

[2] Grove on the Correlation of Physical Forces, p. 10.

[3] 'In the embryo of a flowering plant it is scarcely possible to define the limits even of the stem itself, which loses itself above in the plumule, and below in the radicle.'—*Henfrey's Botany*, p. 23.

shaped expansions, which he was the first to discover and describe (Figs. 23, 24, and 25, p. 21)[1].

Absorbents of Plants.—The club-shaped expansions referred to consist of masses of irregular and imperfectly-united fibrous cells, such as those out of which the vessels are developed. They do not occur in all leaves, and are found in stems and branches that have assumed the function of leaves. They occupy the intercellular spaces between the ultimate venous network of the leaves, into which network they also open. Some of them, however, open outwards towards the air. The vascular club-shaped expansions are thus brought into immediate contact not only with the veins of the leaf, but also the tissues concerned in assimilation. They are found in a less developed form in the root and body of the turnip. The simplest kinds consist of only fenestrated cells, with their ends bent round so as to meet[2]. By the club-shaped expansions a direct connexion is established in the leaf between the vascular tubes found in the branches, stems, and roots; in fact, the free extremities of the tubes may be said to be united in the leaves and roots by a series of vascular expansions resembling the capillary

---

[1] These structures, when present, form the terminations of the vascular system. They are masses of irregular and imperfectly-united fibrous cells, such as those out of which vessels are developed; and they are sometimes slender and sometimes bulky—usually, however, being more or less club-shaped. Speaking of the club-shaped expansion of the *Euphorbia neriifolia*, Mr. Spencer says, ‘Occupying one of the interspaces of the ultimate venous network, it consists of a spirally-lined duct, or set of ducts, which connects with the neighbouring vein a cluster of half-reticulated half-scalariform cells. These cells have projections, many of them tapering, that insert themselves into the adjacent intercellular spaces, thus producing an extensive surface of contact between the organ and the embedding tissues. A further trait is that the unsheathing prosenchyma is either but little developed or wholly absent, and consequently this expanded vascular structure, especially at its end, comes immediately in contact with the tissues concerned in assimilation.’ Further on he observes, ‘Considering the structure and position of these organs, as well as the nature of the plants possessing them, may we not form a shrewd suspicion as to their function? Is it not probable that they facilitate absorption of the juices carried back from the leaf for the nutrition of the stem and roots?’—*Principles of Biology*, vol. ii. p. 559.

[2] ‘It should be added that, while the expanded free extremities graduate into tapering free extremities, not differing from ordinary vessels, they also pass insensibly into the ordinary inosculations. Occasionally, along with numerous free endings, there occur loops, and from such loops there are transitions to the ultimate meshes of the veins.’—Ibid., vol. i. p. 559.

vessels of animals. If this be so—and there is no room for doubt—many of the difficulties connected with the circulation in plants disappear, for the presence of a capillary system in the leaves and roots enables us to reconcile the double set of vessels of Petit Thouars and Gaudichaud with the single set of Mr. Spencer. It also enables us to explain the ascending current in spring, the ascending and descending currents in summer, and the descending current in autumn. Further, it shows us how those currents may be inaugurated, how carried on, how interrupted, and how partly or altogether stopped. In the root one set of cells and vessels absorb and another excrete, the excreting vessels, according to Macaire[1], giving off matters which are detrimental to the soil. In this arrangement we have an indication of two systems and two forces acting in opposite directions (Fig. 1, p. 9).

Whether two distinct systems of vessels exist is immaterial, if, as I have explained, all vessels virtually form syphon tubes. The vessels which convey the sap, as is well known, are arranged in more or less parallel vertical lines. If the vessels are united to each other by a capillary plexus, or, what is equivalent thereto, in the leaves and roots, they are at once, as has been shown, converted into syphon tubes, one set bending upon itself in the leaves, the other set bending upon itself in the roots. As however a certain proportion of the syphon tubes which bend upon themselves in the leaves are porous and virtually open towards the roots; while a certain proportion of the syphon tubes which bend upon themselves in the roots are porous and virtually open towards the leaves; it follows that the contents of the syphon tubes may be made to move by an increase or decrease of moisture, heat, etc., either from above or from below. In spring, the vessels may be said to consist of one set, because at this period the leaves and the connecting plexuses which they contain do not exist. All the vessels at this period may therefore be regarded as carrying sap in an upward direction to form shoots, buds, and leaves, part of the sap escaping laterally because of the porosity of the

[1] Macaire-Princeps, Sur les Excrétions des Racines, Mém. de la Soc. Phys. et d'Hist. Nat. de Genève, tom. v. p. 287. Annales des Sc. Nat., 1st series, xxviii. 402. Brugmans, De Mutata Humorum in Regno Organico Indole.

vessels. In summer, when the leaves are fully formed, the connecting links are supplied by the capillary vascular expansions formed in them—the tubes are, in fact, converted into syphons. As both extremities of the syphons are full of sap in spring and early summer, an upward and a downward current is immediately established. When the downward current has nourished the plant and stored up its starch granules for the ensuing spring, the leaves fall, the syphon structure and action is interrupted, and all the tubes (they are a second time single tubes) convey moisture from above downwards, as happens in autumn. As the vascular expansions or networks are found also in the stems of plants, it may be taken for granted that certain of the tubes are united in spring, the upward rush of sap being followed by a slight downward current, as happens in endosmose and exosmose. As moreover the spongioles of the root and the leaves are analogous structures, and certain tubes are united in the roots, the downward current in autumn is accompanied by a slight upward current. This accounts for the fact that, at all periods of the year, the upward, downward, and transverse currents exist; the upward and downward currents being most vigorous in spring and autumn, and scarcely perceptible in winter. Furthermore, as some of the vascular expansions in the leaves are free to absorb moisture, etc., in the same way that the spongioles are, it follows that the general circulation may receive an impulse from the leaves, or from the roots, or both together, the circulation going on in a continuous current in certain vessels, as explained (see Fig. 36, p. 50).

Analogy between Leaves and Roots.—That leaves and roots have many points in common was shown by the researches of Bonnet [1], who found that plants of mercurialis whose leaves were in contact with water absorbed as much, and, for a time, kept nearly as fresh, as those whose roots were immersed [2]. The hairs on the under surface of leaves absorb

---

[1] Bonnet : Recherches sur l'Usage des Feuilles dans les Plantes. Gotting., 1754.

[2] 'Leaves proceed from the nodes of the axis, and commence as *cellular processes at the extremities of the medullary rays*. The extremities of the roots are composed of *loose cells, which appear to be the terminal tissues of the radicle*, and formed by the elongating root.'—*Balfour's Botany*, pp. 51 and 96. Both leaves and roots are covered by epidermis, and have vessels developed in them. The stomata of the

moisture, and seem to act as cellular rootlets. Nor is this all. Hoffmann[1] showed that, after every fall of rain or dew, the leaves absorbed moisture, which passed downwards in the tracheae and enveloping prosenchyma, and displaced for a time the air usually found in the spiral vessels. In proportion as the absorption was abundant and rapid, the tendency of the moisture to enter the spiral vessels was increased. Almost precisely the same remarks might be made regarding the spongioles of the root. In seasons of drought they absorb and transmit comparatively little moisture. After a rainfall the spongioles drink greedily, and send on crude sap in abundance. Further, excess of moisture sent up by the roots is exhaled by the leaves; excess of moisture, sent down by the leaves, escaping by the roots. If the relation existing between the leaves and roots be disturbed, and exhalation prevented, the plant becomes dropsical. If, on the other hand, the exhalation from the leaves be in excess of the moisture absorbed by the roots, the leaves wither and droop. Leaves and roots both give off gases—the former, oxygen; the latter, according to Wiegmann and Polodorff, carbonic acid. In the epiphytes, or air-growing plants, the roots (aerial of course) are of a green colour, like the leaves, and possess stomata. The stomata are wanting in the roots of aquatic plants, but they are also absent in the submerged leaves. The cuttings of many plants give off *leaf-buds and roots* at the same time. 'In the monocotyledons and ferns, the radicle is abortive, and the efficient roots are really lateral organs, comparable in a certain way to the leaves upon the ascending part of the stem[2].' When the branches and leaves are growing rapidly, the roots are also developing their rootlets, and constantly renewing their delicate absorbing extremities. Aerial roots take on the function of leaves, and obtain nourishment from the atmosphere. In this case they lose their fibrils, assume the appearance of stems, and throw out leaf-buds.

leaves seem to be represented in the roots by hairs. Leaves frequently display hairs, and the stomata are generally absent in submerged leaves.

[1] On the Circulation of the Sap in Plants, in 'Scientific Memoirs,' Nat. Hist. i. p. 46.

[2] Henfrey's Botany, p. 16.

Duhamel proved this ingeniously and very simply. He took a willow and inserted its branches into the soil, where they took root. This done, he pulled up the original root and exposed it to the air. The original root, after a short interval, became transformed into *leaf*-bearing branches. The fibrous rootlets upon the surface of tuberous taproots, like the carrot, parsnip, etc., appear to be mostly *true branches*[1]. Speaking generally, it seems to be a matter of little consequence whether the stem be placed in a vertical or procumbent position. In either case the branches and leaves strike upwards—the roots and spongioles downwards. Roots, like leaves, are sometimes spirally arranged. Roots may produce buds, as shown in the Anemone japonica, and branches may be made to throw out rootlets. The rhizome of Solomon's-seal throws out a bud from its upper surface, and roots from its under; and the strawberry, from its runners, sends leaves up and roots down[2], all which proves very clearly that the spongioles and leaves, and roots and branches, are closely allied both in structure and function— the circulation and the forces which produce it being in either case essentially the same. The intimate relation which exists between the roots and the leaves is well expressed by Mulder, who asserts that all the nitrogenous constituents of plants are absorbed by *the roots* and assimilated there at once, carbon being fixed by the *green organs;* that a continual interchange goes on *from above and from below* between *the leaves and roots,* the roots supplying protoplasmic material which originates all organic phenomena; the leaves on their part sending down the ternary compounds (CHO), which supply the material for cell-membranes, starch, etc. The leaves of plants have the power of attracting and condensing the moisture suspended in the air, and the roots *can pump it up* from the soil from considerable depths. A tree has, as it were, open mouths at both ends; these mouths communicating with open channels, which, in some cases,

---

[1] Henfrey's Botany, pp. 16–18.

[2] 'The strawberry plant produces in the axils of its leaves, buds, which in the same season expand several of their internodes and form long filiform branches, the buds of which give rise to rosettes of leaves and stock root, and thus form independent plants.'—Ibid. p. 33.

traverse the entire length of the tree; at other times they interlace and form loops, which convert them into syphons directed towards the leaves and roots respectively, as already stated. (Fig. 36, p. 50).

The Effects produced on the Circulation by the Swaying of Plants in the Wind: Mr. Spencer's views.—Mr. Herbert Spencer is of opinion that the circulation is influenced to a considerable extent by the swaying of plants and trees in the wind; this oscillation subjecting certain parts of the tree or plant to lateral and longitudinal strain. The effect of the strain, he remarks, is to bend the tree or plant alternately in opposite directions, and from the parts so bent the sap is driven in an upward and downward direction, a certain amount being forced through the coats of the vessels (which are porous) into the surrounding tissues. According to him, a certain proportion of the propelling power is intermittent, confined to no locality, and variable as to intensity.

To reconcile the idea of an upward and downward circulation in a single system of vertical tubes, Mr. Spencer explains, as has been stated, that the vessels of the stem and branches terminate in club-shaped expansions in the leaves; which expansions act as absorbent organs, and may be compared to the spongioles of the root. If, therefore, the spongioles of the root, Mr. Spencer argues, send up the *crude* sap, it is not difficult to understand how the spongioles of the leaf (the club-shaped expansions referred to) send down the *elaborated* sap, one channel sufficing for the transit of both.

From the foregoing, it will be evident that, in Mr. Spencer's opinion, the upward and downward currents take place in different parts of the same tube, and that when one part of the tube is engaged with the up circulation, the down circulation is prevented, and *vice versa*[1]. Now, granting

---

[1] Mr. Spencer observes:—'If, then, returning to the general argument, we conclude that these expanded terminations of the vascular system in leaves are absorbent. organs, we find a farther confirmation of the views set forth respecting the alternating movement of the sap along the same channels. These spongioles of the leaves, like the spongioles of the root, being appliances by which liquid is taken up to be carried into the mass of the plant, we are obliged to regard the vessels which end in these spongioles of the leaves as being the channels of the down current whenever it is produced. If the elaborated sap is

that the upward and downward currents take place in the same tube, it appears to me that both currents may be going on at the same time by a simple process of endosmose and exosmose[1]. I have difficulty in understanding how, in an organised structure, the saps should be driven about in a reckless manner, at irregular intervals, and as it were by accident. I can, however, readily comprehend how, if a porous vertical tube, or any number of such tubes, containing dense fluids, be arranged in parallel lines, and placed in contact with less dense fluids, that the less dense fluids will penetrate the more dense ones in an upward or downward direction, according as the less dense fluids are placed below or above the more dense fluids; the more dense fluids penetrating the less dense fluids always in an opposite direction, so as to produce two distinct and opposite currents, which run from below upwards and from above downwards; the porosity of the vessel occasioning a certain amount of transfusion or lateral circulation. In this we have an arrangement capable of furnishing a steady supply of sap to every part of the tree, quite irrespective of any influence exerted by the wind. In fact, it is necessary to exclude the action of the wind when discussing the question ; for sap ascends, descends, and transudes in trees nailed to walls, in climbing and hothouse plants, where of course the wind is inoperative. Mr. Spencer's argument may be briefly stated. 'If,' he says, 'a trunk, a bough, a shoot, or a petiole is bent by a gust of wind, the substance of its convex side is subject to longitudinal tension, the substance of its concave side being at the same time compressed. This is the primary mechanical effect. There is, however, a second mechanical effect, which

---

abstracted from the leaves by these absorbents, then we have no alternative but to suppose that, having entered the vascular system, the elaborated sap descends through it. And seeing how, by the help of these special terminations, it becomes possible for the same vessels to carry back a quality of sap unlike that which they bring up, we are enabled to understand tolerably well how this rhythmical movement produces a downward transfer of materials for growth.'— *Principles of Biology*, vol. ii. p. 561.

[1] Dutrochet believes, that in endosmosis the two opposite fluids pass through the same capillary canal, the one travelling in one direction, the other in a contrary direction; and that the double movement of transmission takes place by a reciprocal penetration of the two fluids.

more chiefly concerns us. That bend by which the tissues of the convex side are stretched also produces lateral compression of them. It is demonstrable that the tension of the outer layer of a mass made convex by bending, must, by composition of forces, produce at every point a resultant at right angles to the layers beneath it; that, similarly, the joint tension of these two layers must throw a pressure on the next deeper layer, and so on. Hence, if at some little distance beneath the surface of a stem, twig, or leaf-stalk, there exist longitudinal tubes, these tubes must be squeezed each time the side of the branch they are placed on becomes convex. If, then, the sap-vessels are thus compressed, the sap contained by them will move along the lines of least resistance. Part, and probably the greater part, will escape lengthways from the place of greatest pressure; some of it being expelled downwards, and some of it upwards. But, at the same time, part of it will be likely to ooze through the walls of the tubes. If these walls are so perfect as to permit the passage of liquid only by osmose, it may still be inferred that the osmose will increase under pressure; and probably, under recurrent pressure, the places at which the osmotic current passes most readily will become more and more permeable, until they eventually form pores. At any rate, it is manifest that when pores and slits exist, whether thus formed, or formed in any other way, the escape of sap into the adjacent tissue at each bend will become easy and rapid. The lateral oscillation or strain takes place in stems and branches, a longitudinal strain occurring in roots, the circulation being in part due to a rude pumping process, occasioned by the swinging about of different parts of the tree or plant.' On this doctrine Mr. Spencer founds another, viz. that in the region of the strained part, a profuse exudation of sap takes place; this sap going to form woody fibre, which strengthens the yielding part. Unfortunately for Mr. Spencer's hypothesis, the upward, downward, and transverse currents, as has been stated, occur in hothouse and other plants, and in roots which are in no way exposed to winds; wood being formed under these circumstances just as it is out of doors. Indeed, wood is formed in trees nailed firmly to a wall, and in climbing plants which twist themselves

around unyielding structures. Nuts and thorns, and other hard structures, in like manner, are formed in the absence of anything in the shape of strains. Mr. Spencer states that in plants with stems, petioles, and leaves, having tolerably constant attitudes, the increasing porosity of the tubes, and consequent deposit of dense tissue, takes place *in anticipation* of the strains to which the parts of the individual are liable, but takes place at parts which have been habitually subject to such strains in ancestral individuals. If, however, the sap is exuded, and wood formed, before the strain takes place, the strain cannot consistently be regarded as the cause either of the exudation or of the wood. While attaching considerable importance to the effect produced on the circulation by the swaying of plants and trees in the wind, it must be stated that Mr. Spencer gives due prominence to the vital, capillary, and osmotic forces. He writes:—
'The *causes* of circulation are those actions only which disturb the liquid equilibrium in a plant, by permanently abstracting water or sap from some part of it; and of these the first is the absorption of materials for the formation of new tissue in growing parts; the second is the loss by evaporation, mainly through adult leaves; and the third is the loss by extravasation through compressed vessels. Only so far as it produces this last can mechanical strain be regarded as truly a cause of circulation. All the other actions concerned must be classed as *aids* to circulation—as facilitating that redistribution of liquid that continually restores the equilibrium continually disturbed; and of these capillary action may be named as the first, osmose as the second, and the propulsive effect of mechanical strains as the third [1].'

Epitome of Forces engaged in the Circulation of Plants.—Before passing to a consideration of the circulation as it exists in animals, it may be useful to recapitulate very briefly the forces at work in the circulation of plants, and to say a few words with regard to the nature of force generally. Of the forces which produce the circulation in plants, capillarity and osmose undoubtedly play an important part. Capillarity inaugurates, and osmose maintains in a great measure, not only the ascending and descending currents, but also the

---

[1] Principles of Biology, vol. i. pp. 553, 554.

cross currents and the gyration or rotation of the cell contents. Capillary action is induced in an upward or downward direction according as the fluid is presented to the top or bottom of the capillary tube. It may go on either within the vessels of the plant, or in the interspaces between the vessels; and the same may be said of endosmose and exosmose. Endosmose, as has been explained, acts in conjunction with exosmose. The one implies the other. The endosmotic and capillary actions are modified by vital, chemical, and other changes. They produce a swelling of the cells and entire tissues of the plant, as the fluid absorbed by the roots and leaves must be accommodated within the plant. The fluids imbibed produce pressure of the cell-walls, vessels, etc.—these reacting and forcing the fluids in the direction of least resistance. Increase of temperature in the roots, stem, and branches, leads to a similar result; increase of temperature expanding the air which pervades all parts of plants. The expanded air, like the fluids, naturally escapes in the direction of least resistance. From this it follows that the circulation is most vigorous during the day, and least so during the night. The processes of growth and reproduction produce the vacuum into which the fluids urged on by cell, air, and other pressure naturally flow. The presence of sap and air are equally necessary to growing and germinating plants. Growth or vital change involves chemical change. Starch is to be transformed into sugar, and before this can be done, water must flow to the point where the transformation is to take place; the demand for water acts as a *vis a fronte*. The leaves exhale from their surfaces, and here, too, a constant evaporation is going on. A fluid abstracted from the leaves by external heat draws on the fluid in the branches; the fluid in the branches drawing up that in the stem, which, in turn, acts upon that in the roots; the roots being originally supplied by absorption, capillarity, and osmose. This can be proved by direct experiment. If a system of tubes have their lower extremities placed in water, while a portion of moistened bladder is laid across their upper extremities, expanded to receive it, it is found that the quantity of fluid which passes through the tubes is determined by the amount of evaporation. The roots exhale as well as absorb, so that a certain proportion of the fluids are drawn downwards. In other words, the leaves may be said to draw the fluids upwards, while the roots, at stated periods, draw them downwards. The leaves act more especially in conjunction with endosmose, the roots with exosmose. These, again, act in harmony with capillary structures and vito-chemical changes incident to growing plants.

Lastly, the occasional swaying of petioles, branches, and stems, by the wind, exerts, as Mr. Herbert Spencer has shown, an intermittent pressure, to which he attributes an upward, downward, and lateral thrusting of the sap in the direction of least resistance. The strain to which the different parts of the tree are subjected by the swaying in question gives rise, as he explains, to an exudation of sap at the strained point—the exuded fluids making room for other fluids, which, being supplied either by the roots or leaves, result in motion.

I have placed the lateral swaying or pumping process of Mr. Herbert Spencer last, because, as has been already stated, the general and intracellular circulation of plants can go on when no wind is present.

Considerable diversity of opinion exists as to the channels through which the circulating fluids of plants are conveyed. Hoffmann and Unger maintain that in plants possessed of fibro-vascular bundles, the sap in the first instance passes up from the roots chiefly in the parenchymatous cellular constituents of the bundles, and that these juices do not pass by the spiral vessels themselves.

Rainey was of opinion that the intercellular canals, which are more or less continuous throughout the entire length of the plant, are the channels through which the sap principally ascends; and that the descent of the elaborated sap occurs in the vessels, and not in the cells or intercellular spaces. Tetley was inclined to regard the cells and vessels as secreting organs which operated upon the crude sap in the intercellular canals, from which they separated, by vito-chemical actions, liquid and gaseous matters. Schultz maintained that the sap descends through the lactiferous vessels, these being compared by Carpenter to the capillaries of animals. Spencer states from experiment that the spiral, annular, scalariform; and other vessels, form the channels for the ascent of the sap, and he is disposed to believe that the sap descends in the same vessels in which it ascends.

Spencer is further of opinion that there is only one system of vessels, the crude and elaborated saps ascending and descending in the same vessels at different times, a result favoured, but not caused, by the swaying of the different parts of the plant or tree in the wind. Mr. Spencer is quite aware that the ascent and descent of the sap is not occasioned by the swaying referred to, for he remarks, 'Whether there is oscillation or whether there is not, the physiological demands of the different parts of the plant determine the direction of the current[1].' The researches of Petit Thouars, Gaudichaud, De la Hire, Darwin, Knight, and Macaire, favour the idea of a double system of vessels—an ascending and a descending set. However authors differ as to the number and direction of the vessels, they are all agreed in this, that the currents ascend, descend, and transude. The question which naturally presents itself at this stage, is, Are vessels necessary to the circulation in plants? and if so, is there one or two sets of vessels? I pointed out that vessels are not necessary to the circulation, as this goes on in cellular plants where no vessels exist. I also endeavoured to show that when vessels are present, the circulation may go on either within them, or in the intervascular spaces outside of them, provided these, like the vessels, are capillary in their nature. I further attempted to reconcile the views of those who maintain that there is only one set of vessels, with those who believe that two sets are necessary for carrying on the ascending and descending current, by supposing (and we have good warrant for the supposition) that the vessels and intervascular spaces of plants are united in the stem and branches, and at certain periods of the year in the leaves and roots, to form syphons, the free extremities of which are directed alternately in the direction of the leaves and roots. These syphons are infinite in variety and form, and interlace in every conceivable direction. They may be confined to the roots, stem, branches, or leaves, or portions of

[1] Principles of Biology, vol. i. p. 557.

them, the fluids being sent on by relays; or they may extend throughout the entire length of the plant or tree. They consist of rigid capillary tubes with porous walls, *i.e.* walls capable of preventing the ingress of air, while they do not prevent the free ingress and egress of fluids, as witnessed in osmose and evaporation. The long legs of the syphons, or what are equivalent thereto, correspond to the evaporating surfaces, and those surfaces in which an active osmosis is established. The leaves and roots form such surfaces, but they are not confined to those portions of the plant, as they exist in every part of it; the plant breathing and drinking at every pore when it has an opportunity. If you figure to yourselves the vast drying or evaporating surfaces furnished by a tree in full leaf, you will readily comprehend the immense tractile power exerted, and the astonishing force with which the fluids are drawn up in the syphon tubes referred to. If, on the other hand, you regard the leaves and roots, not as evaporating surfaces, but as absorbing surfaces (they are both), *i.e.* surfaces capable of imbibing moisture, you will have no difficulty in understanding that the force exerted by endosmose, which is a pushing force, is equally great. But evaporation and endosmose—in other words, the tractile or *pulling* force, and the propelling or *pushing* force—can, by the syphon arrangement, act together; the one operating upon the one leg of the syphon, the other upon the remaining leg, in such a manner as to cause a continuous flow of fluids through the syphon. It is thus that evaporation and absorption can go on together, and that fluids, or fluids and air, may be made to circulate together. The nutritive juices may be said to invade the tissues of the plant by a process of endosmose, the endosmotic action being favoured by evaporation and transpiration; endosmose pushing and evaporation pulling and giving the fluids right of way through the tissues. No better arrangement can be imagined for the supply of new material and the discharge of effete matter. The tissues are literally irrigated and washed out at the same time.

Precisely the same remarks may be made regarding the animal tissues. It is an error to suppose that the circulation in animals is carried on exclusively by the heart. This is an engine employed for carrying the blood to and from the tissues through considerable distances, but the tissues do their own work, or rather the particles of the tissues are so arranged that they permit certain physical forces, such as capillary attraction, osmosis, evaporation, respiration, chemical affinity, etc., to do the work for them. The organic kingdom avails itself of inorganic power. This may account for the great rapidity with which poisons spread in animal organisms, and also for their mode of elimination. The capillary vessels of animals form syphon loops, as in plants, and the animal syphon loops are porous in the same sense that the vegetable syphon loops are porous. They are, therefore, capable of transmitting a continuous stream of fluid in a given direction, and of absorbing and evaporating at innumerable points—the absorption and evaporation, as already explained, greatly facilitating instead of retarding the general circulation. That the tissues respire has been abundantly proved by the researches of Spallanzani. He found that all the tissues take in oxygen and give off carbonic acid, as the lungs themselves do. The view here advocated is further favoured by the fact that the circulation of animals does not cease the moment the body dies and the action of the heart fails. On the contrary, the tissues draw on the fluids, these being evaporated as before—an arrangement which accounts for the arteries being comparatively void of blood after death, the blood by this process being actually diminished in amount; diminished, because after the death of the body no new blood is being formed, while the old blood is being circulated and used by the tissues so long as the tissues retain their vitality and heat. That the heart is not necessary to the circulation in its widest sense is proved by the fact that it goes on when neither heart nor blood-vessels are present. The heart, therefore, while the major factor in the circulation of animals, may, after all, be regarded as an auxiliary, *i.e.* a differentiation for a purpose. But to return. I was engaged in discussing the syphons and syphon action in plants.

The syphons in plants are sometimes simple, sometimes compound. By the term simple, I mean a syphon consisting of a tube bent upon itself, the one extremity of which is longer than the other (Fig. 39, *r, t,* p. 70). By the term compound syphon, I mean a syphon consisting of several syphons united to each other, the limbs of which are not necessarily unequal in length. The compound syphon may be composed of rigid non-porous capillary tubes, as shown at Fig. 38 ; or of larger tubes with porous walls, as seen at Fig. 39 [1]. When a series of syphons directed in opposite directions are united and open into each other, the circulation becomes more or less continuous, as in animals. Under these circumstances a certain proportion of the syphons are open in

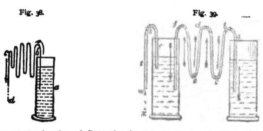

Fig. 38.   Fig. 39.

Fig. 38.—Capillary compound syphon, similar to that found in the interior of plants. The capillary syphon differs from the ordinary syphon in this, that the point at which the fluid escapes *may be much higher* than that at which it enters. Thus the fluid may enter at *a*, and escape at *c*, instead of at *d*. The instant the end of the syphon *b* is placed in fluid, the fluid rises and falls, and travels in the direction *c*, finally escaping at *d*. The compound capillary syphon here figured is equally effective when inverted, the fluid being applied from above instead of from beneath. The compound capillary syphon explains within certain limits the circulation as it exists in plants with well-defined vessels and intervascular spaces. —*Original.*

Fig. 39.—Simple and compound syphons perforated at various points ; the perforations being covered with animal or vegetable membrane, to prevent the ingress of air, while they do not prevent the ingress or egress of fluids by absorption and evaporation.

r, Short leg of simple syphon ; *t*, long leg ditto ; *s*, perforation covered with membrane ; *w, x*, fluids escaping through the syphon.

a Compound syphon, the legs of which are of the same length ; *b, c, d, e, f,* perforations in compound syphon covered with membrane. By elevating the vessel to the right of the figure, the fluid contained within the syphon is made to pass through it, as indicated by the arrows, into the vessel to the left of the figure. (This process may be reversed.) Evaporation or absorption occurring at the points *b, c, d, e, f,* facilitates the transmission of fluids through the syphon. They even generate the movement referred to ; the fluids oscillating now in one direction, now in another, according as one or other prevails. The compound syphon may have its legs of the same length, or the one leg long and the other short, as in the simple syphon. The apertures covered with membrane give the unequal pressure required to produce a true syphon action. These apertures correspond to the leaves, roots, and other surfaces of plants, in which absorption, evaporation, and other physical actions go on.—*Original.*

the direction of the leaves and roots. When I use the term ' open,' I wish it to be understood ' open ' in the sense that they can take in fluids by imbibition or absorption, or give it off by evaporation.

In such a system of syphons, a true syphon action can be induced and maintained ; the vegetable membrane or aggregation of cells, which closes the ends of the syphons, effectually preventing the admission of air from without, but not interfering in the slightest with the passage of fluids from with-

[1] The walls in this case may be flexible as well as porous, made of gut, supported with wire.

out or from within—in other words, with absorption and evaporation.

In the compound capillary syphon (Fig. 38), I find that the moment the one end of it (*a*) is immersed, the fluid fills the several loops of which it is composed, and escapes by the extremity not immersed (*d*). In this case the compound syphon arrangement which I believe exists in plants is nearly but not exactly imitated. The syphons in trees have porous walls in addition to their free open extremities. By porous walls, I mean walls which admit of the passage of fluids through them.

In the compound syphon represented at Fig. 39, the several conditions found in plants are, I apprehend, exactly reproduced. Here we have a syphon made of glass tube with numerous apertures in it. These apertures are of large size, and covered with bladder. They admit of a free evaporation or a free absorption at a great many points. As, however, they are covered with an animal membrane, no air is permitted to enter the syphon to disturb its action.

The syphon action is therefore as perfect as in the syphon in which no apertures are found. In other words, in the novel form of syphon which I have here constructed, fluids and air, if need be, can pass on in rapid and uninterrupted succession; evaporation taking place, and fluids being added at different portions of the syphon, in such a manner as not only not to interfere with the well-known action of the syphon, but, what is very remarkable, actually to favour it. I showed on a previous occasion that if a capillary tube placed in water be expanded at one end and covered with bladder, the fluid rises in the tube in proportion to the evaporation going on in the bladder. I also drew attention to the fact, that evaporation may go on either from above or from below, *i.e.* in the leaves or roots. When evaporation (as in seasons of drought) goes on at both ends of a plant, the fluids contained within the plant are drawn in opposite directions; counter currents being thus established which speedily drain the tree of its juices and cause it to exhibit symptoms of collapse—to make it droop, in fact (Figs. 40 and 41, p. 72).

In this case, the presence of heated air, or the condition of *dryness*, induces opposite currents. But respiring surfaces under certain conditions, say in wet or rainy seasons, may

become absorbing surfaces. This is proved by the fact
that a thin fluid will pass through an animal or vegetable
membrane for which it has an affinity either from above or
from below, according as the thin fluid is placed above or
below the thicker fluid (Figs. 42 and 43).

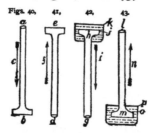

Figs. 40,   41,   42,   43.

Fig. 40.—Tube (*a*) with expanded evaporating surface (*b*) covered with animal or vegetable membrane
directed downwards. The expanded portion corresponds to the roots of plants. When evaporation goes
on at *b*, fluid presented at *a* is drawn through the tube in the direction of the arrow *c.—Original.*

Fig. 41.—Similar tube with expanded portion directed upward. The expanded portion in this instance
corresponds to the leaves of plants. When evaporation occurs at *e*, the fluid presented at *d* is drawn
through the tube in the direction of the arrow *f.* Evaporation is to be regarded as a pulling force.—
Original.

Fig. 42.—Tube (*g*) with expanded absorbing surface (*h*) covered with membrane and directed upwards
to correspond with the leaves of a plant. When a thin fluid (rain or dew) is presented to the membrane,
and to a thicker fluid contained in the tube, it passes by endosmose in a downward direction, as indicated
by the arrow *i.* *k*, Vessel containing the thinner fluid.—*Original.*

Fig. 43.—Tube (*l*) with expanded absorbing surface (*m*) covered with membrane and directed downwards to correspond with the roots of a plant. When a thin fluid (sap from the earth) is presented to
the membrane and to a thicker fluid contained in the tube, it passes by endosmose in an upward direction, as indicated by the arrow *n.* *p*, Vessel containing the thinner fluid. Endosmose is to be regarded
as a pushing force.

Figs. 42 and 43 show how, in wet seasons, plants may be gorged with saps both from the leaves and
from the roots, and how endosmose occurring in the leaves and roots tends to produce currents in
opposite directions. The currents induced by endosmose are always the converse of those induced by
evaporation, so that absorption and endosmose may be going on in the leaves, while evaporation is
going on in the roots; the fluids in this case being pushed and drawn through the plant in a *downward* direction: or absorption and endosmose may be going on in the roots, and evaporation in the
leaves, in which case the fluids are pushed and drawn through the plant in an *upward* direction.—
Original.

From this it follows that evaporation, or the condition of
dryness, draws or sucks the fluids out of the vessels and intervascular spaces, while the condition of *wetness* pushes or propels the fluids into them. Here we have a sucking or pulling
force, and a pushing or propelling force; a *vis a fronte* and a
vis a tergo ; and I am disposed, as already indicated, to claim
a like power for certain of the vessels and for the heart. But
evaporation and absorption do not as a rule go on at the same
surface at the same time. When a surface is absorbing it
evaporates sparingly, and the converse. A free evaporation
and a free absorption may, however, occur at the same time
in different surfaces; and in such cases evaporation and
absorption work together and not against each other (Fig. 36,
p. 50). Dryness and moisture in this way directly influence
the circulation.

In the arrangement which I now advocate, evaporation or the withdrawal of fluids, and absorption or the addition of fluids, may take place at an infinite variety of points, and in such a manner as to favour rather than oppose the passage of the fluids in the capillary tubes and syphons. The syphons are set in operation by the presence of fluids, by capillary action, osmosis, evaporation, and by vital and chemical changes occurring in growing parts.

When the plant is full of fluids, evaporation from the leaves and other parts sucks or draws the fluids up, supplying a *vis a fronte;* endosmose pushing on fluids from below, and acting as a *vis a tergo.* If a superabundance of sap is presented to the roots, and an unusual amount of evaporation is going on in the leaves, the up current is increased in volume and intensity. If these conditions are reversed, the down current is proportionately augmented. The fluid contents of the plant oscillate between either extreme, and the up and down currents are equilibrated when all the forces which operate upon the plant are balanced.

A plant responds to external conditions as an Aeolian harp responds to the wind.

The circulation is literally played upon by the elements. I might push the simile further, and apply the remark to ourselves; for the most exalted natures are ever the most susceptible—susceptible not only to psychical, but also to physical influences.

While engaged in describing the general circulation in plants, I volunteered an explanation of the intracellular circulation; the intracellular movements, as I endeavoured to point out, being in all probability due to evaporation; or to endosmose and exosmose occurring within or outside the cells, the rounded form of the cell converting what would under ordinary circumstances be merely opposite currents into rotatory ones (Figs. 30, 31, 32, p. 34). This led me to infer that certain movements (not necessarily those of gyration) occurring primarily within the cell, inaugurate the general circulation, but that when the general circulation is once established, it contributes to, and may actually produce, gyration in the cells themselves (Fig. 35, p. 47, and Fig. 37, p. 51). Finally I endeavoured to show that all the forces engaged in the circulation of plants, whether vital, chemical, or physical, act together to obtain a common result.

Organic Forces a Modification of Inorganic Forces.—I have dwelt upon the subject of the circulation of plants at much greater length than I intended, or than was perhaps desirable under the circumstances; but it is one of extreme interest, since in it we have the germs of many of the arguments advanced to explain the circulation as it exists even in man himself. Thus we are told that the tissues drink out of the blood and draw it onwards, supplying a *vis a fronte;* that secreting glands produce a similar effect; that the column of blood in the arteries is balanced by that in the veins; that the heart has a sucking and propelling action—in other words, that it pulls as well as pushes; that evaporation assists in determining a flow of blood to the lungs, the movements of respiration assisting the circulation; that the play of the muscles urges the blood forward, much in the same way that the sap is occasionally urged forward in trees in virtue of their stems and branches swaying in the wind. In discoursing of the circulation in an animal or a plant, we are necessarily discoursing of motion as a whole, as it exists in the physical universe. In fact, we are compelled to regard the forces which operate in the inorganic world as essentially the same as those which operate in the organic; for in all animal and vegetable movements we have ultimately to deal with those of the cells and tissues; nay, more, with the ultimate particles of matter composing them. The cells and particles of which an organism is composed may be operated upon singly and act individually; or they may be operated upon conjointly and act in masses. In the former case we have motion as a consequence of endosmose and exosmose, capillary and other attractions, vital and chemical, occurring in the ultimate molecules. In the latter case we have motion proceeding from a battery of force, such as that furnished by the heart; this organ, by its united complex movements, urging on the circulation to a great extent independently. But for the movements primarily occurring in the substance of the heart, the highly differentiated movements representing the diastole and systole of that organ could not take place. The primary molecular movements, if I may so phrase them, always precede those of greater magnitude. In the one we have the particular movement, in the other the general movement; but nature, with infinite wisdom, has so arranged that the general movement shall harmonise with the particular movement. Thus the heart may act in the circulation of an animal as a *vis a tergo*, and the demand for nutritious juices in the tissues as a *vis a fronte*. They may even act separately. The heart may push forward its blood into an artery occluded by a ligature, and the plant may draw on its juices when no heart exists. As all animals and vegetables may be resolved into inorganic atoms, so the physical and vital forces may be referred to a common source. It is thus that we reconcile the circulation in the plant and lower animals with that of the higher animals, and with certain movements which we know exist in the physical universe.

When we come to scan the dim border-land on which life and death struggle for pre-eminence, the most cautious observers and the gravest philosophers are often at fault. Indeed the human faculties only enable us to make very partial advances towards a solution of the great problems of life and motion. We are hedged in on all sides by boundaries which apparently we cannot override. If we advance beyond a certain distance, a veil of greater or less density is interposed. This arises from the fact that even the greatest minds have a limited range, and that nature is as vast in her littleness as in her greatness. The telescope and the microscope have done much, but just in proportion to what has been done, it becomes apparent that so much the more remains to be done. Our most approved instruments, instead of simplifying matters, have actually complicated them. They have revealed wonder upon wonder, and convinced us that there are points which we must either take for granted or prove by analogy. This becomes very evident when we employ a microscope with a high magnifying power, and attempt to make out an ultimate structure; or, what is still more difficult, define the nature of certain movements which take place under our eye, but which we cannot comprehend, as we are at a loss to know whether they are organic or inorganic. Under such circumstances the head becomes confused with thinking and the eye with watching, and all to no purpose. If, for example, we examine a salivary cell, we find apparently deep in its substance a great number of infinitely minute points, each of which is evidently in motion. They are seen after a little careful focussing to quiver and vibrate, and even to rotate. These are the so-called Brunonian movements, and are now regarded as physical in their nature. They afford the first glimmerings of visible motion. If we examine a vegetable or animal infusion after it has stood for a short time, we find a scum or pellicle on its surface. A considerable portion of this scum consists of a molecular mass in which no movement whatever can be detected. In parts of it, however, an aggregation of the molecules has taken place, and when this aggregation occurs, there, of a certainty, movement makes its appearance. The movement is very indistinct, and it requires an experienced eye to detect it. By and by, as the infusion becomes older, the aggregation of molecules becomes more distinct, and the movements exhibited by them more marked. A careful observer will now perceive little dark points and rod-shaped bodies darting about in the field as if by magic. They do not change form, and apparently have no power of contracting and expanding ; nevertheless they advance, recede, pause, advance again, and whirl about with a mad energy which is truly wonderful.

If the infusion be still older, long pointed bodies are found, which advance with a zig-zag or wavy serpentine motion, but still without any trace of contraction or expansion in any part of their substance. These constitute the so-called vibrios and bacteria, concerning which so much has been said lately. As to their mode of production and real nature, there is still a doubt in the scientific mind. All, or nearly all, are agreed that they are living things—a belief favoured by the fact that they increase and multiply. As to their movements there can be no doubt. Still more wonderful, in my opinion, are the movements of the amoeba. This simplest organism consists of a mass of jelly, in which molecules of various sizes are embedded. This transparent creature, which remarkably resembles a white blood-corpuscle, and which is in the ordinary acceptation of the term structureless, has nevertheless the power of changing the shape of every part of its body, and of advancing and retiring in whichever direction it pleases. The movements of this most singular creature are like those of water spilt upon the ground; or the spreading of a drop of fluid in blotting paper. The amoeba causes its body, or a part thereof, to flow out in any direction it pleases. It literally pushes a certain part of its body outwards, and invades a certain portion of territory; the other parts of its body which are not advancing, remaining stationary. Contraction seems to take no part in this movement. When a part of the body is to be advanced, a transparent portion of it bulges, and into this the granules rush in a continuous stream; the knuckle or projection of the body advancing as the granules flow into it. There is no constriction, and nothing that can even suggest the idea of contraction. On the contrary, the parts of the body advanced are invariably wedge-shaped. There is change of form but no diminution of volume. The amoeba has the power of changing form apart from contraction—a power which I believe is also possessed by the sarcous elements of muscles. I am indebted to my friend Dr. M'Kendrick for an opportunity of studying those movements under unusually favourable conditions, and direct attention to them because I am desirous of impressing upon you the necessity, when considering the circulation, of taking into account a large number of vital and a still greater number of physical forces, which all work together to produce it. The tissues have a circulation of their own apart from the heart and blood-vessels, and the presence of a heart, blood-vessels, or indeed of differentiated canals, is not necessary to certain forms of the circulation. Again, the heart, when it exists, impels the blood in virtue of its inherent movements, *i.e.* the movements which occur in its sarcous elements or ultimate particles; these in turn being traceable to nutritive and other changes induced by the circulation itself. In fact, in the circulation, we have before us a very involved problem of vital, physical, and chemical reactions.

Motion a Condition of Matter.—It will greatly facilitate our comprehension of the circulation if we bear in mind that motion is a condition of matter [1]. 'Of absolute rest,' as

---

[1] Many advanced thinkers are of opinion that there is but one force, and that all the others are but modifications of it.

Grove, in his work on the Correlation of Physical Forces, says:—'I believe that the same principles and mode of reasoning as have been adopted in this essay

Mr. Grove eloquently puts it, ' Nature gives us no evidence. All matter, as far as we can ascertain, is ever in movement, not merely in masses, as with the planetary spheres, but also molecularly, or throughout its most intimate structure[1].' Force, like matter, cannot be annihilated ; and where we have the one we have the other. ' Thus, matter and force are correlates in the strictest sense of the word ; the conception of the existence of the one involves the conception of the existence of the other : the quantity of matter, again, and the degree of force, involve conceptions of space and time.' When motion ceases to be visible, *i. e.* when moving masses strike against each other and apparently stand still, motion is redeveloped in the shape of heat, which is invisible motion. In the steam-engine, for example, the piston, and all its concomitant masses of matter are moved by the molecular dilatation of the vapour of the water, the movement of the molecules being imperceptible. If homogeneous substances come together, heat alone is generated ; but if homogeneous and heterogeneous substances come together, electricity is produced ; and some have thought that, whereas the contents of vegetable cells are heterogeneous, and the saps presented to them are nearly if not quite homogeneous, electricity takes part in the circulation. 'Motion,' Mr. Grove observes, 'will directly produce heat ; and electricity, being produced by it, will produce magnetism—a force which is always developed by electrical currents *at right angles* to the direction of those currents[2].' If electricity be permitted to rank as one of the forces in the general—*i. e.* the up-and-down—circulation of plants, magnetism would explain why there should be cross currents also. ' If we now take heat as our starting-point, we shall find that the other modes

might be applied to the *organic* as well as the inorganic ; and that muscular force, animal and vegetable heat, etc., might, and at some time will, be shown to have similar definite correlations. . . . . From Professor Matteucci's experiment it appears that whatever mode of force it be which is propagated along the nervous filaments, this mode of force is definitely affected by currents of electricity. . . . Mosotti has mathematically treated of the identity of gravitation with cohesive attraction, and Plücker has recently succeeded in showing that crystalline bodies are definitely affected by magnetism, and take a position in relation to the lines of magnetic force dependent upon their optical axis or axis of symmetry.'—*Correlation of Physical Forces*, pp. 88, 89.

[1] Grove on the Correlation of Physical Forces, pp. 16, 17, and 104.
[2] Op. cit. p. 23.

of force may be readily produced by it[1].' The heat of spring, by creating a demand for sap in the tree may be said to inaugurate the circulation. Heat produces a movement in distant parts, and bodies coming together from a distance produce heat; inorganic bodies act upon organic ones, and *vice versa*. What is inorganic now may be organic very shortly. The chemistry of the outer and inner world is essentially the same. It is owing to this circumstance that a living body can assimilate, and maintain its position in the world of matter; and this principle of force, which pervades both the organic and inorganic kingdoms, shows how an organised being may live in contact with inorganic or dead matter; how the organic and inorganic may give to and take from each other,—may, in fact, reciprocate with positive advantage to both.

Circulation in Metals.—It would sound somewhat curious if I were to speak of a circulation in metals; but Seebeck has shown, 'that when dissimilar metals are made to touch, or are soldered together and heated at the point of contact, a current of electricity flows through the metals, *having a definite direction*, according to the metals employed; which current continues as long as an *increasing* temperature is gradually pervading the metals, ceases when the temperature is *stationary*, and flows in a contrary direction with the decrement of temperature[2].' The same words might almost be employed in describing the circulation of plants. In spring, when the temperature increases, there is a steady current of sap in an upward direction; in autumn, when the temperature decreases, the current is reversed; in summer, when the temperature may be regarded as stationary, the ascending and descending currents may be said to balance each other or equilibrate. Nor is this all. If a voltaic current be made to act upon electrodes of iron, the molecules of the iron are made to rotate very much in the same way that the cell contents rotate or gyrate in plants. From the foregoing it will be evident that 'heat, electricity, magnetism, chemical affinity,

---

[1] Grove, op. cit. p. 24.

[2] Hitherto it has been customary to regard the electrical current as consisting either of a single fluid idio-repulsive, but attractive of all matter; or else one produced by two fluids, each idio-repulsive, but attractive of the other. Grove is inclined to attribute electrical phenomena to a molecular polarisation of ordinary matter, or to matter acting by attraction and repulsion in a definite direction.

and motion, are all correlative, or have a reciprocal depend-
ence[1].' Animals and plants are especially susceptible to the
influence of light; and it has been supposed, not without
reason, that matter of every description is altered by exposure
to it. Until, therefore, the organic and inorganic kingdoms
are drawn more closely together, both as regards their physical
constitution and mode of action, many of the so-called vital
forces must remain unexplained. A force can only originate
as a transmitted force; it has no existence as a force *per se*[2].
Force may be regarded as *static* or *balanced*, and *dynamic*
or *motive*. Static force in the animal and vegetable
kingdoms represents rest, or a state of equilibrium in the
part. We have this peculiar condition when a flexor and
extensor muscle prevent motion in a joint. When this equilibrium is disturbed, dynamic or motive force preponderates
over the static or balanced force. When a part is in a state
of equilibrium, it is also in a state of tonicity, and ready to act
in whichever direction the force preponderates; and this explains why, in plants, the circulation is now upwards, now
downwards, and how, at other times, it oscillates and becomes
temporarily suspended.

CIRCULATION IN ANIMALS (*Invertebrata*).

*Symmetry of Form in the Organs of Circulation and the
Body generally.*—I now proceed to a consideration of the circulation as it exists in animals; and an attentive examination
of the subject not only induces me to believe that there is a
striking analogy between the circulation in animals and plants,
but that in animals devoid of pulsatile vessels and hearts, it is
in some senses identical, and traceable to the operation of the
same forces. The direction of the force is determined by
influences exerted without or within the animal or plant, or
partly the one and partly the other. Uniformity of action
implies symmetry of form; and it appears to me that plants
and animals are symmetrically constructed in order that the

---

[1] Grove on the Correlation of Physical Forces, p. 13.

[2] 'The term "force," although used in very different senses by different authors,
in its limited sense may be defined as that which produces or resists motion.'—
Correlation of Physical Forces, p. 14.

forces displayed by them may equilibrate or balance each
other, and in order that plants and animals as a whole or
parts of them may experience moments of repose; alternate
activity and repose culminating in those marvellous rhythmic
movements to which I shall have occasion to allude very
shortly. Repose implies a balancing power in the structures in
which it is manifested, and hence the bilateral symmetry which
everywhere obtains in animal organisms, and in organs themselves. I can instance no more beautiful example than the
heart itself. In the ventricles of the mammalian heart, as
you are aware, the muscular fibres are arranged in two symmetrical sets of spiral fibres, so wonderfully and exquisitely
convoluted that each individual fibre has a counteracting or
opposing fibre; each region being equilibrated by an opposing
region; the whole forming a minutely reticulated structure, in
which the fibres cross with mathematical precision at all
conceivable angles, the fibres by their shortening and
lengthening producing a motion which is, in some senses,
unique in the animal economy. Similar remarks may be
made regarding the bilateral nature of the stomach, bladder,
and uterus, and indeed of all parts of the body. The flexors
and extensors, when in a state of equilibrium, are in a state of
rest, and when the flexor shortens the extensor lengthens, and
vice versa. The one movement implies the other. In like
manner the heart has the power of opening and closing[1]. I
employ the terms *lengthens* and *shortens* when speaking of
long muscles, in preference to *relaxes* and *contracts*—contraction literally meaning a diminution of volume, no such
diminution occurring in the movements of a muscle. This is
proved by causing a muscle to contract in a graduated vessel
containing water. The water always remains at the same
level. I employ the terms *opens* and *closes*, when speaking
of hollow muscles, as involving no theory as to the manner in
which a muscle acts. All muscular movements are the result
of *a vital change of shape* in the sarcous elements of which

---

[1] That the one part of the heart *opens* while the other *closes*, is proved by this,
that all parts of the heart act, even when they are deprived of blood. When,
moreover, the heart is acting slowly, the ventricle or ventricles (if there be two)
open before the auricle or auricles, as the case may be, close. I have frequently
seen this in the fish and frog.

G

muscles are composed, the volume of the sarcous elements always remaining exactly the same. Such change is not expressed by the terms contracts and relaxes. Contraction is usually regarded as a vital or *active* movement, relaxation being erroneously regarded as a mechanical or *passive* one.

Respiration and Assimilation connected with the Circulation.—In order to have a just conception of the circulation as it exists in animals, it will be necessary to examine it in connexion with the movements of respiration and nutrition, and the movements of the soft and hard parts generally.

There is a considerable proportion of the lower animals in which no trace of a circulation has yet been detected, the nutritious fluids in such cases being supposed to pass from the alimentary canal by interstitial transudation throughout the entire body, as the sap passes into the substance of cellular plants. One great obstacle to a proper understanding of the circulation in many of the lower forms of organic animal life, is the difficulty experienced in determining whether the currents observed in inclosed spaces within their bodies belong to the circulation of their blood and nutrient juices, or are a means to a very different end, viz. respiration, locomotion, and other widely dissimilar functions. In sponges, which live and grow in water, this element passes in continuous currents through pores and canals in their substance. These currents enter at one point and issue at another, and are not, as Dr. Grant showed, due to the contraction of the canals. He suggested that they might possibly be due to the action of cilia, and Huxley and Bowerbank have succeeded in demonstrating the presence of those structures. It is only when cilia, blood-vessels, or hearts, are present, that the forces assume a visible form.

Ciliary Currents.—Dr. Sharpey, in his admirable paper 'On Cilia,' shows that definite currents may be produced by ciliary movements. He instances two currents, which he found within the tentacula of the actinia; the one running from the base to the point of the tentaculum, the other in an opposite direction. He observed similar currents in the asterias and echinus; and those currents, he remarks, curiously enough, continue after the parts which exhibit them are detached from the animal, from which it follows that they are beyond the reach of the will. The peculiarity of the currents referred to consists in this, that they run in opposite directions as in plants. In the polypi, medusae, planaria, and some entozoa, where a circulation is absent or very obscure, the caeca of the alimentary canal is much branched, and evidently assists in carrying nutritious juices to all parts of the body. It thus performs in a great ·measure the functions of a circulatory apparatus, as well as of an alimentary canal. What fluids are not circulated by the caeca are circulated under such circumstances by a transudation or interstitial movement, as in plants. In several of the medusae no distinct organ of circulation can be detected, the alimentary canal in such cases being of large size, and ramifying in every direction on the surface, or in the substance of the animal. Hitherto I have been dealing with the circulation as it exists in plants, and in the lower forms of animals, where neither contractile vessels nor hearts are present. When vessels are present, as in the cestum and beroe, Eschscholtz has shown that a large loop or ring of vessels surrounds the mouth, from which arteries and veins proceed; branches passing to the fins, which at once serve for respiration and locomotion; the fins in this respect resembling the growing wings of many insects. It is not quite ascertained whether in the beroe, the circulating fluid, which is of a yellowish colour and contains globules, is actually blood. In the diplozoon (a small entozoa), Nordmann made out, with a high magnifying power, currents moving in opposite directions in two sets of vessels occurring on either side of both limbs of the animal. These vessels terminate posteriorly in a kind of sac, and, according to Nordmann and Ehrenberg, they neither contract nor dilate. We have now, you will observe, got distinct vessels in animals minus contractile power as in plants.

In the compound ascidiae, as Mr. Lister has shown, the different individuals of the branched animal are united by a polypiferous stem, and have a common circulation. Each individual is furnished with a heart consisting of a single cavity, which pulsates thirty or forty times per minute. In the common stem two distinct currents are traceable, these running in opposite directions (Fig. 27, p. 29). One of the currents enters the ascidia by its peduncle, and goes direct to the heart. It proceeds thence to the gills and system generally, which having traversed, it leaves the animal by the peduncle at which it entered, and passes into the common stem, to circulate through another ascidian. The direction of the currents is reversed every two minutes or so ; and Mr. Lister found that if an ascidian was separated from the common stem, the separated individual can set up an independent circulation, consisting of two currents likewise running in opposite directions. The circulation in the ascidiae is very remarkable, and closely resembles that in many plants. It occurs in non-contractile tubes, and in the absence of cilia. It is distinguished by an ascending and descending current, free to enter and leave the animal, as the sap is free to enter and leave the tree. The circulation moreover reverses and oscillates, and it may go on independently in an individual or in a community of individuals. Precisely the same remark may be made of the tree, for in this also the circulation oscillates, and if a portion of a tree, say a vine, be forced, it sets up a circulation of its own, while it at the same time maintains a certain relation with the other parts of the tree which are not forced (compare Fig. 8, p. 14, with Fig. 27, p. 29).

In the leech, sand-worm, and earth-worm, the circulation is, if possible, more tree-like. In these the blood (which is red in colour) moves slowly forward in the vessels situated on the dorsal surface of the animal, the direction of the current being reversed in the ventral vessels. If the leech, to which my remarks more especially apply, be placed in a vertical position, the currents of course correspond to the ascending and descending currents of plants. Between the dorsal and ventral vessels are numerous transverse vessels, which carry on a lateral or cross circulation, this too being analogous to what is found in plants. (See Fig. 8, p. 14, and compare with Fig. 44, p. 89).

There are no distinct hearts in the leech, sand-worm, and earth-worm, the circulation being carried on mainly by the closing of the vessels at different points.

Rhythmic Movements—Analogy between Involuntary and Voluntary Movements.—If the vessels closed throughout their entire extent, very little if any movement would occur. If, again, the centre of a long vessel closed, the fluid would be driven away from the constricted point in opposite directions. To insure a circulation of the nutritious juices in a particular direction when valves are not present, the vessels must open and close in parts, in a certain order, in a given direction, and at stated intervals; one part opening while another is closing, and *vice versa.* This is what virtually takes place in the lashing of cilia. First one moves and then another, to form a progressive wave of movement; this in its turn forming a progressive wave of fluid. It is this peculiar kind of movement that de- termines the wave of the pulse. The wave movement of cilia has been aptly compared by Dr. Sharpey to the un- dulating motion produced by the wind on a field of corn, and exactly resembles what I myself have seen in the living mammalian heart. The alternation of movements diametri- cally opposed to each other, if they occur at regular intervals, constitute the so-called rhythmic movements. These move- ments are witnessed in the blood-vessels, the heart, the intestines, the stomach, the bladder, and the uterus. They recur at very long intervals in the uterus, but the element of duration or time does not destroy the nature of the movement; the action of the heart is a rhythmic action, whether the organ beats 50 to the minute or 100 [1]. It is the nature of the movement which settles its claim to be regarded as rhythmic or not. Hollow muscles display rhythmic movements when one part of their substance opens and another closes simultaneously; these movements al- ternating and repeating themselves at longer or shorter periods. Thus the stomach, bladder, rectum, and uterus, close when their sphincters open; and their sphincters close when the viscera open. Minutes, hours, days, weeks, or

[1] The frequency of the heart's action varies greatly in different animals. According to Burdach (Physiologie, vol. iv. p. 251), the number of pulsations per minute in the shark is 7; in the mussel, 15; in the carp, 20; in the eel, 24; in the snake, 34; in the horse, 36; in the caterpillar, 36; in the bullock, 38; in the ass, 50; in the crab, 50; in the butterfly, 60; in the goat, 74; in the sheep, 75; in the hedgehog, 75; in the frog, 77; in the marmot, locust, and ape, 90; in the dormouse, 105; in the cat and duck, 110; in the rabbit and monoculus castor, 120; in the pigeon, 130: in the guinea-pig, hen, and bremus terrestris, 140; and in the heron and monoculus pulex, 200.

months, may elapse between the opening and closing of
the parts of a hollow viscus, but when they do open and
close, its movements are essentially rhythmic in character.
Very similar remarks may be made regarding the voluntary
muscles. The voluntary muscles, like the involuntary, are
arranged in cycles, the closing of one half of the cycle being
accompanied by the opening of the other; in other words,
when the muscle constituting the one half of the cycle
shortens, the other elongates. In the involuntary muscles
the cycle closes in all its diameters, to expel fluid or other
contents. In the voluntary muscles the diameter of the circle
remains the same, the object being to cause the jointed bones
placed within the cycle to move in specific directions. The
motion of the voluntary and involuntary muscles is essentially
wave-like in character—i. e. it spreads from certain centres,
according to a fixed order, and in given directions. Thus the
ventricular portion of the heart closes towards the pulmonary
artery and aorta; the stomach towards the pyloric valve; the
rectum towards the sphincters ani; the bladder towards the
urethra; and the uterus towards the os. It is the same in the
movements of the extremities; the centripetal or converging
muscular wave on one side of the bones to be moved, being
accompanied by a corresponding centrifugal or diverging wave
on the other side; the bones by this means being moved to a
hair's-breadth. The centripetal or converging, and the centrifugal or diverging waves of force are correlated. The same holds
true of the different parts of the body of the serpent when
creeping; of the body of the fish when swimming; of the wing
of the bird when flying; and of our own extremities when
walking. In all these cases, the moving parts are thrown
into curves or waves[1]. It could not be otherwise. If fluids
are to be propelled in certain directions, forces which act
in definite directions must be provided. This also holds true
of locomotion however performed; whether by a living undifferentiated mass, i. e. a mass devoid of nerve, muscle, bone,

---

[1] That an intimate relation exists between the organs of locomotion and the
structures which carry on the circulation and the digestion in the higher animals,
is rendered exceedingly probable by the fact, that the cilia of the infusoria enable
those creatures to move from place to place, and produce the currents which enable
them to seize their food and respire.

etc.; or by an animal in which all these are present. It may seem out of place to refer to the voluntary muscular movements here, seeing I am called upon, strictly speaking, only to deal with the involuntary. It however appears to me, that the two must be studied together: that, in fact, the compound involuntary muscles, such as the heart, stomach, bladder, and uterus, give the cue to the muscular arrangements in the extremities and bodies of animals generally.

Hitherto it has been the almost invariable custom in teaching anatomy, and such parts of physiology as pertain to animal movements, to place much emphasis upon the configuration of the bony skeleton as a whole, and the conformation of its several articular surfaces in particular. This is very natural, as the osseous system stands the wear and tear of time, while all around it is in a great measure perishable. It is the link which binds extinct forms to living ones, and we naturally venerate and love what is enduring. It is no marvel that Oken, Goethe, Owen, and others, should have attempted such splendid generalisations with regard to the osseous system—should have proved with such cogency of argument that the head is composed of expanded vertebrae. The bony skeleton is a miracle of design very wonderful and very beautiful in its way. But when all has been said, the fact remains that the skeleton, when it exists, forms only an adjunct of locomotion and motion generally. All the really important movements of an animal occur in the soft parts. The osseous system is therefore to be regarded as secondary in importance to the muscular, of which it may be considered a differentiation. Instead of regarding the muscles as adapted to the bones, the bones ought to be regarded as adapted to the muscles. Bones have no power either of originating or perpetuating motion. This begins and terminates in the muscles and soft parts. Nor must it be overlooked that bone makes its appearance comparatively late in the scale of being; that innumerable creatures exist, in which no trace either of an external or internal skeleton is to be found; that these creatures move freely about, digest, circulate their nutritious juices and blood when present, multiply, and perform all the functions incident to life. While the skeleton is to be found in only a certain proportion of the animals existing on our globe, the soft parts are to be met with in all; and this appears to me an all-sufficient reason for attaching great importance to the movements of soft parts; to protoplasm, to moving jelly masses, to involuntary muscles such as the oesophagus, stomach, intestine, bladder, uterus, heart, and blood-vessels. It may appear far-fetched to state that the voluntary muscle is a differentiation and further development of the involuntary; that the movements of the oesophagus, stomach, and intestines, prefigure those of the blood-vessels; that the movements of the blood-vessels prefigure those of the heart; that the movements of the heart prefigure those of the chest and abdomen; and that the movements of the chest and abdomen prefigure those of the extremities: but such, I believe, is actually the case[1]. Indeed I hope to be able to show you, before I finish the present course, that if I eliminate the element of bone from the chest and the extremities, the direction of the muscular fibres of those parts will correspond exactly with the direction of the muscular fibres of the ventricles of the mammal; nay, more, that even the bones of the several regions, especially of the extremities, are twisted upon themselves in the form of a double spiral, and in a manner resembling that in which the fibres of the heart are convoluted. This is especially perceptible if the internal fibres of the left ventricle of the heart be compared with the bones of the bird's wing; or the bones of the anterior extremity of the elephant; or the bones of the extremities of any quadruped.

I hope further to be able to point out that the heart within the thorax is a heart working within a greater heart—the thorax itself; the two having a common function, viz. to bring the air and the blood face to face, so as to enable them to reciprocate with the utmost facility and in the most direct way possible[2]. I might make similar observations regarding

---

[1] The extremities are a differentiation of the trunk. They are not necessary to existence; they may be lopped off and the trunk live as before.

[2] As the circulatory apparatus adapted to absorb nourishment for the use of the embryo becomes developed, it is necessary that a respiratory apparatus be provided for depurating the blood. This apparatus is termed the *allantois*. It sprouts from the anterior and lower part of the wall of the belly of the embryo, at first as a little mass of cells, which soon exhibits a cavity so that a vesicle is formed which looks like a diverticulum from the lower part of the digestive cavity. This vesicle in birds has been shown by Vulpian (Journ. de la Physiologie, tome i. p. 619 et seq.) to be possessed of *a distinct contractile power*, and

the stomach, intestine, bladder, and uterus. These are hollow muscles[1] situated within the abdomen, a still greater hollow muscle; and when any of them acts, the abdominal muscles take part in the movement. The hollow muscles and abdomen may however act separately, just in the same way that the heart may act when cut out of the thorax. I have to apologise for these digressions, but the object of my treating the subject of the circulation comparatively is to bring out contrasts, and to eliminate, if possible, from a mass of detail, some principle or principles.

Circulation in the Leech contrasted with that in Plants.— The circulation in the leech affords a good illustration of what may be done by rhythmic movements acting in a given direction; the rhythmic movements of the blood-vessels sufficing for carrying on the circulation within the body of the leech; and, what is not a little curious, the rhythmic movements of the oesophagus of the leech causing the blood of another animal to circulate within its oesophagus and alimentary canal when it feeds[2]. 'In the leech,' Dr. Thompson observes, 'the principal and most highly contractile longitudinal vessels are placed one on each side, and there are also two lesser longitudinal vessels, one superior and the other inferior, all which communicate freely together by small cross branches along the whole body.' (Fig. 44.) According to J. Müller, for a certain number of pulsations, the middle and the lateral vessel of one side

Fig. 44.

Fig. 44.—*a, a,* Principal and most highly contractile vessels of leech. *a*, minor vessels; *e,* cross vessels.

---

soon becomes so large as to extend itself around the yolk-sac, intervening between it and the membrane of the shell, and coming through the latter *into relation with the external air;* but in the embryo of mammalia, the allantois, being early superseded by another provision for the aeration of the blood, seldom attains any considerable dimensions.—*Carpenter's Human Physiology,* Lond. 1864, pp. 800, 801.

[1] The hollow muscles are adapted for transmitting air, fluids, or solids. Usually they only transmit one of these. The intestine transmits all three.

[2] When speaking of the teeth of the common leech, Mr. Dallas remarks, that immediately the teeth, three in number, have sawed through the skin, they are retracted and the blood pumped from the wound by the alternate dilatation and contraction of the muscular oesophagus.—*Natural History of the Animal Kingdom,* by W. S. Dallas, Esq. F.L.S., p. 95.

contract together, and propel the blood into the lateral vessel
on the other side; and then the order is reversed, and the
middle vessel acts along with the lateral vessel of the other
side, so that *one lateral vessel is always dilated, while the
median and opposite lateral ones are contracted*, and *vice versa*.

Some anatomists believe that in the leech there is a simple
oscillation of the blood from side to side, or across the animal;
others that there is, in addition, a general progressive movement of the blood *forwards* in the upper vessel, and *backwards* in the lower one (*vide* arrows). The latter view is
most probably the correct one, for when a vertical and
horizontal system of vessels are united to each other by
innumerable capillary loops, a certain proportion of the blood
necessarily flows round or gyrates. Indeed it would appear
that the blood flows in a circle round the margin of the
animal, much in the same way that the granular contents
of the cell in many plants gyrate; that when the upper
vessel closes, it forces the blood *forwards* and laterally;
the lower vessel, when it closes, forcing the blood *backwards*
and laterally. There is nothing contradictory in this supposition. The principal forces act on opposite sides of a
circle in one and the same direction; the minor forces acting transversely. If the vessel on one side of the animal
closed throughout its entire length, it would certainly force
the blood through the lateral or transverse branches into
the vessel on the opposite side; this again, when it closed,
reversing the movement. In this arrangement the circulating fluid would receive a check, *i. e.* it would have a halt
or dead point between each oscillation. There would be
this further difficulty: the vessel would close at once throughout its entire length, instead of consecutively and in parts.
By adopting the view now suggested, the blood will flow
in one continuous round without halt or dead point, and
be compelled to do so by a kind of vermicular movement,
i. e. by a simultaneous opening and closing of the different
parts of the vessel, akin to swallowing; the wave-like movement travelling in one direction, the cause and the effect
being equally intelligible. The circulation in the leech resembles that in the plant in this, that it consists of an ascending, descending, and transverse current. (Compare Fig. 8,

p. 14, with Fig. 44, p. 89.) There are, however, in addition, well-defined blood-vessels which are endowed with the power of opening and closing for a specific purpose.

The presence of vessels, as has been already shown, is not necessary to the circulation. In young and abnormal tissues, even in animals, the blood tunnels out channels for itself in determinate directions, and around these channels blood-vessels are ultimately formed [1]. The direction of the current of the blood and nutritious juices is determined by processes of growth, by capillarity, osmosis, evaporation, and other changes occurring in the animal. It is however quite natural that when the vascular system becomes differentiated the blood-vessels should be laid down in the exact position of the original currents, the existence of which is as necessary to their own formation as that of the tissues generally.

How the Circulation connects the Organic and Inorganic Kingdoms.—In plants and in the lower animals, the distinguishing feature of the currents constituting the circulation is, that they proceed in the direction of the length of the plant or animal, and transversely—the vertical and horizontal currents running at right angles to each other. The circulation in plants is essentially an interrupted or disjointed circulation. It occurs within capillary or other syphon tubes or spaces, the syphons being directed alternately towards the leaves and the roots, in which direction the extremities of the syphons are united by vegetable membranes, which prevent the ingress of air, and preserve the integrity of the syphon action, while they at the same time facilitate absorption,

---

[1] The vessels are at first solid cylinders made up of formative cells cohering together. By liquefaction of their substance in the interior, these cylinders become tubes, and their central cells thus set free are the primitive blood-corpuscles. —*Quain's Anatomy*, 7th edition, clxxx. In the formation of the Haversian canals in bone, the vessels first pour out the animal matrix, and then deposit in it the bone earth; thus by degrees they come to be surrounded by their own work.—*Holden's Human Osteology*, p. 32.

'We have the fact, that in each plant, and in every new part of each plant, *the formation of sap-canals precedes the formation of wood;* that the deposit of woody matter, when it begins, takes place around the sap-canals, and afterwards around the new sap-canals successively developed; that the formation of wood around the sap-canals takes place when the coats of the canals are demonstrably permeable, and that the amount of wood-formation is proportionate to the permeability.'—*Principles of Biology*, by Herbert Spencer, vol. ii. p. 564.

evaporation, and osmosis. The saps of a plant ascend, descend, advance, and retire, in a series of waves. They rarely gyrate, unless when two systems of alternating syphons unite to form circular spaces, in which case the circulation resembles that within cells or the bodies of animals. Plants grow into the earth and air, or into the water and air. The earth and water operate upon their circulation at one end—the air and its vapours at the other. Plants for the most part are fixed. It is otherwise as a rule with animals. These move freely about on the land, or in the water or air. The circulation in animals is, with few exceptions, a closed or complete circulation—*i. e.* the juices flow in a continuous circle. This is necessary because the forces of the circulation in animals are more strictly speaking a part of themselves.

Digestion and Circulation.—The leech, for example, has no roots to dig into the ground, or leaves to spread out in the sunshine, for the purpose of absorbing and giving off moisture. It however does this indirectly by its mucous linings and skin, by its blood-vessels and by its tissues generally, all of which are capable of absorbing and giving off moisture [1]. It takes in its food and fluids by the mouth; these being made to traverse a distinct alimentary canal. The circulation is, so to speak, without, beyond, or cut off from the nutritious juices supplied by the mouth; these being conveyed to the blood indirectly, and in such a way as would not suffice for carrying on the circulation. In the plant the nutritious juices absorbed by the roots at once suffice for nourishment and for carrying on the circulation. The same holds true of animals very low down in the scale. In the higher animals, however, the food and drink swallowed contribute only indirectly to carrying on the circulation, this being effected by a distinct apparatus specially provided. Indeed between the food as received into the stomach, and the blood as elaborated for nutrition, there is a considerable gap—the gap being traversed by a distinct set of vessels, the so-called lacteals or chyliferous ducts. Through

---

[1] Boerhaave says in one place, An animal is a plant which has its roots (internally) in the stomach. Perhaps some other might with equal propriety play upon this idea and and say, A plant is an animal which has its stomach (externally) in its roots.—*Kant's Lesser Metaphysical Writings.* Leipzig, 1838, p. 62.

these, and through the capillary blood-vessels, the nutritious portions of the food reach the blood. Between the nutrition as carried on in the plant and animal there are what may be regarded as intermediate systems. Thus in the flustra, a form of polype, the particles taken in by the mouth as food rotate within the stomach and rectum, very much in the same way that the contents of certain plant-cells gyrate. Here the food of the animal circulates in a manner analogous to that in which the pabulum of the plant, or the white and red corpuscles of the blood of the mammal, circulate. This shows how very intimately the functions of the circulation and the digestion are related to each other [1]. Indeed the object and aim of the circulation in every case is to provide nourishment for distant parts, and to expose the circulating fluids freely to the air. The circulation connects the plant with the earth and air. It enables it to give to and receive from both, in fact fixes its place in nature. The animate and inanimate kingdoms are by the aid of the circulation enabled to reciprocate. What is said of the plant may also be said of the animal. It is the circulation which more especially connects the animal with the outer world. The pabulum taken in by the mouth of the animal very soon finds its way to the blood, and the circulation insures that the blood duly reciprocates with the air [2]. It is in this way that the peristaltic movements of the stomach and intestines are related to the rhythmic movements of the heart, blood-vessels, and lungs; these, in turn, bearing a certain relation to the voluntary muscles. If the voluntary muscles are set violently in motion, as in running or wrestling, these, as is well known, quicken the movements of both lungs and heart. Looking at the circulation in its entirety,

[1] 'The first rudiment of the heart, which is the earliest of the permanent organs of the embryo that comes into functional activity, consists of an aggregation of cells, forming a thickening of the fibrous coat of the *anterior portion of the intestinal canal*; the innermost cells of which, becoming detached, float in the newly-formed cavity as the first blood-corpuscles, whilst the outer remain to constitute its walls. For a long time after it has distinctly commenced pulsating, and is obviously exerting a contractile force, its walls obviously retain the cellular character, and only become muscular by a progressive histological transformation.'—*Carpenter's Human Physiology*, 1864, p. 799.

[2] In plants the air and circulating fluids are in many cases mixed, and in insects the whole animal is traversed by innumerable air-tubes, which convey air to every part of the body.

we are compelled to take in a wide range of phenomena
and forces, the relations of which are as yet imperfectly
understood. A more extensive acquaintance with the subject,
will, I have no doubt, bring out the interesting fact, that
the phenomena and forces are all correlated to each other.
It is impossible to speak of the circulation apart from the
respiration and the digestion; and these, in the higher animals,
are linked by a silver chain to the nervous system, which,
in its turn, reacts upon all the three.

Cilia, their Form and Function. — While it is impossible
to fix upon any one force which may be said to carry on the
circulation in plants, there are forces at work in the lower
animals which would be quite equal to the task. I speak
of the forces residing in cilia, and which may be classed as
visible forces. Cilia are conical-shaped hair-like processes,
semi-transparent, elastic, and apparently homogeneous. They
occur in incalculable numbers, and are in some instances infinitely minute. They are found on the external and internal
surfaces of the lower animals; and on the mucous lining of
the nostrils, lungs, Eustachian, Fallopian, and other tubes of
the higher. In some cases they are arranged in straight rows,
and in others they form circles or spiral lines. Some observers are of opinion that they contain muscular fibres, or
what are equivalent thereto, in their interior ; and Ehrenberg
showed that they had muscles attached to their roots. Dr.
Grant thought that they were tubular, their movements being
due to the absence or presence of water in their interior. They
are especially deserving of attention as foreshadowing an infinite variety of movements in the animal economy. They
lash about with a vibratile or reciprocating rhythmical motion,
the one after the other, in such a manner as to produce a
waved surface, resembling that produced by wind upon water,
or, as Dr. Sharpey well put it, wind among corn. Their
movements, while they last, are regular and definitely co-ordinated ; *i.e.* they move in certain directions with various degrees of speed, and produce currents which flow in definite
directions[1]. They have thus the power of propelling fluids

---

[1] In some cases the cilia are flattened out so as to resemble the blade of an oar,
the blade in some instances being digitated and resembling the feathers of the
wing of a bird. Under these circumstances they are usually employed as organs

in given directions, over any surface on which they are situated. One of the most remarkable motions, essentially ciliary in character, is witnessed in the spermatozoa of the common earth-worm (*Lumbricus agricola*). Immediately the spermatozoa are extruded from the testes, everything in their proximity becomes ciliated by them; one end becoming fixed, the other vibrating free. They thus actually establish ciliary currents on inanimate surfaces; and if the substance to which they attach themselves is not too large, they drag it about with an undulating motion, and sometimes cause it to gyrate. This is precisely the kind of force which would suffice for carrying on the circulation, in the absence of a heart and pulsatile vessels; but cilia have not hitherto been found either in the vascular tissues of plants or animals, or on the globules either of the blood or lymph. The function of cilia is very varied. They produce currents outside the animal; their presence on the interior of the stomach causing its contents to rotate or gyrate. They serve as organs of locomotion, and some are of opinion that they act as lungs and organs of sense. They are, therefore, endowed with this very remarkable property, that they can produce currents in a given direction on any particular surface; or they can cause the whole animal to move in a line to any given point. They also assist in the processes of digestion and respiration. Here is a multiplicity of function, and it is by regarding such structures that the movements of the blood-vessels and heart are assimilated with those of the intestine, stomach, bladder, and uterus; and the movements of the intestine, stomach, bladder, and uterus, with those of the voluntary muscles.

Cilia are endowed with wonderful vital powers; they live after being separated from the body, and until the parts containing them are on the verge of putrefaction. This shows that they can operate independently of the will. The heart and hollow viscera also act independently of the will, and after being removed from the body, so that both as regards their tenacity of life, their rhythmic movements, and

of locomotion. In the infusoria the cilia are apparently under the influence of the will. There are, however, numerous cases where they are not, and where they vibrate for protracted periods after having been removed from the body.

their involuntary actions, the cilia and heart have many points in common.

Undefined Forces of the Circulation—slowing and quickening of the Circulation, etc.—The inference I draw from the foregoing is this : If in nature there are vital forces which can act independently of the will, and produce continuous or interrupted currents in definite directions, it is not difficult to understand that a plant or animal, or *parts thereof*, may exert vital powers in an equally precise and definite manner although unseen. The life of a plant or animal represents the aggregate movements of its structural elements ; and although we cannot trace with the naked eye or microscope the grouping and combined action of its various molecules, or, what is the same thing, the differentiation of its forces, we are, I think, bound to conclude that the life has much to do with the regulation and distribution of those forces in living organisms. The seed has those forces pent up within itself, and when it is placed in proper conditions they manifest themselves. If however the seed is dead, those conditions do not affect it. It is very probable that when the seed is dead its structure is so changed that the physical forces which would come into play in a living seed are inoperative. If the tissues are composed originally of similar elements variously combined, it is difficult to resist the conclusion, that the life has much to do with the production of each. What other than a vital chemistry could transform a mass of protoplasm into the aqueous humour of the eye ; the ivory of the tusks and teeth ; the hard, resisting bone ; and the actively moving muscle ? It was long before the presence of cilia was detected in parts where we now know they exist, and it is quite possible that auxiliary forces, infinitely minute but spread over large surfaces, may assist the heart and blood-vessels in pushing forward the circulation. There is no absolute necessity for supposing the existence of such forces ; as osmosis, capillary attraction, absorption, evaporation, chemical affinity, etc., aided by pulsating hearts and blood-vessels, are of themselves equal to the task. In a living organism, however, where every part helps every other part, and where all is motion, it is scarcely reasonable to suppose that the *onus* of pushing forward a mass of fluid would be delegated entirely either to the heart or the blood-vessels. In plants, as has been explained, fluids can circulate without either the one or the other; and a portion of skin may be taken from one animal and placed upon an open sore in another, and made to grow; its connexions with the heart and blood-vessels of the animal from which it was removed being completely destroyed. These facts, coupled with the circumstance that sap is determined to the growing parts of plants and animals, form a strong presumptive proof that in the latter, as in the former, a great variety of hidden or invisible forces are at work. This argument is not demolished by saying that if the heart is removed in an animal the general circulation ceases. It may happen that while the invisible forces are inadequate of themselves to carry on the circulation in an animal, they may nevertheless afford invaluable assistance. In the cold-blooded animals the capillaries propel the blood for some time after the heart has been removed. The motion proceeds from the smaller to the larger vessels alike in veins and arteries. Haller, who especially investigated this subject, thought that this phenomenon could not be due to the contraction of the large vessels, to capillarity, nor gravitation. He attributed it to some unknown power residing in the solid tissues which attracted the blood, and also to the action of the globules of the blood upon each other. It may in reality be due to a reverse endosmotic action ; the blood, during the process of cooling, coagulating and becoming thicker than the serum outside the vessels. What originally passed out of the capillaries by endosmose may in part return to them, the return being favoured by the closing of the capillaries and a diminished evaporation due to a loss of animal heat. Dr. Alison believed that the capillaries of animals exerted a peculiar propulsive power apart from contractility, and that the globules of the blood were possessed of the power of spontaneous motion. His hypothesis will be regarded by some as extravagant, but there is nothing ridiculous in it. The ova of fixed plants, as we have seen, leave the parent and lead an itinerant life, until they find a suitable habitat ; the contents of cells gyrate ; and cilia placed on certain surfaces produce currents in definite directions.

On watching the circulation in the mesentery of the frog

some time ago, with my friend Dr. Wyllie, I found it difficult
to believe that the white corpuscles, while they floated in the
blood plasma, were not endowed with a certain amount of
independent movement. They loitered along the margins of
the capillaries, now stopping here, now there, now advancing
a little, and now halting resolutely: attaching themselves to
the inner surface of the vessels, they forced their way in an
outward direction and produced an external bulging, after
which, changing their shape, they pushed themselves right
through the capillary walls. Once outside the vessels, they
reassumed their original form for a brief space, after which
they gradually merged into the adjacent tissues, and became
undistinguishable from them. The growth of the individual
may, in this sense, be regarded as identical with its power
of circulation: the one is correlated to the other. The
organism lives because it has the power of circulating its
nutritious juices. There are many facts which strengthen
the hypothesis that the circulation of the blood within the
capillaries is not entirely due to the action of the heart.
The circulation of the blood may continue in the capillaries after the heart has ceased to act; or it may cease
in parts, the heart acting vigorously the while. The flow of
blood in the capillaries is not regular, which it would be if
entirely dependent on the action of the heart. In some instances the circulation in certain of the capillaries within a
given area is quickened, while in others within the same area
it is slowed, and the direction of the current reversed. In
cold-blooded animals the circulation within the capillaries
goes on after the heart is excised. The arterial system, after
most kinds of natural death, is found emptied of blood. In
death by yellow fever, the external veins often become so
distended, that on puncture the blood gushes forth as from
arteries. Secretions depending upon the circulation within
the capillaries go on after the heart has ceased to beat. In
the early embryo the blood moves in the vascular area before
it is subjected to the influence of the heart—the movement
being *towards* instead of *from* the centre. The heart in some
cases is absent during the whole of embryonic life—the organs
being nevertheless well developed, which of course implies a
capillary circulation. The circulation in the capillaries may

be slowed or stopped by the local application of cold, and by local death or gangrene, which shows plainly enough that there is, as Sir James Paget cautiously puts it, 'some mutual relation between the blood and its vessels, or the parts around them, which, being natural, permits the most easy transit of the blood, but, being disturbed, increases the hindrance to its passage.' Professor Draper[1] thought that 'if two fluids communicate with one another in a capillary tube, or in a porous or parenchymatous structure, and have for that tube or structure different chemical affinities, movement will ensue ; that liquid which has the most energetic affinity will move with the greatest velocity, and may even drive the other liquid before it.' The occult forces, if I may so call them, while they are not equal to carrying on the circulation by themselves, exert, I believe, sufficient power to relieve the heart and blood-vessels from excessive strain. It is, moreover, more natural for the tissues to drink leisurely, and according to desire, than to have blood unceremoniously thrust upon them by a violent *vis a tergo*. Where the blood has to travel long distances before it is utilised, a perfect system of blood-vessels and a heart are necessary for transmitting it to the scene of its labours. Arrived there, another set of forces comes into play. This is in part proved by the absence of the pulse in the capillaries. I may be here met by the statement that the force of a common injecting syringe can cause a fluid to pass through the arteries and capillaries so as to return by the veins. I have had considerable experience in artificial injections, and have invariably found, that unless extreme care is exercised, the capillaries are ruptured in the process. Nor is this due to coarse particles in the injection blocking up the capillaries, for the same pernicious effects follow when water is employed. It is the force that does the mischief, and this is another reason for believing that the circulation within the capillaries differs materially from that in the main arteries and veins. It could not be expected that the delicate capillary vessels, with their thin transparent walls, could resist without injury the same pressure brought to bear upon the aorta ; nor are they called upon to do so, the pressure being diminished in proportion to the increase of area in the capil-

[1] Treatise on the Forces which produce the Organisation of Plants, pp. 22-41.

H 2

laries, as compared with that in the arteries. That the force exerted by the heart is modified as it is transmitted is abundantly proved by the greater thinness of the walls of the great veins, as compared with the great arteries. The slowing of the circulation in the arteries in the direction of the capillaries, and the quickening thereof in the veins in the direction of the heart, render it exceedingly probable that the ventricle, or ventricles, exert a propelling power, and that the auricle, or auricles, exert a sucking power. This is what virtually happens in the more simple forms of the circulation, when one surface absorbs and another respires; fluids entering the tissues by endosmose (which may be regarded as a pushing force), passing through them and escaping by evaporation (which may be regarded as a pulling force). The sucking and propelling power, there is reason to believe, is possessed by each compartment of the heart—a circumstance due to the fact that the opening and closing of the different parts of the heart are equally vital acts. (They are vital in the same sense that the opening and closing of the medusa, and the vacuoles of such plants as the *Volvox globator, Gonium pectorale,* and *Chlamydomonas,* are vital.) Thus the auricle and ventricle, when they close, *propel or push* the blood ; whereas, when they open, they *draw or suck* it. As the auricle closes when the ventricle opens, and *vice versa,* it follows that when the ventricle is pushing, the auricle is pulling ; the auricle pushing when the ventricle is pulling. The two forces, in fact, act together, the object being to cause the blood to flow in a circle. That each compartment of the heart—in other words, each pulsating cavity—has the power of gently sucking in the blood and forcibly ejecting it, seems proved by analogy. If a caoutchouc oval-shaped cylinder furnished with two apertures be compressed by the hand, to exclude the air, and immersed in water, it fills itself when it expands. The water can be extruded by the pressure of the hand, and the operation repeated *ad libitum.* If the apertures of the cylinder have fitted to them two tubes, one of which is supplied with a ball-valve as in some forms of enema syringe, water may be pumped out of a vessel in a more or less continuous stream as by the heart, by immersing that end of the apparatus containing the valve, and applying an interrupted pressure to the cylinder, by alternately closing and opening the hand in which the cylinder is retained. When the cylinder is forcibly closed, it ejects the water; and when it spontaneously opens, it draws it in. Precisely the same thing occurs in the heart of the lobster; the heart in this crustacean consisting of a single muscular sac, which gives off and receives numerous tubes (Fig. 48, *h*, p. 108). This reasoning is not vitiated by the fact that the vessels proceeding to and from the heart are flexible, for I have ascertained by experiment that the vessels may be as thin as tissue paper and not collapse when suction is applied to them, provided always they be full, or moderately full, of blood—blood, like other fluids, being nearly incompressible. If, for example, a piece of gut having a syringe attached to it at either end be immersed, and the gut and one syringe be moderately filled with water, I find that the water in the full syringe can be made to pass to the empty syringe, without in the slightest altering the calibre of the gut. This follows, because the contents of the gut remain always exactly the same. The transference is effected by one operator pushing down the piston of the full syringe, while another draws up the piston of the empty syringe. It is in this way that the vessels are always kept moderately full of blood, and that one compartment of the heart always closes and pushes at the same instant that another compartment opens and pulls. The blood ejected from the one compartment is received by the other, the vessels being always full; one compartment of a single heart (heart consisting of an auricle and ventricle), and two compartments of a double heart (heart consisting of two auricles and two ventricles), being always empty. From this it appears that two pulsating cavities, one of which opens when the other closes, are capable of carrying on the circulation in the absence of elasticity in the vessels. Nor will this occasion surprise. No substance is perfectly elastic; so that if much power was stored up in the vessels by the heart, a considerable proportion of it would be sacrificed. Such vessels as take an active part in the circulation open and close in parts rhythmically, and produce a kind of swallowing movement; this movement being due less to elasticity than vitality in the parts. The elasticity of the vessels is principally of use in causing the blood to flow in a continuous stream, the elasticity acting when the ventricles have ceased to act (*i.e.* between the pulsations) in such a manner as definitely to co-ordinate the ventricular movements. Elasticity is also useful in keeping the vessels open, in permitting them to assume various attitudes, and in yielding to and correcting local congestions. The blood is most economically circulated by an apparatus which opens and closes spontaneously in parts; this arrangement reducing friction and conserving energy. Such an apparatus operates upon the blood and not upon itself. It can operate with or in the absence of elasticity, and performs work in whichever direction it moves. The object of the circulatory apparatus is to convey blood to and from the capillaries where the tissues are fed, and this can be done most conveniently by an apparatus which propels fluid in a circle, one half of the apparatus propelling or pushing the fluid round one half of the circle, the fluid being gradually slowed in its course; while it sucks or draws it round the other half, the fluid being gradually quickened in its course. By this arrangement no time is lost, the blood being slowed in order to afford the tissues an opportunity of taking from and giving to it, and quickened when these interchanges are not necessary. The blood is slowed as it proceeds from the

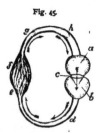

Fig. 45.

Fig. 45.—Diagram representing how the heart pushes and pulls the blood, and how the circulation is slowed and quickened. *a*, auricle. *b*, ventricle (pulsating cavities), of exactly the same size; *c*, auriculo-ventricular orifice guarded by a mitral valve; *d*, artery; *e, f,* capillaries; *g, h,* vein. The ventricle (*b*) propels or pushes the blood towards the capillaries (*e, f*) when it closes; the auricle (*a*) sucks or draws it from them when it opens. The auricle always opens when the ventricle closes, and *vice versa* (one compartment of the heart being always empty when the other is full). The blood is by this means forced in a circle (*vide* arrows). It is slowed in the direction *b, d, e,* and quickened in the direction *f, g, h, a.* The valves *c, g, h,* insure that the blood will always flow in the same direction.—*Original.*

heart, by the breaking up of the arteries into innumerable branches, and from a marked increase in the capillary area; the friction experienced by the blood *in transitu* being correspondingly increased. It is quickened as it proceeds towards

the heart, by the veins converging, and from a marked diminution in the venous area ; the friction experienced by the
circulating fluid being correspondingly diminished. (These
points are shown in Fig. 45.)

Circulation in the Star-fish.—In the star-fish the intestinal
vascular system consists of loops, from which arteries and
veins are given off; these being connected with a dilated
pulsatile canal, which may be regarded as a rudimentary
heart. Similar remarks are to be made of the holothuria, so
that we have at length arrived at what may be regarded as a
visible force, viz. a pulsating vessel. It is a remarkable circumstance that in the mammal those veins which are not
furnished with valves are largely supplied with non-striated
muscular fibres, which run in two directions, viz. across and
in the direction of the length of the vessel. This holds true
of the inferior vena cava, the renal, azygos, and external iliac
veins, and of all the large trunks of the portal venous system,
and of the trunks of the hepatic veins [1]. These vessels have
therefore the power, within certain limits, of opening and
closing [2], and of forcing on the blood independently of valves.
Valves are consequently accessory structures and adjuvants
to the heart in the higher animals.

Circulation in the Spider.—In the spider a large dorsal
vessel makes its appearance, this being dilated posteriorly so
as to resemble a heart. The great propelling organ in the
circulation of animals is now beginning to assume form. The
dorsal vessel gives off lateral branches which ramify through
the body ; the venous blood being collected in open spaces
or sinuses on the abdominal surface. There is as yet only an
arterial system of vessels, the venous one being deficient. The
blood is aerated by tracheae or pulmonary cavities.

Circulation in the Insect.—A similar account may be given
of the circulation in the insect. Here the dorsal vessel is
divided into a series of swellings, each of which is furnished
with valves, and endowed with a pulsatile power, as shown at
h of Fig. 46, p. 104. The dorsal·artery receives lateral currents
from various parts of the body, and is widened out posteriorly.

---

[1] Anatomy, Descriptive and Surgical, by Henry Gray, Esq., F.R.S., p. 401.
[2] Nerves are supplied to the inferior cava and cerebral veins; to the aorta,
pulmonary artery, and many other vessels.

The dorsal vessel opens and closes in parts (one part always opening when the other closes) with a vermicular or wave-like motion—this, in conjunction with the valves (x, r), determining the course pursued by the blood. The blood is returned by two vessels situated on the ventral aspect of the insect (v); these, according to Carus and Wagner, being in many cases absent, and their places supplied by open sinuses, as in the spider. The dorsal and ventral vessels are united anteriorly and posteriorly by loops which, in the immature or larval individual, extend into the antennae, fin-shaped caudal processes, the first joint of each leg, and the immature wing. Under these circumstances the wings, antennae, and caudal appendages, act as respiratory organs.

Fig. 46.

Fig. 46 shows the position of the vessels in the insect. h, great dorsal vessel, consisting of pulsatile swellings which force the blood towards the head. v, vessels situated on the ventral aspect, which collect and transmit the blood in a direction from before backwards. The arrows indicate the direction of the currents in the wings. *, x, r, valves situated in dorsal vessel. Between these the lateral currents enter (*vide* small curved arrows). The valves are pushed aside and opened by the blood as it travels in the direction of the head (*see* arrows directed upwards), and forced towards the axis of the vessel, and closed by the blood when it attempts to travel away from the head (*see* arrows directed downwards).— *After Thomson.*

In the insect the organs of respiration are also the organs of locomotion. The circulation is most complete, as a rule, in the immature insect. It is however quite perfect in not a few adult insects. Carus found it so in the wings of semblis, developed for flight. In the fully matured insect the circulation in many cases becomes circumscribed, the blood being cut off from the several appendages and confined to the body. When the several parts are formed the vessels are either wholly or partly obliterated, as happens in the old vascular bundles of woody tissue in the more central parts of the tree. The insect is by this means rendered stronger and lighter for the purposes of flight. It is by the filling up and obliterating of blood-vessels that organs, such as the branchiae of the frog, and other foetal structures which serve a temporary purpose, are lopped off. As the presence of blood is necessary to the existence of such structures, so its absence results in their destruction. The insect possesses a circulatory apparatus, which compels the blood to flow in given directions. The dorsal vessel of the insect consists virtually of a chain of hearts, which act in unison and in a certain rhythmic order, although they are more or less distinctly cut off from each other by the presence of valves. The caudal heart closes first (that immediately in front of it opening), and so on in regular order, that next the head closing last. The blood is driven forward by a rhythmic wave, or swallowing movement, and the valves are so placed that it must of necessity move in a circle. The peculiarity of the movement consists in the fact, that while one pulsatile cavity closes, another opens; each cavity opening and closing alternately, and every two cavities reciprocating and co-ordinating to produce a common result. In this way the blood, when expelled by the closing of one chamber, is received by another, which opens for the purpose. The dorsal vessel of the insect thus exerts a pushing and pulling power, similar to that exerted by the oesophagus in swallowing.

If any one of the pulsating cavities had, when it closed, forcibly to dilate that anterior to it, much power would be lost. The object to be attained by the closing of any one of the cavities is not to dilate that beyond it, but to force on the blood; and this object is best secured by any two cavities working in unison, the anterior one always opening when that behind it closes. In this way a *vis a fronte* and a *vis a tergo* is supplied. Each pulsating cavity, when it closes, exerts a pushing power, and, when it opens, a pulling power, so that each bead-like swelling of the dorsal vessel of the insect possesses all the attributes of the most highly differentiated hearts; in other words, it reverses its movements, so as to work in both directions, at one time acting as a *vis a tergo*, at another as a *vis a fronte*. This is a point of very considerable importance, as it invests pulsating sacs with a double function, literally no power being wasted. In the lobster, where there is only one pulsating sac, the double function is necessary. The arrangement affords a very good example of the conservation of energy in living tissues.

Fig. 47.

The heart of the chick greatly resembles a segment of the dorsal vessel of the insect. Thus it consists of a tube constricted in three portions; the one portion corresponding to the auricle, a second to the ventricle, and a third to the aortic bulb. These have the power of opening and closing rhythmically. The heart of the chick pulsates at a very early period, while it is yet a mass of nucleated cells, and before muscular fibres are developed in it (Fig. 47).

Fig. 47.—Heart of chick at thirty-seventh hour of incubation, seen from ventral aspect. *a, a,* primitive veins. *b,* auricular portion *of* the heart. *c,* ventricular ditto. *d,* bulbus arteriosus. *e, e,* primitive aortic arches, which subsequently unite to .form the descending aorta. *f, f,* omphalo-mesenteric arteries.—*After Quain.*

Function performed by the Valves.— The valves situated between the pulsatile sacs of the dorsal vessel of the insect facilitate, as stated, the forward movement, but effectually prevent a retrograde or backward movement. As I shall frequently have occasion to allude to the valves as I proceed with the circulation, it may be as well briefly to refer to them on their first appearance. They consist of crescentic reduplications of the lining membrane of the vessels, around the interior of which they are festooned like garlands (Fig. 46, *, *x, r,* p. 104). They diverge from the interior of the vessel in the direction of its axis, and as they are directed obliquely upwards and inwards with reference to the axis, they readily admit of the blood passing through them in the one direction, but effectually prevent its return. They may be compared to the folding-doors placed on the floor of a granary, which are opened by each consignment of grain as it is made to pass from a lower to a higher level, but which flap together the instant the grain is elevated to prevent its passing again in a downward direction. They, in fact, permit motion in only one direction. The valves are flexible elastic sluices, which are for the most part opened and closed mechanically by the blood—a few being closed partly by muscular movements. The free margins of the valves project into the interior of the vessels to such an extent that when the column of blood is at rest, they are more or less in apposition. The slightest reflux therefore instantly and effectually closes them. This action is the more instantaneous from the fact that behind the valves the vessels are scooped out to form sinuses, which contain a large quantity of residual blood ; this, by its mere weight, greatly facilitating the closure. These sinuses I find in both the arteries and veins. They are known in the aorta and pulmonary artery of the human heart as the sinuses of Valsalva (Fig. 49, i, p. 108). The valves are found in infinite variety, and vary as regards the size, shape, number, and structure of their segments in the various orders of animals. As however they all act upon the same principle, and I shall have occasion to describe them minutely hereafter, I shall merely state that, when valves are present, the mystery as to the direction of the current or currents at once disappears ; for it is evident that if a long vessel furnished with valves closes at any given point, the fluid contained in it must move in the direction in which the valves open. (*Vide* arrows directed upwards of Fig. 46, * p. 104.)

The circulation of the insect is remarkable when viewed in connexion with the respiratory system. As you are aware, the body, and indeed every part of the insect, is tunnelled out by an innumerable series of minute elastic tough tubes, the so-called tracheae. By their aid the insect breathes at every pore, very much in the same way that the plant breathes by its vascular and intervascular spaces, when these contain air. This is an interesting circumstance, as it shows the vast importance of constant relays of fresh air for the purposes of the circulation. The presence of air is a *sine qua non ;* the fish has its gills, the reptiles their branchiae or lungs, and so of the birds and mammals. The respiratory and circulatory systems more immediately connect the living organism with the outer world. In the stems of plants there are large air cavities, and not unfrequently the air and nutritive juices circulate together in the vascular bundles. In the lower animals, where the fluids transude, the air enters into combination with them ; and in the higher animals the blood in the lungs and other parts is separated from the air by a membranous film exceedingly delicate in texture. In none of the animals which have hitherto been examined have we met with any one structure which could with propriety be denominated a heart. This, in its simplest form, is to be found in the ascidia, which is provided with a pulsatile sac, consisting of thin membranous walls, apparently devoid of valves.

Circulation in the Lobster. Position of the Respiratory Apparatus in the Lobster, Fish, etc.—In the lobster a structure is found which may be regarded as a true heart, alike on account of its position and shape, and because of the vessels which proceed from and return to it. The structure in question is situated below the posterior margin of the thoracic shield, and consists of an oval-shaped cavity or ventricle with muscular walls, as represented at *h* of Fig. 48.

Fig. 48.　　　　　　Fig. 49.　　　　　　Fig. 50.

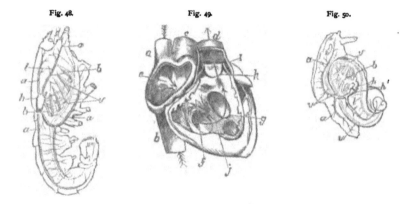

Fig. 48 shows the distribution of the blood-vessels in the lobster. *a, a, a, a,* systemic arteries, *b, b,* branchial veins. *v,* systemic veins and sinuses, from which the branchial veins arise. *l,* artery conveying blood to liver and to branchiae.—*After Thomson.*

Fig. 49.—Pulmonic or right side of human heart. *e,* right auricle. *g,* right ventricle. *a,* superior cava. *b,* inferior cava. *c.* aorta. *d,* Pulmonic artery. *h,* segment of semilunar valve. *i.* sinus of Valsalva. *f,* segment of tricuspid valve. *j.* musculus papillaris. The arrows indicate the direction in which the blood enters and leaves the right or pulmonic heart.—*After Gray.*

Fig. 50.—Heart and vessels of garden-snail. *h,* auricle. *h'* ventricle. *a, a,* arteries. *v, v, v.* veins. *b,* pulmonary sacs which receive the blood from the veins.—*After Thomson.*

The heart of the lobster has the power of opening and sucking or drawing the blood into it, and of closing and ejecting or pushing the blood out of it. These acts are equally vital in their nature[1]. It gives off six systemic arteries, these con-

[1] When the heart closes it completely extrudes its contained blood, and is, to all intents and purposes, a solid muscular mass. If it did not open spontaneously, it is obvious that no pressure exerted by the vessels could force the blood into it; nor must it be overlooked that, in the embryo, the heart acts before it contains blood. The medusa and certain plants, such as the *Volvox globator, Gonium pectorale,* and *Chlamydomonas,* have also the power of opening and closing irrespec-

veying the blood to the system generally, and to the liver (*l*). The arterial blood is collected by veins which open into sinuses situated in the lower or ventral surface of the body. From these the branchial veins, which return the blood which has passed through the gills to the heart, arise. The heart, it will be observed, is a systemic heart, *i.e.* a heart which forces the blood directly through the arteries, and only indirectly through the veins. It resembles, in some respects, the lymphatic hearts of reptiles and birds. When it closes, the blood is forced from the dorsal to the ventral surface of the lobster, the fluid proceeding simultaneously in the direction of the head and tail. It then flows into sinuses or pouches, from which it passes through the gills on its way back to the heart. There is as yet no pulmonic heart present, and by this I mean a heart delegated to force the blood directly into the aerating apparatus, whether this takes the form of gills, branchiae, or lungs. The circulation of the lobster, notwithstanding, naturally resolves itself into two parts, the presence of gills or aerating structures necessitating this degree of differentiation. The gills or aerating apparatus of the lobster are situated on its ventral surface, and in the track of the venous system, towards its termination ; *i.e.* they are interposed between the terminal part of the venous system and the heart—the blood flowing from the heart towards the system, and from the system towards the gills. The same arrangement obtains in the cephalopoda. In the fish, as I shall show presently, an opposite arrangement prevails, the gills being situated at the beginning of the arterial system ; the blood flowing from the heart (ventricle) towards the gills, and from the gills towards the system. It is therefore a matter of little or no importance on what part of the circle representing the circulation the aerating apparatus is situated, so long as it occupies a position favourable to the exposure of the blood to the air. The blood flows in a continuous round, and it suffices if it be aerated at one part of its course, either by the aid of pulmonic sacs, gills, branchiae, or lungs. As the respiratory system be-

tive of anything they contain. The elasticity of the vessels assists the opening or sucking action of the heart, but does not cause it. When the heart consists of two compartments, one of them closes and pushes while the other opens and pulls, the compartments opening and closing alternately.

comes more differentiated, its connexion with pulsating cavities becomes more intimate. Thus in the bird and mammal the lungs are provided with a heart for themselves—the so-called pulmonic or right heart, which consists of two cavities : an auricle which receives the venous blood fromt he system, and a ventricle which forces the blood directly through the lungs (Fig. 49, p. 108). The left or systemic heart of the bird and mammal likewise consists of two cavities : an auricle which receives the aerated blood from the lungs, and a ventricle which distributes the purified blood to the system. The heart of the bird and mammal consequently each consist of four compartments. Between the most highly differentiated heart, as found in the bird and mammal and that of the lobster, there is an infinite number of modifications, these mainly depending on the nature of the respiration. Thus in the fish the heart consists of two cavities—an auricle and a ventricle ; in the serpent of three—two auricles and one ventricle ; in the alligator the cavities virtually amount to four—the single ventricle being divided into two by an imperfect septum. It is therefore necessary to bear in mind, when speaking of the heart of animals, that it may consist of one, two, three, or four cavities.

Circulation in the Brachiopoda and Gasteropoda.—The brachiopoda have two aortic hearts, *i. e.* two pulsating cavities situated on the principal artery of the body. The auricle and ventricle of a single complete heart are thus distinctly foreshadowed. Valves are also present. In the gasteropoda and pteropoda, of the former of which the garden-snail may be taken as an example, there is a well-marked auricle and ventricle : the auricle receiving the blood from the pulmonary sacs, which receive it from the veins ; the ventricle forcing it through the arteries (Fig. 50, p. 108).

In the heart of the garden-snail the movements take place in the same order as in hearts of a higher type. Thus the auricle and ventricle pulsate alternately—the auricle closing when the ventricle is opening, and *vice versa*. The rhythmic peristaltic movement which we beheld ·in the dorsal vessel of the insect reappears in a slightly modified form, the vermicular waves of motion being more isolated, and consequently more distinct. When a wave movement travels rapidly forward in a long vessel, it is difficult to say where it begins and where it terminates. This difficulty is in a great measure removed when, as in the present instance, the one cavity is observed to close, and then the other.

Circulation in the Cuttle-fish.—In the cephalopoda, of which the cuttle-fish may be taken as the representative, we find a muscular systemic heart consisting of one cavity. To this may be added two dilated portions in the two vessels which lead to the branchiae. These close and open like the heart itself, so that there are virtually two branchial cavities and one systemic one—three pulsating cavities in all. The connexion between the circulation and the respiration is now becoming very obvious, and the pulsatile sinuses, situated near the root of the gills, may be regarded as harbingers of the pulmonic or right heart, as it exists in the bird and mammal (Fig. 51).

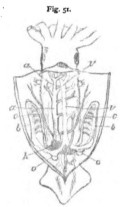

Fig. 51.

Fig. 51.—Heart and vessels of cuttle-fish. *h*, heart. *o, o,* Dilated portions of vessels which lead to branchiae. *b, b ; c, c,* branchial vessels. *a, a,* arteries. *v, v,* veins.—*After Thomson.*

CIRCULATION IN ANIMALS *(Vertebrata).*

Hitherto we have been dealing with the invertebrata. In my remarks on the circulation of those most interesting and variously-constituted creatures, I have confined myself to no zoological classification, but have picked up a link of the chain wherever I found a suitable one. I have been able to show a gradual development of, and differentiation in, the channels and forces of the circulatory apparatus.

In the circulation of the vertebrata, to an examination of which I now hasten, I shall be able to show a still higher degree of differentiation—not so much of the forces themselves, as of the organs or instruments by which the forces make themselves manifest.

Circulation in the Fish.—In the fish we find a muscular heart consisting of two cavities, an auricle and a ventricle. The auricle receives the venous blood from the liver and the system generally, the ventricle forcing the blood through the capillaries of the gills (where it is aerated), into a large artery, which may be regarded as the homologue of the descending aorta in mammals. The blood contained in the great dorsal artery of the fish is arterial, that in the veins and heart venous (Fig. 52, p. 114). In addition to its general or major circulation, the fish has two special or minor circulations; viz. a circulation through the kidneys, and another through the liver. These minor circulations reappear in the reptiles, and are interesting, the more especially as the portal circulation is also to be found in the mammal. When the major circulation is once determined, any number of minor circulations may be added without greatly increasing the complexity. The major circulation, as has been explained, may be represented by a circle—the minor circulation, by one or more loops grafted on the original circle. These loops may be added at any part, and may be increased indefinitely. Thus there may be a capillary circulation, a renal circulation, a portal circulation, a pulmonic circulation, a cephalic circulation, and so on.

The respiratory apparatus of the fish is placed on the arterial system. In the lobster and cuttle-fish, as has been shown, it is placed on the venous. This however occasions no difficulty. The heart of the fish, while consisting of only two cavities, has accessory structures of considerable importance attached to it. Thus the auricle is provided with a great venous sinus, which collects the blood destined to fill the auricle; while the ventricle is furnished with a muscular pulsatile organ, the so-called bulbus arteriosus, which assists the ventricle in forcing the blood through the gills. These several structures are deserving of separate description. The venous sinus, like its congeners, is a mere irregular dilatation or swelling, occasioned for the most part by the converging and flowing together of the principal venous trunks of the system. It may be compared to the venae cavae of the mammal. The auricle is a somewhat irregularly shaped oval or angular chamber, having exceedingly thin muscular walls. The muscular fibres entering into its formation pursue no definite direction, but are grouped in such a manner as to secure great strength, and a large degree of pulsatile power. The shape of the ventricle in the most muscular fishes is that of an inverted three-sided pyramid.

In the heart of the salmon, which I have had an opportunity of dissecting, the ventricular walls are composed of muscular fibres which run in three well-marked directions, viz. vertically, transversely, and from without inwards. The vertical fibres are found on the outside and inside of the ventricle. In addition to being vertical they are also slightly plicate, a certain number of them passing through the wall of the ventricle, in a direction from without inwards or the converse. The vertical fibres, which may be regarded as forming an external and internal layer, are in many cases continuous at the base and apex of the ventricle. The transverse fibres occupy a central position in the ventricular wall, and pursue a more or less circular direction. The fish is thus supplied with an organ of great power, capable of opening and closing with a steady rhythmic movement. The bulbus arteriosus resembles, in its general appearance, the bulb of a hyacinth. It is muscular, and has a structure in many cases analogous to the ventricle itself. It receives the blood from the heart, and assists in forcing it through the capillaries of the gills, and thence through the system. A careful examination of the movements of the heart and bulbus arteriosus in the living pike, eel, trout, flounder, cod, etc., has convinced me that the ventricle and venous sinus close, when the auricle and bulbus arteriosus open, and *vice versa*. The auricle supplements, as it were, the movements begun by the veins and venous sinus; the ventricle, those commenced by the auricle; and the bulbus arteriosus, those commenced by the ventricle. The relation of the auricle, ventricle, and aortic bulb to each other is to be inferred from the presence of valves between these structures, an arrangement which provides for combined and independent movements. Nor is this arrangement uncalled for. The close proximity of the gills to the heart would expose the capillaries of the gills to rupture if the ventricle closed with the violence necessary to force the blood through the entire system. This danger is averted by employing a second pulsatile cavity (the bulbus arteriosus), which, closing as it does with less vigour than the ventricle, keeps up but modifies the pressure

I

within the required limits. We have an example of what mischief may be done by a too sudden and too violent closure of a pulsating cavity in the vicinity of capillaries, in cases of hypertrophy of the right ventricle of the human heart, where the pressure exerted not unfrequently produces rupture of the capillaries of the lungs—the pulmonary apoplexy of pathologists. The branches of the bulbus arteriosus correspond for the most part to the number of gill-plates; these in the cod-fish amounting to four on either side. The number of the branches vary: thus in the *Lophius piscatorius* there are only three, in most osseous fishes four, in the skates and sharks five, and in the lampreys six and seven. It is most interesting to observe that the arrangement of the vessels at the arterial bulb, and the beginning of the descending aorta, if we may so call it, is the same; the gills or respiratory system being introduced into the circulatory system as it were accidentally, or by the way. Thus, in the cod-fish, there are four main vessels given off from the top of the bulb on either side to the gills, a corresponding number being given off from the gills to constitute the first part of what may be regarded as the descending aorta. (Cp. parts marked *a, a, b, b* of branchial plate Fig. 52.)

The arterial bulb of the fish is, in some respects, a remarkable structure. It is especially so as regards the number and nature of the valves contained in its interior. These vary in number, size, and shape, their segments ranging from two to thirty-two. In fact, in this single structure, every valve in the animal series is either indicated or actually represented. I defer a consideration of them till I come to speak of the valves as a whole. The number of the valves is in some measure necessitated by the pulsating properties of the bulb, and the peculiar form of the respiration in fishes. The closing of the bulb is apt to interfere with the perfect action of the valves, and the proximity to the heart of the capillary vessels of the gills predisposes to regurgitation.

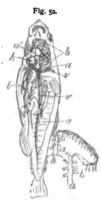

Fig. 52.

Fig. 52.—Heart and vessels of the fish (cod). *h*, ventricle with auricle behind. *a′*, bulbus arteriosus, giving off four branchial vessels (*b*). These converge to form the first part of the descending aorta (*a, a*). *v, v*, systemic veins receiving blood from liver (*l*), kidneys, etc.

In either case an increase in the number of valves is demanded.

The subjoined account of the movements of the heart of the fish, taken from life, may prove interesting. The movements are rhythmical in character, and occur as follows :—

The large veins at the base of the heart close slowly and become paler in colour; the auricle opening and becoming darker in colour. The auricle then closes energetically and suddenly, and changes from a dark purple colour to a reddish hue, the ventricle opening and assuming a dark purple colour. The ventricle now closes suddenly with a vermicular or wave-like motion, and assumes a reddish tinge, the arterial bulb opening and becoming of a purple colour. The bulb when it closes changes from a purple to a bluish or pearly white colour. The change of colour in the parts referred to is due to the presence or absence of blood in their interior. The veins and ventricle close when the auricle and arterial bulb open, and the veins and ventricle open when the auricle and arterial bulb close. The movements of the veins and ventricle co-ordinate those of the auricle and arterial bulb. There are no dead points. Before the veins have ceased to close, the auricle begins to open ; before the auricle has ceased to close, the ventricle begins to open; before the ventricle has ceased to close, the bulbus arteriosus begins to open; and so on in regular and uninterrupted succession. It occasionally happens when the heart is more or less deprived of blood and acting slowly that the auricle opens before the veins close, the ventricle in like manner opening before the auricle closes; a circumstance which, in my opinion, proves that the *opening* of the auricle and of the ventricle is a vital act, in the same sense that the *closing* of each is a vital act. In other words, the opening of the auricle is not due to the closing of the veins, neither is the opening of the ventricle due to the closing of the auricle. The one movement contributes to the other, but does not cause it.

The auricle and ventricle (particularly the latter) open with considerable energy, so much so that the expansile movement may be felt when the heart is grasped between the finger and thumb.

The veins and arterial bulb shorten when they open, and elongate when they close. The auricle and ventricle, on the other hand, elongate when they open and shorten when they close. This difference is due to an excess of circular fibres in the veins and bulb, as compared with the number of these fibres found in the auricle and ventricle. The veins, auricle, ventricle, and arterial bulb, are highly expansile. They flatten slightly when they open, and become rounded when they close. They increase and decrease by about a third during these movements. The veins act with less energy than the bulb, the bulb than the auricle, and the auricle than the ventricle. The action of the bulb is slow and sustained rather than rapid and violent. The auricle, ventricle, and bulb, empty themselves of blood when they close.

The ventricle when closing rotates and screws slightly in the direction of its length. It also becomes shorter and narrower.

The apex of the ventricle describes an ellipse when the ventricle is opening and closing.

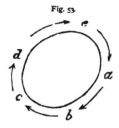

Fig. 53.

Fig. 53.—Track described by the apex of the heart of the fish. Enlarged. *Original.*

I annex a diagram of the ellipse as bearing upon the much-disputed question of the impulse of the heart. The letter *e* (Fig. 53) represents the position assumed by the apex at the time the ventricle is closed and empty of blood. When the ventricle opens and receives the blood from the auricle, the apex travels in the direction *e, a,* and suddenly descends in a downward and outward direction, as shown at *a, b.* When the ventricle closes and ejects its blood, the apex describes the segment of the ellipse *b, c, d, e,* it being thus drawn outwards, upwards, and inwards. The apex impinges against the thorax when it is describing the part of the ellipse *a, b, c, d,* and more particularly at *b, c.* There is no pause in the action of the ventricle from the time the apex leaves the point *e* until it returns to it. The ventricle expands between the points *e* and *b.* The ventricle as a whole flattens itself at this stage, and recedes from the anterior wall of the thorax, but its apex advances slightly towards it. The auricle closes when the apex of the ventricle is travelling from *e* to *b*; and at this time the ventricle is most full of blood. The ventricle begins to close when the apex reaches *b,* the closing becoming more complete as the apex travels in the direction *b, c, d, e.* 'At *e* the closure is perfect and the ventricle empty of blood.' From this it follows that the impulse of the heart of the fish corresponds neither to the diastole nor the systole of the ventricle, but to the termination of the diastole and the beginning of the systole. Of this I have fully satisfied myself.

Circulation in the Aquatic Reptiles.—I now pass to the circulation in the aquatic reptiles, as it is found in the axolotl, proteus, menobranchus, siren, the larva of the frog, salamander, etc. The gills in the axolotl and allied forms are situated outside the body, and are persistent. The gills of the larva of the frog, on the contrary, become covered as the animal develops, so that they assume the position and function of the gills in the fish. The heart in the protean reptiles consists usually of three cavities, viz. two auricles and a ventricle. The great point of interest in these remarkable creatures is the position of the gills, and the mixing of the arterial and venous blood in the ventricle. This is effected in the following manner:—The bulbus arteriosus, which may be compared to the first part of the aorta in mammals, divides into two ; each division giving off three or more branches on either side, which extend along the arches formed by the hyoid bones, and break up into innumerable loops, to form the external gills, two branches, when lungs are present, going to them. The lateral vessels pass through the gills in a direction from before backwards, and reunite to form the descending aorta, so that the gills or respiratory apparatus is situated on the arterial or systemic system of vessels, as in the fish. When lungs are present they are furnished with pulmonary veins which proceed direct to the heart.

The blood is projected from the ventricle into the capillaries of the gills and lungs. As the vessels from the gills reunite to form the descending aorta, the blood in the descending aorta is consequently red or arterialised blood. This pervades the entire body, and is returned to the right auricle by the systemic veins. The blood which circulated through the lungs is returned to the left auricle by the pulmonic veins. When the auricles close, the right one discharges venous blood into the ventricle, the left one arterial blood ; the arterial and venous blood being mixed up in the ventricle accordingly. This result is facilitated by the fact that the interior of the ventricle presents a fretted, uneven, or broken surface, which is especially adapted for the triturating or mixing process. In some of the protean reptiles arterial twigs pass directly from the aortic bulb to the descending aorta. In such cases the blood is mixed in the descending aorta as well as in the heart; the blood which circulates through the body being partly arterial and partly venous. (Fig. 54.)

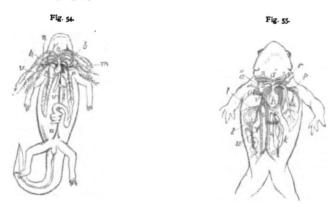

Fig. 54.   Fig. 55.

Fig. 54.—Heart and vessels of axolotl. *h*, ventricle. *m*, right auricle, receiving venous blood from the system generally (*v, v*). *n*, vessels from gills conveying arterial blood to the left auricle. *a* (superior), aortic bulb, dividing into eight branches, six of which go to the gills (*b*), and two to the lungs (*p, p*). *a* (inferior), descending aorta, formed by the reunion of the vessels which go to the gills. *l*, veins from liver.—*After Thomson.*

Fig. 55.—Heart and vessels of frog. *h*, ventricle with auricles above and behind. *a'*, aortic bulb splitting up into branches to supply the system and lungs. Of these some (*a''*) unite to form the descending aorta (*a*); others (those from the first part of the aortic bulb) going directly to the lungs. *v, v*, systemic veins. *l, u, k*, vessels going therefrom to the liver and kidneys.—*After Thomson.*

Circulation in the Frog.—Leaving the aquatic reptiles, which respire principally by gills, I come to speak of those which respire by means of lungs, such, for example, as the chelonia, ophidia, and sauria. The adult frog naturally introduces us to this group. In the frog the circulation is very similar to that just described. Here the heart, as in the protean reptiles, consists of three cavities, two auricles and one ventricle. The lungs derive their vessels directly from the first part of the aorta, branches from the aortic arches uniting to form the descending aorta. The venous blood from the system returns to the right auricle, the arterial blood from the pulmonic veins returning to the left. When the auricles close, the blood is mixed in the ventricle as before. The venous blood, while making the circuit of the system, circulates by a special arrangement through the kid-. neys and the liver (Fig. 55).

The following description of the movements of the heart of the frog is taken from notes made during the life of the animal. The observations on which the description is based were made with extreme care on a large healthy frog im- mediately after capture, and before and after the pericardium was removed. The rhythm of the frog's heart essentially consists of four stages, traceable to the movements of the veins at the base of the heart, and to the movements of the auricles, ventricle, and bulbus arteriosus. The movements are essentially wave-like in character, the blood being forced through the structures referred to, by a kind of swallowing movement. The veins, auricles, ventricle, and arterial bulb, act in pairs, as in the beaded dorsal vessel of the insect. Thus when the veins close, the auricles open; when the auricles close, the ventricle opens; when the ventricle closes, the aortic bulb opens; when the aortic bulb closes, the veins open; and so on in endless succession. These are vital movements, and go on when the heart is deprived of blood. From this it follows that the veins and ventricle open and close together; the auricles and bulbus arteriosus opening and closing together. As however the auricles open when the veins close, and the ventricle opens when the auricles close, while the arterial bulb opens when the ventricle closes, and the veins open when the aortic bulb closes, the sucking and propelling action of the various chambers through which the blood passes is brought fairly and fully into play. The blood is passed on by a series of definitely co-ordinated movements. When the heart is acting normally, one or other part of it is always moving. The instant the large veins begin to close, the auricles begin to open; and the moment the auricles begin to close, the ventricle begins to open. When the ventricle begins to close, the aortic bulb begins to open; and when the aortic bulb begins to close, the veins begin to open; and so on *ad infinitum*. It follows from this that the sounds of the heart are more or less continuous. The veins close slowly, the auricles somewhat suddenly; the ventricle less suddenly than the auricles, and the bulbus arteriosus less suddenly than the ventricle. The closure of the arterial bulb is a slow sustained movement. The veins and auricles open slowly, the ventricle somewhat suddenly; the aortic bulb opens less suddenly than the ventricle, but more suddenly than the auricles.

When the veins close they become of a peach colour, the auricles assuming a deep purple colour from the blood which they contain shining through their semi-transparent walls. When the auricles close a dark wave of blood is seen to enter the ventricle, the auricles becoming of a reddish, the ventricle of a purple, colour. When the ventricle closes it becomes pale red, the aortic bulb, when it opens, becoming a pale purple ; when the aortic bulb closes it becomes of a bluish or pearly white colour, the veins at the base of the heart becoming a deep purple. The colour of the parts referred to depends upon the thickness of their walls and the quantity of blood which they contain at any given time. The veins, auricles, ventricle, and arterial bulb, each reduce themselves by about a third when they close; they increase by a corresponding amount when they open. The different parts of the heart open and close by progressive wave-movements. The opening movement is centrifugal in character, the closing one centripetal. These are the only movements which can increase and diminish hollow chambers. Similar movements are observed in the opening and closing of the mushroom-shaped disc of the medusa, and the vacuoles or spaces of certain plants; those, for instance, of the *Volvox globator, Gonium pectorale,* and *Chlamydomonas.* The presence of muscular fibres is not necessary to such movements. The ventricle opens more suddenly than it closes; a remark which also holds true of the bulbus arteriosus. When the ventricle opens it flattens, its long diameter being increased ; when it closes it becomes rounded, its long diameter being diminished. The apex and anterior wall of the ventricle strike the thoracic parietes towards the end of the diastole, and the beginning of the systole, as in the fish. At this period the apex descends and advances towards the thorax. The apex during the diastole and systole describes an ellipse (Fig. 53, p. 116). The ventricle rotates slightly from right to left during the diastole, and from left to right during the systole.

The long diameters of the veins and auricles increase when those of the ventricle and bulbus arteriosus decrease, and the converse, the contents of the pericardium remaining nearly always the same.

The subjoined account of the movements of a snake's heart, written in 1865, is abstracted from my note-book :—When the heart is exposed, the auricles and ventricle are observed to open and close alternately. The movements in both cases are exceedingly slow, and apparently of about the same duration. The auricles and ventricle, particularly the latter, close in every direction—viz. from above downwards, from below upwards, and from without inwards. When the ventricle closes its anterior wall advances and strikes the internal surface of the thoracic parietes, the impulse being communicated during the ventricular systole.

The reptiles, which breathe chiefly by lungs, exhibit very considerable variation as to the structure of their hearts, the principal feature in which is the possession by many of a more or less complete septum ventriculorum. In this class the heart has virtually another cavity added to it ; and it will be seen, that in proportion as the septum of the ventricle is rudimentary or complete, the circulation gradually advances from a single or mixed circulation to a double one; *i. e.* a systemic and pulmonic.

Circulation in Lacerta ocellata.—In the *Lacerta ocellata* a rudimentary septum makes its appearance.

It virtually divides the ventricle into two portions, these corresponding to the right and left ventricles of the bird and mammal. This necessitates a considerable modification in the arrangement of the great vessels at the base of the heart. In the fish, and protean reptiles, only one vessel proceeds from the ventricle, but in the present instance the anterior or right compartment of the ventricle gives off the pulmonic vessels, while the posterior or left compartment gives off the systemic. Provision is thus made to a great extent for a distinct pulmonic and systemic circulation, the right side of the ventricle forcing the blood through the lungs, the left side forcing it through the system generally. Before leaving the heart of the Lacerta ocellata, it is interesting to observe, that while the vessels emanating from the base of the ventricle are modified to suit the requirements of the almost double circulation, they nevertheless present in their groupings the general appearance presented by the branchial vessels of the fish where the circulation is single. We have here the remnants of an earlier form.

Circulation in the Python, Crocodile, etc. Presence of Septum Ventriculorum.—In the heart of the python the septum ventriculorum is nearly complete; in fact, the right and left ventricles would be quite distinct but for the existence of a small spiral slit in the septum posteriorly.

In the heart of the crocodile (*Crocodilus Lucius*) the septum ventriculorum, as was pointed out by Hentz and Meckel, is fully developed, so that the ventricles of this animal are as perfect as those of either the bird or mammal. The object to be gained by dividing the heart into four distinct compartments is obvious. By having two auricles and two ventricles, one auricle and one ventricle can be delegated to receiving the venous blood from the veins and forcing it through the lungs; the remaining auricle and ventricle receiving the arterial blood from the lungs, and forcing it through the system generally. The lungs on the one hand and the body on the other are each provided with a heart; hence the epithet double circulation, or, what is the same thing, pulmonic and systemic circulation. The peculiarity of the double circulation consists in the fact that the arterial and venous blood circulate separately as such, and are not mixed either in the heart or the vessels. This object, of course, can only be attained by increasing the chambers of the heart, and by keeping them separate from each other.

FOETAL CIRCULATION.

Points of Analogy between the Circulation in Reptiles and that in the Human Foetus.—It is not a little curious, that in the foetal life of mammals many of the peculiarities of the reptilian circulation reappear. Thus in the foetus the auricles communicate with each other by means of the foramen ovale, and the great vessels of the ventricles communicate by means of the ductus arteriosus [1].

[1] These openings occasionally remain pervious in the adult.

In the foetus, therefore, the blood in the auricles and great vessels of the ventricles becomes more or less mixed up. As I pointed out on a former occasion, it is a matter of indifference where the respiratory apparatus is situated. It may occur in the venous system, as in the lobster and doris; or in the arterial system, as in the fish. The respiration of the mammalian foetus affords a striking illustration of the accuracy of this observation. In the foetus in utero the pulmonary organs perform no function whatever. They are ready for work, but, being in an unexpanded condition, are incapacitated. The arterialisation of the blood is therefore effected indirectly by the placenta, which is a temporary structure. To meet the requirements of such an arrangement, the uterine vessels of the mother, and the vessels of the foetus, are specially modified.

The foetal circulation naturally resolves itself into two kinds, viz. the circulation within the body of the foetus, carried on principally by the agency of the foetal vessels and heart (these constituting the visible forces); and the circulation within the placenta and the tissues of the foetus generally, carried on for the most part by absorption, evaporation, endosmose, exosmose, capillarity, chemical affinity, nutrition, etc. (these constituting the invisible forces). I shall first deal with the visible circulation as it exists within the body of the foetus, after which I shall proceed to examine the invisible circulation as it exists within the placenta.

Circulation in the Body of the Foetus.—The circulation within the body of the foetus is a closed circulation; *i.e.* its vessels and capillaries are continued upon themselves in such a manner as to form a series of circles of greater or less magnitude—the blood flowing within those circles in one continuous round. The blood is a mixed blood, being partly arterial and partly venous, the mixing taking place in the vessels and within the heart.

A mixed circulation amply meets the requirements of the foetus, and is a positive advantage, as it places the foetus in the condition of the reptilia, which are very tenacious of life, and endure much hardship without sustaining positive injury—qualities of the utmost importance to the foetus in utero, the position of which is being constantly changed.

The foetal circulation differs from the reptilian circulation, as to the temperature of the fluid circulated (the one being a cold, the other a warm blood); likewise as to the nature of the aerating apparatus, the blood of the foetus not being aerated by branchiae or lungs, but by the placenta, a temporary structure, improvised for the purpose. That the placenta performs the office of a lung to the foetus is in great measure proved by the fact that if the umbilical cord be compressed before delivery the child makes vigorous efforts to respire by the mouth [1]. The placenta has for its object the close apposition of the capillary vessels of the mother and foetus; this apposition enabling the foetus to avail itself indirectly of the lungs of the mother. The foetal circulation further differs from the reptilian in the important circumstance that the blood circulated is not produced and nourished by food taken into the alimentary canal, but by material absorbed from without; this material, in the later stages of pregnancy, being supplied by the blood in the uterine capillary vessels, and by the utricular glands of the mother, and applied indirectly by absorption, osmosis, capillarity, chemical affinity, etc., to the capillary vessels or villous tufts of the foetal portion of the placenta. The foetus in this way indirectly avails itself of the stomach as well as of the lungs of the mother. The placenta consists of two elements; a maternal element and a foetal element, and the function performed by it is essentially that of an alimentary canal and a lung. Professor Goodsir observes that 'the external cells of the placental villi perform during intra-uterine existence a function for which is substituted, in extra-uterine life, the digestive action of the gastro-intestinal mucous membrane. The internal cells of the placental villi perform during intra-uterine existence a function for which is substituted, in extra-uterine life, the action of the absorbing chyle cells of the intestinal villi. The placenta therefore not only performs, as has been always admitted, the function of a lung, but also the function of an intestinal tube [2].'

---

[1] See a remarkable case related by Hecker, and the experiments of Schwartz, etc. *Vide* Casper's Forensic Medicine (New Sydenham Society's Transactions, vol. ii. p. 128, and vol. iii. p. 38).

[2] Structure of the Human Placenta, by John Goodsir, Esq., F.R.S.L. and E., etc. 'Anatomical Memoirs,' p. 460; 1845.

Between the maternal and foetal portions of the placenta there is a line of demarcation, well marked in the earlier stages of pregnancy, but blurred and confused in the later stages; partly because of the very intimate and accurate apposition of the two parts of the placenta, which in not a few instances gives rise to abnormal adhesions; and partly because of the serrated nature of the opposing surfaces, and the presence of certain secretions. The line referred to forms at once the natural line of junction and separation between the mother and foetus, and in a perfectly healthy parturition the foetal portion of the placenta parts from the maternal portion in such a manner as not to rupture or destroy to any extent the mucous lining and capillary vessels of the uterus of the mother. On the other hand, the mucous lining and villous tufts of the foetal portion of the placenta likewise remain intact. This accounts for the fact that in the lower animals, and in a perfectly healthy human female, there is little if any haemorrhage at parturition. The relation which the foetus bears to the mother is that which the plant bears to the ground and the air; and that which the tissues of the adult animal bear to its alimentary canal and lungs, through which it obtains its nourishment and its breath. The capillary or villous tufts of the foetal portion of the placenta represent the roots of the plant; the corresponding capillary tufts of the maternal portion of the placenta, the ground and atmosphere on which the plant subsists. The foetus is in this sense to be regarded as a parasite, for it is a living thing living upon another living thing. This explains why a foetus can take root and live upon other mucous surfaces than those supplied by the uterus, as, for example, those of the Fallopian tube; and I can quite understand that the foetus would thrive on certain portions of the mucous lining of the alimentary canal, if we could only succeed in making a natural transference.

It is this intimate yet independent existence which enables us to consider the circulation of the foetus as a thing *per se*. If we examine the foetal portion of the placenta we find that the arteries and vein of the umbilical cord split up into innumerable capillary tufts, these minute vessels opening into and freely anastomosing with each other. While the capillary vessels of the foetal portion of the placenta communicate with

each other, they do not communicate with corresponding
vessels in the maternal portion of the placenta; so that the
foetal blood, impelled by the foetal heart and other forces,
flows in a circle and gyrates in the body of the foetus precisely as in the adult. The presence of the umbilical vessels
and other foetal structures, and the opening of the chambers
of the foetal heart directly and indirectly into each other, do
not affect this gyration. We may begin at any part of the
circle, but where we begin we must end, if we follow up the
course of the blood. The umbilical vein, for example, extends
between the placenta and the liver. It conveys arterial blood
to the liver [1], and the ductus venosus (a foetal structure), which
opens into the upper part of the vena cava inferior. In this
latter situation the arterial blood originally supplied by the
umbilical vein is mixed with the venous blood of the vena
cava inferior. The vena cava inferior opens directly into the
right auricle, and indirectly into the left auricle by the foramen
ovale (a foetal aperture). The Eustachian valve is, however,
so placed that comparatively little of the blood (some say
none) from the inferior cava finds its way into the right
auricle, by much the greater portion passing through the
foramen ovale into the left auricle. We have now got the
mixed blood supplied by the upper portion of the inferior cava
in the left auricle. This passes by the left auriculo-ventricular
opening into the left ventricle. It proceeds thence into the ·
arch of the aorta, and the right and left carotid and subclavian
arteries; the head and superior extremities of the foetus, which
are comparatively very large and well nourished, being supplied
by a purer blood than that furnished to the trunk and lower
extremities. The blood returns by the jugular and subclavian
veins, and vena cava superior, to the right auricle. It then
passes through the right auriculo-ventricular opening into the
right ventricle. It is impelled thence into the pulmonary
artery; but as the lungs of the foetus are in an unexpanded
condition, and only receive so much blood as suffices for their
nutrition [2], the circulation would be stopped in this direction

---

[1] The arterial blood supplied to the liver is returned to the inferior cava by the
hepatic veins.

[2] In the foetus in utero, the pulmonary organs take no part in the aeration of
the blood. They are ready for work, but being unexpanded are incapacitated.

but for the existence of a temporary canal, the so-called ductus arteriosus, which unites the pulmonary artery and aorta at the aortic arch. Through this canal the more strictly venous blood from the head, superior extremities, and right side of the heart, finds its way. The venous blood from the right side of the heart, and the nearly pure arterial blood from the left side, are thus a second time mixed. (The venous and arterial blood were first mixed in the upper part of the vena cava inferior.) The blood, doubly diluted as it were, proceeds through the descending aorta and supplies the trunk, viscera, and lower extremities. The passage of the blood through the foetal heart is indicated by the arrows in Fig. 56. It is not

Fig. 56.

Fig. 56.—Diagram of the course pursued by the blood in the foetal heart. *y*, superior cava, the blood from which passes into the right auricle ; thence into the right ventricle (*q*) ; thence into the pulmonary artery (*v*); and thence into the ascending (*u*) and descending aorta (*m*). *o*, inferior cava, the blood from which passes behind the Eustachian valve (*r* of Fig. 57, A, p. 129), through the foramen ovale, to the left auricle ; thence to the left ventricle (*r*) ; and thence to the ascending (*u*) and descending (*m*) aorta. *u*, arch of aorta and its branches.—(Compare with similar letters of Fig. 57, A, p. 129.)

necessary to describe the circulation in the lower extremities at length. All that I wish to impress upon you is, that the foetal circulation is a complete or closed circulation. The aorta at its lower part divides into the common iliac arteries, which subdivide into the external, internal, and hypogastric arteries ; the two former supplying the inferior extremities with blood. The venous blood is returned by the corresponding veins to the inferior cava, where it is joined by the arterial blood originally supplied by the umbilical vein. This completes one cycle of the circulation. The other cycle is formed

The probabilities are that the lungs, towards the full term, perform rhythmic movements in anticipation of the function to be performed by them after birth, in the same way that the heart pulsates while yet a solid mass, and before it contains blood.

by the hypogastric and umbilical arteries and vein, these constituting a very remarkable system of temporary canals; further proving, if more proof were required, that the chief function of the vessels is to convey the blood and nutritious juices through long distances. Vessels, as has been already shown, are not necessary to the circulation in the tissues. The chief point of interest in the foetal circulation, as far as the heart is concerned, consists in the right and left auricles opening directly into each other by the foramen ovale; the right and left ventricles opening indirectly into each other by the ductus arteriosus, which unites their great vessels together.

The peculiarities of the circulation within the body of the foetus are shown at Fig. 57, A; those of the circulation within the placenta, at Fig. 57, B (*vide* arrows).

Circulation in the Placenta.—The foetal circulation thus far is not difficult to comprehend. The really difficult problem, and consequently the really interesting one, is the relation which the foetal circulation bears to the maternal circulation. I have explained that the vessels of the mother and foetus remain quite distinct in the placenta, and that in reality they are merely placed in intimate and accurate apposition. I wish you to bear this fact constantly in mind. To understand this relation it will be necessary to recapitulate shortly, and to point out the relation which the external and internal surfaces of animals—*i. e.* skin and mucous membranes—bear to each other, and to corresponding parts of plants.

On a previous occasion I directed attention to the analogy between the branches and leaves and the roots and spongioles of plants, and showed that these parts are essentially the same; roots in some cases giving off branches to produce leaves, and the stems of certain trees giving off branch-like processes which ultimately become roots. I explained that the surfaces exposed by the spongioles and roots, and the leaves and branches, are absorbing, secreting, and evaporating surfaces; the same surfaces at one time absorbing and secreting moisture, and at another, discussing and evaporating it, according to the condition of the plant and the absence or presence of moisture, heat, etc. This arrangement facilitates the circulation by favouring endosmose, exosmose, capillary attraction, and other physical forces, which, we know from experiment, perform an important part in the circulation of plants. The nutritious juices, I pointed out, are applied to the leaves and roots, and also, though to a less

Fig. 57.

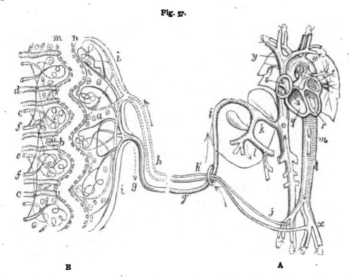

B

A

Fig. 57 A.—Diagram showing the course of the circulation in the human foetus (*vide* arrows). *g'*, *t*, umbilical vein, conveying arterial blood from the placenta. *h'*, umbilical arteries, conveying venous blood to the placenta. *k*, ductus venosus. *l*, vena portae. *o*, vena cava inferior. *y*, vena cava superior. *s*, Eustachian valve and right auricle. *q*, right ventricle. *v*, ductus arteriosus, uniting aorta (*u*) and pulmonary artery. *t*, left auricle. *r*, left ventricle. *m*, descending aorta. *x*, common iliac artery, dividing into external and internal iliac arteries. *j*, hypogastric arteries, continuous with umbilical arteries (*h'*).

Fig. 57 B.—Diagram illustrating the relation existing between the maternal (*m*) and foetal (*n*) portions of the placenta (human). The maternal and foetal surfaces are represented as separated from each other by a certain interval (*m*, *n*) to avoid confusion. They are slightly uneven from the projection into them of the maternal and foetal capillary vessels. (Compare space *m*, *n*, with similar space at *f* of Fig. 60, p. 132.) During pregnancy the two surfaces accommodate themselves so as to dovetail and fit accurately into each other. In the diagram the vessels represented by solid lines contain *arterial* blood; those represented by dotted lines *venous* blood. *m*, mucous lining of uterus, with nucleated cells on its surface. *b*, sub-epithelial, spheroidal, and fusiform corpuscles, embedded in connective tissue. *c*, *d*, utricular glands lined with epithelium, and opening on mucous surface of uterus. They pour utricular secretion into utricular space (*m*, *n*). This space is mapped off, on the one hand, by the villi and coverings of the maternal portion of the placenta : and on the other, by the villi and coverings of the foetal portion of the placenta. The utricular secretion is necessary to a free osmosis between the maternal and foetal vessels. (Compare space *m*, *n*, with similar space at *f* of Fig. 60, p. 132 ; at *e* of Fig. 64, and at *i*, *f* of Fig. 65, p. 134.) *n*, limiting membrane of foetal portion of placenta covered with nucleated cells. *a*, sub-epithelial, spheroidal, and fusiform corpuscles embedded in connective tissue. *i*, *i*, amnion. *g*, umbilical vein, conveying arterial blood to foetus. *h*, umbilical arteries, conveying venous blood from foetus. The umbilical arteries and vein break up to form the villi of the foetal portion of the placenta ; these being directed towards similar villi (*e*, *f*) constituting the maternal portion. The maternal and foetal villi are separated from each other by the utricular space (*m*, *n*) containing utricular secretion ; by two layers of cells, by two membranes, and by a certain proportion of connective tissue, spheroidal, fusiform, and other corpuscles (*a*, *b*). Goodsir regarded the placental villus as consisting of a maternal and foetal portion ; the maternal portion being composed of a membrane and nucleated cells, and corresponding to *m* of diagram ; the foetal portion being composed of a membrane and nucleated cells, and corresponding to *n* of diagram. Between the maternal and foetal portions (as he termed them) of a placental villus, he represents a space which corresponds to the space between *m* and *n* of diagram. This space he regarded as the cavity of a secreting follicle (see *d* of Figs. 61, 62, p. 133). Goodsir has, it appears to me, appropriated the lining membrane of the maternal portion of the placenta (*m* of diagram) and added it to the limiting or lining membrane of the foetal portion (*n* of diagram).— *Original.*

degree, to the stems of plants. I further explained that the animal has no roots to dig into the ground, or leaves to spread out in the sunshine, and that in this case the nutritious fluids

K

and aliments in the majority of instances are applied to an in-
voluted portion of the animal's body, to wit, the mucous surface of its alimentary canal. But the mucous lining or internal
skin of an animal is essentially the same as its external skin;
the two bearing the same relation to each other which the
roots and leaves of plants do; the mucous lining or internal
skin of the animal corresponding to the roots of the plant,
the external or true skin to the leaves of the plant. When
therefore food in a more or less fluid condition is presented to
the stomach and intestine, it is absorbed, and passes by osmosis, capillary attraction, etc., through the animal in a direction
from within outwards, first through the lacteals, and then
through the vascular system and tissues of the body generally[1].
But fluids (in plants and animals) can be transmitted in an
opposite direction, viz. from without inwards. This is shown
in the case of shipwrecked mariners who immerse their bodies
in the sea to slake their thirst, and in the inunction with oil
and other nutritious fluids in cases of starvation from disease.
The transmission of fluids through the body, both from without and from within, is favoured by the respiration of the
tissues, and the fact that evaporation goes on both in the
mucous lining or internal skin and in the external or true
skin, these surfaces, as already stated, being essentially the
same. The circulation within the tissues, as I have endeavoured to explain, is in a great measure independent of
the heart, and due mainly to the operation of certain physical forces, viz. absorption, endosmose, exosmose, capillary
attraction, chemical affinity, evaporation, etc. The heart and
blood-vessels, when they exist, are employed for transmitting
the nutritious fluids through long distances, in order to bring
the blood and other juices face to face with the tissues, the
constituent elements of which are so arranged that each takes
—or one might almost say, has forced upon it, by the physical
forces referred to—those particular ingredients which are best
adapted for its development, maintenance, and reproduction.
The object of these remarks is to show that the placental circulation of mammals is substantially the same as that of the
tissues generally. The ovum is extruded from what may be
regarded a mucous surface, viz. the interior of the ovary. It

---

[1] The lymphatic vessels join the vascular ones—the chyle ultimately becoming
blood.

is grasped by the fimbriated extremity of the Fallopian tube, as by a hand extended to receive it, and conveyed to the interior of the uterus, in the mucous lining of which it is literally planted (Fig. 58, *b.*)

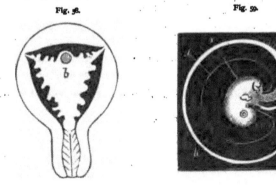

Fig. 58.   Fig. 59.

Fig. 58.—Impregnated human uterus, showing hypertrophy of the mucous lining or uterus (the decidua of authors). The mucous lining is represented in black, and the egg (*b*) is seen at the fundus of the uterus, engaged between two of its projecting convolutions.—*After Dalton.*

Fig. 59.—Human ovum at end of third month, showing placental portion (*a*) of the chorion fully formed. *h*, chorion. *a*, villous tufts proceeding from chorion. These tufts at an early period completely invest the chorion, hence the epithet 'shaggy chorion.' When the chorion is shaggy the placenta is diffuse, as in the mare. *f*, amnion. *x*, foetus. *t*, umbilical vesicle.—*After Dalton.*

The internal surface of the ovum (apparently its external one) is applied to the internal or mucous surface of the uterus; but the internal surfaces of mother and foetus are similarly constituted and perform analogous functions, the two coming together and blending as naturally as the fingers of the hands pass through and fit into each other. After a certain interval processes equivalent to roots and spongioles are sent out from the internal surface of the foetus (chorion) as seen at *a* of Fig. 59. Similar processes, which naturally exist in the uterine mucous membrane of the mother, become hypertrophied and exhibit a greatly increased activity. These processes of the mother and foetus are at first distinct, a certain interval separating the two (Figs. 57 B, *m, n*, p. 129; 58, *b*; and 77, *a, g*, p. 141). Gradually however they approach and interweave until they are accurately adapted to each other; the foetus being as it were grafted on to the mother. Notwithstanding this very intimate relation, the foetus and mother are essentially distinct. The foetus is in some senses out of, or beyond, the mother, from the first. The arrangement is of a purely temporary character. The internal surface of the foetus, or that part of it which

K 2

constitutes the foetal placental area, is quite distinct from the corresponding internal surface or mucous lining of the uterus which constitutes the maternal placental area. In the ruminants this relation is very well seen, the villous tufts which represent the foetal portion of the cotyledon being torn out of corresponding tufts in the mucous lining, representing the maternal portion of the cotyledon, without rupturing the vessels, and in such a manner as to occasion no bleeding whatever. This arises from the fact that the capillary vessels of the foetus and mother are simply laid against each other, *i. e.*

Fig. 60.

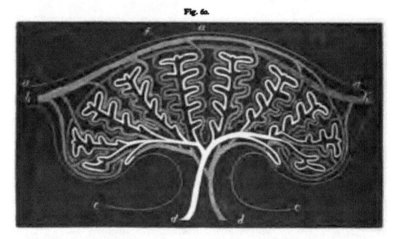

Fig. 60.—Cotyledon of cow's uterus. *a, a*, surface of foetal chorion. *b, b*, blood-vessels of foetal chorion. *c, c*, surface of uterine mucous membrane. *d, d*, blood-vessels of uterine mucous membrane.—*After Dalton.*
f, Secretion from utricular glands (cotyledonous milk) placed between maternal and foetal vessels, and which is necessary to the mutual interchange of gases, nutrient, effete, and other matters, between parent and offspring.—*Author.*

placed in juxtaposition; the two sets of vessels and the mucous linings investing them remaining essentially distinct. With a view to a natural and easy separation, the maternal and foetal tufts in ruminants are arranged in wedge-shaped masses, the apices of the wedge-shaped capillary masses of the foetus dovetailing into the capillary wedge-shaped masses of the mother, an arrangement which admits of very easy extraction. The extraction is further facilitated by the presence of cotyledonous milk between the tufts (Fig. 60).

In man the relation between the foetal villous tufts and those of the mother is more intimate than in any other animal, the tufts themselves being slightly club-shaped ; but even here I am disposed to believe that the foetal and maternal tufts are radically distinct, and that each is provided with its appropriate coverings ; that, in fact, an open space exists between the two. This open space or neutral territory occurring between the maternal and foetal placental tufts, I propose to designate the *utricular space*, from the fact that the utricular secretion or cotyledonous milk is poured into it. It corresponds, in my opinion, in the human subject, to the space marked *d* in Figs. 61 and 62, to *c* of Fig. 63, and to *e* of Fig. 64.

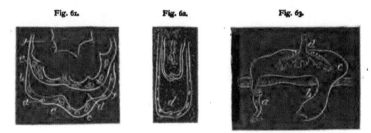

Fig. 61.   Fig. 62.   Fig. 63.

Fig. 61.—The extremity of a placental villus (human). *a*, the external membrane of the villus, the lining membrane of the vascular system of the mother. *b*, the external cells of the villus, cells of the central portion of the placental decidua. *c, c*, germinal centres of the external cells. *d*, the space between the maternal and foetal portions of the villus. *e*, the internal membrane of the villus, the external membrane of the chorion. *f*, the internal cells of the chorion. *g*, the loop of umbilical vessels. —*Goodsir*, 1845.

Fig. 62.—This drawing illustrates the same structure as Fig. 61, and has been introduced to show the large space (*d*) which occasionally intervenes between the internal membrane and the external cells. It would appear that into this space the matter separated from the maternal blood by the external cells of the villus is cast, before being absorbed through the internal membrane by the internal cells. This space therefore is the cavity of a secreting follicle, the external cells being the secreting epithelia, and the maternal blood-vessel system the capillaries of supply. This maternal portion of the villus and its cavity corresponds to the glandular cotyledons of the ruminants, and the matter thrown into the cavity to the milky secretion of these organs.—*Goodsir*, 1845.

Fig. 63.—Diagram illustrating Dr. John Reid's views of the human placenta. *a*, curling artery. *b*, uterine vein. *c*, uterine sinus formed by expansion of artery (*a*) and vein (*b*). *d*, foetal tufts or villi, with inner coat (*c*) of vascular system (*a, b*) of mother enveloping them.—1841.

I have represented the utricular space at *m, n*, of Fig. 57 B (p. 129), and at *e, g*, of Fig. 77 (p. 141). Professor Turner has represented a similar space as occurring between the maternal and foetal portions of the placenta of the whale (*Orca gladiator*), seen at *i, f*, of Fig. 65 (p. 134) ; a corresponding space found in the ox being shown at *f* of Fig. 60 (p. 132).

The utricular space is bounded by certain landmarks which it behoves us to study. They are essentially those of two mucous membranes or two portions of skin. The external and internal skin have many features in common. The former consists of innumerable eminences or papillae, the free surfaces of which display a mass of looped capillary vessels in all

respects analogous to the placental villi or tufts. Between
the papillae an infinite number of tubes with blind convoluted
extremities are found. These tubes open towards the free

Fig. 64.

Fig. 65.

Fig. 64.—Diagrammatic section of human decidua at the termination of pregnancy. *a*, amnion with
epithelium. *b*, chorion. *c*, decidua. *d*, muscular coat. *e*, line of separation of the membranes of the
ovum situated within the cell layer. *f*, cell layer of decidua. *g*, glandular layer of the same with
epithelial cells.—*Friedländer*, 1870.

Fig. 65.—Diagram illustrating the placental arrangements in the whale (*Orca gladiator*). *c*, utricular
gland. *b*, funnel-shaped crypt into which utricular gland opens. *a*, cup-shaped crypt. *f*, *f*, epithelial
layer lining crypts. *d*, fusiform corpuscles. *e*, *e*, spheroidal sub-epithelial corpuscles. *g*, *g*, close
capillary plexus. *h*, *h*, foetal villi projecting from chorion. These villi are invested by an epithelial
layer (*i*, *i*). They consist of connective tissue which contains a layer of sub-epithelial corpuscles (*k*), of
fusiform corpuscles (*l*), and a close capillary plexus (*m*, *m*), derived from the umbilical arteries, which
plexus is continued into an extra-villous chorionic network (*n*, *n*) from which the umbilical vein arises.
The foetal and maternal vessels are not in contact, still less continuous with each other, but are separated
by the layer of sub-epithelial corpuscles of the villus, the epithelial investment of the villus, the epithelial lining of the crypt, and the layer of sub-epithelial corpuscles of the crypt. The space between the
two epithelial surfaces is intended to show the interval between the foetal and maternal portions (of the
placenta) into which the secretion of the uterine glands is poured.—*Turner*, 1871.

surface, and correspond to the sweat-glands. They secrete a
peculiar fluid which is exhaled when we perspire[1]. Precisely
similar remarks may be made of the internal skin or mucous

[1] The number of sweat-glands in the human body is incredibly great. Krause
estimated that, on the skin of the cheeks, posterior portion of trunk, thigh and leg,
they number 500 to the square inch; on the forehead, neck, forearm, back of hands
and feet, and anterior part of trunk, 1000 to the square inch; and on the sole of the
foot and palm of the hand, 2700 to the square inch. This observer estimated the
number of sweat-glands in the body at 2,300,000; the amount of glandular tubing
amounting to 153,000 inches, or something like two and a half miles (Kölliker,
Handbuch der Gewebelehre; Leipzig, 1852, p. 147). Lavoisier and Seguin estimate
the quantity of fluid lost by cutaneous perspiration in twenty-four hours at 13,770
grains, nearly two pounds avoirdupois (Robin and Verdeil, op. cit. vol. ii. p. 145).
According to Dr. Southwood Smith, labourers engaged in gasworks sometimes lose
by cutaneous and pulmonary exhalations as much as three and a half pounds in less
than an hour (Philosophy of Health, chap. xiii; London, 1838). The effect produced on the circulation by the extraction of such large quantities of fluid from the
system must in such cases be very great.

lining of the alimentary canal. Here we have a surface consisting of minute projections, filled with capillary loops, and studded with a vast array of tubular glands, similar, in many respects, to the sweat-glands and to the utricular glands or follicles of the uterus. The structures constituting the external and internal skin are shown in Figs. 66 to 75.

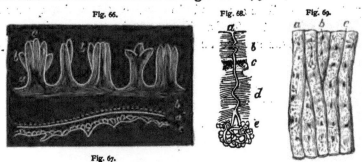

Fig. 66.   Fig. 68.   Fig. 69.

Fig. 67.

Fig. 66.—Compound papillae from palm of human hand (magnified). *a*, base of papilla. *b*, *b*, *c*, branches of papillae. (Compare with Figs. 70 and 73.)—*After Kölliker*.

Fig. 67.—Plan of a secreting membrane. *a*, basement membrane. *b*, epithelium, composed of secreting nucleated cells. *c*, layer of capillary blood-vessels. (Compare with *m*, *n* of Fig. 57 B, p. 129.)—*Quain*.

Fig. 68.—Sweat-gland and duct of human skin, opening upon surface at *a* (magnified). *c*, gland surrounded by fat. *d*, duct of gland passing through corium, through lower (*c*) and upper part (*b*) of epidermis. (Compare with Figs. 71 and 72, and with *c*, *d* of Fig. 57 B, p. 129.)—*After Wagner*.

Fig. 69.—Ridges on epidermis of human skin, with orifices of sweat-glands (magnified). *a*, ridge, *c*, furrow. *b*, orifice of sweat-gland. (Compare with *a* of Figs. 74 and 75, p. 136.)—*After Quain*.

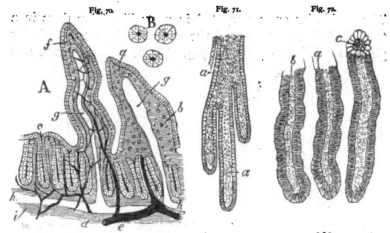

Fig. 70.   Fig. 71.   Fig. 72.

Fig. 70 A.—Vertical section of two villi, from intestinal mucous membrane of rabbit $\frac{150}{1}$. *a*, epithelium covering the villi. (Compare with *m*, *n* of Fig. 57 B, p. 129.) *b*, substance of villi, with lymph-cells. *c*, tubular glands or crypts of Lieberkühn. (Compare with Fig. 72, and with *c*, *d* of Fig. 57 B.) *d*, *e*, capillary artery and vein forming capillary plexus (*f*) in villus. (Compare with Figs. 73, p. 136, and 78, p. 143.) *g*, *g*, lacteal vessels of villi, joining horizontal lacteal (*h*, *h*). *i*, submucous layer.

Fig. 70 B.—Cross section of three tubular glands more highly magnified.—*After Frey*.

Fig. 71.—Deep portion of pyloric gastric gland, lined with cylindrical epithelium (*a*, *a*). From human stomach (magnified).—*Kölliker*.

Fig. 72.—Utricular glands from mucous membrane of unimpregnated human uterus (magnified). *a*, lining of cylindrical epithelium. *b*, interior of utricular gland. *c*, orifice of utricular gland. (Compare with Figs. 68 and 71.)—*Dalton*.

Here then, I submit, we have the elements out of which the placenta, when it exists, is formed, viz. two pieces of skin, or what is equivalent thereto, displaying innumerable eminences and depressions, an inconceivable number of capillary loops, and a vast array of utricular glands corresponding to sweat, gastric, intestinal, and other glands of that type (Fig. 57 B, p. 129.) The mucous lining of the uterus displays a re-- markably rich network of capillary vessels, looped and directed towards the free surface as in every other part of the body.

Fig. 73.

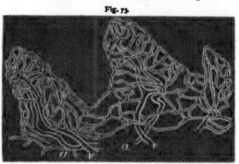

Fig. 73.—Blood-vessels of intestinal villi, magnified (human). *a. a*, arteries. *v, v*, veins. The artery and vein in each villus conducts to an intermediate capillary plexus or network. (Compare with *e, f,* of Fig. 57 B ; with *d, e, f,* of Fig. 70 A, p. 129; and with Fig. 78 A, C, p. 143.)—*From Injection by Lieber-kühn.*

The capillaries are aggregated in parts like fairy rings in a field, and in the centre of the vascular rings the utricular glands or follicles open (Fig. 74). These glands secrete and

Fig. 74.   Fig. 75.

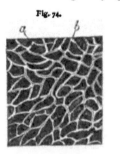
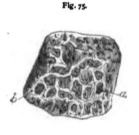

Fig. 74.—Network of capillary vessels (*b*), with orifices of utricular glands (*a*), as seen on surface of mucous membrane of human uterus (magnified). (Compare with same letters in Fig. 75.)—*Farre.*
Fig. 75.—Network of capillary vessels (*b*), with orifices of gastric glands (*a*), as seen on surface of mucous membrane of human stomach (magnified).—*Ecker.*

exude an opalescent slightly viscid fluid resembling milk, and which has from this circumstance been designated cotyledonous milk. The cotyledonous milk of the uterus supplies during gestation the nourishment afforded at a later period by the mammary glands. It also acts as an osmotic medium to the maternal and foetal blood. The uterus and mammae sympathise, and the lacteal fluids which they supply perform analogous functions.

Goodsir describes in the human subject two membranes and two sets of cells as interposed between the capillary loops of the mother and foetus. These membranes and cells he separated from each other by a space, indicated at d of Figs. 61 and 62, p. 133. Turner has described a somewhat similar arrangement in the whale. He represents a foeto-maternal placental space, bounded on the one hand by the vessels and cells of the mother, and on the other by the vessels and cells of the foetus. Thus, proceeding from the space in the direction of the uterus, there is, according to him, 1st, a layer of epithelium, and 2nd, a layer of connective tissue, having embedded in it sub-epithelial, spheroidal, and fusiform corpuscles, and a close capillary plexus. Proceeding in the direction of the foetus, a precisely similar arrangement obtains, there being, 1st, a layer of epithelium, and 2nd a layer of sub-epithelial, spheroidal, and fusiform corpuscles, in which a close capillary plexus is found (Fig. 65, p. 134).

Thus far the relation existing between the maternal and foetal capillary vessels and their coverings is quite intelligible. The theories, however, advanced as to the transformations which the vessels and mucous membrane of the uterus undergo during the process of gestation have strangely, and, I feel assured, unnecessarily, complicated that relation.

First as to the mucous membrane of the uterus. There is nothing peculiar in this membrane, other than arises from an increased development and contact with the villous tufts of the chorion; an ovum evolving as readily in the Fallopian tube as in the uterus. When impregnation takes place the uterine mucous membrane becomes greatly expanded, its component elements becoming excessively hypertrophied. It has, partly from this circumstance, but chiefly because it was erroneously supposed to be discharged at parturition, had its name changed from mucous membrane to decidua [1]. When the ovum

---

[1] In the posthumous work of Dr. William Hunter ('An Anatomical Description of the Human Gravid Uterus'), edited by Dr. M. Baillie in 1794, the decidua is described as under:—'This membrane is an efflorescence of the internal coat of

enters the uterus, Sharpey and Coste believe that the uterine mucous membrane (the decidua of authors) rises up around it in the form of a wall, the free borders of the wall increasing until they unite and form a dome above it; the ovum becoming completely invested by the maternal lining or mucous membrane of the uterus.

Dr. Arthur Farre suggests another explanation. He supposes that the ovum, on entering the uterus, drops into one of the orifices leading to the utricular follicles, and, in growing there, draws around it the already formed, but soft and spongy, uterine mucous membrane constituting the walls of the cavity [1]. The ovum, according to these views, is buried at conception, and requires to be exhumed at parturition.

The mucous membrane of the pregnant uterus has for the foregoing reasons been artificially divided into three parts, known as the decidua vera, decidua reflexa, and decidua serotina. The decidua vera (also termed parietal) corresponds to that part of the mucous membrane which lines the uterus as a whole; the decidua reflexa to that part of it which is supposed to grow around and over the ovum; and the decidua serotina (supposed by some to be a new formation [2]) to that part of it which corresponds to the foetal portion of the placenta, and with which it is directly or indirectly in contact [3] (Fig. 76).

These views, I need scarcely add, are hypothetical, and the terms employed in explaining them arbitrary. As there are no sufficient anatomical proofs that the mucous membrane of

the uterus itself. . . . It may be said to be the internal membrane of the uterus. . . . It is really the internal lamella of the uterus.'

[1] This hypothesis is based upon what may turn out to be a purely accidental occurrence, viz. the discovery by Bischoff of the presence in the guinea-pig of an ovum in the bottom of a uterine follicle.

[2] 'At the part where the uterine expansion of the decidua is interrupted by the reflexion inwards of the decidua reflexa, and where the ovum enters, the place of the decidua vera is supplied by *another layer similar to it*, and connected at its margins with it, the decidua serotina.'—*Kirkes' Physiology*, p. 661, 3rd edition, 1856.

[3] Dr. Arthur Farre is of opinion that the decidua reflexa is in part formed out of the parietal decidua (decidua vera) from the number of orifices of utricular glands seen on its surface. He however admits that much is due to the further development of the elemental decidual tissues, this increase being principally due to the large supply of blood-vessels furnished to the decidua reflexa at an early period.

the uterus during pregnancy deports itself as described, I propose abandoning the terms decidua vera, decidua reflexa, and
decidua serotina. I will therefore, when speaking of the lining
membrane of the uterus, refer to it simply as such, always
specifying the portion meant.

· ·That the uterine mucous membrane does not require to
grow around and over the ovum during pregnancy is proved
by this, that in extra-uterine foetation the uterine mucous
membrane is absent. Similar remarks apply to Fallopian-
tube foetation, although here the conditions more closely resemble those found in the uterus[1]. In pregnancy, whether
extra-uterine or intra-uterine, the mucous membrane, capillary

Fig. 76.

Fig. 76.—x, Chamber occupied by ovum. b, c, decidua vera. d, decidua reflexa. g, decidua serotina.
Compare with same letters in Fig. 77, p. 141.—Original.

vessels, utricular glands, and muscular fibres of the uterus, increase in size and activity. We have two admirable specimens
of Fallopian-tube pregnancy in the Museum of the Royal College of Surgeons, Edinburgh, in which the uterine structures
have become hypertrophied by sympathy ; the os uteri being
curiously enough closed by a plug of mucus. Extra-uterine
and Fallopian-tube pregnancies induce me to believe that the
ovum brings with it or develops its own membranes[2] ; the

[1] As the Fallopian tube opens into the uterine cavity the two are anatomically
continuous.

[2] 'The ovum during its passage along the Fallopian tube acquires a layer of
albumen, and this subsequently coalesces with the zona pellucida to form the
chorion.'—Kirkes' Physiology, p. 676, 3rd edition, 1856. The villi of the chorion
consist at first entirely of cells, bounded by an external layer of textureless membrane, which gives their form. (Goodsir.) If a normal placenta be examined after

conditions necessary being heat, moisture, and a mucous surface, either within or without the uterus. The chick only derives heat from the body of the mother. When the ovum reaches the interior of the uterus, it applies its chorionic (which is in reality its mucous) surface to some portion of the mucous surface of the uterus. At first the two mucous surfaces are quite distinct, the relation being that rather of apposition than actual contact. As pregnancy advances the maternal and foetal mucous membranes, and the vessels which underlie them, become developed (particularly in the region which corresponds to the placental area); the membranes and vessels becoming entangled, adhering, and interweaving in a most remarkable manner (Fig. 57 B, p. 129, and Fig. 77, p. 141).

The advantage of this arrangement consists in the fact that it secures to the mother and foetus an independent and yet a common life—the foetus being to the mother in the relation of a parasite. It further secures independence and community of structure.

Thus the foetus has its mucous lining (*d, e* of Fig. 77), and the mother her mucous lining (*g, b, c* of Fig. 77); the foetus has its capillary zone, consisting of villous tufts (*h, a* of Fig. 77), and the mother has a corresponding capillary zone, the capillaries found on the mucous lining of the uterus (*e, f* of Fig. 57 B, p. 129); the mother has utricular glands (*c, d* of Fig. 57 B, p. 129); the foetus their homologues. The foetus, as parturition advances, concentrates and augments its villous tufts and vascular supply (*a* of Fig. 77, p. 141; *a* of Fig. 59, p. 131; *i, n* of Fig. 57 B, p. 129); the maternal vessels, within the placental area, becoming correspondingly developed (*e, f* of Fig. 57 B, p. 129), and the blood-supply correspondingly increased. This community of structure and of life secures to the ovum and subsequent foetus the fullest opportunities for nourishment and development. In normal pregnancy the ovum, from the time it enters the uterus, is in contact with the uterine mucous lining. It brings with it an independent life and independent structures, and it is the blending of that life and those structures for a certain period with the life

delivery, a distinct membrane can be traced on its uterine surface; *i. e.* the surface corresponding to the uterine placental area. This membrane I am disposed to consider the mucous membrane or lining of the chorion.

and structures of the parent, that constitutes the mystery of conception and gestation.

The mucous membrane of the chorion (the *decidua reflexa* or *decidua ovuli* of authors) increases in the same ratio as the ovum, which it incloses and protects. The receptacle containing the ovum is a small chamber placed within a larger one, viz. the uterine cavity. Those surfaces of the foetal and maternal chambers which are directed towards each other are each provided with a mucous lining. The walls of the

Fig. 77.

Fig. 77.—Plan of section of uterus with fully formed ovum (human). *g*, mucous lining or membrane of uterus, opposite placenta (decidua serotina of authors). *b*, *c*, lining membrane on body of uterus (decidua vera of authors). *d*, lining membrane of foetus (decidua reflexa of authors). This membrane (*e*) is found on the free surfaces of the chorionic villi (*a*), being in fact the mucous lining of the chorion. Such parts of it as are not engaged in covering the chorionic villi become thinned away and disappear towards the full term. It may however always be found on the free or uterine surface of a normal placenta. *a*, chorionic villi constituting foetal portion of placenta. (The maternal portion is formed by capillary vessels found in mucous lining, *g*.) *h*, chorion, from which the chorionic villi spring. *f*, amnion. *i*, umbilical vesicle. *j*, Fallopian tube.

Note.—As pregnancy advances the parts marked *e*, *a*, *g* approach each other, and become accurately apposed. The same holds true of the parts marked *b* and *d*. This apposition and blending of maternal and foetal structures facilitates the exchange (chiefly by osmosis) of nutritive and effete materials between parent and offspring.—*Original.*

foetal and maternal chambers are only in apposition at first; but as development proceeds the foetal chamber becomes fixed to the maternal one, and protrudes from it like a spherical bud. The cavities of the chambers nevertheless remain quite distinct. On the mucous lining of both the foetal and maternal chambers, orifices of utricular glands or their homologues can be made out—a circumstance of considerable importance, as showing that the foetal portion of the placenta is supplied with utricular glands as well as the maternal portion.

A large number of vessels, terminating in minute capillary plexuses, are found on the mucous surfaces of both the foetal and maternal chambers. These interdigitate at an early period. The ovum at first lies loose in the foetal chamber, but becomes fixed in it towards the end of the first month. The fixing is effected by the aid of villous processes which project from all parts of the chorion (hence the epithet shaggy chorion). They suspend and fix the ovum in the foetal chamber as a spider is suspended and fixed by its web. The embryo, surrounded by its amnion, chorion, and mucous lining, in this manner becomes securely anchored in a haven of its own forming. Other changes succeed. As the ovum grows, the villi of that part of it which is in contact with the mucous lining of the uterus increase in size, and become more ramified. The villi of the maternal placental area become correspondingly developed. Dissepiments or partitions of mucous membrane also make their appearance, and divide the maternal and foetal villi into groups, producing that lobed appearance so characteristic of the fully formed placenta. The lobes of the human placenta are in reality the homologues of the cotyledons of the ox.

The ovum brings a certain amount of nourishment with it ; the rest it obtains by imbibition, due to contact with the mucous membrane of the uterus, and the utricular secretion which it there finds. Long before blood-vessels make their appearance in the embryo, a circulation of nutritious juices, similar to that found in plants and the lowest animal organisms, is established. This is effected by osmosis, due to the presence of membranes and fluids of different density. The membranes are seen at Fig. 77, p. 141. They consist of the capillary blood-vessels of the interior of the uterus (e, f of Fig. 57 B, p. 129) the mucous membrane of the uterus (g, b, c of Fig. 77, p. 141) the mucous membrane and capillary blood-vessels of the chorion (e, a, h of Fig. 77), and the amnion (f of Fig. 77). There is every reason to believe that the maternal and foetal membranes when in contact, as in pregnancy, not only act as osmotic media, but also as secreting media. Goodsir attributed a secreting power to the membranes and cells covering the extremities of the placental villi. These, according to him, consist of an external membrane and nucleated cells, and an internal membrane and nucleated cells. Between these a space occurs, which he regards as the cavity of a secreting follicle (Figs. 61 and 62 d, p. 133). The external membrane corresponds to the mucous lining of the uterus, which I believe it really is; the internal membrane to the outer surface of the chorion. This, as explained, I regard as the mucous lining of the chorion.

The chorion and mucous surface of the uterus are, as a rule, highly vascular. I have succeeded in minutely injecting the arteries and veins of the chorion and amnion of the mare[1]; and injections of the membranes of the ox, sheep, and other domestic animals, are to be found in nearly all our museums[2]. The mucous membranes of the uterus and

Fig. 78.

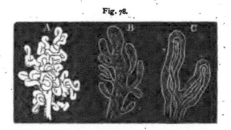

Fig. 78.—A, Extremity of foetal tuft of human placenta. From an injected specimen, magnified forty diameters. Compare with vessels in Fig. 57 B, p. 129.
B, Compound villosity of human chorion, with ramified extremity. From a three months' foetus, magnified thirty diameters.
C, Extremity of villosity of chorion more highly magnified, showing the arrangement of the blood-vessels in the interior.—*After Dalton.*

chorion, with their cells and blood-vessels, may with great propriety be compared to secreting structures composed of a basement membrane, nucleated cells, and capillaries (Fig. 67, p. 135); and it appears to me that they only require to be brought together to inclose a space to enable them to assume the secreting function.

The desired space is obtained immediately the ovum comes in contact with the mucous lining of the uterus. At first the uterine mucous membrane and utricular glands are more especially engaged in secreting; the product passing by

[1] These and other preparations bearing upon the placenta are to be found in the Hunterian Museum of the Royal College of Surgeons of London.
[2] Particularly fine specimens of placentae and membranes are to be seen in the Anatomical Museum of the University of Edinburgh, the majority of them injected by Goodsir.

endosmose and imbibition directly into the ovum ; the ovum
returning its peculiar fluids by exosmose. The transference
of liquid materials is greatly facilitated by the formation, in
the first month of pregnancy, of the shaggy chorion. This
structure is composed of an immense number of villous tufts,
consisting of a membrane of nucleated cells within which
capillary blood-vessels are ultimately developed (Fig. 78,
A, B, C, p. 143).

The villous tufts are at first short club-shaped processes
of uniform size. They are not attached to the mucous lining
of the uterus, so that the embryo floats freely and obtains its
nourishment after the manner of water-plants, viz. by imbibition. The club-shaped villi, as Goodsir pointed out, elongate
by additions to their extremities as in the roots of plants;
cells passing off from the germinal spots situated on the ends
of the villi. Goodsir demonstrated that blood-vessels appear
in the chorion and chorionic villi when the allantois reaches
and applies itself to a certain part of the internal surface of
the chorion. At this stage of development the umbilical
vessels communicate with vascular loops in the interior of the
villi. The injections of Schroeder van der Kolk showed a
profusion of capillary vessels in the chorionic villi as early as
the third month ; and at later periods of gestation up to the
sixth month, Dr. Arthur Farre succeeded in displaying
without difficulty, by the aid of fine injections, a very abundant supply of these vessels. At a later period, a large
proportion of the fine capillaries within the villi disappear,
the long, tortuous, varicose loops described by Goodsir alone
remaining. From this it follows that the blood-vessels engaged
in nourishing the foetus have a period of development, a
period of increased activity, and a period of decay; the
period of decay heralding, if not actually producing, parturition. These changes are necessary to inaugurate the circulation of the foetus, to unite the circulation of the foetus
with that of ·the mother, and to separate that connexion at
the period of parturition.

The fluids concerned in the nutrition and well-being of the
foetus are such as are supplied by the utricular glands and by
the various secreting surfaces, maternal and foetal. The
utricular glands in the early months of pregnancy supply a

milky fluid, nutritive in character, which, as has been explained, acts as an osmotic medium to the fluids contained without and within the foetal chamber. Of the fluids contained within the foetal chamber the substance of the embryo imbibes freely. In the later stages of pregnancy, when the placenta is fully formed, the utricular secretion produces an osmotic action between the blood contained in the placental villi of the foetus and that contained in the capillaries of the placental area of the mother (*vide* Fig. 79).

There is reason to believe that, even in advanced pregnancy, the surface of the foetus imbibes nutritive materials from the fluids in which it is suspended, and by which it is

Fig. 79.

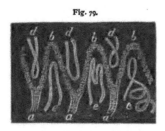

Fig. 79.—Diagram showing the placental relations of the maternal and foetal capillaries, and the position occupied by the utricular secretion. *a, a, a,* utricular glands, pouring out utricular secretion (*b, b, b*). *e, e, e,* maternal capillary plexuses (with artery and vein) as seen on interior of uterus. *d, d, d,* foetal capillary plexuses with artery and vein as seen on surface of placenta, directed towards interior of uterus. The maternal and foetal linings and epithelial corpuscles which separate the maternal and foetal villi are not represented. The presence of the utricular secretion (*b. b, b*) between the maternal and foetal vessels necessitates a free interchange of the ingredients peculiar to each. See also under *f* of Fig. 60, p. 132.—*Original.*

constantly bathed. This it can readily do, as the external skin of the foetus is so delicate that it in some respects resembles the mucous membrane of the adult. The external skin of the foetus in intra-uterine life in all probability absorbs and exercises a secreting function; whereas in extra-uterine life it respires and exercises an excreting function. As I showed in plants, certain surfaces may act either as absorbing or respiring surfaces, according as they are exposed to the influence of moisture or air (Figs. 30, 31, p. 34, and Fig. 36, p. 50).

I have stated that Goodsir divided the membranes and cells found by him on the extremities of the placental villi into an external and internal set; and that, in my opinion, the external membrane and cells constitute the mucous or lining membrane of the uterus.

Goodsir has, it appears to me, transferred the mucous lining

L

of the uterus to the mucous lining of the chorion; a not unnatural transference, when it is remembered that, in not a few instances, particularly in highly civilised females, artificial adhesions are formed, and the foetal part of the placenta drags with it at parturition a portion or all of the maternal part. To this circumstance, in all probability, is to be traced the difficulty experienced by anatomists in determining whether the uterus does, or does not, shed its mucous membrane after each parturition [1]. This would explain why there should be a space between the external and internal membranes covering the extremities of the placental villi, as described by Goodsir; the space being the natural line of junction and separation between the maternal and foetal portions of the placenta [2]. It would also account for the belief entertained by him, by Reid, Ecker, and others, that the maternal blood-vessels (arteries and veins) within the placental area become enormously expanded, and envelop

[1] In man the tissues, as a rule, are more highly elaborated than in animals—a circumstance which renders their separation more difficult. Dr. Arthur Farre, in his work ' On the Uterus and its Appendages,' states that ' in the latter months of pregnancy, the parietal decidua (i. e. the mucous lining of the uterus) becomes thinner, and loses much of its spongy character, except immediately around the placenta, where this is still most distinct. It ultimately becomes blended with the outer surface of the foetal membranes, and is partly thrown off with them in the act of birth, while a part remains, forming a honeycomb layer attached to the uterine muscular coat.' Now it appears from this that the decidua of the placental area admits of division, one part being shed with the placenta at parturition, the other remaining on the interior of the uterus. In reality the placenta takes its own mucous lining with it, the uterus retaining the mucous lining which belonged to it before conception took place. If we examine a normal placenta when thrown off at full term, we find a membrane on its free or uterine surface; and if we examine the placental area of the uterus which corresponds thereto, we find a similar membrane. This is what we would a priori expect. Why should the placenta at parturition drag off any part of the decidua or mucous lining of the uterus? The maternal and foetal structures are distinct from the first, and so remain. They separate as naturally and with as little inconvenience as they come together.

[2] From the foregoing it will be evident that I do not regard the placenta as structurally united to the uterus, but simply as in apposition and adhering, the union being of the most intimate description, from the fact that the maternal and foetal villi pass through each other so thoroughly that they form with their contained blood a semi-fluid mass. The placenta is to the foetus what the roots are to a parasitic plant (the mistletoe, for example). The foetus, by its placenta, literally plants itself on the inner surface of the uterus, this supplying it with nutritious juices and with air.

by bladder-like dilatations the villi of the foetal portion of the placenta (Fig. 63, p. 133, and Fig. 80). If, as I presume, in the specimens examined by Goodsir, Reid, Ecker, and others, the villi of the foetal portion of the placenta dragged with them at parturition the villi of the maternal portion, the result would be exactly that figured and described, viz. a large spongy mass, containing blood sinuses, with occasional villi proceeding from or dipping into them. During pregnancy the vessels of the uterus, particularly the veins, assume gigantic proportions, the blood contained within the organ causing it in some respects to resemble a lung; but the blood-vessels

Fig. 80.

Fig. 80.—Diagram illustrating the arrangement of the placental decidua (human). *a*, parietal decidua. *b*, a venous sinus passing obliquely through it by a valvular opening. *c*, curling artery passing in the same direction. *d*, lining membrane of the maternal vascular system, passing in from the artery and vein, lining the bag of the placenta, and covering (*e*, *e*) the foetal tufts, passing on to the latter by two routes, first by their stems from the foetal side of the cavity; and, secondly, by the terminal decidual bars (*f*, *f*) from the uterine side, and from one tuft to the other by the lateral bar (*g*). This membrane is in contact with decidual cells, unless along the stems of the tufts and the foetal side of the placenta. (Compare with Fig. 63, p. 133.)—*Goodsir, 1845.*

increase in a progressive ratio with the nerves, glands, muscular, mucous, and other tissues, and there are no sufficient grounds, anatomical or physiological, for supposing that during the hypertrophy which occurs during pregnancy, the maternal capillary vessels corresponding to the placental area, cease to exist as such; in other words, become converted into the bladder-like expansions referred to. Such a metamorphosis would remove the human placenta out of the category of mammalian placentae; a removal which neither its origin, progress, nor final dehiscence warrants [1].

[1] When the human chorion is shaggy, the placenta is diffuse, as in the mare; and this is a reason why even in its most matured condition, *i.e.* in its concentrated and localised form, the human placenta is not to be regarded as a thing *per se*, but a modification of other placentae, all of which are formed on a common plan. In the mare the villous tufts of the chorion are applied to the mucous lining

One naturally inquires, when contemplating the enormous maternal vascular expansions represented by Reid (Fig. 63, p. 133), Goodsir (Fig. 80, p. 147), and Ecker, where the material comes from which produces them? The additional material required on the part of the curling arteries and veins of the uterus, to envelop every villous tuft contained in the foetal portion of the placenta, is such as virtually to render the hypothesis untenable. So far as known to me, there is no other example of a modification on a similarly gigantic scale in any natural structure. If the terminal portions of the curling arteries and veins of the uterus were expanded to the extent described, and if, moreover, they embraced and became locked within the villous tufts of the foetal portion of the placenta, as figured, then of necessity the whole of that portion of the interior of the uterus corresponding to the placental area would be converted into an open wound when the placenta was removed; the wound exhibiting on its surface an incredible number of large bleeding vessels, which no degree of contraction on the part of the uterus could either modify or restrain. What however is the real state of things? During a healthy parturition scarcely any blood is lost, and on examining that portion of the interior of the uterus corresponding to the placental area, it is found covered with a mucous membrane somewhat resembling a honeycomb—an appearance caused by the apposition and interpenetration of the mucous membrane and villi of the foetal portion of the placenta. On examining the free or uterine surface of the placenta, a similar membrane is discovered; the one, in fact, being the counterpart of the other[1]. If a normal full-term placenta is injected with size after its removal, there is little

---

of the uterus as a whole. In the tiger a band of villous tufts invests the chorion at its middle; the villi in this band only being applied to the mucous lining and capillaries of the uterus. In the ox the villous tufts of the chorion are grouped together, and appear as isolated patches, varying from an inch to an inch and a half in diameter. These form so many placentulae. In man the villous tufts of the chorion are ultimately aggregated into one large oval mass, to which the name of placenta has been given. The human placenta is, so to speak, a concentration and higher development of all the other forms. Its great general features are however the same, and the manner of its application to the mucous lining and capillary vessels of the uterus in no respect differs from the others.

[1] See note 1, p. 146.

if any extravasation from its free or uterine surface; plainly showing that it is bounded by its own peculiar mucous membrane. All the difficulties and dangers referred to are avoided by regarding the foetal and maternal portions of the placenta as essentially distinct, not only in the early but also in the later months of .pregnancy. The structures in question are simply in temporary apposition (Fig. 57 B, p. 129). This view insures, as stated, an independence and community of structure. It assimilates the human with the placentae of other mammals. It accounts for the fact that a foetus may be developed in the Fallopian tube, or outside the uterus altogether. It in especial explains how the ovum can be applied to the incubating chamber of the mother, and how the foetus may be separated from it, without causing either injury or inconvenience. Lastly, it shows that the maternal and foetal evolutions which constitute a pregnancy are correlated, the one advancing *pari passu* with the other.

As a proof that the relation subsisting between the maternal and foetal placental surfaces and vessels in man is not that figured by Reid, Goodsir, Ecker, and others, I may state, that wherever I have had an opportunity of injecting the utero-placental area with the parts *in situ—i.e.* with the placenta adhering to the mucous surface of the uterus—I have found an arrangement closely resembling in its general features that found in the mammalia as a class. It is only when the uterus and placenta are partially or altogether separated that the appearances described and figured are observed. In 1863 I destroyed and carefully injected a pregnant monkey, as being likely to throw additional light on this complicated and much disputed question. The monkey was near the parturient period, the foetus being large and well formed. In the monkey the placenta remarkably accords with that found in man. In the present instance I injected the uterus, and then, having ascertained the site of the placenta within the uterus, I made an incision through the uterine wall at a considerable distance from it, through which I pulled the foetus. I then injected the placenta from the umbilical vessels. The placenta consisted of a large oval isolated mass, which might have been taken for a human placenta at the sixth or seventh month. At a little distance from the placenta proper there was a placentula or little placenta, the vessels from which converged and united with the main vessels of the principal one. The placentula I regarded as an accidental formation. On making microscopical sections of the placental area, so as to embrace the maternal and foetal vessels, their coverings, cells, glands, etc., the appearances observed were substantially those represented at Fig. 57 B, p. 129; this figure, as already explained, embodying my views of the structure and physiological relations of the human placenta.

I am not therefore disposed to acquiesce in the commonly received opinion that in man the placental foetal tufts are covered by an expansion of the corresponding vessels of the mother. I disagree—1st, Because there is no analogy to support this view. 2nd, Because it is giving to the foetus what I believe in reality belongs to the mother. 3rd, If the vessels of the mother are so expanded, they are necessarily destroyed when the placenta is removed, this relation involving the laceration and destruction of the mucous lining and capillary vessels corresponding to the maternal placental area—a proceeding which would expose the mother (notwithstanding the vigorous contraction of the uterus) to serious and probably fatal haemorrhage. 4th, That portion of the mucous lining of the uterus corresponding to the placental area is, as Dr. Matthews Duncan has shown, not removed in parturition. 5th, In a healthy parturition there is almost no blood lost, a circumstance which could not occur if the arrangement figured by Reid, Goodsir, Ecker, and others, obtained, as, in this case, not only large vessels, but large sinuses containing blood, would be exposed. 6th, In the lower animals no blood is lost at parturition; but in these we know the maternal and foetal capillary vessels or tufts are simply placed in apposition, the two separating with the utmost facility. 7th, The blood-sinuses of the uterus (and by these I mean the maternal vascular expansions said to envelop the foetal placental villi) are not necessary to gestation. That these sinuses are not necessary to the evolution of the foetus is abundantly proved by this,—that a foetus (as in extra-uterine foetation) can live and thrive where they do not exist. 8th, I have never been able to detect a foetal placental tuft or villus in a uterine maternal sinus (containing maternal blood), where the utero-placental relations were intact, *i.e.* where the natural line of union between the maternal and foetal portions of the placenta was inviolate.   In such cases I have found an occasional foetal villus in a utricular gland whose orifice was dilated ; the uterine gland, as explained, opening on the free or mucous surface of the placental area.   9th, and lastly, Nothing is gained physiologically by the unnatural thinning and dilatation of the maternal vessels for the purpose of investing with bladder-like expansions the placental foetal villi.   A moment's reflection will show that such an arrangement would not bring the blood of the mother any closer to that of the foetus than it would be if the maternal vessels remained unexpanded and normal.   There are good grounds for believing that the placental villi (maternal and foetal) simply fit into each other, and, by a process of interweaving and dovetailing, ultimately form a more or less solid mass. As the maternal and foetal vessels by this arrangement are laid against each other in every conceivable attitude, a more perfect (and I will add a more extensive) osmotic action between the maternal and foetal blood is induced than could otherwise be obtained.   The osmotic action is favoured by the presence of a thin layer of utricular secretion between the maternal and foetal villi and their appropriate coverings, as already explained.

The belief that the maternal uterine vessels do not expand to embrace the foetal placental villi, as recorded by Reid, Goodsir, Ecker, and others, has been recently confirmed by the researches of Dr. Braxton Hicks, the President of the Obstetrical Society of London[1].   This gentleman argues against the existence of blood in the so-called maternal sinus system, and the sinus system itself, from finding that neither are present in extra-uterine foetation.   He inveighs against the presence of blood in the sinous system in normal pregnancy, as he can detect no trace of that fluid when the relations between the placenta and uterus are undisturbed. By the sinus system is here meant that space (or spaces)

---

[1] *Vide* Lancet for 18th May, 1872; also memoir by Dr. Robert Lee. 'On the Structure of the Human Placenta and its Connexion with the Uterus,' Phil. Trans. 1832.

occurring between the foetal villi of the chorion, which, according to commonly received opinions, is lined by the expanded uterine vessels of the mother. Dr. Hicks dissected four specimens. In two not a trace of blood was found. In the others there was a trace. In one of them the origin was clearly traced to a small clot extravasated among the villi ; in that which remained to a laceration of the villi themselves. Dr. Hicks adduces further evidence derived from three placentae called 'fatty.' In these the decidual vessels were highly distended with blood, nevertheless the intervillal space was absolutely free.

So much for the vessels of the maternal portion of the placenta.

With regard to the vessels constituting the foetal portion of the placenta (particularly their coverings), there is considerable diversity of opinion. Some say that the foetal vessels and villi are bare ; others that they are covered by a chorionic layer of cells; others that the chorionic cells are covered by a layer of decidual cells ; others that, in addition to all the foregoing, there is a layer derived from the internal membrane of the vascular system of the mother.

Dr. Arthur Farre holds that the blood of the foetus is separated from the blood of the mother, 1st, by the walls of its own capillaries ; 2nd, by the gelatinous membrane in which these ramify, and 3rd, by the external, non-vascular, nucleated sheath derived from the chorion. With the latter alone, he remarks, the blood of the mother is brought into contact.

There are, as you observe, grave discrepancies in the explanations given both of the maternal and foetal elements of the placenta ; and I cannot help thinking that the truth will be evolved more readily if we discard a certain amount of detail and keep to general principles. Analogy, comparative anatomy, and development induce me to believe that the relation of the maternal to the foetal portion of the placenta is not so complicated as authors have laboured to make it, and that the actual relation, as already explained, is that which one portion of skin or mucous lining, furnished with glands, capillary vessels, a limiting membrane, and epithelium, bears to another similarly constituted when the two are brought face to face and laid against each other[1].

Not less conflicting are the views advanced as to the manner in which the foetus is nourished and respires. Goodsir is of opinion that the foetal placental villus consists of an external and internal membrane, each provided with nucleated secreting cells, and that between the two membranes there is a space which he regards as the cavity of a secreting follicle. The cells of the external membrane of the placental villus, according to him, secrete from the blood of the mother by means of the uterine capillaries the nutritive matter absorbed through the internal membrane by the internal cells, and conveyed thence to the foetus by the foetal placental tufts or villi. The secretion he compares to the cotyledonous milk of ruminants.

Ercolani advocates another view. 'He admits that the utricular glands do furnish materials for the nutrition of the embryo, but only in the early period of development; and he strives to prove that, from a transformation and greatly increased growth of the uterine mucous membrane, and of the sub-epithelial connective tissue, a new maternal glandular organ is formed, which in its simplest form consists of secreting follicles, arranged side by side and opening on the surface of the mucous membrane. In the human subject, he says, the typical form of the glandular organ is wanting, but the cells of the serotina, which invest the chorionic villi, represent the fundamental portions of the gland organ. Into these new-formed secreting follicles, and not into the utricular glands, the villi of the chorion penetrate, and are bathed by the fluid secretion, which they absorb for the nourishment of the foetus[2].' Ercolani's hypothesis is ingenious, but there is no necessity for supposing that a new maternal glandular organ is formed, as existing structures very slightly modified can perform the work said to be performed by the new structure. Turner does not believe with Ercolani that

---

. [1] See a curious case of 'a placenta partially adherent to a naevus occupying the scalp and dura mater.'—Lond. Med. Chir. Soc. Trans. xxii. 1829, pp. 300-309.

[2] Ercolani, as rendered by Turner, in his memoir 'On the Gravid Uterus, and on the Arrangement of the Foetal Membranes in the Cetacea (*Orca gladiator*).'—Trans. Roy. Soc. of Edin. vol. xxvi. p. 500 (1871).

the utricular glands cease to perform their functions at an early period of embryonic life. On the contrary, he states that in the Orca, 'although the foetus had reached an advanced state of development, the vascularity of the glands, their epithelial contents, even the presence of plugs of epithelium or inspissated secretion projecting through the orifices—all gave one the impression of structures in a state of active employment. If this be the case, then the secretion would be poured out into the crypts, and brought in contact with the villi of the chorion. . . . I am disposed, therefore,' he adds, 'to conclude that, in all those forms of placentation in which the utricular glands preserve their structural characters within the placental area, they play an important, if not the whole part, in the nutrition of the foetus, not merely in the early[1], but throughout the whole period of uterine life[2].' Turner does not believe that the sub-epithelial corpuscles represented by himself (Fig. 65, e, k, p. 134) on the uterine and chorionic surfaces of the placenta, and which closely correspond to the external and internal cells of the placental villus of Goodsir (Fig. 61, b, e, p. 133), have a secreting function. He is inclined to regard them as lymphoid bodies which have wandered out of the adjacent capillaries into the connective tissue, to whose nutrition and growth they adminster.

According to Goodsir, as has been explained, 'the external

---

[1] 'When the ovum, with its villous chorion, reaches the uterus, the villi becomes embedded in the secretion poured forth by the enlarged follicular glands of the mucous membrane of that organ; and from this they doubtless derive the nutriment on which the embryo at first subsists. . . . Coincidently with the increasing size of the follicles, the quantity of their secretion is augmented, the vessels of the mucous membrane become larger and more numerous, while a substance composed chiefly of nucleated cells fills up the intrafollicular spaces, in which the blood-vessels are contained. The object of this increased development seems to be the production of nutritive materials for the ovum; for the cavity of the uterus shortly becomes filled with secreted fluid, consisting almost entirely of nucleated cells, in which the villi of the chorion are embedded. . . . After impregnation the glands of those parts of the mucous membrane which come into immediate relation with the ova greatly enlarge, while the extremity of each compound gland, just before it opens on the surface of the uterus, dilates into a pouch or cell, filled with whitish secretion, within which is received a process of the chorion.'—*Kirkes' Physiology*, 3rd ed. 1856.

[2] On the Gravid Uterus, and on the Arrangement of the Foetal Membranes in the Cetacea (*Orca gladiator*).—Trans. Roy. Soc. Edin. 1871, pp. 501, 502.

cells of the foetal placental villi perform, during intra-uterine existence, a function for which is substituted in extra-uterine life the digestive action of the gastro-intestinal mucous membrane. The internal cells of the foetal placental villi perform during intra-uterine existence a function for which is substituted in extra-uterine life the action of the absorbing chyle-cells of the intestinal villi. The placenta, therefore, not only performs, as has been always admitted, the function of a lung, but also the function of an intestinal tube[1].' Dr. John Reid, as has been pointed out, believed that the uterine capillary vessels expanded to such an extent that they invested the foetal capillary tufts (Fig. 63, *d*, p. 133), the foetal villi being bathed by the blood of the mother much in the same way that the gills of aquatic reptiles are bathed by water. The placenta, Dr. Reid observes[2], is therefore not analogous in structure to the lungs, but to the branchial apparatus of certain aquatic animals[3]. If the views suggested in the text, and illustrated by Fig. 57 B (p. 129), and Fig. 77 (p. 141), be adopted, the opinions of Goodsir, Reid, Ecker, Ercolani, Turner, and others, may readily be reconciled, as the utricular glands secrete a fluid which assists in nourishing the foetus, while it at the same time acts as an osmotic medium. The membranes and cells found on the surfaces

[1] Anatomical and Pathological Observations, by John Goodsir, Esq., F.R.S.E. etc.; Edin. 1845, p. 63.

[2] Physiological, Pathological, and Anatomical Researches, by Dr. John Reid, 1848, p. 327. Reid's paper On the Blood-vessels of the Mother and Foetus (Human) originally appeared in the Edin. Med. and Surg. Journal (No. 146) for January 1841.

[3] If this analogy be admitted, the following difference is to be noted :—The branchiae of the aquatic reptile are in the immediate vicinity of the heart, whereas the placenta is widely removed, not only from the heart, but even the body of the foetus. In this sense the placenta is outside and beyond the foetus; hence the necessity for that remarkable system of canals which constitute the umbilical cord. This cord might be of any length, it being a mere tunnel to enable the circulation of the foetus and mother to reciprocate. Similar remarks may be made regarding the principal arteries and veins of all the higher animals. The really effective circulation occurs within the capillaries and tissues, and the large vessels stand in the same relation to the heart as aqueducts to their reservoirs. The longest vessels of all are to be found in trees. The umbilical cord consists of two arteries and one vein; but it is not to be inferred from this that the arteries and their radicles contain arterial blood, and the vein and its radicles venous blood. On the contrary, the vein contains arterial blood, and the arteries mixed blood.

of the maternal and foetal portions of the placenta secrete, by a double process, from the capillaries (maternal and foetal), which they cover, the substances necessary to the well-being alike of parent and child,—the placental membranes and utricular glands working together. The placental membranes and cells, as I have shown, enclose a space which, from the fact of the glands pouring their secretion into it, I designate the '*utricular space*.' The space in question contains the utricular secretion or cotyledonous milk. To this cotyledonous fluid I am disposed to attach considerable importance, as it is one of the sources from which the foetus derives its nourishment in the early months of pregnancy, before its blood-vessels are formed, and the medium through which the blood of the mother operates on the blood of the foetus and *vice versa*, when the maternal and foetal villi are fully developed. In short, I regard the utricular space, with its glandular secretion, as performing at once the office of a stomach, a lung, and an *osmotic medium*.

The capillary blood-vessels of the mother and foetus are entirely distinct, and separated, as has been stated, by two membranes and two sets of cells. Here we have the conditions necessary for a vigorous osmotic action. Both sets of vessels contain blood, but, as the blood of the mother and foetus are very similarly constituted, they can only act upon each other when a third and thicker fluid is present, on the principle 'ex nihilo nihil fit.' This thicker fluid the utricular glands supply. It is the thinner portions of the maternal and foetal blood which flow out of the vessels by a process of endosmose into the utricular space, where they commingle; part of the mixed fluid returning by a process of exosmose to the vessels alike of the mother and foetus. By this means a free interchange of nutritious and effete matters is permitted, the mother and foetus participating equally. This would account for the influence exerted by the mother on the foetus, and the converse; the foetus, as is well known, altering the constitution of the mother, and affecting even her future progeny[1]. The foetal and maternal

---

[1] When a white mother bears a child to a black father, the future offspring, even if begotten by a white father, is, as a rule, coloured. John Hunter relates

vessels abut against each other in every conceivable position, and as they are only separated from one another by an osmotic medium and certain membranes and cells, the maternal and foetal blood yield up their peculiar ingredients to each other,—gases, especially when in a state of solution, like fluids, readily passing through certain membranes. The blood of the foetus, there is reason to believe, is by this means nearly as well aerated as the blood of the mother.

In a previous lecture I described at length the peculiarities of the foetal circulation. On that occasion I explained that two kinds of forces are employed, viz. the visible and invisible,—the visible forces carrying on the circulation within the body of the foetus, the invisible forces carrying on the circulation within the placenta. In the present and subsequent lectures I shall occupy myself solely with the visible forces, and with the machinery, if I may so phrase it, in which the visible forces manifest themselves, viz. the heart, blood-vessels, nerves, etc. A consideration of the visible forces necessarily involves details ; but I shall strive to put them in such a way as not to prove irksome. Hitherto we have been dealing with the machinery of the circulation as a whole, now it behoves us to become acquainted with the different parts of that machinery. In describing the several structures employed, I must ask your forbearance if at times I repeat myself. I only do so because nature repeats herself, and because, in dealing with the highest form of the circulation as it exists in the bird and mammal, I am necessarily dealing with essentially the same materials and forces employed in the lowest. It is this circumstance which makes the comparative anatomy and physiology of the circulation laborious and long ; but the same circumstance, it appears to me, imparts to the circulation, as it exists in ourselves, its chief interest.

In my remarks on the foetal circulation, I directed attention to the fact that the cavities of the heart of the foetus open into each other,—the two auricles communi-

a curious case of an English mare covered by a quagga horse. The offspring displayed the quagga stripes, and these stripes reappeared in the future progeny of the mare when put to English horses.

cating directly by the foramen ovale, the two ventricles indirectly by a canal extending between their great vessels, viz. the ductus arteriosus. On a previous occasion I stated that a somewhat similar arrangement obtains in the reptile, where the two auricles open into a single ventricle,— this ventricle, in certain cases, being partially divided into two by a rudimentary septum ventriculorum. The circulation in the foetus and reptile is from this circumstance a mixed circulation — *i. e.* the blood circulated is partly arterial and partly venous. The reptiles are cold-blooded animals; and the foetus might be classed under this heading also, were it not for the fact that the foetus inherits the temperature of the mother, and the blood of the parent is virtually that of the offspring. To obtain a warm blood, such as is found in the bird and mammal, the chambers of the heart must be walled off from each other, and thus it is that in birds and mammals the cavities of the right and left halves of the heart do not intercommunicate. A warm blood is the result of a complete arterialisation, and this can only be produced where the lungs and breathing apparatus are sufficiently differentiated, and when a complete pulmonic and systemic heart are present. I use the term 'breathing apparatus' in its widest sense, for we know that the tissues respire, and that the blood is always warmest where its oxidation goes on most vigorously [1]. That the differentiation of the heart into four distinct chambers has something to do with maintaining the blood at a certain temperature is proved by this,—that in morbus ceruleus, where the cavities of the heart communicate abnormally, the temperature of the body is very considerably reduced. The temperature of the blood bears a fixed relation to the activity of respiration; the respiratory power and temperature being highest in birds, then in mammals, then in reptiles and fishes, and lastly in the invertebrata [2]. Mr. Newport has pointed out

---

[1] Sir Benjamin Brodie, in the Croonian Lecture for 1810, and in the Philosophical Transactions for 1812, cited experiments to show that the maintenance of animal temperature is directly or indirectly under the influence of the nervous system.

[2] In birds, according to Tiedemann and Rudolphi, the average temperature is 107°; the temperature in the linnet rising to 111·25°. In mammalia the average temperature is 101°; in the bat (Vespertilio pipestrella) 106°; in the narwhal 96°.

the very interesting fact that the larvae of insects with small respiring organs have a lower temperature than the perfect insect; and that the flying insects, because of their possessing a large respiratory apparatus, have a higher temperature than the non-volant ones. During sleep and hibernation the respiration and temperature decrease.

Distribution of the Great Vessels in Reptiles, Birds, and Mammals.—I have alluded to the general distribution of the vessels proceeding from the ventricle or ventricles, as

Fig. 81.　　　　　　　　　　　　　　Fig. 82.

Fig. 81.—Anterior aspect of turkey's heart. with right and left ventricles opened to show auriculo-ventricular valves. *a*, aorta arching to right side and dividing into three branches, two of which (*b*) go to right side, and one (*c*) to left side. *d*, pulmonary artery dividing into two, and sending a branch to right and left lungs. *i*, muscular or fleshy valve which occludes right auriculo-ventricular orifice. *f*, musculus papillaris of fleshy valve (compare wth *g*). *e*, portion of septum to which valve is applied when closed. *f*, left ventricle. *v*, tendinous valve which occludes left auriculo-ventricular orifice. *g*, musculus papillaris with chordae tendineae attached to tendinous valve —*Original.*

Fig. 82 shows the distribution of the great vessels at the base of the human heart, seen anteriorly. Contrast with Fig. 81. *u*, aorta giving off innominate, left carotid, and left subclavian arteries. *m*, descending aorta. *v*, pulmonary artery dividing and giving branches to right (*p'*) and left (*p*) lungs. *a*, trachea bifurcating and dividing in right (*p'*) and left (*p*) lungs. *y*, descending cava. *o*, ascending cava, *s*, right auricle. *q*, right ventricle. *t*, left auricle. *r*, left ventricle.

the case may be, of the reptile, and it is important that I should now direct attention to their arrangement in the heart of the bird, and to the construction of the descending aorta, as this forms one of the connecting links between the circulation of birds and reptiles on the one hand, and birds and mammals on the other. The aorta of birds is very short, and divides into three principal branches almost before it leaves the left ventricle (Fig. 81, *a, b, c*). The aorta of birds arches in the direction of the right bronchus;

In reptiles it is 82·5°, when the surrounding medium is 75°. In fish (the tunny tribe excepted) and in the invertebrata it is the same as the medium in which they live. The mammalia and birds, as Mr. Hunter ascertained, have a certain permanent heat in all atmospheres, while the temperature of the other is variable with every atmosphere.

whereas in mammals it arches towards the left bronchus. (Compare *b* of Fig. 81, with *u* of Fig. 82, p. 159.) Of the three branches of the aorta in birds, one arches towards the right axilla, and the other to the left, these being analogous to the single arteria innominata of man, the birds having virtually two innominates. The pulmonary artery of birds divides into two branches as in the mammal, one going to the right lung, the other to the left. (Fig. 81, *d*; compare with *v* of Fig. 82, p. 159.)

In all reptiles the descending aorta is formed by the union of two branches—the right and left aortic branches. The right corresponds with the systemic aorta of birds, and arises from the left ventricular compartment. The left arch leads generally from the right ventricular cavity into the descending aorta, and joins the right arch towards the back. The number and distribution of the great vessels proceeding from the heart become fewer and less complicated in the mammal. Here the great vessels are reduced to two ; the aorta proceeding from the left ventricle and giving off the innominate, left carotid, and left subclavian arteries, which in conjunction with the descending aorta and branches, convey arterial blood to all parts of the system ; and the pulmonary artery, arising from the right ventricle, which sends blood exclusively to the lungs. Although the great vessels of the mammalian and human heart are reduced to two, it is worthy of remark that the tendency to an arched or branchial arrangement distinctly recurs. Thus the aorta and pulmonary artery are plaited upon each other, the aorta arching from right to left; the pulmonary artery subdividing and arching equally to right and left (Fig. 82, p. 159).

In birds and reptiles there are two superior cavae, a similar number being found in the mammalia which approach nearest to the oviparous vertebrata, as the monotremata and marsupiata, and in some of the rodentia, as for example the porcupine. The heart of the bird, like that of the mammal, consists of four distinct cavities, the cavities being separated from each other by valves and muscular partitions ; the former occurring in the auriculo-ventricular orifices, and isolating the right and left auricles from the right and left ventricles; the latter separating the right auricle from the left auricle, and the right ventricle from the left ventricle. The right auricle of the bird is comparatively very large, and the right ventricle highly differentiated, it being supplied with a wonderfully perfect muscular valve (Fig. 81, *i*, p. 159), which takes the place of the tricuspid valve in mammals (Fig. 84, *f*, p. 174). The elaboration of the right heart of the bird is, no doubt, connected with the very perfect and very extensive respiration of that animal.

Valves in the Heart of the Bird.—The system of valves in the heart of the bird is very complicated and very complete. The inferior cava is guarded at its orifice by a semilunar valvular fold, which separates it from the orifice of the left superior cava. The orifices of the inferior and left superior cavae are further protected by the large valves which guard the mouth of the coronary sinus. ' In the emu a strong oblique semilunar *muscular fold* commences by a band of muscular fibres running along the upper part of the auricle, and, expanding into a valvular form, extends along the posterior and left side of the sinus, terminating at the lower part of the fossa ovalis. A second semilunar *muscular valve* of equal size extends parallel with the preceding along the anterior border of the orifice of the sinus, its lower extremity being fixed to the smooth floor of the auricle, its upper extremity being continued into a strong muscular column running parallel to the one first mentioned across the upper and anterior part of the auricle, and giving off from its sides the greater part of the musculi pectinati[1].'

The other valves of the bird's heart—viz. the aortic, pulmonic, and mitral (Fig. 81, *v*, p. 159)—closely resemble those of the mammal, a description of which will be given further on. The aortic and pulmonic valves of the bird consist of three semilunar cusps or segments—the valves which occupy a similar position in the reptiles having only two cusps. The remarkable feature in the valves of the heart of the bird consists in the amount of muscular fibres mixed up with

[1] Comparative Anatomy and Physiology of Vertebrates, by Professor Owen.

M

them, some being partly, and others wholly, muscular. The arrangement of the muscular fibres in the heart of the bird closely resembles that in the heart of the mammal, to be described subsequently.

Respiration and Circulation in Birds.—The differentiation perceptible in the cardiac valves of the bird is necessitated by the highly developed condition of the lungs, the lungs being more capacious than in any other class. The increased capacity of the lungs becomes a *sine qua non* when it is remembered that birds require to make great exertions in launching themselves into the air from a level surface, and also in diving. A bird exerts its greatest power in rising. When fairly launched in space the weight of its body acts upon the twisted inclined planes formed by the wings, and does the principal part of the work[1]. The air cells and spaces in birds extend in many cases to every part of the body, not excepting the bones[2] and muscles ; and a bird can respire for a short time after the trachea is closed if the humerus be perforated. The great air-sacs in connexion with the lungs of birds, as I have ascertained from artificial injections, have arteries and veins in considerable numbers ramifying on their surface, the arterial and venous blood contained in the vessels being equally exposed to the influence of the air contained in the air-sacs. The air-sacs, which are apparently mere appendages of the lungs, are in reality the harbingers and types of all lungs. They closely resemble, in their rudimentary form, the hollow viscera of vertebrates[3]. The fish has its

---

[1] 'On the Mechanical Appliances by which Flight is attained in the Animal Kingdom,' by the Author, Trans. Lin. Soc. vol. xxvi. 'On the Physiology of Wings,' by the Author.—Trans. Roy. Soc. Edin. vol. xxvi.

[2] 'In the gannet and pelican the air enters all the bones with the exception of the phalanges of the toes, and in the hornbill even these are permeated by air.'—*Comp. Anat. and Phys. of Vertebrates*, by Professor Owen, vol ii. p. 214.

[3] 'In all the air-breathing vertebrata the respiratory membrane is formed by a prolongation of the internal tegumentary or mucous membrane from the upper part of *the digestive tube*; and this also holds true in the aquatic vertebrata or the fishes. When the expanded respiratory membrane is placed at some distance from that portion of the mucous membrane of the digestive tube with which it is continuous, as is especially the case in mammalia and birds, this mucous membrane is prolonged to the part where its expansion occurs, in the form of a tube strengthened on the outer surface by elastic textures, to enable it to withstand the atmospheric pressure. Along this tube (trachea) and its branches (bronchi and bronchial tubes) the air

swimming bladder—a closed sac containing air instead of urine, but which, like the urinary bladder, can open and close. 'In the water-newt, the lungs consist of a pair of elongated sacs, without any internal laminae or folds. In the frogs these membraneous sacs present ridges on their inner surface, especially at the upper part; and in the lungs of the turtle and crocodile these ridges increase in number and in size, and form partitions dividing the interior of the lungs into numerous cells communicating with each other.' The differentiation is carried still further in the bird and mammal; and there are grounds for believing that these, like the more simple air-bladder of the fish, have the power of opening and closing within certain limits.

The Air-sacs of Birds, etc.—The air-sacs of birds have nothing whatever to do with flight, as they are found in birds which do not fly, and flight can be performed by the bat in their absence. Sappey enumerates as many as fifteen air-sacs. They open the one into the other, and as they have a peristaltic action, currents of air are continually passed throughout the entire substance of the body, very much as in the tracheae of insects and in the older vascular bundles of plants. The peristaltic movements of the air-sacs of birds show the intimate relation existing between the lungs and the heart; the one circulating air, the other blood. The air-sacs of birds were described by John Hunter as early as 1774. Somewhat analogous membraneous expansions are found in connexion with the lungs of serpents—the python, for example; so that the lungs of birds, which represent the highest development of pulmonary organs, have certain affinities with the lungs of reptiles, which are not differentiated to anything like the same extent.

The only peculiarities in the circulation of birds to which allusion is necessary are to be found in a modification of the portal circulation and the possession of a distinct renal circulation. The veins of birds anastomose very freely. One of these anastomosing branches extends between the united caudal, haemorrhoidal, and iliac veins to the vena portae, so that the blood from the viscera and posterior part of the body

passes to and from the proper respiratory membrane on the inner surface of the lungs.'—*Cyc. of Anat. and Phys.* 'Arterial Respiration,' vol. iv. p. 331.

flows either into the vena portae or vena cava inferior. The
renal circulation of birds was discovered by Professor Jacob-
son. It is venous in character, branches of the inferior cava
proceeding to the interior of the kidneys[1]. Other investigators
have found what virtually amounts to a renal circulation in
reptiles and fishes.

Circulation in the Mammal.—What has been said of the
heart of the bird applies, with slight modifications, to the
heart of the mammal. This, too, consists of four distinct
cavities—two auricles and two ventricles ; the auricles and
ventricles in the adult being separated from each other by
valves and by muscular partitions or septa. In virtue of this
arrangement the heart of the mammal is often spoken of as
consisting of a right or pulmonic heart composed of the right

Fig. 83.

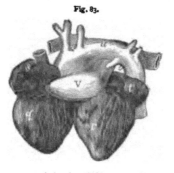

Fig. 83.—Heart of dugong seen anteriorly : shows bifid apex. *s*, right auricle. *q*, right ventricle, *t*, left
auricle. *r*, left ventricle. *u*, aorta giving off innominates, left carotid and left subclavian arteries. *v*, pulmonary artery bifurcating and proceeding to right and left lungs. (Compare with human heart, Fig. 82,
p. 159.)—*Owen.*

auricle and ventricle, and a left or systemic heart composed
of the left auricle and ventricle. The terms pulmonic and
systemic have been employed because the right heart receives
the venous blood from the system and forces it into the lungs ;
the left heart receiving the arterial blood from the lungs and
forcing it into the system. This arrangement provides for
what may be regarded a distinct venous circulation, and a
distinct arterial circulation ; the two kinds of blood, viz. the
arterial and the venous, being no longer mixed either in the
vessels or in the heart (Fig. 82, p. 159).

In the dugong, the systemic and pulmonic hearts are very

---

[1] I have had opportunities of injecting the kidneys of birds, and the degree of
vascularity is in some cases quite remarkable.

distinct—the right and left ventricles being widely separated
from each other at their apices, and only joined towards their
bases, as shown at Fig. 83. This virtually divides the organ
into a left or systemic, and a right or pulmonic heart. The
auricles of the heart of the dugong are of equal size, and the
ventricles closely resemble each other in their general configuration. The heart of the whales and dolphins more closely
resembles that of the other mammals. The arteries of the
whale, as John Hunter pointed out, are remarkable for their
tortuosity and convoluted arrangement. Vast plexuses of tortuous vessels are found under the pleura and between the ribs
and their muscles on each side of the spine. Similar plexuses
surround the medulla spinalis, more especially where it comes
out from the brain. In the porpoise the veins, which are for
the most part devoid of valves, display a similar tortuosity,
particularly on either side of the spine below the kidneys.
When artificially injected the venous plexuses present a very
unusual appearance[1]. Hunter was of opinion that the cetacea
contain more blood in proportion to their size than other
mammals; and the vast arterial and venous expansions referred to certainly favour this view. He thought the expansions had something to do with the habits of the animals—
the cetacea remaining submerged for long intervals, and devoting very short periods to breathing and aerating their
blood. He thought, in fact, that the plexuses acted as reservoirs for oxygenated blood, and prevented asphyxia when the
animals dived. This may form a partial, but is not the whole
explanation; as I have succeeded in injecting similar arterial
and venous plexuses in the arms and legs of the sloth, the
arms, legs, and tail of the spider-monkey, and the testicles of
the ram—where, of course, no such aggregation of oxygenated
blood is required[2]. Sir Charles Bell believed that the plexusus
and increased vascular supply were necessary to parts performing a large amount of work, or undergoing strain; such
parts requiring a more liberal supply of nutritive material.
The tortuosity of the vessels quite explains the absence of

---

[1] In illustration, see specimens prepared by the author, deposited in the Museum
of the Royal College of Surgeons, London.

[2] These preparations are deposited in the Hunterian Museum of the Royal ·
College of Surgeons of London, where they may be consulted.

valves in the veins; the plexuses of veins in the porpoise resembling varicose veins in ourselves, where the valves are
diseased or broken down. The circulation in the cetacea is
especially remarkable for its magnitude. The enthusiastic
and justly-renowned Hunter found in the circulation of the
cetacea a subject worthy of his scalpel. He says—'In our
examination of particular parts, the size of which is generally
regulated by that of the whole animal, if we have only been
accustomed to see them in those which are small or middle-
sized, we behold them with astonishment in animals so far
exceeding the common bulk as the whale. Thus the heart
and aorta of the spermaceti whale appeared to be prodigious,
being too large to be contained in a wide tub, the aorta mea-
suring a foot in diameter. When we consider these as applied
to the circulation, and figure to ourselves that probably ten or
fifteen gallons of blood are thrown out at one stroke, and moved
with an immense velocity through a tube of a foot diameter,
the whole idea fills the mind with wonder[1].'

In order, as it were, to make the differentiation between the
systemic and pulmonic circulation more obvious, the systemic
circulation is carried on within vessels termed arteries, and the
venous circulation within vessels termed veins. These are
separated from each other at the periphery of the body and
the organs thereof, by minute plexuses of vessels, which, from
their small size, are denominated capillaries. They are separated at the heart by muscular and valvular septa. The
arteries begin at the heart and terminate at the capillaries;
the veins begin at the capillaries and terminate at the heart.
Between and around the capillaries, a very minute system
of vessels, the hyper-vascular canals, are found. The arteries
break up, branch or bifurcate, and become smaller and smaller
as they proceed from the heart; the veins, on the other hand,
converge and unite, and become larger as they near the heart.

The arterial and venous systems may not inaptly be compared to a cone, the apex of which is directed towards the
heart; or to a tree, which bifurcates near its roots, and whose
stem and spreading branches represent the arterial and venous
vessels lying side by side. The arterial system is in some

[1] Phil. Trans. 1787, p. 415.

respects the converse of the venous. The arteries have thick walls, are elastic in the direction of their length and breadth, and, if the aortic semilunar valve be excepted, are not furnished with valves. They are also comparatively narrow. The veins have thin walls, are less elastic than the arteries, and are·provided with numerous valves which may consist of from one to four or more segments. The veins are, comparatively speaking, very wide. The presence of valves in the veins and other structures is to ensure that the circulating fluid shall always proceed in one direction. They are the sluices or floodgates which are thrown open by the advancing tide, but which are closed the instant it attempts to retrogress or recede [1].

With the peculiarities of the circulation in the mammal most of you are familiar. I will however take the liberty of briefly adducing the leading facts connected with it, as an enumeration of these will enable me to introduce some new matter which may prove interesting.

Auricles, Ventricles, Valves, Septa, etc., of Mammalian Heart.—The mammalian heart (of which the human may be taken as an example) is a conical-shaped, hollow, muscular mass, slightly twisted upon itself, particularly at the apex [2]. It is divided into four distinct compartments—a right auricle and a right ventricle, and a left auricle and a left ventricle. The right auricle is separated from the left auricle by a muscular partition, a similar partition running between the right and left ventricles. The right and left auricles are separated from the right and left ventricles by valvular septa (the mitral and tricuspid valves), which, when the heart opens and closes,

---

[1] 'In man the valves are very numerous in the veins of the extremities, especially the lower ones, these vessels having to conduct the blood against the force of gravity. They are absent in the very small veins, also in the venae cavae, the hepatic vein, portal vein and its branches, the renal, uterine, and ovarian veins. A few valves are found in the spermatic veins, and one also at their point of junction with the renal vein and inferior cava in both sexes. The cerebral and spinal veins, the veins of the cancellated tissue of bone, the pulmonary veins, and the umbilical vein and its branches, are also destitute of valves. They are occasionally found, few in number, in the venae azygos and intercostal veins.'—*Anatomy, Descriptive and Surgical*, by Henry Gray, Esq., F.R.S., etc., p. 401.

[2] In mammalian hearts the apex is slightly notched, the notch varying in different animals. In the dugong it is so deep as to separate the right and left ventricles throughout half their extent. The notch in question forms the boundary between the apices of the right and left ventricles. (Fig. 83, p. 164.)

rise and fall like diaphragms (Figs. 84, *f*; 85, *m*, *i*, *n*; p. 174). The cavities of the heart are of nearly the same size, the walls of the right auricle being so thin in parts as to be nearly transparent. Those of the left auricle are a little thicker. The walls of the right ventricle are about twice the thickness of those of the right auricle ; while those of the left ventricle and septum are nearly twice as thick as those of the right ventricle. The thickness of the walls of the auricles and ventricles is in exact proportion to the work to be performed by them—the left ventricle having a greater amount of work to do than the right ventricle, and the left auricle than the right. This is proved by the fact that in the foetus, where there is no distinct pulmonic and systemic circulation, the walls of the ventricles, until quite towards the full term, are of nearly the same thickness. It is also proved by hypertrophy of the right ventricle in cases of disease of the lungs, which, obstructing the passage of the blood through the pulmonic vessels, necessitates an increase of power in the propelling organ. In order to understand the course pursued by the blood in the right or pulmonic and the left or systemic heart of the mammal, it is necessary to be familiar with its entrances and exits.

Right Heart of Mammal.—The blood enters the right auricle by two principal openings : the one communicating with the superior cava, through which it receives the venous blood from the head and upper extremities ; the other communicating with the inferior cava, through which it receives the venous blood from the trunk and lower extremities. (Fig. 84, *a*, *b*, p. 174). These openings are not provided with valves, so that the reflux of the blood when the right auricle closes is prevented in part by atmospheric pressure, by the closing of the valves of the large veins of the upper extremities and neck, and in part by the closure of the cavae themselves, which are supplied with muscular fibres for this purpose. In addition to the openings of the superior and inferior cavae, there are those of the coronary sinus and foramina Thebesii, through which the venous blood of the heart itself finds its way into the right auricle. These constitute the entrances into the right auricle. There is only one exit. The venous blood passes from the right auricle into the right ventricle by the right auriculo-ventricular orifice, which is guarded by the tricuspid valve (f). Once in the right ventricle, the blood is expelled through the funnel-shaped canal known as the infundibulum or conus arteriosus into the pulmonary artery (d), the orifice of which is guarded by the pulmonic semilunar valve (h). It thence finds its way into the lungs, where it is arterialised; and there we leave it for the present. The right auricle and ventricle form a through route for the venous blood, this being collected in the right auricle, which, when it closes, forces it into the right ventricle, the right ventricle in turn forcing it into the lungs. (*Vide* arrows of Fig. 84, p. 174.)

The Blood urged on by a Wave-Movement; Heart and Vessels Open and Close in Parts.—The blood is projected by a progressive wave-movement, which begins in the cavae and extends to the right auricle, and thence to the right ventricle; the right auricle opening as the cavae close, and the right ventricle opening as the auricle closes. The blood is thus forced on by a *vis a tergo*, aided by a sucking or *vis a fronte*, movement. The *vis a tergo* or closing movement acts in conjunction with the elasticity of the vessels; the *vis a fronte* or sucking movement in conjunction with atmospheric pressure and the demand set up by the tissues for nourishment. If the different parts of the heart have the power of expelling their contents, they should, *ceteris paribus*, have the power of opening to receive a new supply. Dr. Carson believed that the different parts of the heart relaxed after being contracted; the relaxation being favoured by the distribution of the muscular fibres, by the elasticity of the lungs, and by a diminution of atmospheric pressure on the *outer or convex surface* of the heart, the pressure of blood on the great veins which conduct to the organ, and which act on its *inner or concave surface*, being increased. In other words, he was of opinion that the relation between the lungs, pleura, heart, and pericardium was such, that the different parts of the organ were opened in a great measure mechanically by a simultaneous withdrawal and increase of atmospheric pressure on its outer and inner surfaces[1]. While agreeing with Dr. Carson that the heart exerts a pulling and pushing power, I differ from him as to the *modus operandi*. In short, I attribute the opening and closing powers possessed

[1] An Enquiry into the Causes of the Motion of the Blood, by James Carson, M.D., 1815.

by the different parts of the heart to an inherent vitality. That the movements in question are not due to a rhythmic pressure exerted outside and inside the organ is obvious from this, that the heart acts when it is cut out of the body and deprived of blood, the atmospheric pressure on its outer and inner surfaces being equal. That the heart regulates its movements irrespective of atmospheric pressure is further apparent from the fact that its different parts move at different times—the hearts of some of the lower animals, by the mere vermicular movements of their walls, transmitting two kinds of blood through a single chamber. Thus Goodsir [1] observed that there is a slight asynchronism between the movements of the right and left auricles in the heart of the lizard [2], and that the contraction of the ventricle begins at its right side, in the neighbourhood of the pulmonary artery, and terminates at the left or arterial sinus of the ventricle. Brücke, in his memoir in the Vienna Transactions, has, curiously enough, described a ventricular arrangement by which venous blood only passes into the pulmonary artery in reptiles; the ventricle beginning to contract on the right side, and afterwards on the left.

Many are of opinion that the closing of the auricle produces the opening of the ventricle, the closing of the ventricle in turn dilating the auricle. This would be a mere waste of power; and, besides, unless the ventricle opened spontaneously, the blood from the auricle, which is the distending medium, would be denied admission. The ventricle when it closes becomes a solid mass, to which no fluid, however great the pressure exerted by it, can gain access (Fig. 93, *b*, p. 190) [3]. Nor must it be overlooked that occasionally, when the heart is acting slowly, the ventricle opens before the auricle closes, and the converse. Furthermore, the several parts of the heart open and close when cut out of the body and deprived of blood. There is, therefore, no sufficient ground for believing

[1] Anatomical Memoirs, vol. i. p. 443.

[2] Similar asynchronism was observed in the auricles of the turtle and frog.

[3] In discharging my duties as Pathologist to the Royal Infirmary of Edinburgh, I occasionally open hearts, the ventricular cavities of which are quite obliterated. The extent of centripetal or closing power possessed by the hollow viscera is very remarkable. I have at present in my possession a human stomach, the calibre of the body of which is not greater than that of the small intestine. The patient died of starvation, induced by cancer of the oesophagus.

that the opening of the ventricle is due to the closing of the auricle, and *vice versa*. On the contrary, observation and experiment tend to prove that the different compartments of the heart open and close spontaneously by vital and independent acts. The probabilities are, that there is no such thing as a violent closing of one part of the circulatory apparatus producing a violent opening of another part [1]. That the different parts of the heart and vessels are endowed with the power of opening and closing is in great measure proved by this, that in the lower animals, where there are no hearts, the vessels pulsate and carry on the circulation by themselves. Similar pulsating vessels, as has been already explained, are found when hearts are present; as in the mesenteric vessels of the frog, the veins of the bat's wing, the caudal vessels of the tail of the eel, the saphenous veins of the rabbit; and the chances are, that the vessels generally perform an important part in the visible circulation of vertebrates [2]. The caudal vessels of the eel display a sacculation which may be regarded as a venous heart. The power of the vessels to open and close in parts decreases as the elastic properties of the vessels increase.

[1] Dr. Hoggan, in a recent number of the Edinburgh Medical Journal (October, 1872), states his belief that the heart dilates or expands in virtue of the blood forced into its parietes at each systole. This doctrine is, I believe, founded in error. The heart in the embryo pulsates while yet it is a solid mass of nucleated cells—*i. e.* before it is supplied with blood-vessels and before cavities are formed in it. In the adult it pulsates after it is removed from the body, its cavities, which contain the blood, and which, according to Dr. Hoggan, indirectly force it into its ventricular walls, being laid open. The presence of blood is moreover not necessary to rhythmic movements, as plants and the lower orders of animals, which are devoid of blood, exhibit them. Dr. Hoggan's theory is not more satisfactory when applied to the lungs. If the lungs are expanded by the forcing of blood into their capillary vessels, then the lungs of the foetus should be expanded, as their vessels are pervious, and the foetal heart acts vigorously. Again, in the case of the adult lung, collapsed from fluid or air pressure exerted from without (the carnified lung of pathologists), the heart acts normally, but fails to arrest the mischief. If a lung be deprived of its residual air, it is impossible to inject it. In conclusion, if the blood in the vessels and capillaries of the lungs and heart caused their expansion, it is evident that this fluid, which is constant in amount in both, would prevent their contraction and destroy their rhythmic movements—that is to say, would render the alternate increase and diminution of the volume of the heart and lungs impossible. Dr. Liebermann, of Vienna, who wrote after Dr. Hoggan, but published before him, virtually endorses Dr. Hoggan's views.

[2] The small vessels are largely furnished with nerves. They diminish their calibre on the application of cold, and increase it on the application of heat.

The inferior vena cava, the renal, azygos, and external iliac veins, and the large trunks of the portal venous system and hepatic veins, as Dr. Gray has shown, contain longitudinal and circular non-striated muscular fibres, so that they have a structure resembling that of the intestine, the power of which to transmit solid, semi-solid, or fluid contents is well known. In addition, the inferior cava and the pulmonary artery and aorta at their origins are abundantly supplied with nerves—an arrangement which assimilates the great vessels situated at the root of the heart to the bulbus arteriosus of fishes, which, as has been shown, is endowed with rhythmic power. The vessels aid the circulation indirectly by their elasticity and resiliency. By receiving and storing up part of the impulse communicated to the blood by the heart at each systole, and by expending the power thus imparted gradually between the pulsations, they tend to equalise the current, and give continuity of movement. That the calibre of the great vessels increases when the ventricles close is proved by placing a ring of metal with a slit in it round the carotid of the horse or other large animal. The slit is widened during the systole, and diminished during the diastole.

If rigid vessels were compatible with the movements of animals, they would be preferable to elastic ones for carrying on the circulation, as, in this case, the heart would merely require to force on the blood without having to dilate the vessels. If, even with our imperfect knowledge of mechanics, we were asked to transmit fluid from one point to another, we would never dream of employing an elastic tube (a tube which can open and close in parts is quite another matter). Still less would we think of distending the elastic tube with the power which should transmit the fluid, delegating the transmission at second hand to the recoil of an elastic apparatus. This, I repeat, with our imperfect knowledge of mechanics, we would not do. Can it be thought, then, that nature, perfect in every direction, would employ a method to which we, with our limited knowledge and crude methods, would object? The vessels or ducts must of necessity be flexible: they form part of a living, moving mass, and must yield to accommodate themselves to the varying postures and shapes assumed by the organism to which they belong. It does not however follow from this that they are to be regarded as simply elastic tubes : on the contrary, we know that some of them pulsate—*i. e.* open and close in parts. We know further that all of them are supplied with nerves, and many of them with longitudinal and circular muscular fibres similar to those found in the intestines ; the intestines exhibiting vermicular movements. Nor must it be forgotten that the presence of nerves and of muscular fibres are not necessary to the so-called contraction and relaxation of parts. The heart opens and closes while yet it is a mass of cells (neither cavities nor blood being present) ; and the vacuoles or spaces in many plants open and close with a regular rhythm—the closure being rapid and the opening slow, as in the different parts of the heart. Here of course neither muscle nor nerves are present. It is therefore exceedingly improbable that the blood-vessels take no part in the circulation other than is produced by a mechanical recoil.

If there is any truth in the theory that living structures accommodate themselves to the conditions in which they are placed, it is reasonable to conclude that the vessels of animals, being opened and allowed to close at brief intervals through innumerable lives (some of them very protracted), come ultimately to open and close of themselves, and to act either independently or in conjunction with the heart. If the vessels were rigid and non-resilient, the blood would be forced along them by successive jerks, each jerk corresponding to the closing or systole of the ventricles. This is what actually happens when the heart is acting so feebly that it fails to distend the vessels, and evoke their elastic properties. Under these circumstances a very distinct venous pulse is felt, the elasticity which begets a continuous current being inoperative. The fact that a feeble heart can make its pulsations felt in the veins proves that considerably less power would suffice for carrying on the visible circulation if the vessels were rigid (they are virtually so in this non-distended condition). When the heart is acting normally, the column of blood in the vessels receives during the systole a smart tap, similar to that which a hammer produces when made to strike the end of a column of wood or other rigid material. This follows because fluids are very slightly compressible even under high pressures. The incompressibility of the fluid column of blood accounts for the extreme rapidity with which the pulsation communicated during the systole travels, the impulse at the heart and extremities being nearly synchronous. This rapidity of travel is accounted for by the blood ejected from the ventricles displacing that immediately in front of it, this in turn displacing the blood in front of it, and so on *ad infinitum*, until the capillaries are reached by the advancing column on the one hand, and the heart by the receding column on the other. The transmission of the different portions of blood meted out by

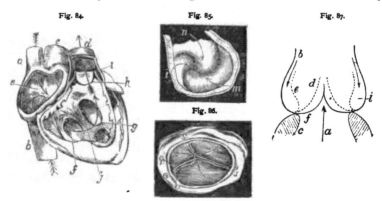

Fig. 84.   Fig. 85.   Fig. 87.

Fig. 86.

Fig. 84.—Pulmonic or right side of human heart. *e*, right auricle. *g*, right ventricle. *a*, superior cava. *b*, inferior cava. *c*, aorta. *d*, pulmonic artery. *h*, segment of pulmonic semilunar valve, *i*, sinus of Valsalva. *f*, segment of tricuspid valve. *j*, musculus papillaris. The arrows indicate the direction in which the blood enters and leaves the right or pulmonic heart.—*After Gray.*

Fig. 85.—Tricuspid valve in action seen from above (human). The segments are folded and twisted into each other by a screwing wedging motion (*vide* arrows *m*, *i*, *n*), occasioned by the spiral movements of the ventricles and the spiral impulse communicated to the blood contained within the right ventricle.—*Original.*

Fig. 86.—Semilunar valve of pulmonary artery in action, seen from above (human). Shows how, when the valve is closed the segments *rs*, *so*, *or*, are folded upon themselves, and spirally wedged towards the axis of the vessel (*vide* arrows). To produce a perfect closure the margins (*a*, *b*) of the segments must flatten against each other, the extent of the flattening increasing as the pressure exerted by the blood is augmented.—*Original.*

Fig. 87.—Diagram showing sectional view of the sinuses of Valsalva (*i*) in the human pulmonary artery. Shows also the different positions assumed by the segments of the pulmonic semilunar valve when at rest and in action. *a*, arrow indicating the course taken by the blood on leaving the right ventricle. The blood in its passage pushes aside the segments (*f*) of the valve, until they assume the positions *d* and *e*. *d* represents the position of the segments when at rest and floating in blood; *e* their position when pushed aside by the advancing tide; and *f* their position when closed. The arrow *b* indicates the direction taken by the blood when it retrocedes and closes the valve; *c* base of right ventricle (infundibuliform portion).—*Original.*

the ventricles, at each systole, may be compared to the water and debris contained in the buckets of a dredging-machine, where each bucket is pursued by every other bucket in a continuous round. The all but incompressible nature of the fluid column of blood in the vessels, taken in connexion with the fact that the blood is moved on in relays, enables the heart, as has been stated, to exert a sucking as well as a propelling power.

Valves of Right Heart of Mammal.—To facilitate the circulation of the blood through the heart, the valves, sluices, or gateways of the heart are constructed to open in only one direction ; thus, the tricuspid valve opens towards the right ventricle (Fig. 84, *f*), and the semilunar one (Fig. 84, *h*) towards the pulmonary artery; the blood is consequently compelled to travel from the right auricle (Fig. 84, *a*) to the right ventricle (*g*), and from the right ventricle to the pulmonary artery (*d*) and lungs. It is only when the valves are diseased and incompetent that even a slight amount of regurgitation is possible, either in the tricuspid (Fig. 85) or semilunar valve (Fig. 86).

When the blood is being forced from the right ventricle, it is projected as a fluid wedge (the infundibulum is wedge-shaped). The fluid wedge throws the segments of the semilunar valves back into the sinuses of Valsalva, as opening folding-doors are forced into recesses formed for their reception (Fig. 87, *i*). This has the effect of increasing the orifice of the pulmonary artery very considerably. But the recesses or sinuses of Valsalva (Fig. 87, *i*) have yet another function. They are large enough always to contain a certain amount of residual blood, which by its mere weight tends to force the segments towards the axis of the pulmonary artery, the instant the systole of the right ventricle ceases. This movement is favoured by the sucking power exerted by the right ventricle when it expands (*vide* arrow *b* of Fig. 87). The segments of the semilunar valve, in addition, incline towards the axis of the vessel when left to themselves (Fig. 87, *d*). In virtue of this mechanical adaptation, the margins of the segments are forced towards each other by the slightest reflux; the reflux, when it increases, producing a folding or wedging of the segments into each other, as shown at Fig. 86. The tricuspid valve acts on the same principle (Fig. 85), but has a more complicated function to perform, from its guarding the right auriculo-ventricular orifice, the size of which varies as the heart opens and closes, and from the fact that it is geared by a series of tendinous bands, the chordae tendineae [1], to

---

[1] In the substance of the pulmonic semilunar valve, similar bands are found ; and in certain cases of disease they are dissected out, and greatly resemble the chordae tendineae of the tricuspid. Both valves are evidently formed on the same type.

actively-contracting structures, viz. the musculi papillares (*f,j*, of Fig. 84, p. 174).

The action of the tricuspid valve is therefore vito-mechanical, while that of the semilunar is nearly, if not wholly, mechanical. The parts which correspond to the sinuses of Valsalva in the right ventricle are the spaces to the outside of each of the segments of the tricuspid.

The blood is forced by the right ventricle into the lungs with considerable energy. Much of the force exerted is however dissipated by the rapid bifurcation of the pulmonary arteries, these dividing and subdividing at such short distances as effectually to slow the current before it reaches the delicate capillaries of the lungs. This is a wise provision, for in cases of hypertrophy of the right ventricle, it happens not unfrequently that some of the smaller vessels of the lung are ruptured, and pulmonary apoplexy induced [1].

Safety-valve action of Tricuspid.—It has been thought by some [2], that, in order to prevent injury to the pulmonary organs, the tricuspid valve is never exactly competent, and that, when the right ventricle closes, the blood, which cannot be forced into the lungs without producing mischief, escapes into the right auricle, and thence into the cavae. I am not disposed to look favourably on this argument, as it assumes an imperfection in the circulatory apparatus, which I do not believe exists. In the fish, where there is no reason to suspect a regurgitant action, the gills are situated in close proximity to the heart, but no harm accrues from the proximity, although the ventricle and bulbus arteriosus are both exceedingly powerful structures [3]. The walls of the right and left ventricles of the mammal, as has been already stated, are of the same thickness in the foetus until quite near the full term. Towards the end of the full term and after birth, when the pulmonic circulation is established, the right ventricular walls thin, while the left ventricular walls thicken. Here is an accommodating process which produces the exact amount of pressure required

[1] Pulmonary apoplexy is usually associated with disease and constriction of the mitral valve, the constriction obstructing the flow of blood into the left ventricle, and damming it up in the lungs.

[2] Mr. T. W. King, in Guy's Hospital Reports for April, 1837, No. IV.

[3] For explanation of the manner in which the ventricle and bulbus arteriosus of the fish act, see under ' Circulation in the Fish,' p. 113.

for forcing the blood without danger through the lungs and through the system. If the blood which should be forced into the lungs was allowed to regurgitate into the right auricle, and thence into the cavae, it would tend to disturb the whole circulation, for any impediment at one part would necessarily react upon every other part. We have, moreover, direct proof that the tricuspid valve is competent. If, *e.g.*, I push a rigid tube past the semilunar valve of the pulmonary artery and fix it firmly in that vessel, and then sink the right heart in water, I find that, by blowing into the tube, the segments of the tricuspid are gradually floated up by the water, approximated, and apposed so perfectly that not a single drop of fluid is permitted to regurgitate (Fig. 85, p. 174).

I have repeatedly performed this experiment, and always successfully. If regurgitation is a serious matter in the bicuspid and semilunar valves, it would be illogical to infer it was harmless in the tricuspid. The express function of the tricuspid and all other valves is to prevent regurgitation. Not only is the ·power of the right ventricle exactly suited to the requirements of the pulmonic circulation, but the pulmonic vessels are provided with that degree of elasticity and of vital movement which enables them to reciprocate with the utmost nicety. In virtue of this arrangement the blood arrives at the capillaries of the lungs, and the vessels of the entire system, at the speed and in the quantity best suited for each. The slowing of the current is necessary for the purposes of respiration, nutrition, growth, waste, etc. The slowing of the blood in the delicate capillaries of the lungs increases the opportunities afforded this fluid for taking in oxygen and giving off carbonic acid and other matters. These interchanges effected, the blood is urged on, partly by the closure of the right ventricle, partly by the opening of the left auricle, and partly by atmospheric pressure, into the pulmonary veins, which debouch by four openings into the left auricle.

Left Heart and Valves of Mammal.—As there are no tissues to be nourished by the blood in the pulmonary veins, it follows that these can exert no influence in drawing the blood into the left auricle. This function is performed by the closing of the right ventricle, by the vital expansion of the left auricle, aided by atmospheric pressure and by the movements of the lungs

N

themselves.   Once in the left auricle, the arterial blood is projected thence by the closing of the left auricle through the left auriculo-ventricular opening into the left ventricle, which simultaneously expands to receive it.   It is then forced by the closing of the left ventricle through the aorta, and by means of its branches through the whole system.   The course of the current through the left heart is determined as in the right by the presence of two sets of valves, viz. the bicuspid or mitral and the aortic semilunar valve.   These valves resemble the tricuspid and pulmonic semilunar valves just described so closely, that further allusion to them at this stage is unnecessary.

Circulation in the Head, Liver, and Erectile Tissues.—In mammals the circulation in the head, liver, and erectile tissues is worthy of a separate description.   The supply of blood to the brain is comparatively very large[1].   It is furnished by the two internal carotid and the two vertebral arteries.   These spread out on the base of the brain to form the circle of Willis, which may be regarded as a reservoir for providing a regular supply of blood to the arteries of the organ.   The arteries break up into an infinite number of minute branches in the pia mater, from whence they betake themselves to the brain-substance.   The blood is returned by numerous small veins to the venous sinuses, which are remarkable for their great size, and the fact that they are formed on the one aspect by the tough dura mater, and on the other by the inner table of the cranium, so that their walls may, in a great measure, be regarded as incompressible.   This led to the belief that the quantity of blood in the brain is always the same.   Dr. Kellie endeavoured to establish this view by experiment.   He found that if an animal was bled to death the quantity of blood in the brain remained the same, while the system generally was drained; but that if the cranium was perforated, and air admitted to the brain before the bleeding took place, the brain and system generally were blanched equally.

[1] Dr. J. Crichton Browne, in a recent and able article 'On Cranial Injuries and Mental Diseases,' referring to a case where a portion of bone two inches by one had been removed from the upper part of the right frontal region on account of injury, states that the cicatrix pulsated visibly, and that the vascular changes were so rapid and considerable, as to impress him with the idea that the brain in some respects resembles erectile tissue.   (*West Riding Lunatic Asylum Medical Reports*, vol. ii. pp. 101, 102; 1872.)

Dr. Burrows obtained opposite results, so that the question is still *sub judice*. The erectile organs are rendered tense by a determination of blood to the very extensive and complicated venous plexuses contained in their interior. Professor Kölliker is of opinion that the plexuses during the non-erectile state are compressed by the habitual contraction of organic muscular fibres, and that in the erectile state the action of these fibres is suspended by nervous influence, the blood being permitted to distend the plexuses mechanically. It is more natural to suppose that the organic muscular fibres alluded to by Kölliker are not in a state of habitual contraction, *i. e.* constant activity, in the non-erectile state, but resting ; the muscles being active and expanding during the erectile state. It is difficult to understand how a muscle should be called upon to perform work constantly, when the same result might be obtained by occasional effort exerted at long intervals. Instead of regarding the muscle as habitually contracted, we have only to imagine that it occasionally expands. These remarks are equally applicable to the class of sphincter muscles. It seems irrational to invest a muscle with the power of contracting or closing, and to divest it of the power of elongating and expanding.

The venous blood of the principal abdominal viscera passes through the liver on its way to the heart. The following is the arrangement :—' The blood supplied by the cœliac and mesenteric arteries to the abdominal viscera is not returned directly to the heart by their corresponding veins, as occurs in other parts of the body. The veins of the stomach and intestinal canal, of the spleen, pancreas, mesentery, omenta, and gall-bladder, unite together below the liver into one large vessel, the trunk of the vena portae, which branches out again and distributes to the liver by its ramifications the whole of the venous blood coming from the above-mentioned organs. The blood of the vena portae, being joined in the minute branches by that of the hepatic artery, passes into the smallest ramifications of the hepatic veins, by the principal trunks of which the venous and arterial blood circulated through the liver is carried to the inferior vena cava, and thus reaches at last the right side of the heart.'

The great arteries are important accessories of the circulation of the mammal, inasmuch as they transmit the blood to and from the heart, which is the central engine for its propulsion. They are, however, as has been stated, only accessories. The most important functions performed by the vessels are delegated to the capillaries, a mazy labyrinth of minute vessels which ramify and inosculate in every conceivable direction. It is within those delicate capillary tubes that the blood meanders and literally irrigates the tissues, each tissue selecting and drawing through the capillary walls whatever it requires; or what comes very much to the same thing, having forced upon it by an osmotic action those peculiar fluids for which it has an affinity, and which are best adapted for its support, nourishment, and decay. The capillaries are therefore deserving of very particular attention, the more especially as their structure and movements indicate the structure and movements of the larger vessels; these, again, indicating the structure and movements of the heart, which in its turn curiously enough foreshadows the structure and movements of all the other muscles, voluntary and involuntary.

The Lymphatic and Capillary Vessels of Animals.—The capillaries furnish the simplest form of vessel. They may be divided into two kinds, viz. such as convey red blood, and such as convey a pale watery or milky fluid, the lymph or chyle. The lymphatics are intimately connected with the process of digestion in the alimentary canal and tissues generally. 'The *lymph*,' Mr. Huxley observes, 'like the blood, is an alkaline fluid, consisting of a plasma and corpuscles, and coagulates by the separation of fibrine from the plasma. The lymph differs from the blood in its corpuscles being all of the colourless kind, and in the very small proportion of its solid constituents, which amount to only about five per cent. of its weight. Lymph may, in fact, be regarded as blood *minus* its red corpuscles and diluted with water, so as to be somewhat less dense than the serum of blood, which contains about eight per cent. of solid matters. A quantity of fluid equal to that of the blood is probably poured into the blood daily from the lymphatic system. This fluid is in great measure the mere overflow of the blood itself—plasma which has been exuded from the capillaries into the tissues, and which has not been taken up again into the venous current; the rest is due to the absorption of chyle from the alimentary canal.' In reptiles and birds the lymphatics are provided with pulsating sacs or hearts and valves—an arrangement which insures that the lymph shall travel in only one direction, viz. towards the general circulation. The lymph in man is discharged into the general current of the circulation by two apertures situated between the angles of junction of the right and left internal jugular and right and left subclavian veins. The openings by which the lymph is discharged into the general circulation are each provided with a pair of valves to prevent regurgitation of the venous blood. The lymphatic vessels are to be regarded as the feeders of the vascular vessels, in the same sense that the vessels of the roots of a tree are to be considered the feeders of the vascular vessels in the trunk of the tree. In this respect the sanguineous circulation is to be

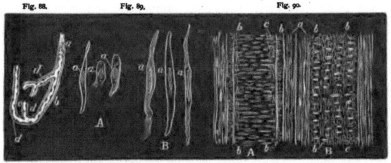

Fig. 88.　　　　　Fig. 89.　　　　　　　　　　Fig. 90.

Fig. 88.—A minute artery (a), ending in (b) larger and (c) smaller capillaries. d, nuclei embedded in the walls of the capillaries. Magnified 200 diameters.

Fig. 89.—A, epithelial cells of the arteries. a, the nucleus. B, muscular fibres of the arteries: the middle one, having been treated with acetic acid, shows more distinctly the nucleus (a). Magnified 300 diameters.

Fig 90—A, a small artery. B, a small vein, both treated with acetic acid; a fibrous coat; b, nuclei of the muscular coat; c, nuclei of the epithelial coat. Magnified 300 diameters.—After Huxley.

looked upon as an evolution or development of the chyliferous. The colourless corpuscles, which are so abundant in the lymphatic vessels, reappear in the capillaries of the vascular system, and are known as the white corpuscles of the blood. They are possessed of independent movements and change shape. They have attracted an usual share of attention of late from the power they possess of forcing themselves through the thin walls of the capillaries. The capillaries vary in size from $\frac{1}{1800}$ to $\frac{1}{3000}$ of an inch in diameter, and form an infinite variety of minute loops, being now straight, now slightly waved, and now tortuous. They generally form a network so dense that the point of a pin cannot be introduced without lacerating some of them. The capillaries of the vascular system lie midway between the arteries and veins—the arteries conducting to and the veins from them. Around and between the capillaries is a system of still more minute vessels, the hypervascular canals.

The capillaries form a sort of neutral territory, in which the blood meanders more slowly in order to afford the tissues the fullest opportunity of imbibing nourishment and discharging effete matter. They form a through route for the blood, but one with numerous convenient stages for the interchange of the good and bad things of the economy. The circulation in these minute vessels may not inaptly be compared to a river which carries a blessing wherever it goes, giving freshness and beauty to the country, and purifying the city by removing its sewage. The capillaries of the lymphatic system, so far as known at present, do not form a through route, but begin in the tissues by blind ends, resembling the spongioles of the roots of plants. The lymphatic system would therefore appear to be the precursor of the vascular system, and to form a connecting link between the vegetable and animal. The lymphatics are eminently adapted alike for conveying new and old ingredients into the blood. Like the roots of plants they are endowed with selective powers, certain of their terminals taking up new matter, others matter which has been partially used, and others effete or waste matter.

Structure of the Capillaries and Small Arteries and Veins: Vessels close and elongate, and open and shorten.—The walls of the capillaries are composed of a thin, structureless membrane, in which small oval bodies, termed nuclei, are embedded. They bear a considerable resemblance to the walls of the cells and young vascular bundles of plants.

The capillaries differ from the small arteries and veins in being of a uniform calibre, and in having very delicate thin permeable walls. The thin permeable walls permit the fluid contents of the capillaries to escape into the surrounding tissues, which are in this manner irrigated and nourished very much in the same manner that the growing parts of a plant are nourished by the imbibition of saps. In either case, the growing parts, *i.e.* the ultimate particles of the plant and animal, are outside the vessels [1]. In this sense the foetus is

[1] There are portions of the body, such as the nails, hair, teeth, cartilage, epi-

also outside the circulation of the mother. The capillaries further differ from the small arteries and veins in this, that the latter possess a more complex structure and thicker walls. Thus, proceeding from without inwards, the walls of the smaller vessels consist, first, of a sheath of fibrous tissue, the fibres of which pursue a more or less longitudinal direction [1]; second, of a muscular layer composed of flattened spindle-shaped bands, with elongated nuclei, these bands running transversely or across the vessels [2]; and, third, of a layer of very delicate, elongated, epithelial cells, the oval nuclei of which are arranged longitudinally or at right angles to those of the muscular fibres [3].

This arrangement accounts for the reticulated appearance presented by the smaller vessels (Fig. 90, p. 181), and for the fact, first promulgated by John Hunter, that the vessels are extensile and retractile in their length and breadth. As the walls of the vessel become thicker, they lose the permeability which is a distinguishing feature of the capillaries. The vessels, however, have what may be regarded an equivalent added, viz. muscular fibres and nervous twigs, which regulate their calibre and consequently the exact amount of blood supplied to the capillaries and to the tissues.

When the muscular layer of a small vessel closes in a direction from without inwards, the vessel is lengthened and narrowed, and the fluid contents ejected, from the fact that all muscles, when they shorten in one direction, lengthen in another and opposite direction; muscular movements being

thelium, epidermis, etc., which are not supplied with vessels at all. These structures are still further removed from the circulation, but, like the others, they are not beyond the reach of its influence.

[1] The external or areolar fibrous coat consists of areolar tissue and longitudinal elastic fibres; it also contains, in some of the larger veins, a longitudinal network of non-striated muscular fibres, as in the whole length of the inferior vena cava, the renal, azygos, and external iliac veins, and in all the large trunks of the portal venous system, and in the trunks of the hepatic veins.—*Gray's Anatomy*, p. 401.

[2] The middle layer in the *larger* vessels, according to Gray, consists of numerous alternating layers of muscular and elastic fibres, the fibres of the former running across the vessel, those of the latter in the direction of its length. This layer is thicker in the arteries than in the veins.

[3] The internal layer in the *larger* vessels consists, in Gray's opinion, of an epithelial lining, supported on several laminae of longitudinal elastic fibres. This layer is less brittle in veins than in arteries.

due not to any increase or diminution in the volume of muscles, but to a change of shape in their sarcous elements. The fibres of the central or transverse muscular layer of a small vessel are arranged, as explained, at right angles to the fibres composing the external fibrous layer, and the delicate elongated epithelial cells constituting the internal 'layer. When, therefore, the fibres of the central or transverse muscular layer close or shorten, they elongate and stretch the elements composing the external and internal layers; these, in virtue of their elasticity, the instant the closure ceases, assisting the central layer in regaining its normal dimensions. We have thus two forces at work—the muscular force and the elastic force. As however these forces act at right angles to each other, and the structures in which they reside ar geared together, it follows that when the one acts the other must act also. It is thus that muscular and elastic force can act in unison, and by their united efforts produce a common result (Fig. 90, p. 181).

Elastic and Vital Properties of Vessels.—The influence exerted by the elasticity of vessels in producing a steady continuous flow of blood is well marked. There is however reason to believe that the elastic properties of vessels have been overrated. It must never be overlooked that the movements in vessels have their origin in muscles, either the muscles of the heart, or the muscles of the vessels themselves. Nor must it be forgotten that the muscular layer of even the smallest vessel can by itself increase or diminish the calibre of the vessel, the muscular fibres determining the amount and direction of the movement. This is proved by the fact that a small artery may be made to diminish its circumference by the application of cold, and increase it by the application of heat. That the closing or partial closing and elongating of a small vessel is directly due to the shortening of the muscular fibres comprising the central layer of the vessel, is evident from the direction of the muscular fibres (they are circular, and invest the vessel transversely). That the opening or partial opening of a small vessel is only partly due to the recoil of the fibrous and elastic elements, is apparent from this, that they invest the vessel in the direction of its length. At most, therefore, the elastic elements, when they spring back, shorten the vessel. It remains for the muscular element to elongate, and by its elongation to expand and widen the vessel. The power to increase and diminish the size of the vessel resides chiefly if not exclusively in the muscular fibres, these, as already explained, having a centrifugal and centripetal action. The elastic structures are more developed in the vessels than in the heart and other hollow viscera, these organs being comparatively inelastic. The voluntary muscles, on the other hand, are less elastic than the involuntary ones. In proportion as the muscular movements become exact the elastic structures disappear. In order to have a perfect co-ordination in muscular movements, all the parts of the muscles involved, whether these be extensors or flexors, pronators or supinators, abductors or adductors, must take part. Nothing is left to chance, and as a consequence elasticity is reduced to a minimum. If a vessel was composed solely of muscular fibres it would not be so strong, neither would its movements be so rapid or continuous, as one composed partly of muscular and partly of elastic fibres. A muscle is capable of acting in two directions; it can first elongate and then shorten itself; but these are opposite movements, and between them a pause or halt (the dead point of engineers) inevitably occurs. Elasticity gets the muscle over this dead point, and decreases the duration of the pause. The value of elasticity in interrupted or rhythmic movements, such as those employed in the circulation, becomes therefore very obvious. There are many examples to prove that elasticity plays a part not only in involuntary movements, but likewise in voluntary ones. The wing of a bird, for instance, is flexed almost exclusively by the action of powerful elastic ligaments, extending between the shoulder and wrist, and between the elbow and hand. These ligaments gradually close or flex the wing towards the termination of the down-stroke,[1] and are put upon the stretch towards the termination of the up-stroke, by the shortening of the powerful pectoral and other muscles. Nearly half of the wing movements are therefore performed by a purely mechanical

---

[1] They are prevented from closing the wing suddenly, after the manner of springs, by the resistance offered by the air to the expanded wing as it descends.

arrangement[1]. Numerous other examples might be cited, but this is a very obvious one. It suffices, when elastic structures are present, if the muscles stretch them when they shorten; the elastic structures, when they shorten, assisting in the elongation of the muscular ones. The elastic and muscular structures mutually operate on each other. What would be a purely vital act is by this arrangement rendered more or less mechanical, and no better illustration can be given of the fact that animate, and what may be regarded as inanimate, matter can be made to reciprocate and work in harmony. The difference (but it is an all-important one) between a living vessel and an elastic tube amounts to this: The walls

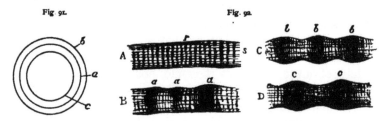

Fig. 91.   Fig. 92.

Fig. 91.—Diagram showing how the walls of a vessel or of a hollow viscus may oscillate on either side of a given line. a, position of rest of walls of vessel or heart. b. walls of vessel or heart when expanded. c, ditto when partly closed —Original.

Fig. 92 shows an elementary fibre of the skate in the uncontracted and contracted state.
A.—Fibre in the condition of rest. r, transverse markings or cleavage. s, longitudinal markings or cleavage.
B.—a a a, one side of fibre contracting or shortening.
C.—b b b, both sides of fibre contracting or shortening. All parts of the fibre become involved in succession. Thus the constrictions between b b b of C become the swellings c c c of D.—After Bowman.'

of a living vessel can oscillate or vibrate on either side of a given line, this line corresponding to their position of rest[2]. An elastic tube, on the other hand, can only be made to vibrate on one side of a given line. In other words, it can be made to open by being artificially distended, but it cannot be made to close. Thus if the circle a of Fig. 91 be made to represent an elastic tube, it may be stretched until it assumes the dimensions b, but it cannot be made to assume the dimensions c. This the living vessel can readily do from the power it possesses of oscillating on either side of the circle a.

[1] 'On the Mechanical Appliances by which Flight is attained in the Animal Kingdom,' by the Author; Trans. Lin. Soc. of London, vol. xxvi. 'On the Physiology of Wings,' by the Author; Trans. Roy. Soc. of Edinburgh, vol. xxvi.

[2] Precisely similar remarks may be made of the parietes of the different compartments of the heart.

All attempts therefore at reproducing by merely elastic tubes and cavities the structure and forces employed in the circulation, are more or less fallacious. Another marked difference between a hollow muscle and an elastic tube is to be noted. An elastic tube, when allowed to return to its position of rest after being put upon the stretch, is active throughout its entire substance at one and the same time. A living muscle, on the contrary, moves in parts—its action being a progressive wave action. Bowman is very explicit on this point. He states, 1st, That active contraction never occurs in the whole mass of a muscle at once, nor in the whole of any one elementary fibre, but is always partial at any one instant of time. 2nd, That no active contraction of a muscle, however apparently prolonged, is more than instantaneous in any one of its parts or particles; and therefore, 3rd, That the sustained active contraction of a muscle is an act compounded of an infinite number of partial and momentary contractions, incessantly changing their place and engaging new parts in succession; for every portion of the tissue must take its due share in the act. From this it follows that a muscle rests in its sarcous elements or ultimate particles even when it is working. These points are illustrated at Fig. 92.

Structure of the large Arteries and Veins.—As the vessels increase in size and their walls become thicker and more complex, the structures composing them are arranged at right angles and obliquely, but always in pairs and symmetrically. Regarding the composition of the veins, there is considerable difference of opinion, authorities not being agreed either as to the number or nature of the coats. This may in part be explained by the variation in the thickness of the coats themselves, these, according to John Hunter[1], becoming thinner and thinner in proportion to the size of the vein, the nearer the vein approaches the heart. In moderate sized veins an external, a middle, and an internal coat are usually described; the first consisting of cellular, fibrous, and elastic tissue, interlacing in all directions; the second, of waved filaments of areolar tissue, with a certain admixture of non-

---

[1] Hunter on the Blood, pp. 180, 181.

striped muscular fibres, which run circularly, obliquely, or even longitudinally[1]; the third, consisting of one or more strata of very fine elastic tissue, minutely reticulated in a longitudinal direction, the innermost stratum (when several are present) being lined by epithelium. Of these layers the second and third, from the fact of their contributing to the formation of the venous valves, are the most important. The coats of the veins, as has been long known, are tough, elastic, and possessed of considerable vital contractility *i.e.* they have the power of opening and closing within certain limits. Of these qualities, the toughness prevents undue dilatation of the vessel when distended with blood; the elasticity and the power the vessel possesses of opening and closing assisting the onward flow of that fluid, and *tending to approximate the segments of the valves*. As the valves of the veins are very ample and very flexible, they readily accommodate themselves to the varying conditions in which they are placed by the elasticity and vital properties of the vessel, and by the reflux of the blood.

The coats of the arteries, as is well known, are comparatively much thicker than those of the veins, while the layers composing them are more numerous. The external coat, according to Henle, consists of an outer layer of areolar tissue in which the fibres run obliquely or diagonally round the vessel, and an internal stratum of elastic tissue; the middle coat in the largest arteries, according to Raüschel, being divisible into upwards of forty layers. The layers of the middle coat consist of pale, soft, flattened fibres, with an admixture of elastic tissue; the fibres and elastic tissue being disposed circularly round the vessel. The internal coat is composed of one or more layers of fibres, so delicate that they constitute a transparent film, the film being perforated at intervals, and lined with epithelium. From this account it will be obvious that the large veins and arteries possess a

---

[1] Dr. Chevers says, that in the deep as well as in some of the superficial, veins of the trunk and neck, the middle coat is composed of several layers of circular fibres, with only here and there a few which take a longitudinal course; while the middle coat of the superficial and deep veins of the limbs consists of a circular layer, and immediately within this of a strong layer of longitudinal fibres.—*Med. Gazette*, 1845, p. 638.

much more complex structure than the smaller vessels—
these again being more highly differentiated than the capillaries. The large arteries and veins, in fact, present a structure
remarkably resembling that found in the ventricles of the
mammalian heart; thus they have fibres running longitudinally, obliquely, very obliquely, and transversely; the fibres
intersecting at a great variety of angles, and arranged with a
view to co-ordinating each other. The arteries, as might be
expected from their structure, and as was proved by the
admirable experiments of John Hunter, whose beautiful
preparations I have had an opportunity of examining, possess,
in addition to the vital powers peculiar to them, a considerable
degree of elasticity, and are extensible and retractile both in
their length and breadth; the power of recovery, according to
that author, being greater in proportion as the vessel is nearer
the heart. From this it follows that the pulmonary artery
and aorta are most liable to change in dimensions. As
however any material alteration in the size of the pulmonary
artery and aorta at their origins would interfere with the
proper function of the semilunar valves situated at their
orifices, it is curious to note that the great vessels arise from
strong and comparatively unyielding fibrous rings. These
rings (particularly the aortic one) are so dense as to be almost
cartilaginous in consistence, and Professor Donders[1] has lately
discovered that they contain stellate corpuscles similar in
many respects to those stellate and spicate corpuscles found
in many forms of cartilaginous tumours. They have been
more or less minutely described by Valsalva[2], Gerdy[3], Dr.
John Reid[4], and Mr. W. S. Savory[5], and merit attention
because of their important relations to the segments of the
semilunar valves. The following description of them has
been drawn up chiefly from an examination of a large number
of human hearts. Each ring consists, as was shown by Reid,
of three convex portions. Each convex portion is directed

---

[1] 'Onderzockingen betrekkeligh den bouw van het menchclijke hart,' in Neder-
landsch Lancet for March and April 1852.
[2] Opera Valsalvae, tom. i. p. 129.
[3] Journal Complimentaire, tom. x.
[4] Cyc. Anat. and Phys., article 'Heart,' pp 588, 589. London, 1839.
[5] Paper read before the Royal Society in December 1851.

from above downwards, and from without inwards, and as it unites above with that next to it, the two when taken together form a conical-shaped prominence which is adapted to one of the three triangular-shaped interspaces occurring between the segments of the semilunar valves. The ring surrounding the pulmonary artery is broader, but not quite so thick as that surrounding the aorta, and both are admirably adapted for the reception of the large vessels which originate in three festooned borders (Fig. 94).

Fig. 93.   Fig. 94.

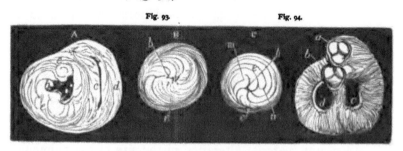

Fig. 93.—Transverse sections of ventricles of heart of deer. Shows how the right and left ventricles obliterate their cavities during the systole. Fig. 93 A, transverse section near the base of the ventricles; *b*, left ventricular cavity obliterated by the heads of the musculi papillares; *c*, cavity of right ventricle obliterated by the approximation of the right ventricular wall (*d*); *e*, *e*, circular fibres of left ventricle exercising their centripetal function. These fibres powerfully contribute to the closing of the left ventricular cavity. Fig. 93 B, transverse section near apex of ventricles; *b*, *e*, fibres which form the musculi papillares of left ventricle, curving towards ventricular cavity (*b*), which they obliterate by a centripetal action. Fig. 93 C, transverse section at apex of ventricles; *b*, left ventricular cavity obliterated by the centripetal action of the circular fibres (*e*, *e*) and those of the musculi papillares (*m*, *n*).—*Original.*
Fig. 94.—Base of ventricles of heart. *a*, *b*, Cartilaginous festooned rings, to which pulmonary artery (*a*) and aorta (*b*) are attached. Within these the pulmonic and aortic semilunar valves in their closed condition are seen. *c*, fibrous ring partly surrounding right auriculo-ventricular orifice. *d*, ditto surrounding left auriculo-ventricular orifice. To these rings the tricuspid and mitral valves, and a certain number of the superficial fibres of the ventricles are attached. The larger proportion of the fibres of the ventricles are continuous alike at base and apex.—*Original.*

Structure of the Heart of the Mammal; the Arrangement of the Muscular Fibres in the Auricles and Ventricles.—The auricles of the mammalian heart, as already explained, are two in number, a right and a left. They are irregularly shaped muscular pouches or receptacles which collect arterial and venous blood, the right communicating with the ascending and descending cavae, the left with the pulmonary veins. The cavae and pulmonary veins are invested with muscular fibres of considerable strength, which confer on these vessels a certain amount of vermicular movement. The muscular fibres of the auricles are arranged at right angles and obliquely as in the ventricle of the fish and reptile (Figs. 95 and 97, p. 192). The fibres in the auricular appendages are disposed in ridges to form the musculi pectinati. Where most plentiful, they are arranged in layers. They are circular in some cases, looped in others, and occasionally plicate. They are specially ar-ranged to procure strength, and with a view to opening and closing the auricular cavities, which they do by alternate cen-trifugal and centripetal movements. The auricles when closed contain a certain amount of residual blood, and in this respect they differ from the ventricles, which have the power of com-pletely expelling it (Fig. 93, A, B, C). The auricles serve as reservoirs, and are to be regarded as intermediate structures between the large veins and ventricles. The auricles are ana-tomically distinct from the ventricles, and in boiled hearts the auricles and ventricles may be separated from each other with-out rupturing a single fibre. The auricles are structurally continuous with the large veins (the cavae and pulmonary veins), from which they are not separated by valves as the auricles are separated from the ventricles. From this it fol-lows that when the auricles close, the pressure exerted by them is away from, as well as towards, the ventricles ; an indirect proof that the auricles by their closure do not forcibly dilate the ventricles. It ought however to be stated that the veins are more or less closed at the commencement of the auricular contraction. The great veins and auricles exhibit sponta-neous and rhythmical movements, the veins closing when the auricles open, and *vice versa*. Analogy favours the belief that the great vessels conducting from the heart (pulmonary artery and aorta), as well as those conducting to it (venae cavae and pulmonary veins), participate in those rhythmical movements. The bulbus arteriosus of fishes and reptiles (the homologues of the first part of the aorta in mammals), as I have already shown, opens and closes like the different parts of the heart itself. The muscular fibres composing the auricles are more plentiful in some regions than in others. In some places they are so sparse as to render the walls of the auricles transparent, while in others they are grouped and superimposed, the walls under these circumstances being quite an eighth of an inch in thickness. (Figs. 95 and 97, p. 192).

The ventricles of the mammalian heart, like the auricles, are two in number, a right and a left. They form a wedge-shaped hollow muscular mass, which is slightly twisted upon itself, particularly at the apex. The base of the wedge is directed upwards, and to this portion the auricles are attached, the auricles fitting into the right and left auriculo-ventricular openings as stoppers into the necks of bottles. The auricles adhere to the fibrous rings investing the auriculo-ventricular orifices (Fig. 94, *c*, *d*, p. 190), but none of the muscular fibres of the auricles are continuous with those of the ventricles. The arrangement of the muscular fibres in the ventricles is exceedingly intricate, and requires careful description. Considered as a muscle, the heart, especially the ventricular portion of it, is peculiar. Being in the strictest acceptation of the term an

Fig. 95.   Fig. 96.   Fig. 97.

Fig. 95.—Anterior aspect of the auricles, showing the distribution of the muscular fibres (human). *a*, pulmonary veins *b*, vena cava superior. The great vessels (*a* and *b*) are invested with muscular fibres, and have distinct movements.—*After Gerdy*.

Fig. 96.—Ideal transverse section of the ventricles, showing how the septum which divides the right and left ventricles from each other is formed. The heart originally consists of a single tube. At an early period it is divided by a longitudinal and transverse fold into four c mpartments, two auricles and two ventricles. The ventricles (*b* and *c*) are separated from each other by the fold (*a*) passing in an antero-posterior direction until it touches the posterior wall (*d*) of the ventricles, into which it penetrates and becomes fixed. The two halves of the fold likewise interpenetrate, the septum becoming of nearly the same thickness as the left ventricle, which is the typical ventricle This accounts for the fact that the muscular fibres are continuous on the posterior aspect of the ventricles, and interrupted on the anterior aspect, and hence the old idea that the ventricles are two muscles enveloped in a third. These points are explained at length in my memoir ' On the Arrangement of the Muscular Fibres in the Ventricles of the Vertebrata ;' Phil. Trans. 1864.—*Original*.

Fig 97.—Posterior aspect of the auricles, showing the distribution of the muscular fibres (human). *a a*. pulmonary veins. *c*. vena cava inferior. These are surrounded by muscular fibres, and take part in forcing the blood into the auricles.—*After Gerdy*.

involuntary muscle, its fibres nevertheless possess the dark colour and transverse markings which are characteristic of the voluntary muscles. Unlike the generality of voluntary muscles however, the fibres of the ventricles, as a rule, have neither origin nor insertion ; *i. e.* they are continuous alike at the apex of the ventricles and at the base. They are further distinguished by the almost total absence of cellular tissue as a connecting medium [1] ; the fibres being held together partly by

[1] The little cellular tissue there is, is found more particularly at the base and

splitting up and running into each other, and partly by the minute ramifications of the cardiac vessels and nerves [1]. The manner in which the fibres are attached to each other, while it necessarily secures to the ventricles considerable latitude of motion, also furnishes the means whereby the fibres composing them may be successfully unravelled ; for it is found that by the action of certain reagents, and the application of various kinds of heat, as in roasting and boiling [2], the fibres may be prepared so as readily to separate from each other in layers of greater or lesser thickness. The chief peculiarity consists in the arrangement of the fibres themselves—an arrangement so unusual and perplexing that it has long been considered as forming a kind of Gordian knot in anatomy. Of the complexity of the arrangement I need not speak ; suffice it to say that Vesalius, Albinus, Haller [3], and De Blainville [4] all confessed their inability to unravel it.

Having, in the summer of 1858, made numerous dissections

apex of the ventricles, and is so trifling in quantity as to be altogether, though wrongly, denied by some.

[1] When the vessels of the ventricles are injected in the cold state with some material which will stand heat (as, for example, a mixture of starch and water), and the heart boiled, the larger trunks from either coronary artery are seen to give off a series of minute branches which penetrate the ventricular wall in a direction from without inwards. These branches, when the dissection is conducted to a certain depth, resemble so many bristles transfixing the ventricular wall. As moreover the cardiac nerve-trunks accompany the trunks of the coronary vessels, while the nerve-filaments cross the smaller branches of the vessels and the muscular fibres (to both of which they afford a plentiful supply of nerve-twigs), the influence exerted by the vessels and nerves in uniting or binding the muscular fibres to each other is very considerable. *Vide* Inaugural Prize Dissertation, by the Author, ' On the Arrangement of the Cardiac Nerves, and their connexion with the Cerebro-spinal and Sympathetic Systems in Mammalia,' deposited in the University of Edinburgh Library, March, 1861.

[2] Of the various modes recommended for preparing the ventricles prior to dissection, I prefer that of continued boiling. The time required for the human heart and those of the small quadrupeds, as the sheep, hog, calf, and deer, may vary from four to six hours ; while for the hearts of the larger quadrupeds, as the horse, ox, ass, etc., the boiling should be continued from eight to ten hours ; more than this is unnecessary. A good plan is to stuff the ventricular cavities loosely with bread-crumbs, bran, or some pliant material before boiling, in order, if possible, to distend without overstretching the muscular fibres. If this method be adopted, and the ventricles soaked for a fortnight or so in alcohol before being dissected, the fibres will be found to separate with great facility. Vaust recommended that the heart should be boiled in a solution of nitre ; but nothing is gained by this procedure.

[3] El. Phys., tom. i. p. 351.   [4] Cours de Physiologie, etc., tom. ii. p. 359.

O

of the ventricles, upwards of a hundred of which are preserved in the Anatomical Museum of the University of Edinburgh [1], I have arrived at results which appear to throw additional light on this complex question, and which seem to point to a law in the arrangement, simple in itself, and apparently comprehensive as to detail [2].

The following are a few of the more salient points demonstrated in connexion with this investigation.

I. By exercising due care, I ascertained that the fibres constituting the ventricles are rolled upon each other in such a manner as readily admits of their being separated by dissection into layers or strata, the fibres of each layer being characterised by having a different direction.

II. These layers, owing to the difference in the direction of their fibres, are well marked, and seven in number—viz. three external, a fourth or central, and three internal.

III. Therè is a gradational sequence in the direction of the fibres constituting the layers, whereby they are made gradually to change their course from a nearly vertical direction to a horizontal or transverse one, and from the transverse direction back again to a nearly vertical one. Thus, in dissecting the ventricles from without inwards, the fibres of the first layer, which run in a spiral direction from left to right downwards, are more vertical than those of the second layer, the second than those of the third, the third than those of the fourth— the fibres of the fourth layer having a transverse direction, and running at nearly right angles to those of the first layer. Passing the fourth layer, which occupies a central position in the ventricular walls, and forms the boundary between the external and internal layers, the order of arrangement is reversed, and the fibres of the remaining layers, viz. five, six, and seven, gradually return in an opposite direction, and in an inverse order, to the same relation to the vertical as that maintained by the fibres of the first external layer. This remarkable change in the direction of the fibres constituting the

---

[1] These dissections obtained the Senior Anatomy Gold Medal of the University in the winter of 1859.

[2] ‘On the Arrangement of the Muscular Fibres in the Ventricles of the Vertebrate Heart, with Physiological Remarks,’ by the Author; Philosophical Transactions, 1864.

several external and internal layers, which is observed to occur in all parts of the ventricular walls, whether they be viewed anteriorly, posteriorly, or septally, has been partially figured by Senac[1], and imperfectly described by Reid[2], but has not hitherto been fully elucidated. It has not had that share of attention bestowed upon it which its importance demands.

IV. The fibres composing the external and the internal layers are found at different depths from the surface, and from the fact of their pursuing opposite courses cross each other, the fibres of the first external and last internal layers crossing with a slight deviation from the vertical, as in the letter X; the succeeding external and internal layers, until the fourth or central layer, which is transverse, is reached, crossing at successively wider angles, as may be represented by an ⋈ placed horizontally (Figs. 98, 99, and 100).

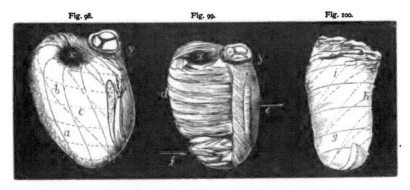

Fig. 98.   Fig. 99.   Fig. 100.

Figs. 98, 99, 100, which are skeleton drawings copied from photographs of my dissections, illustrate the peculiarities in the direction of the fibres of the left ventricle, which I regard as the typical one.
The solid lines (a) of Fig. 98 represent the external fibres constituting the first layer; the dotted lines (i) of Fig. 100 representing the corresponding internal fibres forming the seventh layer. The interrupted lines (b) of Fig. 98 represent the fibres of the second layer, the interrupted lines (h) of Fig. 100 the fibres of the sixth or corresponding layer. The dotted lines (c) of Fig. 98 represent the fibres of the third layer, the continuous lines (g) of Fig. 100 the fibres of the fifth or corresponding layer. At d, e of Fig. 99 the fibres constituting the central or fourth layer are seen; all the fibres to the outside of this layer being external, all to the inside of it internal. The fibres are spiral in their nature, and Fig. 99 is particularly interesting as showing the point at which the external fibres reverse their course and become internal. They wind in the direction d, e (vide arrow) round the left apex, and reappear at f. x, left auriculo-ventricular opening. y, aortic orifice, with semilunar valve closed.—Original.

V. The fibres composing corresponding external and internal layers, such as layers one and seven, two and six, etc., are continuous in the left ventricle at the left apex (Fig. 102, p. 197), and in the right ventricle in the track for the anterior

---

[1] Traité de la Structure du Cœur, de son Action, etc. Paris, 1749.
[2] Cyc. of Anat. and Phys., art. 'Heart.' London, 1839.

coronary artery ; the fibres of both ventricles being for the most part continuous likewise at the base [1] (Fig. 94, p. 190).

VI. From this distribution of the fibres it follows that the first and seventh layers embrace in their convolutions those immediately beneath them, while these in turn embrace those next in succession, and so on until the central layer is reached —an arrangement which explains alike the rolling movements and powerful action of the ventricles. It also accounts for the spiral shape of the ventricular cavities, and the fact that the blood is literally wrung out of the ventricles during the systole.

VII. The fibres of the right and left ventricles anteriorly and septally are to a certain extent independent of each other ; whereas posteriorly many of them are common to both ventricles ; *i.e.* the fibres pass from the one ventricle to the other —an arrangement which induced Winslow [2] to regard the heart as composed of two muscles enveloped in a third (Fig. 96, p. 192). It will be evident from this distribution of the fibres, that while the ventricles are for obvious reasons intimately united, they nevertheless admit of being readily separated (Fig. 101, p. 197).

VIII. If the hinge-like mass of fibres (common fibres) which unite the right ventricle to the left posteriorly be cut through, and the right ventricle with its portion of the septum detached, the left ventricle, which consists of four sets of conical-shaped spiral fibres—two external and two internal sets—will be found to be nearly as complete as it was before the separation took place (Figs. 98, 99, and 100, p. 195). The right ventricle, and its share of the septum, on the other hand, will be found to consist of only conical-shaped spiral fragments of fibres, or at most of flattened rings—a circumstance which has induced me to regard the left ventricle as the typical or complete one, the right ventricle being a mere segment or portion nipped off at some period or other from the left (Fig. 96, *c*, p. 192).

[1] The late Dr. Duncan, jun., of Edinburgh, was aware of the fibres forming loops at the base, but seems to have had no knowledge of the continuity being occasioned by the union of the fibres of corresponding external and internal layers, or that these basal loops were prolongations of like loops formed by similar corresponding external and internal layers at the apex—a view which the author believes is here set forth for the first time.

[2] Mémoires de l'Académie Royale des Sciences, 1711, p. 197.

IX. If the right ventricular walls be cut through immediately to the right of the track for the anterior and posterior coronary arteries, so as to detach the right ventricle without disturbing the septum, and the septum be regarded as forming part of the left ventricular wall, it will be found that the fibres from the right side of the septum, at no great depth from the surface, together with the external fibres from the left ventricular wall generally, enter the left apex in two sets (Fig. 102); and if their course in the interior (Fig. 103, *m*, *n*) be traced, they are observed to extend in

Fig. 101.   Fig. 102.   Fig. 103.

Fig. 101.—Right and left ventricles of mammal seen posteriorly (human). Shows how the fibres issue from the right and left auriculo-ventricular openings (*c*, *d*); the fibres from the left opening passing from the left ventricle (*e*) across septum (*f*) to the right ventricle (*g*). Of these some curve in a downward direction and disappear in the left apex; others curve round anteriorly and disappear in the anterior coronary groove. Compare with Fig. 96, p. 192. *b*, orifice of pulmonary artery.—*Original.*

Fig. 102 shows how the two sets of external fibres (*a b*, *c d*) of the left ventrical curve round and form a beautiful whorl prior to entering the left apex to become the two sets of internal fibres known as the musculi papillares, seen at *m*, *n* of Fig. 103. The fibres twist into each other at the apex in the same way that the segments of the mitral, tricuspid, and semilunar valves twist into each other at the base. Compare with Figs 85 and 86.—*Original.*

Fig. 103.—Musculi papillares (*m*, *n*), chordae tendineae and mitral valve (*v*, *v*) of left ventricle of deer. Shows how the musculi papillares, which are continuations of corresponding external fibres, are spiral in their nature, and how, when they alternately elongate and shorten, they alternately liberate and drag upon the segments of the mitral valve in a spiral manner; this, in conjunction with the blood, causing the segments to wedge and screw into each other, first in an upward and then in a downward direction (Fig. 85). The segments of the mitral and tricuspid valves rise and fall like diaphragms when the ventricles open and close. They alternately increase and diminish the cavities of the ventricles. Similar remarks may be made of the semilunar valves situated at the orifices of the pulmonary artery and aorta. Compare Fig. 85 with Fig. 86.—*Original.*

the direction of the left auriculo-ventricular opening, also in two sets; in other words, the left ventricle is bilateral. I wish particularly to direct attention to this bilateral distribution, as it has been hitherto overlooked, and furnishes the clue to the arrangement of the fibres of the left ventricle.

X. The double entrance of the fibres of the several layers at the left apex, and their exit in two portions from the auriculo-ventricular openings at the base, are regulated with almost mathematical precision; so that while the one set of fibres invariably enters the apex posteriorly, and issues from the auriculo-ventricular opening anteriorly, the other set as invariably enters the apex anteriorly and escapes from the auriculo-ventricular opening posteriorly. But for this disposition of the fibres, the apex and the base would have been like the barrel of a pen cut slantingly or lop-sided, instead of bilaterally symmetrical as they are.

XI. The two sets of fibres which constitute the superficial or first external layer of the left ventricle, and which enter the left apex in two separate portions or bundles, are for the most part continuous in the interior with the musculi papillares (Fig. 103, *m, n*, p. 197), to the free ends of which the chordae tendineae are attached. The musculi papillares, as will be seen from this account, bear an important relation to the segments of the mitral valve (*v, v*), to which they are directly connected by tendinous bands. The musculi papillares from this circumstance merit a more particular description than that given of the other fibres.

On looking at the left auriculo-ventricular opening, the fibres of the first layer are seen to arise from the fibrous ring surrounding the aorta (Fig. 94, *b*, p. 190), and from the auriculo-ventricular tendinous ring (*d*) in two divisions: the one division proceeding *from the anterior portions of the rings*, and winding in a spiral, nearly vertical, direction, from before backwards, to converge and enter the apex *posteriorly* (Fig. 102, *b*, p. 197); the other set proceeding *from the posterior portions of the rings*, and winding in a spiral direction from behind forwards, to converge and enter the apex *anteriorly* (Fig. 102, *d*, p. 197). Having entered the apex, the two sets of external fibres are collected together, and form the musculi papillares and carneae columnae; the one set, viz. that which proceeded from the auriculo-ventricular orifice anteriorly and entered the apex posteriorly, curving round in a spiral direction from right to left upwards, and forming *the anterior musculus papillaris* (Fig. 103, *n*, p. 197), *and the carneae columnae next to it;* the other set, which proceeded from the auriculo-ventricular orifice posteriorly, and entered the apex anteriorly, curving round in a corresponding spiral direction, and forming *the posterior musculus papillaris* (Fig. 103, *m*, p. 197) *and adjoining carneae columnae.* As the external fibres converge on nearing the apex, so the internal continuations of these fibres radiate towards the base; and hence the conical shape of the musculi papillares (*m, n*). I am particular in directing attention to the course and position of the musculi papillares, as they have always, though erroneously, been regarded as simply vertical columns, instead of more or less vertical *spiral* columns. The necessity for insisting upon this distinction will appear more evident when I come to speak of the influence exerted by these structures on the segments of the bicuspid valve. It is worthy of remark that while the left apex is closed by two sets of spiral fibres (Fig. 102, p. 197), the left auriculo-ventricular orifice is occluded during the systole by the two spiral flaps or segments constituting the bicuspid valve (Fig. 105, *m, n*, p. 200). (Compare with Figs. 85 and 86, p. 174.) The bilateral arrangement, therefore, which obtains in all parts of the left ventricle and in the musculi papillares, extends also to the segments of the bicuspid valve, and hence its name. What has been said of the arrangement of the fibres in the left ventricle applies with slight modifications to the fibres of the right one; and many are of opinion (and I also incline to the belief) that the tricuspid valve (Fig. 85, p. 174) is in reality bicuspid in its nature. It is so in not a few cases, as shown at *g, h* of Fig. 105, p. 200. The shape of the ventricular cavities of the heart of the mammal greatly influences the movements of the mitral and tricuspid valves, by moulding the blood into certain forms, and causing it to act in certain directions. A precise outline of the ventricular cavities is obtained by filling the ventricles with wax or plaster of Paris, these substances when allowed to harden furnishing an accurate cast of the parts (*vide* Figs. 104–106, p. 200).

The form of the left ventricular cavity, which, as already stated, I regard as typical, is that of a double cone twisted upon itself (Fig. 104, p. 200); the twist or spiral running from right to left of the spectator, and being especially well marked towards the apex[1]. The cone tapers towards the apex of the left ventricle (*y*), and also towards the base (*b*); and the direction of its spiral corresponds with the direction of the

[1] In this description the heart is supposed to be placed on its apex, with its posterior aspect towards the spectator.

fibres of the carneae columnae and musculi papillares (Fig. 104, x, y). As the two spiral musculi papillares project into the ventricular cavity, it follows that between them two conical-shaped spiral depressions or grooves· are found (Fig. 104, q, j). These grooves, which appear as spiral ridges in the cast, are unequal in size ; the smaller one (Fig. 104, j) beginning at the right side of the apex, and winding in an upward spiral direction to terminate at the base of the external or left and smaller segment of the bicuspid valve (Fig. 105, n) ; the larger groove (Fig. 104, q) beginning at the

Fig. 104.   Fig. 105.   Fig. 106.

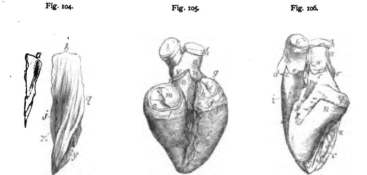

Fig. 104.—Wax cast of left ventricle (b) and portion of right ventricle (a) of deer. Shows spiral nature of the left ventricular cavity,—the spiral courses or tracks of the musculi papillares (x, y), and how, between the musculi papillares, two spiral grooves (j, q) are found (they are spiral ridges in the cast), which conduct the blood to the segments of the mitral valve in spiral waves.—*Original.*

Fig. 105.—Plaster of Paris cast of right and left ventricles of zebra, seen posteriorly. Shows the mitral (m, n) and tricuspid (g, h) valves in action, and how the blood, when these are closed, assumes a conical form (o) for pushing aside the segments of the semilunar valves, and causing them to fall back upon the sinuses of Valsalva (v, w). It also shows how the right ventricular cavity (c) curves round the left one (x), and how the pulmonary artery (b) and aorta (h) pursue different directions. a, beginning of aorta. l, portion of left ventricle adhering to plaster of Paris. f, ditto of right ventricle, q, spiral groove conducting to aorta.—*Original.*

Fig. 106.—Plaster of Paris cast of right and left ventricles of zebra, as seen from the left side. Shows infundibulum or conus arteriosus (i) of right ventricle, and analogous portion of left ventricle (p, a) ; also three prominences on each (d, e, k, r, v), corresponding to the sinuses of Valsalva. It also shows the double cone formed by the left ventricular cavity, the one apex pointing towards the apex of the heart (j), the other towards the aorta (h). y, portion of anterior musculus papillaris adhering to plaster of Paris. x, portion of posterior musculus papillaris. n, spiral groove between musculi papillares corresponding to q of Fig. 104. c, portion of muscular wall of septum. l, portion of base of left ventricle. x, conical space of pulmonary artery where two of the segments of the semilunar valve join each other. w, point where coronary artery is given off. b, pulmonary artery. h, aorta.—*Original.*

left side of the apex, and pursuing a similar direction, to terminate at the base of the internal or right and larger segment (Fig. 105, m).

Running between the grooves in question, and corresponding to the septal aspect of the ventricular cavity, is yet another groove, larger than either of the others (Fig. 105, q). The third or remaining groove winds from the interior of the apex posteriorly, and conducts to the aorta (a), which, as you are aware, is situated anteriorly. The importance of these grooves physiologically cannot be over-estimated, for I find that in them the blood is moulded into three spiral columns, and that, during the systole, the blood in the two lesser ones is forced in an upward direction in two spiral streams upon the under surfaces of the segments of the bicuspid valve, which are in this way progressively elevated towards the base, and twisted and wedged into each other, until regurgitation is rendered impossible (Fig. 105, *m*, *n*). When the bicuspid valve is fairly closed, the blood is directed towards the third and largest groove, which, as has been explained, communicates with the aorta. The spiral action of the mitral valve, and the spiral motion communicated to the blood when projected from the heart, are due to the spiral arrangement of the musculi papillares and fibres composing the ventricle, as well as to the spiral shape of the left ventricular cavity.

What has been said of the conical shape of the left ventricular cavity and aorta applies, with slight alterations, to the right ventricular cavity and pulmonary artery (Figs. 105 and 106, *c*, *i*), the cones formed by the latter being flattened out and applied to or round the left ones.

Analogy between the Muscular Arrangements and Movements of the Hollow Viscera (Heart, Stomach, Bladder, Uterus, etc.), and those of the Trunk and Extremities of Vertebrates.— The distribution and direction of the muscles and muscular fibres of the trunk and extremities of vertebrates accords in a wonderful manner with that just described in the ventricles of the heart of the mammal; the arrangement of the muscular fibres in the ventricles closely corresponding with that in the stomach, bladder, and uterus. This is a remarkable circumstance, and merits the attention of all interested in homologies. If, *e.g.*, the thoracic portion of the human trunk be examined, we find longitudinal, slightly oblique, oblique, and transverse muscles, arranged symmetrically and in pairs as in the ventricles. Thus, in the region of the thorax anteriorly we have the symmetrical muscular masses constituting the pectorals and deltoids, the fibres of which are arranged vertically, transversely, and at various degrees of obliquity. The fibres of these muscles if produced would intersect as in the ventricles. Beneath the pectorals and deltoids we find the external and internal intercostal muscles running obliquely and crossing each other as in the letter X ; while the serrati muscles run transversely and nearly at right angles to both (Fig. 107).

In the region of the abdomen this arrangement is repeated. Thus, we have the recti muscles running in the direction of the length of the trunk ; the transversales abdominis running across the trunk or at right angles to the recti ; and the external and internal oblique muscles running diagonally between the recti and transversales and crossing each other (Fig. 109).

Fig. 107.   Fig. 108.   Fig. 109.

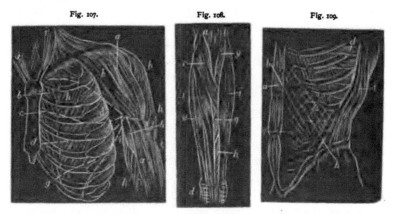

Figs. 107, 108, and 109 show how the muscles of the human chest, arm, forearm, and abdomen run in vertical, slightly oblique, oblique, and transverse directions, as in the heart (left ventricle), and cross, or tend to cross, each other. Compare the letters of these figures with corresponding letters of Figs. 98, 99, and 100, p. 195.—*Original.*

Proceeding to the posterior and lateral aspect of the thoracic region of the trunk a similar arrangement presents itself. Thus, in the trapezii we have the homologues of the pectorals with fibres running in a more or less longitudinal direction, obliquely and transversely, and which would intersect if produced. Beneath the trapezii we have the rhomboidei and splenii crossing obliquely as in the letter X. The longitudinal muscles of this region are represented by the levatores anguli scapulae, the accessorii, the longissimi dorsi, spinales dorsi, and semi-spinales dorsi. The slightly oblique muscles are represented by the levatores costarum, the multifidi spinae, the transversales colli, etc. ; and the transverse muscles by the serrati.

Proceeding to the loins and the region corresponding to the abdomen behind, the arrangement again repeats itself. In the quadrati lumborum, erectores spinalis, and sacri lumbalis, we have longitudinal muscles; in the multifidi spinae, slightly oblique muscles; and in the latissimi dorsi, oblique muscles. If therefore I eliminate the element of bone from the thorax and abdomen, there will remain a muscular mass with fibres running longitudinally, slightly obliquely, obliquely, and transversely; the longitudinal muscles intersecting the transverse muscles at right angles, the slightly oblique muscles intersecting each other at acute angles, and the oblique ones at obtuse angles, symmetrically as in the ventricles of the heart. We have consequently in the thorax and abdomen two hollow muscular masses closely allied to the auricles and ventricles of the heart; the one opening when the other closes, and *vice versa*. This follows because the bones of the trunk, while they transmit, do not originate movement. Nor does the resemblance stop here. Between the thorax and abdomen there is a movable muscular partition—the diaphragm, which descends when the thorax opens and the abdomen closes. A precisely similar function is performed by the mitral and tricuspid valves of the heart, two tendinous structures situated between the auricles and ventricles. The thoracic and abdominal movements are correlated for the reception and discharge of air, food, urine, faeces, etc., in the same way that the movements of the auricles and ventricles are correlated for the reception and discharge of blood. The thorax may be said to pump and suck air; the heart blood. In the diaphragm, the muscular fibres are arranged at right angles, slightly obliquely, and obliquely, as in the ventricles, thorax, and abdomen. This curious muscle may consequently be compared to half a heart, half a stomach, or half a bladder. The diaphragm, like the hollow viscera, chest, abdomen, etc., acts by alternately shortening and elongating its fibres. When it elongates its fibres, it ascends and diminishes the floor of the thorax; when it shortens them, it descends and enlarges the floor of the thorax. This arrangement provides for the diaphragm oscillating on either side of a given line. The diaphragm ascends when the ribs descend, and *vice versa*. The ascent of the diaphragm and the descent of the ribs diminish the capacity of the thorax, and increase that of the abdomen; the descent of the diaphragm and the ascent of the ribs increase the capacity of the thorax, and diminish that of the abdomen. When the thorax expands and the abdomen closes, a wave of motion passes from the symphysis pubis in the direction of the ensiform cartilage; a reverse wave passing from above downwards when the abdomen expands and the thorax closes. The lines representing these waves of motion cross each other figure-of-8 fashion in forced expiration and inspiration. The muscular arrangement described in the hollow viscera and in the human trunk appear in a simpler form in the body of the fish. They are seen to advantage in the body of the manatee, a sea mammal in which the extremities are rudimentary [1]. They reappear in the extremities when these are sufficiently developed. Thus, in the human arm the biceps represents the longitudinal fibres, the supinator longus and flexor carpi radialis the slightly oblique fibres, the pronator radii teres and flexor sublimis digitorum the oblique fibres, and the pronator quadratus the transverse fibres (Fig. 108, p. 202).

Stranger than all, the bones of the extremities are twisted upon themselves and correspond to the mould or cast obtained from the cavity of the left ventricle, which shows that the bones mould and adapt themselves to the muscles, and not the converse. The muscles of the extremities are arranged around their bones as the muscles of the ventricles are arranged around their cavities. These points are illustrated at Figs. 110–112, p. 205.

As the soft tissues precede the hard in the scale of being, I am disposed to tabulate the muscles thus:—1st, The heart and hollow muscles, which act independently of bone; 2nd, The muscles of the trunk, which act in conjunction with bone; 3rd, The muscles of the extremities, also geared to bone. I place the hollow muscles first, because they are found before any trunk proper exists; the trunk muscles second, because the thorax and abdomen precede the limbs; and the muscles of the extremities third, because the limbs are differentiations which are only found in the higher animals.

[1] *Vide* a very splendid memoir on this rare animal by Dr. James Murie, Trans. Zool. Soc. vol. viii. plate 21.

As bones appear comparatively late in the scale of being, I am inclined to regard the hollow involuntary muscles as typical of the solid voluntary muscles, both as to the direction of their fibres and mode of action. The term solid is here applied to the voluntary muscles from the fact that they invest bones and have no cavities in their interior; the involuntary muscles, on the other hand, surround cavities and have no connexion with bone. The fibres of the ventricles, as explained, are arranged longitudinally, transversely, and at various degrees of obliquity, symmetrically, and with something like mathematical accuracy. The fibres are not to be

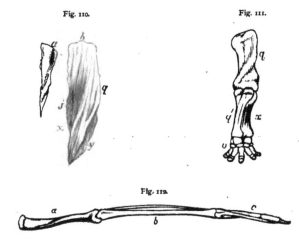

Fig. 110.   Fig. 111.

Fig. 112.

Fig. 110.—Photograph of a cast of the left ventricle of the heart of a deer. Shows the spiral nature of the left ventricular cavity. (For further description see Fig. 104.)—*Original.*
Fig. 111.—Bones of the anterior extremity of the elephant. Shows the spiral arrangement of the bones of the fore leg. (Compare with Fig. 110.) *q*, humerus. *x*, *q′*, radius and ulna. *o*, bones of foot.—*Original.*
Fig. 112.—Bones of the wing of a bird. Shows their spiral arrangement. (Compare with Figs. 110 and 111.) The bones of the human arm resemble those of the fore-limb of the elephant and the wing of the bird. *a*, humerus. *b*, radius and ulna. *c*, bones of the hand.—*Original.*

regarded as in any sense antagonistic. Thus the longitudinal fibres do not pull against the transverse, or the various oblique fibres against each other. On the contrary, the fibres act together and consentaneously. When the ventricle is to be closed, all the fibres shorten and broaden; when it is to be opened, they all elongate and narrow. These movements are definitely co-ordinated. The muscles do not exhaust themselves in a suicidal warfare. The function of the ventricles is to draw in and eject blood, and this can only be done economically in the manner explained. In like manner analogy and a variety of circumstances, to be alluded to presently, incline me to believe that the muscular masses found in the thorax, abdomen, and extremities, are not arranged to antagonise each other, and that the flexors, pronators, and abductors do not when they shorten forcibly drag out the extensors, supinators, and adductors. On the contrary, I believe that all these movements are co-ordinated as in the heart; the extensors, supinators, and adductors elongating when the flexors, pronators, and abductors shorten, and *vice versa;* there being, in short, no such thing as antagonism in muscular movements. It does not follow that because one muscle is situated upon one aspect of a bone or bones, and a second muscle upon another and opposite aspect of the same bone or bones, that therefore the two muscles antagonise or contend with each other. When a muscle by its shortening is intended to stretch another substance, that substance as a rule is simply elastic, *i.e.* it has no power of originating movement. We have examples of this in the blood-vessels and the wing of the bird.

The chief function of the voluntary muscles is to move bones. To move bones effectually and avoid waste there must be conservation of energy. To conserve energy, the muscles of necessity act upon the bones to be moved and not upon each other. The muscles consequently are correlated and their movements co-ordinated. To say one muscle acts against another muscle, is equivalent to saying a muscle acts against itself, and of this we have no proof. In the penniform and other compound muscles, where the fibres meet at a variety of angles and tend to cross, all the fibres shorten and elongate at the same time as in the heart. In the muscular masses investing universal joints, such as are found at the shoulders and pelvis, precisely the same thing happens. The fibres, whatever their length, strength, or direction, act together, and by their united efforts produce an infinite variety of movements. These masses, when acting in conjunction with the muscles of the extremities, can rotate the bones to which they are attached in the same way that the heart can wring out its blood and tilt its apex.

Before leaving the subject of muscular arrangements, it may be useful to recapitulate very briefly.

In the smallest blood-vessels only one set of muscular fibres is present, these running around the vessels. In the larger blood-vessels two sets of muscular fibres are found, these being arranged at right angles to each other; the one set running across the vessels, and the other in the direction of their length[1]. The same arrangement obtains in the intestine, the muscular tunic of the worm, and many simple structures. In the ventricles of the heart, the stomach, bladder, uterus, thorax, abdomen, and the extremities, the muscular fibres are arranged at right angles and obliquely, but always symmetrically and in pairs. The muscles of the tongue afford a good example. In this organ a large proportion of the inherent muscles are arranged in the form of a St. Andrew's cross. Thus there are longitudinal fibres which traverse the tongue from side to side; others which traverse the tongue from above downwards or vertically. Between these two sets of fibres, which intersect each other at right angles, there are others, which converge towards the axis of the organ, and which intersect or tend to intersect at gradually increasing angles, but always in pairs, as in the heart. To these are to be added a sheath of longitudinal fibres which traverse the tongue in the direction of its length. The universality of the movements of the tongue is well known. The tongue certainly possesses an inherent power of elongating and shortening; indeed in many of the ruminants it takes the place of a hand. When the tongue elongates, its cross fibres shorten and broaden; in other words, elongate in the direction of the length of the tongue; the longitudinal fibres elongating in the

---

[1] In some of the larger veins, there are two sets of muscular fibres, the one running in the direction of the length of the vessel, the other across it. Thus in addition to the circular fibres always present in the central layers, there are longitudinal fibres mixed up with the areolar tissue and longitudinal elastic fibres of the external layer, which extend the whole length of the inferior vena cava, the renal, azygos, and external iliac veins, and in all the large trunks of the portal venous system, and in the trunks of the hepatic veins. Muscular tissue is also abundantly developed in the veins of the gravid uterus, being found in all three coats, and in the venae cavae and pulmonary veins it is prolonged on to them from the auricles of the heart. Muscular tissue is wanting in the veins of the maternal part of the placenta, in most of the cerebral veins and sinuses of the dura mater, in the veins of the retina, in the veins of the cancellous tissue of bones, and in the venous spaces of the corpora cavernosa.—*Anatomy, Descriptive and Surgical*, by Henry Gray, F.R.S. etc.; p. 401.

same direction and at the same time. These movements are reversed when the tongue shortens. The muscles situated at the root of the tongue are arranged on a similar principle; these, when they elongate, pushing out the tongue, and when they shorten drawing it in. This follows because the major portion of the muscles of the tongue are not attached to bone, and therefore have no fixed points.

Structure and Properties of Voluntary and Involuntary Muscles.—The voluntary and involuntary muscular systems at first sight appear to have few things in common. In reality they have many; the one being a modification or differentiation of the other. The common parent of the involuntary and voluntary muscle is the nucleated cell, and to this both may be referred [1].

Involuntary Muscle.—The fibres of the involuntary muscles are non-striated or unstriped, *i.e.* they possess no transverse markings. They consist of elongated spindle-shaped fibre-cells, which are flat, clear, granular, and brittle, so that they break off suddenly, and present a square extremity. Many of them display a rod-shaped nucleus in their interior. They occur in the arteries, lymphatics, stomach, intestine, bladder, the pregnant uterus, the ducts of glands, the gall-bladder, vesiculi seminales, etc.

Voluntary Muscle.—The fibres of foetal voluntary muscle display in their substance the nuclei of the cells from

---

[1] 'The researches of Valentine and Schwann have shown that a muscle (voluntary) consists in the earliest stages of a mass of nucleated cells, which first arrange themselves in a linear series with more or less regularity, and then unite to constitute the elementary fibres. As this process of agglutination of the cells is going forward, a deposit of contractile material gradually takes place within them, commencing on the inner surface and advancing to the centre till the whole is solidified. The deposit occurs in granules, which as they come into view, are seen to be disposed in the utmost order *in longitudinal and transverse rows*. From the very first period these granules are part of a mass, and not independent of one another. The involuntary fibres are apparently homogeneous in texture. They however, in some cases, present a mottled granular appearance, the granules being arranged in a linear series. This condition Bowman is inclined to regard as an approximation towards the structure of the striped or voluntary fibre; the granules being of about the same size as those in the voluntary fibres. In the simple muscles of the lower animals, consisting in some cases of only one or two rows of sarcous elements, a transition from the striped towards the unstriped fibres may be perceived; the transverse markings under these circumstances being irregular, broken, or faintly marked.'

which they are developed (Fig. 113 B, *a*, *a*); these corresponding to the rod-shaped nuclei of the involuntary muscle (Fig. 113 A, *a*). The striae are very faintly marked (Fig. 113 B, C). The fibres of the adult voluntary muscles, on the other hand, are distinctly striated or striped, *i.e.* they display a series of symmetrical, longitudinal, and transverse markings, as shown at Fig. 113 D, E, F, G, H, I.

A voluntary fibre consequently consists of an aggregation of square particles arranged with great regularity in symmetrical rows (Figs. 113 D, H). Each fibre is covered by a thin transparent elastic membrane, the sarcolemma, which isolates the one fibre from the other (Fig. 113 E, *a*). The involuntary

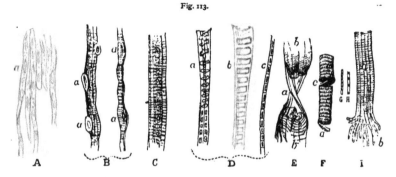

Fig. 113.

A   B   C   D   E   F   I

Fig. 113.—A, Unstriped elementary fibres from human colon ; treated with and without acetic acid. B, elementary fibres from pectoral muscle of foetal calf, two and a half months old, showing corpuscles *a*, *a*, magnified 300 diameters. C, elementary fibres from larva of dragon-fly, in an early stage of development, showing central row of corpuscles, magnified 300 diameters.—*Bowman*. D, muscular fibrils of pig, magnified 720 diameters. *c*, single fibril, showing quadrangular outline of component particles, their dark central part and bright margin and their lines of junction crossing the light intervals. *b*, longitudinal segment of fibre, consisting of a number of fibrils still connected together, *a*, other smaller collections of fibrils.—*From a Preparation by Mr. Leatham, after Dr. Sharpey.*

E.—Fragment of an elementary fibre of the skate, held together by the untorn and twisted sarcolemma. *a*, sarcolemma ; *b*, *b*, opposite fragments of the fibre.

F.—Fragment of striped elementary fibres, showing transverse cleavage (*c*, *d*) of sarcous elements. The longitudinal cleavage is seen at *b* of I. G, H, appearances presented by the separated single fibrillae. At G the borders are scalloped and the spaces bead-like. At H the borders and transverse lines are all perfectly rectilinear, and the included spaces perfectly rectangular. The latter is the more common.—*After Bowman.*

fibre is not invested with this membrane. The voluntary differs from the involuntary fibre in being of a cylindrical shape.

Much confusion unfortunately exists as to the utimate composition of the voluntary muscles, and the nature of the striation. Some are of opinion that the elementary particles of which a fibrilla is composed consist of rows of corpuscles or discs connected by a homogeneous transparent material; others believing that they consist of little masses of pellucid

P

substance, possibly nucleated cells, which because of the pressure to which they are subjected, present a rectangular outline, and appear dark in the centre. Bowman, who has devoted much attention to this subject, describes and figures a longitudinal and transverse cleavage (Fig. 113 I, F, p. 209). He says, 'Sometimes the fibre will split into discs only (Fig. 113 F, *c, d,* p. 209), more often into fibrillae only (Fig. 113 I, *b,* p. 209) ; but there are always present in it the transverse and the longitudinal lines which mark the two cleavages' (Fig. 113 I, *a,* p. 209). He delineates two fibrillae, in one of which the borders and transverse lines are all perfectly rectilinear, and the enclosed spaces perfectly rectangular (Fig. 113 H, p. 209) ; in the other, the borders are scalloped, and the spaces are bead-like (Fig. 113 G, p. 209). When most distinct and definite the fibrilla presents the former of those appearances. The ultimate particles, or sarcous elements, as they have been termed, are merely indicated when the fibre is entire ; the dark and light squares being blended together and forming a continuous structure. It is only when the fibre is injured, and partly disintegrated, that the alternate squares can be seen to advantage (Fig. 116, p. 218). The squares in question exist under all circumstances ; their number and form being imprinted in the very structure of the fibre in its perfect state. In virtue of the longitudinal and transverse cleavage which takes place, a muscle may be separated into its longitudinal fibrillae and transverse discs. 'To detach a fibrilla entire is to remove a particle from every disc, and to take away a disc is to abstract a particle of every fibrilla.' The dark and light markings are due not to an actual difference in colour in the sarcous elements, but to unequal refracting power. This can be shown by altering the focus of the microscope ; the dark and light lines being by this means made to change places. Some aver that in living muscle no lines are visible ; but the fact that the dead muscle coagulates and disintegrates, or breaks up into square patches, tends to prove that the sarcous elements differ in some way from the material which connects them, and that there are at least two substances in an ultimate muscular fibre. I direct attention to the sarcous elements so admirably described and figured by Bowman, because I think they furnish us with a means of explaining the manner in which voluntary and involuntary muscles shorten and lengthen.

Mixed Muscles.—Between the involuntary and voluntary muscles are a mixed class which run the one into the other· by gentle gradations. Thus the mammalian heart, the lymphatic hearts of reptiles and birds, the stomach and intestines of some fish, and the upper part of the oesophagus, are all involuntary muscles, and yet they possess the transverse markings distinctive of the voluntary muscles. The movements of the voluntary and involuntary muscles likewise run into each other. Thus 'many involuntary movements are performed by muscles which are subject to the will; and many muscles that are commonly independent of the will are liable to be affected by it or by other acts of the mind. More than all, whether a muscle is involuntary or not, depends not on itself, but on the nervous system; for if the brain be removed or inactive, all the muscles become involuntary ones.'

Muscles can act in Two Directions; Sarcous Elements of Muscle—Peculiar Movements of.—The first fact to be fixed in the mind when attempting to comprehend the action of a muscle, is the remarkable one, that when a muscle contracts or shortens, it bulges out laterally, and elongates transversely. This follows, because when a muscle acts, its volume remains always the same.

In order that a muscle may shorten in the direction of its length and elongate in the direction of its breadth, and the converse, its ultimate particles, whatever their shape, must have the power of acting in two directions, viz. in the direction of the length of the muscle, and across it.

Muscular Motion as bearing on the Functions performed by the Heart, Blood-vessels, Thorax, Extremities, etc.—With a view to forming a just estimate of the manner in which muscles act, it is necessary to take a wide survey of those substances which we know are capable of changing shape, and which take part in locomotion and other vital manifestations. This becomes especially necessary when we remember that some physiologists maintain that even the striation in voluntary muscles is due not to the presence of two substances, but simply to unequal refraction and the play of light. The advocates of this view regard the substance of voluntary

muscle as homogeneous; the dark and light sarcous elements
or squares constituting the longitudinal and transverse striae
being in their opinion all of the same colour. The striae,
as stated, are absent in involuntary muscles, and very faintly
indicated in young voluntary muscles, so that we must not
lay too much stress on the transverse markings, which may,
after all, be an optical delusion. When I employ the term
sarcous element, cube, or square, I wish it to represent
a definite portion of the muscular mass having that particular form. The dark and light sarcous elements may or
may not have exactly the same chemical constitution, but
this does not interfere with the property which both possess
of changing shape, and this it is which distinguishes muscular and all other forms of movement occurring in the
tissues. The movements of the voluntary and involuntary
muscles are in some senses identical. As voluntary muscle
is a development and differentiation of involuntary muscle,
so voluntary movements are to be regarded as higher manifestations of involuntary movements. In the involuntary
muscle there is a recognisable structure (Fig. 113, A, p. 209), and
in the voluntary muscle that structure apparently becomes
more elaborate (Fig. 113, D, p. 209); but movements definitely
co-ordinated, and very precise in their nature, can occur in
tissues which are structureless or homogeneous; and this is
a point not to be overlooked when studying the movements
of the voluntary and involuntary muscles, for it shows that
structure, in the ordinary acceptation of the term, is not
necessary to motion. Thus, the amoeba, which consists of
a soft jelly mass, can change its shape in any direction it
pleases. It can, as I have ascertained from actual observation, push out or draw in a knuckle of any part of its
body. These movements are not due to contraction in the
ordinary sense of the term, for the portion of the body
protruded is wedge-shaped; no trace of constriction being
anywhere visible. They are doubtless referable to a centripetal and centrifugal power inhering in the protoplasmic
mass which enables the creature to advance or elongate,
and withdraw or shorten, any part of its body. At times
the amoeba elongates its entire body by a wave-like movement, after which it sends out lateral processes which

exactly correspond with the bulgings produced on a muscular fibre when it is made to contract or shorten under the microscope. When it sends out the lateral processes or elongates in the direction of its breadth, the body of the animal is shortened. When the lateral processes are shortened, the body of the animal is elongated. The analogy between the movements of an amoeba and those of a muscular fibre, or a portion thereof, is therefore complete. Indeed there is every reason to believe that the movements of the amoeba and the sarcous elements of a muscle are identical. Both can change their form, elongation in one direction entailing shortening in another and opposite direction. In either case change of form does not involve change of volume, this always remaining exactly the same. Similar properties are possessed by the mushroom-shaped disc of the medusa. This consists of a jelly mass devoid of muscular fibre. The animal advances by a deliberate opening and closing of its disc; these movements, as I have fully satisfied myself from an attentive examination of living specimens, being quite independent of each other. The disc opens slowly and closes rapidly, as in the heart; the disc when it closes forcing itself from the surface of a fluid wedge with considerable energy. Here the centripetal and centrifugal power which I am disposed to claim for muscle, and especially for hollow muscles—such as the heart, stomach, bladder, uterus, blood-vessels, etc.,—is seen to perfection. When the disc closes, the substance of the animal converges and seeks the centre; when the disc opens, its substance diverges and avoids the centre. The closing movement is the result of a vital converging, closing, or shortening of all the particles composing the body; the opening movement being the result of a vital diverging, expanding, or elongating of the same particles. This follows because the fluid in which the medusa is immersed can take no part either in the closing or opening of the disc. The movements of the *Salpa cristata* still more closely resemble those of the heart (Fig. 114, p. 214). The salpa may very properly be compared to the left ventricle. Thus it is a conical-shaped bag supplied with two apertures; one of which, situated at the extremity of the animal (*b*), corre-

sponds to the auriculo-ventricular orifice; the other, situated
at the mouth (*a*), to the orifice of the aorta. The orifice
corresponding to the auriculo-ventricular

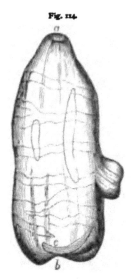

Fig. 114.

opening is supplied with a valve (*c*)
which may be compared to the mitral
valve. When the animal wishes to advance it expands, and draws or sucks
water into its body by the aperture
furnished with the valve. It then by
a centripetal movement closes its body
and the valve, and by so doing forces
the water out of its interior at the
aperture which corresponds to the orifice
of the aorta. By this expedient the
salpa confers on its body a retrograde
movement. The fact to be attended
to in the movements of this simple
creature is the power it possesses of
expanding and drawing water into its
interior, which it subsequently forcibly
ejects. It thus exerts a pulling and
pushing power, similar to that exercised
by the left ventricle or any other compartment of the heart.

Fig. 114.—Salpa cristata. *a*, orifice at mouth. *b*, orifice corresponding in situation to anal aperture. *c*, valve guarding orifice *b*, which permits water to enter in the direction of the mouth, but prevents its return in an opposite direction.

The centripetal and centrifugal movements adverted to
are not confined to animals, and we must descend still
further in the scale of being if we would see them in their
most rudimentary forms. They occur in such plants as the
Volvox globator and Chlamydomonas, the vacuoles of
which open and close with time-regulated beat [1]. They
are the same which cause the leaves and flowers of certain
orders of plants to open and close at various periods of the
day and night. If therefore structureless masses have the
power of opening and closing, or, what is the same thing,

[1] That a jelly-like mass, apparently devoid of structure, is capable of shortening and elongating, is proved by a very remarkable experiment made by Kühne.
This distinguished physiologist took the intestine of a cockchafer and stuffed it
with living protoplasm from a living plant. He applied electricity to the gut so
prepared, and found, to his surprise, that it exhibited all the phenomena peculiar to
to muscle when artificially stimulated—the intestine shortening suddenly when
the stimulus was applied, and elongating slowly after it was withdrawn.

of elongating and shortening, it is not too much to claim
a similar power for a muscular fibre and the sarcous elements
of which it is composed ; the more especially as we know
from observation and experiment that the muscular fibre
when it shortens in one direction elongates in another
direction, the fibre and its component particles possessing
the power of abandoning and returning to their original
form. If it be true that when a muscle shortens it elongates in the direction of its breadth, and if further it be
true that when a muscle elongates it shortens in the direction of its breadth, it follows that all the particles in the
mass obey the same laws. Thus when a muscle shortens in
the direction of its length, all its particles, whatever be their
composition, colour, or original form, elongate in the direction
of the breadth of the muscle. When, on the other hand, a
muscle elongates in the direction of its length, all its particles
shorten in the direction of the breadth of the muscle. But
the particles of a muscle are free to change shape in any
direction, for it is well known that if a long muscle be
artificially stimulated it shortens and after a while regains
its original dimensions, so that by repeating the stimulus
it may be made to shorten a second time. This happens
even when the long muscle is cut away from its connexions,
and when it is removed from the influence supposed to be
exerted upon it by what is termed its antagonist muscle.
This tends to prove that the power which all muscles possess
of alternately shortening and elongating inheres in their
substance or sarcous elements, the movements being essentially vital in their nature, and independent of each other.
That a muscle or fibre, or their component particles, are
endowed with universality of motion, is apparent from the
fact that when a muscle or a muscular fibre shortens, it is
thrown into rugae or swellings, the long axes of the particles of the swelled portions being arranged at right angles
to the long axes of the particles representing the constrictions or narrow parts. But those parts of the muscle or
fibre which form the constrictions the one instant become
the swellings the next, the direction of the long axes of the
particles or sarcous elements of the muscle or fibre being
in this case reversed. Muscular movements are therefore

the result of a rhythmic motion in their ultimate particles, in all respects analogous to the rhythmic movements of the heart. The movements of muscles are characterised by two forces acting at right angles to each other; the one force flying a fixed point, while the other seeks it (Fig. 115).

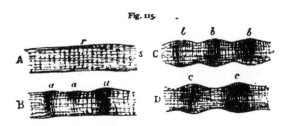

Fig. 115.

Fig. 115 shows an elementary fibre of the skate in the uncontracted and contracted state.
A.—Fibre in the condition of rest. *r*, transverse markings or cleavage. *s*, longitudinal markings or cleavage.
B.—*a, a, a*, one side of fibre contracting or shortening.
C.—*b, b, b*, both sides of fibre contracting or shortening. All parts of the fibre become involved in succession. Thus, the constrictions between *b, b, b* of C become the swellings *c, c* of D.—*After Bowman.*

In reality the ultimate particles or sarcous elements of a muscle are correlated and definitely co-ordinated, neighbouring particles or groups of particles exercising a centrifugal and cen‑tripetal power which causes one set of particles to advance in one direction, while a corresponding set recede in an opposite direction. This is what virtually happens in the voluntary system of muscles. When one muscle shortens on one side of a bone, that on the opposite side elongates. By assign‑ing a centrifugal and centripetal power to a moving mass, we can readily understand how structureless tissues open and close. Without such a power even elaborate tissues would have difficulty in moving. From the foregoing it follows, that from the time the particles of a muscle leave their position of rest and begin to change their form until they return to their original position and assume their original shape, they are in a state of activity. This is proved by the fact that when a muscle or sarcous element shortens in the direction of its length, it broadens or lengthens in the direction of its breadth, and *vice versa*. If we assign to muscles, or their sarcous elements, the power of changing form in one direction, it is unphilosophic to assume that they have not the power of changing form in another and opposite direction. Even structureless masses of protoplasm are endowed with this power, and the amoeba, which may be regarded as an aggregation of such masses, can elongate and shorten its body with equal facility, can contract or close in one direction and expand or open in another—can make a temporary cavity in its substance to serve the purpose of a temporary stomach, and then obliterate it. Similar attributes inhere in the white blood corpuscle. The majority of physiologists of the present day deny that muscles are endowed with the power of elongating. They say that muscles can only contract or shorten, and that when they elongate their elongation is due to elasticity, or they are drawn out by antagonist muscles; a flexor drawing out its extensor the one instant, the extensor drawing out the flexor the next. If this were so, the muscles, as already indicated, would act upon and against each other, instead of upon the bones they are intended to move. The waste of muscular energy under such circumstances would be inordinate. The prevailing theory of muscular action is thus stated by Bowman :—'The contraction of a muscle will be permanent if no force from without be exerted to obliterate it by stretching, for a contracted muscle has no power of extending itself.' Much of the obscurity regarding muscular movements is, I believe, traceable to the employment of the terms *contraction* and *relaxation*, contraction primarily signifying a shrinkage or diminution in volume, which does not occur in muscular movements; relaxation, an abandonment of the contracted state. An example may be useful. According to prevailing opinions a flexor, when it contracts or shortens, drags out or elongates its extensor; the flexor being *active*, the extensor *passive*. Another way of putting it is this: When the flexor *contracts* the extensor *relaxes*, *i. e.* offers no opposition to being drawn out by the flexor. This however is avoiding the difficulty by taking refuge in terms. Either a muscle (or parts thereof) is or is not active. When it is not in a state of activity, it is in the condition of rest, so that the phrase *passive contraction*, so frequently employed, has no meaning. I propose therefore for these and other reasons to abandon the terms *contraction* and *relaxation*, as being inapplicable to muscular movements, and to substitute for them the more simple ones of *shortening* and *elongating*, as applied to long muscles ; and *closing* and *opening*, as applied to hollow muscles. By the shortening or closing of a muscle, I mean its centripetal action, that action by which its particles converge and crowd towards a certain point ; by the elongating or opening of a muscle, I mean its centrifugal action, that action by which its particles diverge or escape from a certain point. These movements are not equally rapid, but they are equally independent and vital in their nature[1]. My meaning will be obvious from the annexed woodcuts.

Fig. 116.   Fig. 117.

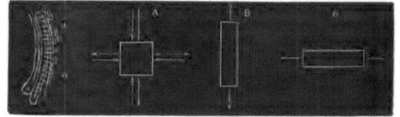

Fig. 116.—Elementary fibres from leg of newly-born rabbit after having been exposed to the action of spirit. Shows longitudinal and transverse cleavage, and the manner in which the sarcous elements or cubes (*a, a*) may become detached.—*After Bowman.*

Fig. 117.—A, sarcous element or cube capable of changing shape in any direction (*vide* arrows). B, same element when elongated vertically. C, ditto when elongated horizontally. The position of rest, and the form of B and C when at rest, is that represented at A.—*Original.*

At Fig. 117 A, a sarcous cube or integral portion of a muscle is represented. This cube, like the amoeba, is en-

[1] Dr. Martin Barry endeavoured to explain muscular actions by assuming that the sarcous elements were arranged as in a spiral spring; but neither the disposition of the dark and light squares, nor their mode of action, favours this view. The late Professor Alison attributed the contraction and relaxation of muscle to the attraction and repulsion of its ultimate particles. Thus he states that contraction essentially consists in a greatly increased attraction among the particles, or globules constituting the muscular fibres, and alteration in the direction in which the attraction acts, rapidly communicating from one particle to another, both along the same fibre and among adjacent fibres, and rapidly succeeded by repulsion or return to the previous state of cohesive attraction existing among those particles; and Dr. C. B. Radcliffe (Nature, Jan. 2, 1872) expresses a belief 'that living muscle is kept in a state of elongation by the presence of an electrical charge, and that contraction is nothing more than the action of the fibres, by virtue of their elasticity, when liberated by discharge from the charge which kept them elongated previously.' Matteucci had come to a similar conclusion at an anterior date, and expressed his belief that muscular action is accompanied by a discharge of electricity analogous to that of a torpedo. This view, Dr. Radcliffe adds, has received confirmation from the new quadrant electrometer.

dowed with universality of motion. Thus it can, by a
conjoined centripetal and centrifugal movement (see solid
arrows), assume the shape represented at B; or it can by
a similar but opposite movement (*vide* dotted arrows) assume
the shape represented at C. In the case of the open or expanded heart, the long axes of the sarcous elements of the
more vertical fibres are arranged as at B, those of the more
transverse fibres as at C. When the heart closes, the sarcous
elements of the more vertical and transverse fibres assume
the shape A. In the case of an open hollow muscle with
a closed sphincter, the long axes of the sarcous elements
of the nearly vertical and horizontal fibres forming the body
of the muscle are arranged as at B and C, the sarcous elements
of the fibres forming the sphincter having the shape indicated
at A. When the hollow muscle closes, the sarcous elements
of the vertical and horizontal fibres assume the shape A, those
of the sphincter assuming the shape C (see Fig. 128, p. 231).
The same arrangement obtains in the voluntary muscles.
When a flexor and extensor muscle are at rest, their sarcous
elements or cubes assume the form figured at A. When the
flexor shortens, its sarcous elements take the form C; the
sarcous elements of the extensor, when it elongates, taking the
form B. When the extensor shortens, its particles assume
the form C; the particles of the flexor, when it elongates,
assuming the form B. The change of shape in the sarcous
elements is necessary to produce the shortening of the flexor
and the elongation of the extensor, and the converse; the
one muscle, as explained, always shortening when the other
elongates, and *vice versa*. The particles of the muscle, like
the muscles themselves, as already stated, are co-ordinated.
They work together and not against each other. The cube
figured at A consequently not only represents the position
of rest for the sarcous elements of both flexor and extensor
muscles, but also the line on either side of which they oscillate
or vibrate when the muscles are in action. The shape of
the sarcous elements, as seen in the biceps and triceps in
flexion of the arm, is shown at Fig. 118, p. 220.

That muscles possess a centripetal and centrifugal power
—*i. e.* a power by which they alternately shorten and elongate—and that one set of muscles is never employed for

violently pulling or drawing out another set, is abundantly proved by the action of the heart and the hollow muscles with sphincters, such as the stomach, bladder, rectum, uterus, etc. The heart pulsates in the embryo while yet a mass of cells, and before it is provided either with cavities, blood, or muscular fibres. The different compartments of the heart open and close after the organ is cut out of the body, and when it is deprived of blood ; but the deprivation of blood prevents the auricles acting upon the ventricles, and the converse. The auricles and ventricles are to be regarded as anatomically and functionally distinct. That the auricles when they close do not forcibly distend or open the ventricles, is evident from the fact that the ventricles open

Fig. 118.

Fig. 118 illustrates how the forearm is fixed or folded on the arm by the combined action of the biceps and triceps. When the biceps (*a*) shortens and the triceps (*b*) lengthens, flexion is produced. When the triceps shortens and the biceps lengthens, extension is produced. In flexion the long axes of the sarcous elements of the biceps muscle (*a*) are directed transversely ; those of the triceps (*b*) longitudinally. These conditions are reversed in extension. At *a* the centripetal action of muscle is seen (*vide* arrows marked *i*) ; at *b* its centrifugal action (*vide* arrows marked *j*). (Compare with arrows of Fig. 130.) *d*, coracoid process of scapula from which the short head of the biceps arises. *e*, insertion of the biceps into the radius. *f*, long head of the triceps. *g*, insertion of triceps into the olecranon of the ulna. *h*, hand.—*Original.*

and close spontaneously when the auricles are removed; Further it occasionally happens when the heart is intact, *in situ*, and acting slowly, that the ventricles open before the auricles close. Finally the ventricles, which are very powerful structures, obliterate their cavities when they close, so that the auricles, which are very feeble structures, have not the requisite power to force the blood which they contain into the solid muscular mass formed by the ventricles at the termination of the systole. That the ventricles do obliterate their cavities when they close is a matter of observation. Ever and anon, when making post-mortem examinations at the Royal Infirmary of Edinburgh, I find

the ventricles rolled together in the form of a solid ball.
Even the stomach is endowed with the power of all but
obliterating its cavity, and I have at present in my possession a human stomach, the body of which has a diameter
not greater than that of the small intestine[1]. The movements
of the hollow muscles with sphincters also support the view that
muscles have the power of elongating as well as shortening ;
in other words, have a centrifugal and centripetal action.
When the stomach, bladder, or rectum close, their sphincters
open, and *vice versa.* But the closing of the stomach,
bladder, and rectum, is occasioned by the simultaneous
closing, shortening, and broadening of all the fibres composing the bodies of the viscera ; the opening of the sphincters
being occasioned by the simultaneous opening, elongating,
and narrowing of all the fibres which go to form the
sphincters. As the sphincters are powerful structures which
guard narrow apertures, and the bodies of the viscera
are comparatively feeble, it follows that no effort on the
part of the bodies of the viscera, acting upon their fluid
contents, could force a passage. Such force is not required,
as the sphincters open spontaneously when the bodies of
the viscera close. The movements are co-ordinated in the
same way that the movements of the different parts of the
heart or those of the flexor and extensor muscles are co-
ordinated. These movements are however only possible in
structures which alternately open or elongate, and close or
shorten ; *i. e.* exert a centrifugal and centripetal power.
They occur in muscular and other tissues.

The opening and closing of the rectum and its sphincters
are represented at Figures 119 and 120, p. 222.

Another element calculated to introduce confusion into our
ideas of muscular movements is the arrangement of the
muscular fibres, and the muscles themselves. Hitherto, and
by common consent, it has been believed that whereas a
flexor muscle is situated on one aspect of a limb, and its
corresponding extensor on the other aspect, these two muscles
must be opposed to, and antagonise each other—must, in

---

[1] The patient to which this stomach belonged died of inanition, occasioned by
stricture of the oesophagus. The stomach itself is quite healthy.

fact, work against each other. Now there can be no greater fallacy than this. Nature never works against herself. The voluntary muscles—whether flexors and extensors, or abductors and adductors, or pronators and supinators—form cycles, one segment of the cycle being placed on one side of the bone to be moved, the remaining segment of the cycle on the opposite side of the bone. When the one side of the cycle closes or shortens, the opposite side of the cycle opens or elongates (*vide* Fig. 118, p. 220). Muscular energy is thus conserved to the utmost, and the bones are made to vibrate

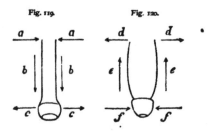

Fig. 119.   Fig. 120.

Fig. 119 shows how the rectum closes and the sphincters open to discharge the faeces. In the act of defecation the rectum closes, and narrows in the direction *a, a* and elongates in the direction *b, b*; the sphincters opening and widening in the direction *c, c*. The arrows indicate the direction in which the forces engaged in discharging the faeces operate. The assistance derived from the co-operation of the abdominal muscles is not estimated.—*Original.*

Fig. 120 shows how the rectum opens to receive the faeces, and how the sphincters close to prevent their escape. In this case the rectum opens in the direction *d, d,* and shortens in the direction *e, e*; the sphincters closing in the direction *f, f.* Here the arrows indicate the direction in which the forces act to retain the faeces.—*Original.*

within their muscular cycles with marvellous precision and exactitude. But for this arrangement the delicate manipulations required in the manufacture of watches, philosophical instruments, etc., could not be performed. The opening and closing, say of the flexor and extensor arcs of the cycles, are in all respects analogous to the opening and closing movements which occur in the different parts of the heart and in the hollow muscles with sphincters. It is thus that the movements of the voluntary and involuntary muscles may be assimilated and referred to a common source.

The involuntary hollow muscles supply the type or pattern on which the voluntary muscles are formed. Nor is this all. In idiots whose nervous system is deranged, the involuntary movements return in the voluntary muscles; and it is by no means an uncommon thing to see in our large lunatic asylums poor demented creatures exhibiting rhythmic movements in different parts of their persons. Thus you will find a considerable number of patients who for hours together move their head, trunk, or limbs, backwards and forwards, or laterally, with a steady see-saw motion, automatically and unconsciously. I was particularly struck with these rhythmic movements in voluntary muscles on a recent visit to the West Riding Lunatic Asylum, where owing to the courtesy of my distinguished friend, Dr. J. Crichton Browne, the medical superintendent of the institution, I had an opportunity of studying them under unusually favourable conditions.

I am well aware that elasticity is assigned a high place in muscular movements by modern physiologists, but there are grounds for believing that its power has been greatly over-rated ; the sarcous elements, of which muscles are composed, being arranged to act either with or without elastic substances [1].

Elasticity is to be regarded as an auxiliary of muscular manifestations, a modification to confer continuity of movement. All muscular movements are interrupted movements—*i.e.* muscles act first in one direction, and then in another. In order that muscles may reverse their movements, they are endowed with a certain amount of elasticity to assist them over their dead points. That however elasticity is quite a secondary matter is evident from this : elasticity cannot generate a movement, muscular movements beginning and terminating in the muscles themselves. Elasticity is to a prime mover (such as a muscle) what an echo is to a sound. It repeats, or tends to repeat, movements generated without or beyond the substance in which it inheres. The blood-vessels are endowed with a greater share of elasticity than the hollow muscles and involuntary muscles generally, the involuntary muscles having a greater share than the voluntary ones. In proportion as muscles become differentiated, and their movements exact, their elastic properties disappear. By assigning a centripetal and centrifugal action to muscles, as apart from elasticity and antagonism, we secure to the

---

[1] When the sarcous elements have departed as far as they can from their original shape and position of rest, elasticity assists the particles in reversing their forces, and gives continuity of motion. The elementary particles may be said to vibrate, and elasticity is calculated to help them over their dead points.

muscles, and the sarcous elements composing them, absolute rest when they are not engaged in shortening or lengthening. There is no necessity for supposing, as hitherto, 'that muscles are kept upon the stretch by the nature of their position and attachments, and by a state of *passive contraction* which opposes their elongation by antagonists.' It is more natural to assume that the muscles which form opposite sides of muscular cycles, instead of maintaining their relative positions by a state of passive contraction, as it is termed, are simply in a state of inaction. By assigning, as I have done, to the muscles and their sarcous elements the power of acting in two directions at right angles to each other, we get rid of the passive contraction of authors, and the necessity for one muscle or sarcous element, when it shortens, dragging out another muscle or element which has been regarded as its antagonist, but which in reality is its correlate. It is impossible to understand how a muscle can be resting in a state of even passive contraction. A healthy muscle is firm in absolute inaction, but its hardness is not due to contraction. A muscle enjoys a greater degree of repose than is usually imagined. It is in a state of absolute rest when not shortening or elongating. But the sarcous elements of a muscle, even when shortening and elongating, have intervals of repose, from the fact that they do not all act at once, but alternately and successively. As a muscle moves in its ultimate elements, so it rests therein. This explains how the heart can go on without pausing as long as life lasts; how a muscle during its action produces a sound, the so-called susurrus; and how it develops heat, the ultimate particles triturating each other as they advance or recede.

How Muscular Fibres open and close the Vessels, the Compartments of the Heart, the Stomach, Bladder, Thorax, Abdomen, etc.—In the smallest capillary vessels no muscular fibres are to be detected. In the larger capillaries faint traces of circular fibres make their appearance. It is only in the smaller arteries and veins that a circular layer of muscular fibres becomes well marked. Every vessel furnished with circular muscular fibres can open and close. When the circular muscular fibres shorten, they elongate the vessel and diminish its calibre. When they elongate, they shorten the vessel and increase its calibre. This follows because the circular fibres form closing rings, and any change in their shape produces either an elongation and narrowing of the vessel, or a shortening and widening thereof (Fig. 124, p. 231). The circular fibres are capable of acting by themselves, or in conjunction with elastic structures arranged in the direction of the length of the vessel. When elastic structures are present they are stretched when the circular fibres shorten. As elastic structures tend to regain their original form when the force which extended them has ceased to act, they assist the circular fibres in elongating. They confer rapidity and continuity of movement by assisting the muscle over its dead points : muscle, of necessity, acting first in one direction and then in another.

In the larger vessels a longitudinal layer of muscular fibres is added to the circular one. Under these circumstances, the two sets of fibres are arranged at right angles, and work together. When the vessel is to be narrowed and elongated, the circular fibres shorten and the longitudinal ones lengthen ; when it is to be widened and shortened, the circular fibres lengthen and the longitudinal ones shorten. The two sets of fibres take part in both movements, and do not antagonise or act against each other (Fig. 125, p. 231). The same thing happens in the vermicular movements of the intestine and the creeping of the earthworm (*Lumbricus agricola*), to which they are likened. The muscular tunics of the intestine and worm are composed of longitudinal and circular fibres, so that they exactly resemble certain of the blood-vessels. I have studied the movements of the worm with considerable attention, as being likely to throw some light upon similar movements in the vessels. Prior to moving, the earthworm draws itself together, and shortens and thickens its whole body (Fig. 121 A, p. 226). It then elongates and narrows, telescopic fashion, the first inch or so (Fig. 121 B, *a*, p. 226). In this movement the rings representing the circular fibres are separated from each other and thickened, the part moving being of a paler colour than the rest of the body. This shows that while the circular fibres shorten and broaden, the longitudinal ones lengthen and narrow, both sets of fibres taking a nearly equal share in the work. The power possessed by the worm of elongating a part of its body is undoubted. When the first instalment of the body is sent forward, it is corrugated or gathered together (Fig. 121 C, *a*), and securely fixed on the ground by the assistance of the setae or hairs situated on the ventral aspect of the animal. A second inch or so is now elongated, telescopic fashion, and sent on precisely as in the first instance (Fig. 121 C, *b*). The second instalment is not drawn forward, as is generally believed, but pushed forward as described. When the second instalment is gathered to the first, and both fixed to the ground by the setae, a third instalment is sent on, the worm not beginning a second step until the tail instal-

Fig. 121.

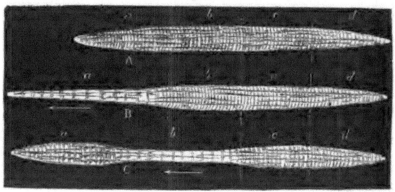

Fig. 121.—A represents the worm as drawn together prior to commencing a step, and divided into four equal portions, *a*, *b*, *c*, *d*.—*Original*.
  B shows the first part of the worm as elongated or pushed out (*a*); the parts *b*, *c*, *d* acting as fulcra.—*Original*.
  C shows the first part of the worm (*a*) shortened, corrugated, and fixed on the ground, the second part of the worm (*b*) being elongated or pushed out; the parts *c* and *d* acting as fulcra.—*Original*.

ment is forwarded and added to the body. The worm advances by a peristaltic or wave movement. It pushes itself forward upon the ground, and in this respect resembles all other animals with terrestrial habits. If the worm had not the power of elongating and pushing its body forward, it is evident that it could never begin a step (Fig. 121 B, *a*).

The movements of the worm are exceedingly interesting, as showing that a muscular mass composed of circular and longitudinal fibres (each set continuous upon itself) has the power of elongating even in the absence of fixed points. The locomotion of the worm is performed by two forces, which always act at right angles to each other. Thus when the first part of the body is sent forward, the circular fibres exert their centripetal power, the longitudinal ones their centrifugal power. When this portion of the body is shortened and corrugated prior to being fixed on the ground by the setae, the circular fibres exert their centrifugal power, and the longitudinal ones their centripetal power. The sarcous elements of the circular and longitudinal fibres alternately seek and fly the centre of the moving parts. It follows from this that the part of the worm which is corrugating and broadening may be compared to a sphincter muscle which is opening; while that part of the worm which is elongating and narrowing may be compared to a hollow muscle closing. In these two movements, both of which are necessary to the locomotion of the worm, the elongating and shortening power possessed by muscle is clearly shown. One part of the worm elongates while another part shortens, and but for this consentaneous double movement (which is a co-ordinated rhythmic movement) no locomotion can take place. The same holds true of the voluntary muscles. When bones are to be moved, one part of the muscular cycle must shorten when the other elongates, and *vice versa*. If any part of the worm attempted to shorten and lengthen at the same instant, it is evident that no locomotion would ensue. In like manner, if the voluntary muscles situated on one aspect of a bone or bones acted against the muscles situated on the opposite aspect, the bones would remain *in statu quo*. The commonly-received opinion, that muscles have only the power of shortening, and cannot elongate, is, I believe, founded in error. The belief is no doubt traceable in a great measure to the incautious use of artificial stimuli. If, *e.g.*, electricity is applied to the first part of the worm when in the act of elongating, it instantly shortens. This however is no proof against the elongating power of muscle. It is simply the sudden substitution of an abnormal for a normal movement. If artificial stimuli produced natural movements they would, when applied to a muscle in the act of elongating, cause it to elongate more rapidly; in other words, they would quicken its movements, and in no instance check or reverse them. Muscle is not the only substance which shrinks or retires within itself on being assailed by a troublesome neighbour.

Q 2

The sensitive plant does the same [1]. The worm elongates its body on the withdrawal of the stimulus, and the sensitive plant regains its original shape. The return movements are therefore vital and normal. In the same way a muscle, when cut out of the body and made to shorten by an irritant, regains its original shape when the irritant is withdrawn, and may be made to shorten many times in succession. When the muscle returns to its original shape it elongates, the elongation being necessary to a repetition of the muscular movement. A long muscle when it shortens virtually reproduces the movements observed in the body of the worm when creeping, one part of the muscle swelling out or broadening by a centrifugal movement, while another portion thins or narrows by a centripetal movement. This accounts for a long muscle being thrown into *ampullae* when it shortens (Fig. 115 C, D, p. 216).

Similar movements to those described in the worm occur in the tentacles of the gasteropoda. In murex, the tentacles are thick solid fleshy stems, composed of various strata of circular, longitudinal, and oblique muscular fibres. These are elongated and retracted at pleasure (Fig. 122, p. 229). In the garden-snail (*Helix pomatia*), the tentacles are hollow tubes, composed of circular bands of muscle. Within each tentacle is a long muscular slip (Fig. 123, *c*, *d*, p. 229), extending between its free extremity and the common retractive muscles of the foot. When the muscular slip (*c*) shortens, the circular muscular fibres elongate, and the tentacle is invaginated (*a*). The same thing happens in invagination of the intestine. A reverse action takes place when the tentacle is protruded (*b*), the enclosed muscular slip (*d*) elongating, and the circular fibres shortening. That the evagination or protrusion of the tentacle is not due to the contraction or shortening of the circular fibres alone, is evident from this. If the tentacle is half invaginated (*a*), the shortening or closing of the circular fibres by themselves tends rather to invagination than evagination. To complete the process the longitudinal muscular slip (*c*) must elongate and push slightly.

---

[1] Desfontaines once carried a sensitive plant with him in a coach, with the following curious result. The jolting of the machine caused it at first to curl up its leaves. When however it became accustomed to the movement, it expanded them.

When a garden-snail elongates its tentacles, we feel that the act is a voluntary and a vital one. The moment however they touch a foreign body, they shrink[1]. The alarm passes away, and again the tentacles are cautiously elongated. The same thing happens in the sea-anemone. When this magnificent creature expands its tentacles like a gorgeous flower opening to the sunlight, it pushes them out with exquisite grace like so many microscopic telescopes. If, however, foreign matter be dropped into the water upon the anemone,

Fig. 122.   .   Fig. 123.

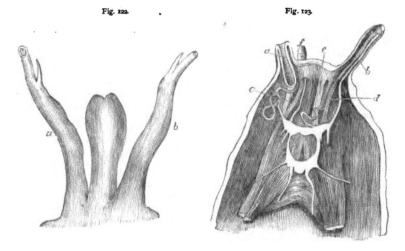

Fig. 122 shows tentacles of murex (a, b) in elongated state.—*Adapted.*
Fig. 123 shows the four tentacles of garden snail (a, b, e, f), one of which (a) is invaginated, and its muscle (c) shortened; a second one (b) being evaginated or pushed out, and its muscle (d) elongated.—*Adapted.*

the tentacles instantly retreat into the interior of the animal. The power of elongating and shortening possessed by the tentacles is, I believe, possessed by every muscle, by every one of its fibres, and by every one of its sarcous elements. If we grant to muscles the power of alternately shortening and elongating, we have an explanation of the multifarious movements which we behold in our own bodies. We can comprehend how the heart, blood-vessels, and hollow viscera act; how we are capable of migrating from one place to another;

---

[1] In phthisical patients, as Dr. Stokes has shown, a smart tap on a muscular part is followed by a contraction and swelling of the part struck. The part struck is surprised, and contracts or rolls itself together.

and how the hand is supplied with its cunning. All are vital manifestations. The elongation and shortening of the tentacles are analogous to the opening and closing of the heart, the extending or flexing of the arm, or the protruding and retracting of the tongue.

To take another example :—the mouth of the gasteropoda in most instances presents the appearance of a prehensile and retractile proboscis. This remark, I may observe, applies to the mouth and lips of a great many animals, the oval aperture and lips being pushed out and retracted at pleasure.

In the gasteropoda, which have no jaw or masticating apparatus, the moveable proboscis consists of a muscular tube composed of longitudinal and circular fibres as in the intestine. By means of this simple structure, every possible kind of movement is effected, the tube seizing the food, and, by alternately opening and closing, forcing it into and along the alimentary canal, just as the blood is forced along a vessel endowed with rhythmical movements. The retraction of the proboscis is occasioned by the shortening of the longitudinal fibres, and the expansion or elongation of the circular ones ; the elongation being effected by a counter and contrary movement. The tongue, as has been stated, is also endowed with the power of elongating and shortening ; the organ being employed by the ox for seizing the grass, and by the chameleon for securing insects.

By investing the sarcous elements of muscle with the power of shortening and elongating, longitudinal and circular fibres can be made to act by themselves or in combination, and so of every form of oblique fibres. If circular fibres are to act by themselves and diminish the calibre of a vessel, they shorten in the direction of the breadth of the vessel. If the same function is to be performed by longitudinal and circular fibres arranged at right angles, the circular fibres shorten in the direction of the breadth of the vessel, the longitudinal fibres elongating in the direction of its length. These movements are reversed if the vessel is to be widened. If a cavity is to be obliterated by longitudinal and circular fibres, the fibres shorten longitudinally and transversely. If it is to be opened, they elongate. If oblique fibres are present, they are accessories, and deport themselves in exactly the same way as the others. In hollow muscles the fibres require to be continuous upon themselves, and this accounts for the fact that in the heart, stomach, bladder and uterus, the fibres have neither origin nor insertion. (*Vide* Figs. 124—130.)

Fig. 124.   Fig. 125.   Fig. 126.   Fig. 127.

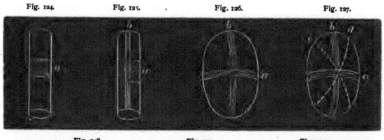

Fig. 128.   Fig. 129.   Fig. 130.

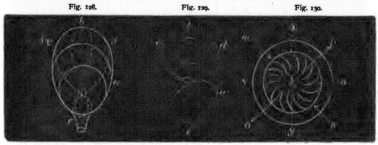

Fig. 124.—Vessel supplied with circular or transverse fibres (*a*), capable of increasing or decreasing its calibre, and of shortening or elongating it.—*Original.*

Fig. 125.—Vessel supplied with circular (*a*) and longitudinal (*b*) fibres, capable of increasing or diminishing its calibre, and of shortening or elongating it.—*Original.*

Fig. 126.—Hollow muscle provided with circular (*a*) and longitudinal (*b*) fibres capable of increasing and diminishing its cavity so as to take in and eject fluid.—*Original.*

Fig. 127.—Hollow muscle provided with circular (*a*), longitudinal (*b*), and oblique (*c, d*) fibres, capable of opening and closing, and of taking in and ejecting fluid. In this case the opening and closing, because of the presence of the oblique fibres, is more perfect than in Fig. 126.—*Original.*

Fig. 128.—Hollow muscle (human bladder) provided with circular (*a*), longitudinal (*b*), and oblique (*c, d*) spiral fibres, continuous at base (*b*) and apex (*e*), in which latter situation they form a sphincter. When the fibres constituting the body of the muscle close, the continuations of those fibres which form its sphincter open, and *vice versa*. Such a muscle can receive, contain, and eject fluid.—*Original.*

Fig. 129.—Hollow muscle (left ventricle of heart of mammal) provided with circular (*a*), longitudinal (*b*), and oblique (*c, d*) spiral fibres, continuous at apex (*e*) and base (*b*). These fibres, by their united efforts, can open or close the muscle, and can cause it to suck in and eject the blood alternately.—(Compare with Figs. 98, 99, 100, p. 195.)—*Original.*

Fig. 130.—Transverse section of left ventricle of heart (mammal), showing it in the open and closed condition. *v*, ventricle when open. *w*, ventricle when closed, and cavity (*y*) obliterated. *x*, imaginary line, on either side of which the walls of the ventricle vibrate when the ventricle closes and opens, and when the ventricular fibres exercise their centripetal (*m, n*) and centrifugal (*o, p*) action.—*Original.*

The heart differs slightly from the blood-vessels, inasmuch as when it closes, all its diameters are shortened ; whereas, when it expands, all its diameters are elongated. In the opening and closing of the different compartments of the heart we have two diametrically opposite conditions. To produce this apparently impossible result in the ventricles, the fibres and the sarcous particles of the fibres are arranged vertically, transversely, and obliquely, in continuous spirals, as shown at Fig. 129, p. 231. Fig. 130, p. 231, v, shows a transverse section of the left ventricle of the heart in the expanded or dilated condition ; w, of the same figure, showing a transverse section of the left ventricle when its cavity is obliterated. The arrows m n, o p of Fig. 130, p. 231, indicate the centripetal and centrifugal force possessed by the heart, in virtue of which it acts as a sucking and propelling organ. The heart has the power of forcibly expanding itself, as it has of forcibly closing itself. It can therefore in virtue of its rhythmic movements alternately suck in and eject blood—the auricles attracting it while the ventricles are repelling it, and *vice versa.* When the walls of the ventricle travel beyond the circle represented by x of Fig. 130, p. 231, in an inward direction, they push the blood out of the ventricular cavity; when they travel beyond the same circle in an outward direction, they suck the blood into it. A common caoutchouc bag, if immersed in water and squeezed at intervals, will do the same. The order in which the closure occurs in the vessels and hearts of the lower animals and in the heart of the mammal favours this view. In the cold-blooded animals the large veins (even to the venae hepaticae) close first; then the auricle or auricles, as the case may be; then the ventricle; and lastly the bulbus arteriosus. In the warm-blooded animals the terminations of the pulmonary veins and cavae (superior and inferior) close first ; then the auricles, then the ventricles, and then the large vessels in the vicinity of the heart; these vessels, as already pointed out, being supplied with an elaborate plexus of nerves. The blood is, as it were, manipulated while it is being transmitted. Thus, it is drawn into and seized by the large veins leading to the heart; then by the auricles, then by the ventricles, and then by the large arteries leading from the heart. No sooner, however, is it seized than it is dismissed, the seizure and the dismissal being alike necessary to the circulation. The blood is not permitted to wander about at pleasure in the cavities of the circulatory apparatus. On the contrary, it is made to flow in a continuous onward stream, by a series of very wonderful peristaltic movements, very much in the

same way that the blood is forced into the alimentary canal
of the leech by the simultaneous opening and closing in
regular succession of the different portions of its muscular
oesophagus. Nay more, it is made to open and close the
doors which lead to and conduct from the chambers through
which it passes. It is customary, when speaking of the
action of the heart, to refer only to the closure of the organ,
its opening being regarded as comparatively unimportant
and depending indirectly on the closing. The opening of
the heart however is as necessary to the circulation as its
closing; and but for the fact that one part of the heart
opens while the other closes, the blood could not be made
to perform its endless round without quite an extravagant
waste of power. The blood, like other fluids, is nearly incompressible, and if it is ejected from one place it must be
received in another of nearly, I might safely say of exactly,
the same dimensions. These are but so many proofs of
arrangement and design. When the veins close, the auricles
open; when the auricles close, the ventricles open; when
the ventricles close, the arteries and veins open, and so on
ad infinitum. The blood is alternately pushed and pulled.
That the vessels may take a part in and modify the circulation is evident from the researches of Marey and Garrod,
who show that any obstruction or narrowing in the small
vessels slows the action of the heart.

*Analogy between the Movements of the Thorax, Abdomen,
and Heart.*—The primary function of the thorax is alternately to suck in and eject air; but it has a second function,
it attracts or determines blood to the heart. In fact, the
movements of the chest and heart are essentially the same,
the object of both being to bring relays of air and blood
into intimate contact within a given area. In breathing
the air does not simply rush into the lungs: it is drawn
in by a vital act. It is likewise expelled by a vital act.
In like manner the blood is drawn into the auricles and
forced out of the ventricles by vital acts. This follows
because the chest and heart have the power of alternately
opening and closing. If the air rushed into the lungs mechanically, and was expelled thence by the mere elasticity
of the lungs, we could not regulate the supply of air admitted

into and sent from the lungs in inspiration and expiration. There would moreover be an absence of the rhythm which characterises the chest movements. We can arrest both the inspiration and expiration, which shows that these actions are voluntary and vital as well as involuntary and mechanical. That an intimate relation exists between the thorax and heart appears from this : by arresting the re-spiration, we can also arrest the circulation. M. Groux, who had a congenital fissure of the sternum, could arrest the pulsation · of his subclavian and rodial arteries by making a full inspiration, and then by holding his breath for a short interval. If he held his breath for a few moments after a full expiration, the pulsating tumour which appeared at the cleft sternum became larger, apparently from the heart becoming unusually distended with blood.

During inspiration the great veins entering and contained in the chest—viz. the subclavian, jugular, and superior and inferior cavae—are full of blood, the blood being attracted by inspiratory effort. During expiration the vessels are comparatively flaccid. These changes are not confined to the chest ; thus the radial pulse is weaker and less voluminous during inspiration, and stronger and more voluminous during expiration. The pulse is weakened during inspiration, from the fact that when air is inspired a large mass of blood is attracted to the chest, which has the effect of relieving the plethora of the arterial system—the blood being as it were dammed up in the arteries during expiration. The inspiratory and expiratory acts affect all the vessels of the body, the respiratory influence being most marked in the vessels of the head, chest, and trunk, and least in those of the extremities. This is rendered obvious by the fact that when the brain, which contains a very large number of vessels, is exposed, it is seen to shrink and recede during inspiration, and to swell out or expand during expiration. The attraction of the blood to the chest, and the consequent draining of the capillaries of the brain, sufficiently account for the diminution of its volume during inspiration ; the absence of that attraction and the gorging of the capillaries accounting for the opposite condition during expiration. The rise and fall of the brain here referred to is not to be confounded with similar but minor changes induced by the action of the heart itself, as the two sets of phenomena occur at different periods. The celebrated Hales made this a matter of experiment. By causing the blood of horses and dogs to enter a vertical graduated tube, he found that with each beat of the pulse the haemostatic column rose and fell two, three, or four inches; but that when the animals respired deeply or struggled, it rose and fell from twelve to fourteen inches. Here again the principal rise and fall of the column coincided exactly with the inspiratory and expiratory acts, the column being lowest during inspiration, and highest during expiration. Another proof that the inspiratory act draws the blood towards the chest is to be found in the fact that when a wound is made in a vein anywhere in the vicinity of the thorax, the air is most apt to enter during sighing, or when deep inspirations are made.

Dr. Buchanan, of Glasgow[1], attaches great importance to respiration as an auxiliary of the circulation, and states his conviction that asphyxia is less due to the poisoning of the blood than to the fact that, when the breathing ceases, the heart is unable to carry on the circulation by itself[2]. I am not disposed to go thus far; for while admitting that respiration forms one of the forces of the circulation in the mammal, I cannot overlook the fact that in some of the lower animals the circulation is carried on where no respiration proper exists. The respiration may be divided into three kinds—viz. (a) the respiration due to the action of the chest and laryngeal muscles; (b) that due to the action of cilia, situated on the trachea and bronchial tubes; and (c) that occasioned by the diffusion of gases. The two former correspond to the visible vascular circulation; the latter to the invisible. The diffusion of gases in the lungs is analogous to the diffusion of fluids in the tissues. The chest and lungs

[1] The Forces which carry on the Circulation of the Blood, by Andrew Buchanan, M.D., etc., Professor of Physiology, University of Glasgow.

[2] Professor Alison is of opinion that the effects of asphyxia first show themselves in the lungs, that the arterialisation of the blood has the power of attracting that fluid to the lungs, and of drawing it on through the capillaries, and that when this auxiliary to the circulation is cut off, the blood stagnates in the lungs. He assigns to the absorption and exhalation which goes on in the lungs in a state of health a power similar to that claimed by most physiologists for the tissues.

form an apparatus for supplying fresh relays of air, just as the heart and blood-vessels form an apparatus for supplying fresh relays of blood. When once the air is inside the lungs it is manipulated, and caused to pass in two directions, by the pulmonary cilia, and the tendency which the carbonic acid and the oxygen in the lungs have to diffuse or pass through each other. The ciliary movements produce currents within the air-passages and lungs akin to those produced within a bee-hive by the fanning of the wings of the bees at the entrance. The ciliary movements and passage of gases in opposite directions produce the primary circulation of air as it exists in the lowest animals; and it is not a little curious to find that, as the circulation of the blood becomes differentiated, so the breathing apparatus becomes complicated. Thus, to the ciliary movements and the mechanical diffusion of gases found in the lower animals, there are added in the higher a complex muscular and bony apparatus.

The movements of the chest, like those of the heart, are said to be active and passive; the expansion or opening of the chest and glottis being due, it is stated, to the contraction of the diaphragm, the intercostal muscles, and the crico-arytenoid muscles; the diminution or closing of the chest and glottis being due to the relaxation of these muscles, to the resiliency of the costal cartilages, and the elasticity of the pulmonic substance and vocal chords. Dalton states that the movement of expiration is entirely a *passive* one. I am however disposed to regard the movement of expiration as well as that of inspiration as vito-mechanical. Dalton evidently experiences a difficulty in regarding expiration as a purely passive act; for he says, in expiration the muscles of both chest and glottis are relaxed, while the elasticity of the tissues, by a kind of *passive contraction* (observe, passive contraction), restores the parts to their original condition [1]. If contraction is active in inspiration, it must also be active in expiration, otherwise there is a contradiction in terms. It is worthy of remark that, according to current views, a vital act *opens* the chest, while it *closes* the heart. But why this

[1] Dalton's Treatise on Human Physiology, p. 206.

-discrepancy, seeing the movements of the thorax and heart are involuntary and rhythmic in character, and in this sense identical[1]? There is plainly a difficulty here, which requires to be cleared up, and which only disappears when the opening and closing of the thorax and heart are regarded as vital in their nature. The presence of cartilage and bone in the thorax may be thought by some to afford a sufficient explanation, but these need not be taken into account, as the muscles of the thorax are arranged in such a manner as would enable them to open and close the chest even in the absence of the hard parts. Nor must it be forgotten that the movements of the thorax are muscular movements, and that whatever change is induced in the hard parts is referable to prior change in the soft parts[2]. If we attend to the inspiratory and expiratory movements in our own persons, and convert what are naturally involuntary movements into voluntary ones, we find that in inspiration we draw in the air by a vital act, and that in expiration we expel it by a vital act. This is proved by the fact that if we interfere either with inspiration or expiration, the movements are arrested. If we make a forcible inspiration, we must also, if we would avoid discomfort, make a forcible expiration.

The Movements of the Mammalian Heart, interrupted and yet continuous. How the Heart rests.—Having described the direction and distribution of the muscular fibres composing the heart of the mammal, the order in which the several compartments of the heart act, and the change of shape induced in all muscles, whether voluntary or involuntary, in a state of activity, we are now in a position to speak of the general and particular movements of the heart. The following are the appearances observed in the living heart of a puppy one day old. The large veins at the base of the heart close in the direction of the auricles, and the auricles slowly open. The auricles then close in the direction of the ventricles with

[1] Inspiration corresponds to the opening of the heart; expiration to its closing. The former act is performed more slowly than the latter.

[2] Since the above was written, Dr. Arthur Ransome has assigned an outward, forward, or pushing movement to the chest in inspiration; and an inward, backward, or pulling movement in expiration. These movements are seen to most advantage in women and children, where the ribs and costal cartilages are softest.—*Proceedings of the Royal Society*, November 21, 1872.

a vermicular wavy movement, somewhat suddenly, the ventricles opening meanwhile. Finally, the ventricles close suddenly and with great energy, a wave movement travelling in spiral lines from the apex to the base, and then from the base in the direction of the apex. When the heart is in motion it rotates on its long axis alternately to right and left, the extent of the rotation being rather more than a quarter of a turn either way. When the ventricles open, the left apex is elongated and pushed downwards by a peculiar screwing motion, similar to that witnessed when a screw is being forced into wood. When the ventricles close, the left apex is shortened and elevated by a remarkable screwing motion, which exactly corresponds with that observed when a screw is being extracted from wood. The left apex, while this screwing motion is taking place, describes an irregular ellipse; the apex impinging against the thorax, particularly towards the termination of the systole, when it gives a sudden bound in an upward and forward direction as if from recoil [1]. The auricles close simultaneously, and so of the ventricles; the auricles always opening when the ventricles close, and vice versa. These structures increase and diminish by about a third when they open and close. They also change colour slightly. This is due to a diminution or increase in the quantity of blood in the walls of the heart and within its cavities at any given time. It is trifling when compared with that observed in the heart of the frog or fish. The ventricles completely empty themselves during the systole. Of this there can be no doubt, as the ventricles are occasionally found so firmly closed after death that their internal or endocardial surfaces are in contact throughout. Analogy also favours this view; the ventricles of the fish and frog completely emptying itself of blood and becoming pale during the systole. When the heart is beating normally, one or other part of it is always moving. When the veins cease to close and the auricles to open, the auricles begin to close and the ventricles to open, and so on in endless succession. In order to admit of these changes, the auriculo-ventricular valves, as has been stated, rise and fall like the diaphragm in respira-

---

[1] In the fish and frog the impulse of the heart, as has been explained, corresponds with the termination of the diastole and the beginning of the systole.

tion; the valves protruding now into the auricular cavities and now into the ventricular ones. There is in reality no pause in the heart's action. The one movement glides into the other as a snake glides into grass. All that the eye can detect is a quickening of the gliding movements at stated and very short intervals. A careful examination of the sounds of the heart shows that the sounds like the movements glide into each other. There is no actual cessation of sound when the heart is in action. There are periods when the sounds are very faint, and when only a sharp or an educated ear can detect them, and there are other periods when the sounds are so distinct that even a dull person must hear: but the sounds —and this is the point to be attended to—merge into each other by slow or sudden transitions. It would be more accurate, when speaking of the movements and sounds of the heart, to say they are only faintly indicated at one time, and strongly emphasized at another, but that neither ever altogether ceases.

If however the heart is acting more or less vigorously as a whole, the question which naturally presents itself is, How is the heart rested? There can be little doubt it rests as it acts, viz. in parts. The centripetal and centrifugal wave movements pass through the sarcous elements of the different portions of the heart very much as the wind passes through leaves: its particles are stirred in rapid succession, but never at exactly the same instant; the heart is moving as a whole, but its particles are only moving at regular and stated intervals; the periods of repose, there is every reason to believe, greatly exceeding the periods of activity. The nourishment, life, and movements of the heart are in this sense synonymous. That the different parts of the heart act consecutively and in regular order was proved by Mr. Malden. He found that if a part of the ventricle of a frog or turtle was irritated exteriorly, it instantly contracted, the contraction spreading from the irritated point in every direction. He found moreover that before the contractile wave had spread over the entire ventricle, the part originally irritated, and which contracted first, expanded or bulged out to form a sacculation; thus showing that the act of dilatation is as much a vital movement as the act of contraction. In proof of this, some poisons apparently kill the heart by destroying its expanding power, the organ in such cases being found firmly contracted after death. The older observers, as Pechlin, Perrault, Hamberger, and more recently Bichat and Dumas, expressed their belief that the dilatation or expansion of the heart is a vital act in the same sense that its contraction is a vital act ; and it appears to me that modern physiologists have fallen into a grave error in stating that the contraction of the heart represents its only period of activity; the heart being passive when it expands, or, as they term it, relaxes. The heart no doubt must rest like every other part of the body, and the most convenient explanation of the phenomenon is to suppose that when the heart is contracting and forcing out the blood it is active, but that when it is receiving the blood it is passive, *i.e.* resting. This however, as I have endeavoured to show, is not the real explanation, the heart performing work not only when it closes, but also when it opens. The heart cannot be said to be resting when it is returning to its position of rest, for if the sarcous elements are doing work from the time they leave their position of rest, it is obvious that they must be doing work until they return to it. The position of rest moreover of the ventricular walls does not correspond to that assumed by them during their diastole or opening, any more than to that assumed by them during their systole or closing. It corresponds to a line midway between both, as shown at *x* of Fig. 130, p. 231. In like manner the position of rest of the voluntary muscles is semi-flexion or semi-extension ; the muscles being in a state of activity in complete flexion and complete extension. During repose the limbs are always slightly bent.

Size of the Cavities of the Heart (Mammal).—The auricles and ventricles increase in all their diameters when they open, and decrease when they close. As however the auricles are always closing when the ventricles are opening, and the contrary, the actual contents of the pericardium fluctuate very little. This circumstance renders it somewhat difficult to determine whether the long diameter of the heart as a whole varies. This was a question keenly debated by the Montpellier and Parisian anatomists and physiologists, but is practically of little importance. There are several subjects which hinge on the degree of opening and closing which occurs in the heart. One of these is the comparative size of the auricular and ventricular cavities. Winslow, Senac, Haller, and Lieutaud, maintain that the disparity in the size of the auricles and ventricles is considerable; Laennec, Bouillaud, Meckel, and Portal, that it is trifling; Lower, Sabatier, and Andral, that there is no difference whatever. The latter is most probably the correct opinion, as it is natural to suppose that the auricles contain the exact quantity of blood to be injected into the ventricles; these forcing out into the large arteries (aorta and pulmonary artery) a corresponding amount, which in due time is returned to the auricles by the large veins (venae cavae and pulmonary veins). This opinion is in a great measure corroborated by the practically incompressible nature of the blood. If a certain quantity of blood is forced out of one chamber, it is natural to suppose (seeing fluids are virtually incompressible) that a chamber of exactly the same size is prepared to receive it. A contrary supposition would tend to disturb the even tenor of the circulation. It is quite impossible, as I know from experience, to determine the size of the cavities of the heart after death, and there is no means of accurately ascertaining it during life. The parietes of the heart after death yield to such an extent that they may be distended at pleasure; a uniform pressure giving anything but a uniform expansion, as the ventricular walls, because of their varying thickness, become unequally stretched.

Impulse of the Heart (Mammal).—Another subject arising out of the degree of opening and closing occurring in the living heart is the impulse or beat of the organ against the anterior wall of the chest. Is this due to the closing or opening of the heart? The heart during the diastole has its apex pushed deeper into the chest; and if to this circumstance be added the fact that at this particular period the organ is enlarged, we *a priori* arrive at the conclusion that the heart is impelled against the thorax during the diastole of the ventricles. Pigeaux, Burdach, and Beau, entertain this belief. There can be no doubt, however, that the impulse in the mammal is communicated, not during the diastole of the ventricles, but during the systole. The illustrious Harvey found it so in man when the heart was exposed by disease. I have not had an opportunity of examining the human heart thus disclosed, but I have made observations on an anaesthetised living monkey, in which the pericardium was opened sufficiently to enable me to witness without disturbing the cardiac movements. The heart in this case beat with great regularity and apparently quite normally. The heart when it opened and closed, rotated on its long axis in opposite directions, to the extent of nearly a quarter of a turn either way. The ventricles elongated themselves during the diastole, and shortened themselves during the systole; a spiral wave of motion travelling from the apex towards the base, and from the base towards the apex. The left apex had a distinct screwing motion. The left apex and the middle third of the right ventricle impinged against the thorax during the systole: the former structure describing an ellipse, as in the fish and frog. Senac stated correctly enough that the impulse is communicated during the systole, and endeavoured to prove his position by averring that the heart is suspended from two curved tubes, viz. the pulmonary artery and aorta; these tubes, when the blood is forced through them by the closing of the ventricles, endeavouring to straighten themselves, and causing the apex of the heart to impinge against the thorax. This is the principle on which the steam-gauges at present employed for registering steam-pressure are constructed. The explanation is ingenious, but the large vessels, as Shebeare and Corrigan have shown, curve in such a manner that their recoil would not force the apex of the heart in the direction indicated, but just the opposite. There is this further objection, the ventricles are shortened in their long diameter during the systole. Senac seems to have been aware of this difficulty, for he endeavoured to strengthen his position by adding that the impulse was partly due to the expansion of the left auricle, which, because of its situation between the spine and the left ventricle, tended to force the apex of the heart outwards. The heart, however, tilts forwards when the large vessels are cut through, and it is altogether removed from the body; in which case, of course, neither the straightening of the vessels nor the swelling of the blood within the left auricle could produce any effect. The true explanation is, I believe, to be found in the shape of the ventricles, and in the distribution and direction of their muscular fibres. The ventricles form a twisted cone, which is flattened posteriorly and truncated obliquely in this direction at its base. The anterior fibres of the ventricles are consequently much longer than the posterior fibres; and as muscular fibres shorten in proportion to their length, this accounts for the heart tilting when removed from the body—the apex, as stated, describing a more or less perfect ellipse. A similar explanation was suggested by Professor Alison, and accepted by Mr. Carlisle and Dr. John Reid.

The Valves of the Vascular System.

Before proceeding to a consideration of the sounds of the heart, it will be necessary to describe somewhat minutely the structure and movements of the cardiac valves.

These are important and interesting, in a medical point of view, from the fact that they are frequently the seat of morbid lesions which inaugurate a long list of painful complaints, very bewildering to the physician, and especially dangerous to the patient. In order fully to comprehend the nature and uses of the highly elaborated cardiac valves as they exist in man, a knowledge of the relations, structure, and functions of the more rudimentary valves found in the veins of mammals and in the hearts of the lower animals is necessary [1].

Venous Valves—their Structure, etc.—The valves of the veins vary as regards the number of the segments composing them. In the smallest veins, and where small veins enter larger ones, one segment only is present. In the middle-sized veins of the extremities two segments are usually met with; while in the larger veins, as the internal jugulars of the horse, three and even four segments are by no means uncommon. (Fig. 131 A—J, p. 244.)

The segments, whatever their number, are semilunar in

---

[1] *Vide* Memoir 'On the Valves of the Vascular System in Vertebrata,' by the Author; Transactions of the Royal Society of Edinburgh, vol. xxiii. part iii., 1864. The preparations on which this investigation is based are preserved in the Hunterian Museum of the Royal College of Surgeons of London.

shape (Fig. 131 A, B, C, H), the convex borders being attached to the wall of the vessel; the crescentic or concave margins, which are free and directed towards the heart, projecting into it. When a valve is composed of one segment, the segment is placed obliquely in the vessel, its attached convex border occupying rather more than a half of the interior. When the segment occurs at the junction of a smaller with a larger vein (Fig. 131 H), its convex border (*a*) is attached to a half or more of the orifice of the smaller

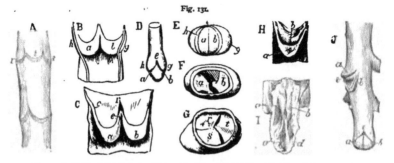

Fig. 131.

Fig. 131 A. External jugular vein of horse inverted. Shows valve, consisting of three (*r, s, t*) segments.—*Original.*

B. Section of external jugular vein of horse. Shows valve consisting of two segments (*a, b*), with dilatations (*g, h*) corresponding to the sinuses of Valsalva in the arteries.—*Original.*

C. External jugular vein of horse opened, to show the relations of the segments (*a, b*) where they come together (*e*), and are united by fibrous tissue (*r*). The free margin of one of the segments is seen at *c*, the attached margin at *a*.—*Original.*

D. Portion of femoral vein distended with plaster of Paris. Shows dilatations (*h, g*) in the vessel behind the valve; *a, b,* segments of valve; *e,* point where the segments come together when the valve is acting.—*Original.*

E. Shows venous valve, consisting of two segments (*a, b*) in action; *h, g,* bulgings corresponding to sinuses of Valsalva; *e,* line formed by the margins of the segments flattening against each other.—*Original.*

F. The same, not in action.

G. Venous valve from external jugular of horse, consisting of three segments (*r, s, t*).—*Original.*

H. Venous valve of one segment situated at the confluence of a small with a large vein. *a,* attached convex border; *b,* free crescentic border.—*Original.*

I. Venous sinus from the auricle of a sturgeon. *a, b,* muscular walls of sinus; *c, d,* muscular fasciculi which assist in opening and closing the sinus—*Original.*

J. Femoral vein distended with plaster of Paris. Shows two sets of venous valves in action; the one set (upper *a, b*) where a small vein enters a larger one; the other (lower *a, b*) in the principal vessel; *e,* line of junction between the segments of the venous valves. The segments are flattened when they come in contact, so that, if forcibly separated, they display a smooth crescentic surface, represented at E, *e* of Fig. 132.—*Original.*

one where it joins the larger, its free margin (*b*) running transversely to the larger trunk. In such cases the segment acts as a moveable partition or septum, common alike to both vessels; but its position and relations are such, that while it readily permits the blood from the smaller vein to enter the larger one, it effectually prevents its return.

When the valve consists of two segments they are semilunar in shape, and very ample, the vertical measurement of each being not unfrequently nearly twice that of the diameter of the vessel. In such cases both segments are usually of the same size, so that they divide the vessel into two equal parts (Fig. 131 B, C, F). They are placed across the vessel, their free margins being inclined towards the heart and the mesial plane of the vessel. The free margins, when the vessel is placed in fluid, run parallel with each other (Fig. 131 E, *e*; Fig. 132 E, *e*, p. 248). The attached margins, on the other hand, diverge to form festoons in the interior of the vessel (Fig. 131 A, *r*, *s*, *t*). This is necessary, as the attached margins must accommodate themselves to the interior of the vessel, which is more or less circular. The free margins of the segments, like the attached ones, start from a common point (Fig. 131 C, *r*); but the shape of the segments, and the angle at which they are placed with regard to each other and the mesial plane of the vessel, are such that the free margins do not diverge to the same extent as the attached ones, but run in a nearly straight line across the vessel. I was much struck, on injecting the external saphenous vein of the human subject from the dorsum of the foot, to find, on dissection, that the free margins of the segments of some of the valves were in contact throughout; clearly showing that when the segments are allowed to float in a fluid, they are more or less parallel, and so projected against each other that even the slightest reflux instantly closes them. This relation of the segments is in part accounted for by the presence of a fibrous structure (Fig. 131 C, *r*), which extends from the wall of the vessel into the interior, and supports them at a certain distance from the sides of the vessel. The fibrous structure referred to is well seen in the semilunar valves of the pulmonary artery and aorta (Fig. 133 A, *b*, p. 252), and seems to have escaped observation. In a line corresponding to the attached border of each of the segments, the middle and internal coats of the vein are thickened, as may be ascertained by a vertical section, or by introducing coloured plaster of Paris into the vessel [1]. I particularly direct atten-

---

[1] I have derived much information from the employment of this material; its use having enabled me to determine with accuracy the relation of the segments of the valves to each other when in action, and other points connected with the physiology of the heart.

tion to this circumstance, as the thickenings referred to form fibrous zones which extend for a short distance into the substance of the segments, and afford them a considerable degree of support (Fig. 131 E, *h*; C, *r*, p. 244). They further assist in preserving the shape of the segments, and in enabling them to maintain the proper angle of inclination, the said angle inclining the segments towards each other in the mesial plane of the vessel (Fig. 131 E, *e*, p. 244). When a valve con-sisting of two segments is situated at the junction of a smaller with a larger vein, one of the segments is usually placed between the two vessels at the point of juncture (Fig. 131 J, upper *b*, p. 244), the other on the wall of the smaller vein (upper *a*). The position of the segments in such instances varies, their long diameter sometimes running parallel with the larger vessel, sometimes obliquely, but more commonly transversely. When the valve consists of three segments (Fig. 131 A and G, p. 244), the segments, as a rule, are unequal in size, one of them being generally a little larger (*t*) than either of the other two (*r*, *s*). They are semilunar in shape, as in the smaller and middle-sized veins, and differ from the latter in being less capacious. The tri-semilunar valves in the veins may therefore be regarded as intermediate between the fully developed bi-semilunar valves found in the veins of the ex-tremities and the fully developed tri-semilunar valves which occur at the origins of the pulmonary artery and aorta. The existence of valves in the veins is indicated externally by a dilatation or enlargement of the vessel (Fig. 131 D, *h*, *g*, p. 244; Fig. 132 A, *h*, *g*, p. 248), the dilatation consisting of one, two, or three swellings, according as the valve is com-posed of one, two, or three segments. These dilatations or swellings are analogous to the sinuses of Valsalva in the arteries (Fig. 133 A, B, *d*, p. 252). They form, with the segments to which they belong, open sinuses or pouches which look towards the heart, and as they extend nearly as far in an outward direction as the segments project inwardly, they give a very good idea of the size and shape of the segments themselves. The object of the swellings is evidently two-fold,—firstly, to cause the blood to act on the segments of the valve from without inwards, *i. e.* in the direction of the mesial plane, or of the axis of the vessel, according as there are two or three segments present ; and secondly, to increase the area over which the pressure exerted by the reflux of the blood extends.

The segments of the venous valves are exceedingly flexible, and so delicate as to be semi-transparent. They possess great strength and a considerable degree of elasticity [1]. Usually they are described as consisting of a reduplication of the fine membrane lining the vessel, strengthened by some included fibro-cellular tissue, the whole being covered with epithelium. This description, however, is much too general to convey an accurate impression of their real structure, and the following, drawn up from the examination of a large number of specimens taken from man, the horse, ox, sheep, and other animals, may prove useful.

When one of the segments of a well-formed bi-semilunar valve removed from the human femoral vein is stained with carmine, fixed between two glasses, and examined microscopically, I find the following :—

1st, The lining membrane of the vessel which forms the investing sheath of the segment, and which is covered with epithelium.

2nd, Large quantities of white fibrous tissue mixed up with areolar and yellow elastic tissue, and a certain amount of non-striped muscular fibres from the middle coats of the vessel. The distribution of the fibres is represented at B, C, D of Fig. 132, p. 248.

Thus running along the concave or free margin of the segment (Fig. 132 B, *a*, p. 248), as likewise on the body, especially where the segments join each other (*b*), is a series of very delicate fibres, consisting principally of yellow elastic tissue. These fibres proceed in the direction of the long diameter of the segment, but transversely to the course of the vessel, and may be denominated the horizontal fibres.

Running in a precisely opposite direction, and confining themselves principally to the body of the segment, is a series of equally delicate fibres (*c*), having a like composition, and which, for the sake of distinction, may be described as

---

[1] Hunter denies the elasticity of the segments, on the ground that the valvular membrane is not formed of a reduplication of the lining membrane of the vessel—an opinion at variance with recent investigation.—*Treatise on the Blood*, pp. 181, 182.

the vertical series. These two' sets of fibres are superficial, and to be seen properly a power magnifying from 200 to 250 diameters is required.

Radiating from the centre of the segment (Fig. 132 C, *e*), towards its attached border (*i, j*), and seen through the more delicate horizontal and vertical ones, is a series of stronger and deeper fibres, composed of white fibrous and yellow elastic tissue, the former predominating. Still stronger and deeper than either of the fibres described, and proceeding from the attached border of the segment (Fig. 132 D, *s, t*), is a series of oblique fibres, continuous in many instances with corresponding fibres in the middle coat of the vessel. These fibres cross each other with great regularity, and form the principal portion of the segments. They are most

Fig 132.

Fig. 132 A. Vertical section of vein distended with plaster of Paris. : Shows the nature of the union between the segments (*e*). A. *g*, pouches behind the segments (*a, b*).—*Original.*
E. The same, the section being carried between (*e*) instead of across or through the segments. *e*, portion of segment flattened against corresponding segment, which in this case is removed. *b*, portion of segment not flattened by pressure. *g*, bulging of wall of vein behind segment.—*Original.*
B, C, D, show the structure of the venous valves.—*Original.*

strongly marked at the margin of the convex border of the segment, where they form a fibrous zone or ring, which, as has been explained, supports the segment, and carries it away from the sides of the vessel into the interior. I have also detected, in the vicinity of the attached border of the segment, some non-striped muscular fibres. The segment of a venous valve, it will be observed, is a highly symmetrical and complex structure, the fibrous tissues composing it being arranged in at least three well-marked directions; viz. horizontally, vertically, and obliquely. The great strength which such an arrangement is calculated to impart to the segment is readily understood.

The segment is thinnest at its free margin, and thickest towards its attached border. This follows because the free margins of the segments support each other when the valve is in action—the strain falling more upon the attached borders.

The Venous Valves in Action.—The manner in which the venous valves act is well seen when a vein is suspended perpendicularly overhead, and water, oil, glycerine, or liquid plaster of Paris, poured into it by an assistant from above. In order to witness this experiment properly, that part of the vein beneath the valve should be cut away, the better to expose the segments to the view of the spectator. When the valve consists of one segment only, the fluid is observed *to force it obliquely across the vessel,* and to apply its free crescentic margin to the interior or concave surface of the vessel with such accuracy as to prevent even the slightest reflux. When two segments occur in the course of a vein · *they are forced by the fluid simultaneously towards each other in the mesial plane of the vessel* (Fig. 131 E, *e*; J, *e*, p. 244), the sinuses behind the segments becoming distended, and directing the current and regulating to a certain extent the amount of pressure. The closure in this instance is almost instantaneous, and so perfect that not a single drop escapes. It is effected by *the free margins of the segments, and a large portion of the sides* coming into accurate contact, the amount of contact increasing in a direct ratio to the pressure applied. If liquid plaster of Paris be employed for distending the vein, and the specimen is examined after the plaster has set, one is struck with the great precision with which the segments act (Fig. 131 E, *a, b*; J, *a, b*, p. 244; Fig. 132 A, *a, b*, p. 248), these coming together so symmetrically that they form by their union *a perpendicular wall or septum* (Fig. 132 A, *e*) *of a beautifully crescentic shape*[1] (E, *e*). This fact is significant, as it clearly proves that the free margins of the segments and a considerable proportion of the sides are pressed against each other when the valve is in action, a circumstance difficult to comprehend, when it is remembered that the attached

---

[1] In order to see the perpendicular wall formed by the flattening of the sides of the segments against each other when the valve is in action, the vein and the plaster should be cut across immediately above the valve, and the segments forcibly separated by introducing a thin knife between them. In Fig. 132 E one of the segments has been so removed.

borders are applied obliquely to the walls of the vessel, and
that the segments, when not in action, incline towards each
other at a considerable angle. When three segments are
present, as happens in the larger venous trunks, the closure
is effected as in the semilunar valves of the pulmonary artery
and aorta. The fluid employed, in virtue of the direction
given to it by the venous sinuses, causes each of the segments
(Fig. 131 G, *r, s, t,* p. 244) to fold or double upon itself at an angle
of something like 120°; the three lines formed by the folding
and union of the three segments dividing the circle corresponding to the wall of the vessel into three nearly equal
parts. (Compare with Fig. 86, p. 174). In the folding of the
segments upon themselves, each segment regulates the amount
of folding which takes place in that next to it, and as the
free margins of the segments so bent advance synchronously
towards the axis of the vessel, they mutually act upon and
support each other. As the three segments are attached
obliquely to the wall of the vessel, while the free margins,
after the folding has taken place, are inclined towards and
run parallel with each other, they form a dome, the convexity
of which is always inclined towards the heart. The dome
consists of three nearly equal parts, the margins of the segments, and a certain portion of the sides, when the pressure of
the refluent blood is applied, flattening themselves against each
other to form three crescentic partitions or septa[1], which run
from the axis of the vessel towards the circumference. (Compare with *r s t, v w x,* of Fig. 134, p. 253.)

The tri-semilunar valve, as will be seen from the foregoing
description, is closed in a somewhat different manner from
the bi-semilunar one. The occlusion of the vessel, however, is
not the less complete; the segments, when three are present,
*being wedged into each other from without inwards and away
from the heart.* As the apices of the wedges formed by the
doubling of the segments whilst in action are composed
principally of the flexible and •free crescentic margins, and
are at liberty to move until the wedging process is completed,
a careful examination has satisfied me *that they rotate to a*

[1] The crescentic partitions, as they occur in the semilunar valves of the
pulmonary artery and aorta, are shown at Fig. 133 C, *b*, p. 252.

greater or less extent before the valve is finally closed. This spiral movement, which is simply indicated in the venous valves, is more strongly marked in the semilunar ones of the pulmonary artery and aorta (Fig. 134, *r s t, v w x*, p. 253), and attains, as will be shown subsequently, a maximum in the auriculo-ventricular valves of the mammal (Figs. 140—143, pp. 268, 281).

By whatever power the blood in the veins advances— whether impelled by the heart alone, or aided by the shortening and lengthening of muscles in different parts of the body, or by rhythmic movements which take place in the vessels themselves, or by respiratory efforts, or by atmospheric pressure, or by combinations of all of these,—there can be no doubt that this fluid, in its backward or retrograde movement, acts mechanically on the valves as described. It ought however to be borne in mind that the veins and the valves are vital structures, and that, although a perfect closure may be effected by purely mechanical means in the dead vein, it is more than probable that, in the living one, the coats of the vessel, with their included nerves, exercise a regulating influence.

Arterial or Semilunar Valves, their Structure, etc.—The arterial valves may be regarded as occupying an intermediate position between the venous valves on the one hand, and the auriculo-ventricular valves on the other. The segments composing them are three in number, and resemble the segments of the venous valves in their shape, position, mode of attachment, and movements; whereas structurally they are more nearly allied to the segments of the auriculo-ventricular, *i. e.* the mitral and tricuspid, valves. Like the venous valves, the arterial occupy the interior of vessels, and are crescentic in shape. Thus the segments have a free crescentic thin margin, and a thicker convex attached margin. The convex margin is firmly secured to the scalloped aortic and pulmonic fibrous rings already described (Fig. 94, *a, b*, p. 190). The segments are surrounded by a fibrous framework, which enables them to maintain their shape and relative position to each other. This framework carries the segments away from the interior of the vessel, and inclines their free margins towards its axis, so that if the vessel, with its semilunar valve, be submerged, the free margins of the segments are naturally more or less in contact—an arrangement which insures the immediate closure of the valve the instant the blood regurgitates. The great vessels are thickened where the segments approach each other (Fig. 133 A, *b*), and thinned and dilated behind each segment (B, *i*), to form three large cavities or sinuses, known as the sinuses of Valsalva (B, *d*). These sinuses contain a considerable amount of residual blood, which by its weight and pressure assists in closing and wedging the segments together during the diastole. They are also the receptacles which receive the segments during the systole—an arrange-

Fig. 133.

Fig. 133 A. Section of pulmonary artery and right ventricle of human heart between the segments of the semilunar valve. Shows the variation in the thickness of the vessel (*a*, *b*), and how it bifurcates (*r*) at its origin. *s*, segment of valve. *c*, *b*, *t*, *f*, fibrous framework surrounding it. *d*, sinus of Valsalva. *e*, pulmonic fibrous ring. *v*, ventricle.—*Original.*

B. Similar section carried through pulmonary artery (*a*, *b*) and middle of segment (*s*). Shows the thinning of the vessel in this situation (*i*). *c*, portion of fibrous framework. *d*, sinus of Valsalva. *c*, pulmonic fibrous ring. *v*, ventricle.—*Original.*

C. Human semilunar valve distended with plaster of Paris, and one of the segments (*g*) removed to show the shape of the lunulae or opposing surfaces which come together when fluid pressure is applied to the segments. *n*, aorta. *m*, flattened portion of segment. This flattening increases with the pressure, as at *b*. The flattening represents the degree of contact between the segments. It is much greater than is usually supposed.—*Original.*

D. Shows how the segments of the semilunar valve are folded, flattened, and spirally wedged into each other when the valve is closed. *v w x*, direction in which the blood flows down upon the segments to fold them. *o r s*, line of union between the segments. *c a b*, nature and amount of flattening occurring along the free margins of the segments.—*Original.*

ment which increases the diameter of the great vessels at their origins at this particular period (Fig. 87, *e*, p. 174). When the reflux of the blood occurs, the segments of the semilunar valves fold or bend at their central portions in such a manner that their free crescentic margins become accurately applied to and flattened against each other, the flattening increasing according to the pressure. This arrangement effectually prevents regurgitation in healthy valves. (Fig. 133 A, B, C, D.)

The sinuses of Valsalva are not disposed in the same plane. They are moreover unequal in size. The highest and smallest is placed anteriorly, that which is intermediate in size posteriorly, the lowest and largest being directed towards the septum. They correspond in situation and dimensions to the segments behind which they are found, and differ from the venous sinuses in being more capacious, a section of the sinus and its segment (which is likewise very ample) giving a sweep of nearly half a circle. As a result of this amplitude, those portions of the segments which project into the vessel are, during the action of the valve, closely applied to each other throughout a considerable part of their extent (Fig. 133 C, *b*; D, *a, b, c*), the great size of the sinuses furnishing an increased quantity of blood for pressing the segments from above downwards, and from without inwards, or in the direction of the axis of the vessel. *The sinuses of Valsalva curve*

Fig. 134.

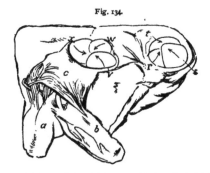

Fig. 134.—Base of heart, with right and left ventricles removed to show the pulmonic, aortic, and mitral valves. The pulmonic and aortic valves (*r s t, v w x*) have been closed by pouring liquid plaster of Paris into them. The mitral valve (*c*) is open, it always happening that when the semilunar valves are closed, the auriculo-ventricular ones are open. The segments of the pulmonic and aortic valves (*vide* arrows *r s t, v w x*) are spirally wedged into each other. *a, b*, right and left musculi papillares of left entricle. *c*, aortic segment of mitral valve. From photograph.—*Original.*

towards each other in a spiral direction; and this ought to be attended to in speaking of the action of the semilunar valves, as the sinuses direct the blood spirally on the mesial line of each segment (Fig. 133 D, *v, w, x*), and cause the segments to twist and wedge into each other, as shown at *r s t, v w x*, of Fig. 134. In order to determine this point, I procured a fresh pulmonary artery and aorta, and after putting the valves in position with water, caused an assistant to drop liquid plaster of Paris into the vessels. The greater density of the plaster gradually displaced the water, and I was in this way furnished with accurate casts of the sinuses and of the valves. The segments of the semilunar valves are unequal in size, and consist of a reduplication of the fine membrane lining the pulmonary artery and aorta, strengthened by certain tendinous bands, and, as was first satisfactorily demonstrated by Mr. W. S. Savory, of a considerable quantity of yellow elastic tissue [1]. Some of the older anatomists, among whom may be mentioned Lancisci[2], Senac[3], Morgagni[4], Win-

Fig. 135.

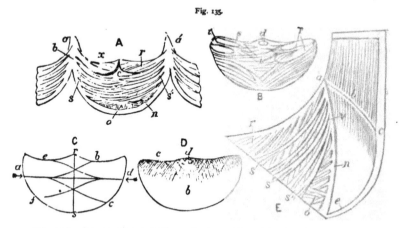

Fig. 135 A. Segment of human semilunar valve (pulmonic) suspended from fibrous band (a, a'). x, r, lunulae which, when the valve is in action, become accurately applied to corresponding lunulae in the two remaining segments. c, portion of segment. The thickening is absent in young healthy valves. n, thickened convex border attached to fibrous ring of pulmonary artery. o, thinner portion of segment. s, s', fibrous bands which split up in the mesial line of the segment, in order to support and strengthen it. These structures are better seen at E, which represents the terminal portion of the aorta of a whale with a half segment of one of the semilunar valves attached. a, b, c, thickened portion of aorta. e, thinned portion. a, n, fibrous ring attaching segment of valve to aorta. r, free margin or delicate lunula of segment. o, thicker portion of segment. v, s, s', s'', thickest portion of segment, consisting of fibrous bands which break up into brush-shaped expansions, and at once strengthen and support the segment. A scheme of the arrangement of these bands is given at C. r, s, mesial line of segment. a, band splitting up into b and c. d, band splitting up into e and f. At B a semilunar segment (v) is shown, where the bands which split up (s, t) are separated by a very delicate membrane (r), and so resemble chordae tendineae. This segment is abnormally thickened and presents a well-marked corpus Arantii (d). At D a segment (b) is shown with its free crescentic borders (e) thickened. This too presents a corpus Arantii (d).—Original.

slow[5], and Cooper[6], believed that they had detected the presence of carneous or muscular fibres; but Haller[7], and many since his time, have gravely doubted the accuracy of their observations. Mr. Moore[8] has figured two sets of mus-

---

[1] Purkinge and Räuschel had detected elastic tissue in the corpora Arantii, but knew nothing of its existence throughout the other portions of the valves. Of its presence I have frequently satisfied myself.

[2] De Motu Cordis.

[3] Traité de la Structure du Cœur. Livre i.

[4] Adversaria Anatomica Omnia.

[5] Exposition Anat. de la Structure du Corps Humain, p. 592.

[6] Myotomia Reformata.

[7] Elementa Physiologiae. Liber iv. sect. 10.

[8] Med. Gazette, March 8, 1850.

cular fibres, which he has termed, according to their supposed action, dilators and retractors; and Dr. Monneret[1] has described two similar sets, which, for like reasons, he has named elevators and depressors. I have sought in vain for the muscular fibres in question, and am inclined to think that when found, they have been mistaken for the tendinous bands accidentally stained with blood. The tendinous bands have hitherto been regarded as following three principal directions, —one band being said to occupy the free margin, and to be divided into two equal parts by the nodulus or corpus Arantii, otherwise called corpusculum Morgagni, and corpus sesamoideum ; a second band, proceeding from points a little above the middle of the segment, and curving in an upward direction towards the corpus Arantii; the third band, which is the thickest, surrounding the attached border of the segment. A careful examination of a large number of mammalian hearts, particularly those of man, has induced me to assign to the semilunar valves a more intricate structure. (Fig. 135 A—E.)

In a healthy human semilunar valve[2] taken from the pulmonary artery, the following seems to be the arrangement. Proceeding from the attached extremities of the segment above, and running along its free margin, is a delicate tendinous band, which gives off still more delicate slips (Fig. 135 A, x, r), to radiate in a downward and inward direction, $i. e.$ in the direction of the mesial line and body of the segment. These fine slips interdigitate in the mesial line, and are attached below to the uppermost of a series of very strong fibrous bands which occupy the body of the segment (s, s'). In the interspaces between the slips the valve is so thin as to be almost transparent. Those portions of the segments included within the delicate fibrous band, running along the free margin and the uppermost of the stronger bands occupying the body, are somewhat crescentic in shape (r), and have, from this circumstance, been termed lunulae. They do

---

[1] Lancet, Dec. 29, 1850.

[2] It is comparatively a difficult matter to get a perfectly healthy human aortic semilunar valve, especially if the patient is at all advanced in years. Out of twenty adult hearts examined by me, nearly half of that number had the valves abnormally thickened.

not form the perfect crescents usually represented in books, the horns of the crescents directed towards the mesial line of the segment being much broader than those directed towards the extremities, or where the segments unite above. The object of this arrangement is obvious. The broader portions of the crescents are those which, when the segment is folded upon itself during the action of the valve, are accurately applied to corresponding and similar portions of the two remaining segments (Fig. 133 C, *b*; D, *a, b, c,* p. 252). If however the lunulae had been symmetrical—in other words, if they had terminated in well-defined horns towards the mesial line, or where the segments fold upon themselves—then the union between the segments in the axis of the vessel (Fig. 133 D), where great strength is required, would have been partial, and consequently imperfect.

Proceeding from the attached extremities of the segments at points a little below the origins of the marginal band, and curving in a downward and inward direction, is the first of the stronger bands (Fig. 135 A, *b,* p. 254). The band referred to splits up into brush-shaped expansions as it approaches the mesial line (*c*), where it interdigitates and becomes strongly embraced. Other and similar bands, to the extent of three or four (*s*), usually the latter number, are met with, and as they all curve in a downward and inward direction, and have finer bands running between them in a nearly vertical direction, they suspend the body of the segment; so that when blood or water is directed upon it, the various parts of which it is composed radiate from the attached or convex border (*b, s*) like a fan, each band dragging upon that above it; the whole deriving support from the thickened convex margin. The bands, which are thus from five to six in number, are best seen on that aspect of the segments which is directed towards the sinuses of Valsalva. The surfaces of the segments directed towards the axis of the vessel are perfectly smooth, and so facilitate the onward flow of the blood. The bands are thickest at their attached extremities, where they interlace slightly, and are mixed up to a greater or less extent with the pale soft flattened fibres and elastic tissue of the central layer of the vessel. The several points alluded to are well seen in Fig. 135 E, p. 254.

As the bands under consideration are exceedingly strong when compared with those occurring in other portions of the segments, and project in an inward direction, or towards the axis of the vessel, when the preparation is sunk in water, their function, as ascertained from numerous experiments on the semilunar valves of a whale (*Physalus antiquorum*, Gray), seems to be the following :—

1st, *They carry the bodies of the segments away from the sides of the vessel, and incline their free margins towards each other at such an angle as necessitates the free margins of neighbouring segments being always more or less in apposition.* In this they are assisted by the thickened portion of the pulmonary artery which projects between the segments, where they unite above, and by the fibrous zones which correspond to the convex border of each segment.

2nd, *The stronger fibres suspend the bodies of the segments from above, and permit the reflux of blood to act more immediately upon the mesial line of each segment where thinnest and where least supported,* to occasion that characteristic folding of the segments upon themselves when the valve is in action. The closure of the valve is in part due to the weight of the blood, in part to the sucking action of the right ventricle when opening, and in part to the elastic properties of the artery.

From the foregoing it will be perceived that the segments of a semilunar valve are bilaterally symmetrical, and constructed on a plan which secures the greatest amount of strength with the least possible material (Fig. 135 C, p. 254).

On some occasions the tendinous bands proceeding from the marginal one are abnormally thickened (Fig. 135 B, *s*, *t*), and terminate in brush-shaped expansions in the body of the segment (*v*); the body under such circumstances projecting in an upward direction towards the corpus Arantii (*d*). In such cases, those portions of the valve which occur between the thickened bands proceeding from the marginal one, are exceedingly thin, and in some diseased conditions altogether awanting (*r*), so that the segment very much resembles one of the segments of the mitral or tricuspid valve, with its chordae tendinae. That there is an analogy between the semilunar and the mitral and tricuspid valves, and that the tendinous chords are a further development, seems probable from the fact that in the bulbus arteriosus of certain fishes, as the gray and basking sharks, lepidosteus, etc., the semilunar valves are furnished with what may be regarded as rudimentary chordae tendineae (Figs. 137 and 138, *b*); the auriculo-ventricular valves of fishes, which have hitherto been regarded as semilunar, exhibiting tendinous chords in various stages of development (Fig. 136, *c*).

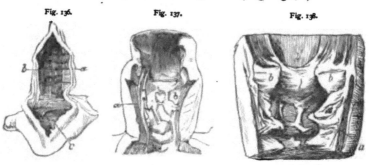

Fig. 136.   Fig. 137.   Fig. 138.

Fig. 136.—Bulbus arteriosus and ventricle of sturgeon ; the former (*a*) displaying five rows of semilunar valves (*b*), the latter an auriculo-ventricular valve (*c*), with numerous tendinous bands running into it.—*Original.*

Fig. 137.—Bulbus arteriosus and portion of ventricle of lepidosteus. Shows the great thickness of the bulb (*a*), and of the valves (*b*), between which tendinous bands run.—*Original.*

Fig. 138.—Portion of bulbus arteriosus of basking shark. Shows the great thickness of the bulb (*a*) and of the valves (*b*), and how the latter support each other.—*Original.*

The corpus Arantii is never present in a perfectly healthy semilunar segment; nor will its absence occasion surprise, when it is remembered that its presence materially interferes with the folding of the segments upon themselves when the valve is in action. That its existence is not necessary to the perfect closure of a semilunar valve, is proved by its complete absence in the segments of the human pulmonic valve, in the segments of the pulmonic and aortic semilunar valves of the lower animals, and in all veins. In the semilunar valve of the whale, where one would have naturally expected the corpus Arantii in perfection, I could not detect even a trace of it. I am therefore disposed to regard it as a morbid condition, due to irritation and subsequent deposit.

What has been said of the semilunar valves of the pulmonary artery may with equal propriety be said of those of the aorta ; the only difference being that the segments of the aorta are stronger and more opaque, to harmonise with the greater strength of the left ventricle.

The Arterial or Semilunar Valves in Action.—As the manner in which the semilunar valves are closed does not seem to be well understood, an account of some experiments conducted by me some time ago with various fluids and liquid plaster of Paris may prove interesting :—

When the aorta is cut across an inch or so above the aortic semilunar valve, and water introduced, the segments, if watched from beneath, are seen to act with great alacrity, the smallest segment, which is situated highest, descending with a spiral swoop, and first falling into position; the middle-sized segment, which is placed a little lower, descending in like manner, and fixing the first segment by one of its lunulae or crescentic surfaces; the third and largest segment, which occupies a lower position than either of the others, descending spirally upon the crescentic margins of the other two, and wedging and screwing them more and more tightly into each other. The spiral movement, as has been already explained, is occasioned by the direction of the sinuses of Valsalva, which curve towards each other, and direct the blood in spiral waves upon the mesial line of each segment (Fig. 133 D, *v w x*, p. 252 ; Fig. 134, *v w x*, p. 253).

From the foregoing description of the venous and arterial semilunar valves in mammalia, it will be evident that there is nothing either in their structure or relations to betoken any great degree of activity on their part. That these structures are, on the contrary, to a great extent passive, seems certain from the fact that a stream of water or other fluid directed upon them from above as recommended at once closes the orifices which they guard. Thus far my remarks have been confined to the so-called venous and arterial semilunar valves of the mammal. I will now say a few words regarding similar structures in the fish, reptile, and bird.

Semilunar and other Valves of the Fish, Reptile, Bird, etc.— The semilunar valves in the bulbus arteriosus of the fish, and the auriculo-ventricular valves in the fish and reptile, differ from the venous and arterial semilunar valves of the mammal in being, for the most part, exposed, either directly or indirectly, to the influence of muscular movements. The bulbus arteriosus is a muscular structure which opens and closes like the other parts of the heart. As a consequence, the valves situated in its interior are opened and closed by vito-mechanical movements. The segments vary as regards number, size, and shape, apparently with a view to meeting the requirements of the structure in which they occur. Thus, in the frog-fish (*Lophius piscatorius*), the origin of the bulbus arteriosus is guarded by a semilunar valve, consisting of two ample and very delicate segments, resembling those found in the middle-sized veins; while in the sun-fish (*Orthagoriscus mola*, Schneider) the same aperture is guarded by a semilunar valve consisting of three segments, the segments being analogous in every respect to those found in the largest veins, and in the pulmonary artery and aorta. As the valve in these cases is situated between the actively moving bulbus arteriosus and ventricle, it is surrounded by a fibrous ring similar to that occurring at the origin of the pulmonary artery and aorta in man. The movements of the valve are consequently not affected by the movements of the bulbus arteriosus and ventricle to any great extent. The semilunar valves in the frog-fish and sun-fish are to be regarded as connecting links between the venous and arterial ones in the bird and mammal, and that more complex system of analogous valves which is found in the bulbus arteriosus of fishes generally. In the bulbus arteriosus of the skate (*Raia batis*), the segments occupy the whole of the interior of the bulb, and are arranged in three pyramidal rows of five each. As the segments in this instance are very small, and cannot obliterate the cavity of the arterial bulb, they must be looked upon as being useful only in supporting the column of blood; it being reserved for the segments at the termination of the bulb, which are larger and more fully developed, to effect the closure. The action of the segments in the bulbus arteriosus of the skate is rendered more perfect by the pressure from without, caused by the closure of the bulb itself. In the bulbus arteriosus of the sturgeon (*Accipenser sturio*), the segments are arranged in four rows of eight each (Fig. 136, *b*, p. 258). They are more delicate, and less perfectly formed than in the skate. In the bulbus arteriosus of the American devil-fish (*Cephalopterus giorna*), the segments increase to thirty-six, are more imperfect than in any of the others, and are supported by three longitudinal angular muscular columns. As the segment-bearing columns, from their shape, project into the cavity of the bulb, and almost obliterate it when the bulb closes, they in this way bring the free margins of the segments together. The orifice of the bulbus arteriosus, however, is not closed by the imperfect segments referred to; this being guarded by two well-formed and fully-developed trisemilunar valves, the one of which is situated at the beginning, the other at the termination, of the bulb. In the bulbus arteriosus of the gray shark (*Galeus communis*), we have a slightly different arrangement, the two rows of segments of which the valve is composed being connected with each other by means of tendinous bands, resembling chordae tendineae. In the bulbus arteriosus of the lepidosteus (Fig. 137, *b*, p. 258), and that of the basking shark (Fig. 138, *b*, ib.), the same arrangement prevails; the segments being stronger and less mobile, and the tendinous bands which bind the one segment to the other more strongly marked. As the tendinous bands referred to are not in contact with the wall of the bulbus arteriosus, but simply run between the segments, and are in some instances, as in the basking shark, very powerful, they must be regarded in the light of sustaining or supporting structures; their function being probably to prevent eversion of the segments. Other examples might be cited, but sufficient have been adduced to show that the form, as well as the number and arrangement, of the segments is adapted to the peculiar wants of the structure in which the segments are situated; and it ought not to be overlooked, that when a multiplicity of segments is met with in an actively moving organ, the muscles and valves act together.

If we now direct our attention to the auriculo-ventricular valves of the fish and reptile, similar modifications as regards the number of the segments, and the presence or absence of chordae tendineae and analogous structures, present themselves. Thus, in the heart of the serpent (*Python tigris*), the two crescentic apertures by which the blood enters the posterior or aortic division of the ventricle are each provided *with a single semilunar valve.* The same may be said of the aperture of communication between the left auricle and ventricle of the crocodile (*Crocodilus acutus*) and of the sturgeon (*Accipenser sturio*, Linn.). In the heart of the Indian

tortoise (*Testudo Indica,* Vosmaer), the left auriculo-ventricular orifice is guarded *by a single membranous fold,* the right
orifice having in addition *a slightly projecting semilunar ridge,*
which extends from the right ventricular wall, and may be
regarded as the rudiment of the fleshy valve which guards
the same aperture in birds (Fig. 139, *i, j,* p. 264). In the heart
of the bulinus, frog-fish, American devil-fish, gray shark, and
crocodile, the auriculo-ventricular orifice is guarded by a
semilunar valve consisting *of two cusps or segments;* while in
the sturgeon, sun-fish, and others, it is guarded *by four, two
larger and two smaller.*

So much for the number of the segments constituting the
auriculo-ventricular valves in fishes and reptiles; but there
are other modifications which are not less interesting physiologically. In the bulinus, frog-fish, and crocodile, the segments of the valves are attached to the auriculo-ventricular
tendinous ring, and to the sides of the ventricle, and *have no
chordae tendineae.* In the sun-fish the valve is likewise
destitute of chordae tendineae; but in this instance the
muscular fibres are arranged *in the direction of the free
margins of the segments of the valve,* and no doubt exercise
an influence upon them. In the gray shark the membranous
folds forming the segments *are elongated at the parts where
they are attached to the ventricular walls,* these elongated
attachments being more or less split up, so as to resemble
chordae tendineae.

In the American devil-fish the auriculo-ventricular valve
consists of two strong well-developed membranous folds,
which, like the preceding, are attached by elongated processes to the interior of the ventricular wall; *these processes
consisting of distinct tendinous slips,* which are attached *to
rudimentary musculi papillares.*

In the sturgeon *three tendinous chords from rudimentary
musculi papillares* are seen to extend into the half of each
of the segments; while in the left ventricle of the dugong,
*six chords proceeding from tolerably well-formed musculi
papillares are distributed to the back, and six to the margins
of each of the segments.* It is however in the bird and
mammal, particularly the latter, that the musculi papillares
are most fully developed, and the chordae tendineae most

numerous—the number of tendinous chords inserted into each of the segments amounting to eighteen or more. As the chordae tendineae of the auriculo-ventricular valves are attached either to the interior of the ventricle, or to the musculi papillares or carneae columnae, it is evident that the closure of the ventricle must influence both valves and chords to a greater or less extent. That, however, the presence of muscular substance does not impair the efficiency of the valves appears from this—that some valves are partly muscular and partly tendinous, a few being altogether muscular. Thus, in the heart of the cassowary, the right auriculo-ventricular orifice is occluded by a valve, which is partly muscular and partly tendinous; the muscular part, which is a continuation of two tolerably well-formed musculi papillares, extending into the tendinous substance of the valve where it gradually loses itself. In the right ventricle of the crocodile, a muscular valve, resembling that found in the right ventricle of birds, exists.

In some birds the right auriculo-ventricular valve is alto-gether muscular. It is usually described as consisting of two parts, from the fact of its dependent or free margin being divided into two portions by a spindle-shaped muscular band, which connects it with the right ventricular wall. As however the valve consists of one continuous fold towards the base, and the two portions into which its free margin are divided are applied during the systole not to each other but to the septum, the valve in reality consists of a singular muscular flap or fold, as shown at *i* of Fig. 139, p. 264.

The muscular flap or fold extends from the edge and upper third of the septum posteriorly to the fleshy pons anteriorly. It opens towards the interior of the ventricle in a direction from above downwards, and is deepest at the edge of the septum posteriorly. As it gradually narrows anteriorly (*i*), it is somewhat triangular in shape, its dependent and free margin describing a spiral which winds from behind forwards, and from below upwards. The valve, from its shape and structure, might not inappropriately be termed the musculo-spiral valve. It is well seen in the right ventricle of the emu, swan, turkey, capercailzie, and eagle. The muscular valve of the bird is composed of the fibres entering into the formation of the several layers of the right ventricular wall (the ventricular wall in fact bifurcates or splits up towards its base) ; the external layers forming the outer wall of the valve, the internal layers, which are slightly modified, forming the inner. If the muscular valve be regarded as an independent formation, which it can scarcely be, it will be best described as a structure composed of fibrous loops, these loops being of three kinds, and directed towards the base— the first series consisting of spiral, nearly vertical fibres, forming a somewhat acute curve ; the second series consisting of slightly oblique spiral fibres, forming a larger or wider curve ; and the third series consisting of still more oblique fibres, and forming a still greater curve. As the fibres composing the different loops act directly upon each other

Fig. 139.

Fig. 139.—Anterior aspect of turkey's heart, with right and left ventricles open to show auriculo-ventricular valves. *a*, aorta arching to right side and dividing into three branches, two of which (*b*) go to right side, and one (*c*) to left side. *d*, pulmonary artery dividing into two, and sending a branch to right and left lungs. *i*, muscular or fleshy valve which occludes right auriculo-ventricular orifice. *j*, musculus papillaris of fleshy valve (compare with *g*). *e*, portion of septum to which valve is applied when closed. *f*, left ventricle. *v*, tendinous valve which occludes left auriculo-ventricular orifice. *g*, musculus papillaris with chordae tendineae attached to tendinous valve.—*Original.*

when the ventricles close, the object of the arrangement is obviously to supply a movable partition or septum which shall occlude the right auriculo-ventricular opening during the systole. The manner in which the several loops act is determined by their direction. Thus, the more vertical ones, in virtue of their shortening from above downwards, have the effect of flattening or opening out the valvular fold, and in this way cause its dependent or free margin to approach the septum. The slightly oblique fibres, which shorten partially from above downwards, but principally from before backwards, assist in this movement by diminishing the size of the right auriculo-ventricular orifice in an antero-posterior direction,—it remaining for the very oblique and transverse fibres, which shorten from before backwards and from without inwards, to complete the movement by pressing the inner leaf of the fold directly against the septum—an act in which the blood plays an important part, from its position within the valve; this fluid, according to hydrostatic principles, distending equally in all directions, and acting more immediately on the dependent or free margin of the valve, which is very thin and remarkably flexible.   When a vertical section of the fold forming the right auriculo-ventricular valve of the bird is made, that portion of it which hangs free in the right ventricular cavity is found to be somewhat conical in shape, the thickest part being directed towards the base, where it has to resist the greatest amount of pressure; the thinnest corresponding to its dependent and free margin, where it is applied to and supported by the septum. The upper border of the fold is finely rounded, and in this respect resembles the convex border which limits the right ventricle of the mammal towards the base.

The spindle-shaped muscular band (Fig. 139, *j*, p. 264), which from its connexion may be said to command the upper and lower portions of the right ventricle interiorly, is obviously for the purpose of co-ordinating the movements of the muscular valvular fold (*i*); and as its position and direction nearly correspond with the position and direction of the musculus papillaris situated on the right ventricular wall of the mammal, it is more than probable that it forms the homologue of this structure.   Indeed this seems almost certain from the fact that if the ventricles of the bird be opened anteriorly and the band referred to (*j*) contrasted with the anterior musculus papillaris of the left ventricle (*g*), both are found to occupy a similar position.   The fleshy band is therefore to the muscular valve of the right ventricle, what the anterior musculus papillaris and its chordae tendineae are to the segments of the mitral valve.   Compared with the tricuspid valve of the mammal, the muscular valve of the right ventricle of the bird is of great strength.   As, moreover, it applies itself with unerring precision to the septum (*e*), which is slightly prominent in its course, its efficiency is commensurate with its strength. The prominence on the septum alluded to is very slight, and might escape observation, were it not that immediately below the prominence the septum is hollowed out to form a spiral groove of large dimensions. This groove, like the valve, runs in a spiral direction from behind forwards and from below upwards, and when the valve is applied to the septum during the systole, converts the right ventricular cavity into a spiral tunnel, through which the blood is forced, on its way to the pulmonary artery. The efficiency of the right auriculo-ventricular muscular valve in birds, clearly shows that large apertures may be occluded by purely muscular arrangements and by vital movements; and it is important to bear this fact in mind, as it shows how the musculi papillares in mammals, by their elongating and shortening, may take part in the opening and closing of the mitral and tricuspid valves. In addition to the muscular valve of the bird described, it may be well to state that in the serpent the opening between the right and left ventricles occurs as a spiral slit in the septum. It is guarded by two projecting muscular surfaces, which are rounded off for the purpose. The orifices of many of the venous sinuses are closed by purely muscular adaptations; the fibres in such instances running parallel with the slit-like opening (Fig. 131 I, a, b), and being continuous with two or more bundles of fibres (c, d), which supply the place of musculi papillares. From the great variety in the shape and structure of the auriculo-ventricular valves, and from the existence in almost all of tendinous chords, which connect them with actively moving structures, there can, I think, be no doubt that these valves possess an adaptive power traceable in a great measure to the centripetal and centrifugal power residing in muscle.

As it would obviously occupy too much time to give a detailed account of the numerous auriculo-ventricular valves, to which allusion has been made, I have selected for description the auriculo-ventricular valves of the mammal, and those of man more particularly.

Intricate Structure of the Mitral and Tricuspid Valves in Mammalia; Relations of the Chordae Tendineae to the Valves and to the Musculi Papillares. — The auriculo-ventricular valves, known as the mitral or bicuspid and tricuspid valves, are composed of segments which differ in size, and are more or less triangular in shape. They are much stronger than the segments composing the aortic and pulmonic semilunar valves, which in some respects they resemble in structure as well as function. The segments of the mitral and tricuspid valves are very dense, and quite opaque, unless at the margins and apices, where they are frequently remarkably thin. They unite at the base where thickest, to form tendinous zones, which are attached to one or other of the fibrous rings surrounding the auriculo-ventricular orifices (Fig. 94, c, d, p. 190). The auriculo-ventricular fibrous rings have been variously described, the majority of investigators regarding them as strongly pronounced structures, which afford attachment, not only to the valves, but to all the muscular fibres of the auricles and ventricles. A careful examination of these rings in boiled hearts has led me to a different conclusion. They afford attachment to the muscular fibres of the auricles and to the valves, *but to almost none of the muscular fibres of the ventricles.* They are most fully developed anteriorly, and on the septum, where they form a dense fibrous investment. The left ring, like everything else pertaining to the left ventricle, is more fully developed than the right; but neither the one nor the other can compare in breadth or thickness with the pulmonic or aortic fibrous rings (Fig. 94, a, b, p. 190). The influence exerted by the auriculo-ventricular fibrous rings in conferring rigidity on the auriculo-ventricular orifices is consequently immaterial. The position of the segments of the mitral and tricuspid valves in the auriculo-ventricular orifices, and their relation to the musculi papillares, is deserving of attention. The left auriculo-ventricular orifice is provided with a valve consisting of two major or principal segments, and two minor or smaller segments which are placed between the principal ones. The major segments are unequal in size and form; their shape and depending position resembling a bishop's mitre inverted, hence the epithet *mitral* or *bicuspid* applied to this valve. The larger of the major segments is suspended obliquely between the left auriculo-ventricular and aortic openings, and occupies a somewhat internal and anterior position; the smaller one, which runs parallel to it, occupying a more external and posterior position. The right auriculo-ventricular orifice, on the other hand, is supplied with a valve composed of three major or principal segments, and three minor or smaller intermediate segments. From this it follows that the right auriculo-ventricular valve has been denominated *tricuspid* to distinguish it from the mitral or bicuspid one. The three principal segments forming the tricuspid valve vary in size,— the smallest running parallel with the septum; the largest being placed anteriorly and inclined to the right side; the one which is intermediate in size occupying a more posterior position. The segments, whatever their size, are attached by their bases to the auriculo-ventricular fibrous rings, and by their margins and apices (by means of the chordae tendineae) to the spiral musculi papillares.

Fig. 140.

Fig. 140.—Anterior segment of human mitral valve. Shows the threefold distribution of the chordae tendineae from above downwards, and from the mesial line towards the margins of the segment. *s*, base of segment. *x*, apex ditto. *r r'*, *s s'*, chordae tendineae from anterior portions (*a, c*) of right and left musculi papillares, bifurcating and losing themselves in margins of segment. *b, d*, posterior portions of right and left musculi papillares, which send chordae tendineae to posterior segment of mitral valve.— *Original.*

The segments of the mitral valve, to which the following description, drawn from an extensive examination of mammalian hearts[1], more particularly applies, consist of a reduplication of the endocardium, or lining membrane of the heart, containing within its fold large quantities of white fibrous tissue, and, as was pointed out by Mr. W. S. Savory,

[1] Of the hearts examined, those of man, the elephant, camel, whale (*Physalus antiquorum*, Gray), mysticetus, horse, ox, ass, deer, sheep, seal, hog, porpoise, monkey, rabbit, and hedgehog, may be mentioned.

and after him by Professor Donders[1], of a moderate amount of yellow elastic tissue. The white fibrous tissue greatly preponderates, and is derived principally from the chordae tendineae, which split up into a vast number of brush-shaped expansions, prior to being inserted into the segments. The fibrous expansions, which assume the form of bands, may consequently be regarded as prolongations of the chordae tendineae. They are analogous, in many respects, to similar bands in the semilunar valves (Fig. 135 B, *s*, *t*, p. 254); the only difference being, that in the semilunar valves, the bands referred to, instead of being free, as in the present instance (Fig. 140, *r r'*, *s s'*, p. 268), are involved in the valvular substance.

As each of the segments composing the bicuspid or mitral valve, like the left ventricle itself, is bilaterally symmetrical, it will be convenient, when speaking of these structures, to describe in the first instance only the half of one of the segments; and in order to do this the more effectually, it will be necessary to consider each musculus papillaris as essentially consisting of two portions[2], *an anterior portion* (Fig. 140, *c*, p. 268), which gives off two (more commonly three) chordae tendineae (*r*, *r'*) to *that half of the anterior segment* of the mitral valve which is next to it; and a *posterior portion* (*d*), which also gives off three tendinous chords, these being inserted into the adjacent *half of the posterior segment*. The three tendinous chords which proceed from the anterior portion subdivide, and are inserted by brush-shaped expansions into the half of the anterior segment in nine different places[3]. Of these, three are inserted into the mesial line of the segment, viz. into the base, central portion, and apex; three into the basal, central, and apicial portion of the free margin; and three into intermediate points between the mesial line and the margin. On some occasions, as in the mitral valve of the whale, a slightly different arrangement prevails; three chordae tendineae being inserted into the

---

[1] Professor Donders describes the yellow elastic tissue as being most abundant in the upper surface of the segments.

[2] The musculi papillares in the human and other hearts either bifurcate or show a disposition to bifurcate at their free extremities, so that the division of the chordae tendineae into two sets is by no means an arbitrary one.

[3] The number of insertions varies in particular instances. In typical hearts, however, it is remarkably uniform.

mesial line of the segment at the base, at the centre, and at the apex; an additional chord *going to the free margin near the apex;* three into intermediate points between the mesial line and the margin; a second additional chord *going to the central portion of the margin.* A third and independent chord *goes to the base of the margin.* In the whale, as will be observed, the arrangement is virtually the same as that first given; the insertions being nine in number,—three into the mesial line, three into the free margin, and three into intermediate points. The tendinous chords pursue different directions prior to insertion; the three which are inserted into the mesial line of the segment (r), and are the longest and strongest, being less vertical than those which are inserted nearer the margin (r'); these in turn being less vertical than the ones inserted into the margin, which are the shortest and most delicate. The basal chord of each set (z), on the contrary, is more vertical than that beneath it, or nearer the apex (x); the apicial chords being more or less horizontal. As there is a disposition on the part of the higher and more central chordae tendineae to overlap, by their terminal brush-shaped expansions, those below and to the outside of them, the segment is found to diminish in thickness from the base (z) towards the apex (x), and from the mesial line towards the periphery or margin; the basal and central portions of the segment being comparatively very thick, the apicial and marginal portions very thin; so thin, indeed, that in some hearts, particularly in the right ventricle, they present a cobwebbed appearance. As the marginal portions form the counterparts of the lunulae in the semilunar valves, and are those parts of the segments which come into accurate apposition when the valve is in action, they are from this circumstance entitled to consideration. When a perfectly healthy mitral valve from an adult, or still better, from a foetus at the full time or soon after birth, is examined, the portions referred to are found to be of a more or less crescentic shape (*vide* that part of the mitral valve to which the chordae tendineae marked r', Fig. 140, p. 268, are distributed), and so extremely thin, that the slightest current in the fluid in which they are examined causes them to move like cilia. The physiological value of this delicacy of structure, and consequent mobility, is very great; as the most trifling impulse causes the marginal parts of the segments, which are naturally in juxtaposition, to approach towards or recede from each other. The half of one of the segments of the mitral valve, it will be seen, consists of a reduplication of the endocardium or lining membrane of the heart, supported or strengthened in all directions by nine or more tendinous brush-shaped expansions; these expansions being arranged in three vertical rows of three each, with much precision, and according to a principle which is seldom deviated from. In addition to the reduplication of the lining membrane and the tendinous expansions described, Lancisi[1], Senac[2], and Kürschner[3] have ascertained that there is a slight admixture of true muscular fibres[4]. When a segment of the mitral valve is examined by being held against the light, or by the aid of a dissecting lens, it is found to consist of tendinous striae running transversely, obliquely, and more or less vertically; the striae of opposite sides being so disposed that they mutually act upon and support each other—an arrangement productive of great strength, and one which secures that the segments shall be at once tightened or loosened by the slightest shortening or lengthening of the musculi papillares. The minor or accessory segments of the mitral valve resemble the principal ones in structure and general configuration. They are, comparatively speaking, very thin; and the chordae tendineae inserted into them differ from those inserted into the principal segments, in having a more vertical direction, and in being longer and more feeble. The description given of the bicuspid valve applies, with trifling alterations in particular instances, to the tricuspid, if allowance be made for an additional large segment, and three or more accessory segments. With regard to the smallest of the three large segments forming the tricuspid, I have to observe that, in all probability, it is simply an over-developed accessory segment; the so-called tricuspid valve being in reality a bicuspid one. Nor is this to

[1] De Motu Cordis.
[2] Traité de la Structure du Cœur, livre i. p. 76.
[3] Wagner's Handwörterbuch, art. 'Herzthätigkeit.'
[4] According to Mr. Savory's observations the muscular fibre is found more particularly at the upper or attached border of the valves.

be wondered at, when I remind you that the right ventricle
is a segmented portion of the left, and partakes of its bilateral
symmetry even in matters of detail. The opinion here
advanced is by no means new, but it appears to me that the
point has not been sufficiently investigated, and we are in
want of statistics regarding it. In ten human hearts which I
examined for this purpose, no less than four had well-marked
bicuspid valves in both ventricles (Fig. 144, p. 281): and on
looking over a large collection of miscellaneous hearts in the
Museum of the Royal College of Surgeons of England, I found
that nearly a third of them had the peculiarity adverted to;.
if indeed that can be called peculiar, which seems to me to be
typical. When two principal segments, with two or more
accessory segments, occlude the right auriculo - ventricular
orifice, the chordae tendineae are arranged as in the segments
of the bicuspid valve already described. When there are
three principal segments, with as many or more accessory
segments, the distribution is varied to meet the exigencies of
the case: there being a tendency in each of the chordae
tendineae to divide into three; one of the chords so divided
being inserted by one of its slips into the mesial line of the
segment at the base; by another into the margin of the
segment, likewise at the base; and by the remaining slip
into a point intermediate between the mesial line and the
margin. Other chords, similarly divided, are inserted at
intervals in a direction from above downwards, or from base
to apex, the insertions in each case proceeding from the
mesial line towards the margin. The segments of the tricuspid valve are thinner than those of the bicuspid. This is
traceable to the fact that the right heart is more feeble, and
has less work to perform, than the left one. As the chordae
tendineae are inserted into every portion of the bicuspid and
tricuspid valves, and freely decussate with each other in all
directions, by means of their terminal brush-shaped expansions; as, moreover, the chordae tendineae are of infinite
variety as regards length and strength, those at the base of
each segment being long and exceedingly strong, while those
at the margins and towards the apices are short, and in some
instances as delicate as hairs, it follows that every part of the
mitral and tricuspid valves is under the control of the conical-

shaped spiral musculi papillares, whose power to shorten and lengthen is now well established[1]. There can be little doubt, therefore, that the chordae tendineae are to be regarded as the satellites of the constantly moving musculi papillares, under whose guidance they have to perform, not only a very important, but a very delicate function, and one which could not by any possibility be accomplished by a simply mechanical arrangement.

The Mitral and Tricuspid Valves of the Mammal in Action.—The theories which have long divided the attention of physiologists as to the action of the mitral and tricuspid valves are two in number; one sect maintaining that the valves *are acted upon mechanically by the blood,* as if they were composed of inanimate matter; the other believing that *they form part of a living system,* their movements being traceable to their connexion with the musculi papillares, which, as explained, have the power of elongating and shortening.

According to the mechanical theory, the segments of the valves are supposed to be *passively* floated up by the blood, which acts upon them from beneath during the systole, and brings their edges or free margins into such accurate apposition as enables the segments completely to occlude the auriculo-ventricular orifices. In these movements *the musculi papillares and carneae columnae* are said *to take no part;* the chordae tendineae acting *mechanically,* like so many stays, to prevent eversion of the segments in the direction of the auricles.

According to the vital theory, the segments of the valves are supposed to be from the first *under the control of the musculi papillares;* these structures, when they shorten, drawing the lips or free margins of the segments closely together in the axes of the auriculo-ventricular openings to form two impervious cones, the apices of which project downwards into the ventricular cavities.

---

[1] Dr. John Reid states from experiment, that the carneae columnae act simultaneously with the other muscular fibres of the heart, and that the *musculi papillares* are proportionally more shortened during their contraction than the heart itself taken as a whole. He attributes this to the more vertical direction of the musculi papillares, and to their being free towards the base and in the direction of the ventricular cavities.

In these movements, it is said, *the blood takes no part*, the chordae tendineae, which are regarded as the proper tendons of the musculi papillares, acting as adjusters or adapters of the segments, a function which their varying length and strength readily enables them to perform.

I need scarcely add that these theories are diametrically opposed to each other.

In the valvular controversy, as in most others, a certain amount of truth is to be found on either side; and I have to express my conviction that both theories (conflicting though they appear) are virtually correct so far as they go, but that neither the one nor the other is sufficient of itself to explain the gradual, and to a certain extent self-regulating, process by which the auriculo-ventricular valves are closed and kept closed. On the contrary, I believe that the closure is effected partly by *mechanical* and partly by *vital* means. In other words, that the blood towards the end of the diastole and the beginning of the systole forces the segments in an upward direction, and causes their margins and apices to be so accurately applied to each other as to prevent even the slightest regurgitation; whereas during the systole, and towards the termination of that act, the valves are, by the shortening of the musculi papillares, dragged down by the chordae tendineae into the ventricular cavities to form two dependent spiral cones.

Granting that my explanation is correct, there is yet another point *as to the manner of the closure*, to which I am particularly anxious to direct attention, as it is of primary importance, and appears to have hitherto escaped observation. I refer to the spiral form assumed by the blood in the ventricular cavities, which, as has been already explained, causes it, towards the end of the diastole and the beginning of the systole, to act in *spiral waves* (Fig. 104, *j*, *q*, p. 200) mechanically on the under surface of the segments, with the effect of *twisting and wedging them into each other in a spiral upward direction* (Figs. 142, 143, *m i n, r s*, p. 281). The segments of the aortic and pulmonic valves are twisted and wedged into each other by the refluent blood in a direction from above downwards (Fig. 141, *v w x, r s t*, p. 281). I allude also to the spiral course pursued by the musculi papillares (Fig. 103, *m n*, p. 197); these structures as the systole advances shortening in such a manner as occasions the spiral descent of the segments into the ventricular cavities (Fig. 141, *m n, r s*, p. 281), to form *two spiral dependent cones*, the apices of which are directed towards the apices of the ventricles.   As the decrease of the blood in the ventricles is followed, as has been stated, by a corresponding increase in the auricles, the blood in the auricles assists in keeping the free margins and apices of the segments from being everted by the uniform pressure exercised on them by the blood in the ventricles during the systole.   From this account of the closure of the auriculo-ventricular valves it will be evident that the bicuspid and tricuspid valves form two movable partitions or septa, which rise and fall during the diastole and systole of the heart, in the same way that the diaphragm rises and falls during expiration and inspiration.   The advantage of such an arrangement is obvious.   *When the ventricles are full of blood*, and the auricles empty, or comparatively so, the valvular septa are convex towards the base of the heart, and protrude into the auricular cavities (Figs. 143, 144, p. 281). When, on the other hand, *the auricles are full of blood*, and the ventricles all but drained of it, the valvular septa are dragged downwards into the ventricular cavities to form inverted cones (Fig. 141, p. 281). Certain portions therefore of the auriculo-ventricular cavities are common alike to the auricles and to the ventricles ; and it is important to note this fact, as the valvular septa, by their rising and falling, at one time increase the size of the ventricular cavities, while they diminish the auricular ones, and *vice versa*.   The principal object gained by the descent of the segments into the ventricles is the diminution of the ventricular cavities towards the base ; the dependent cones formed by the valves fitting accurately into the conical-shaped interspaces situated between the slanting heads of the musculi papillares and the auriculo-ventricular fibrous rings.   As the musculi papillares, when the ventricles close, mutually embrace and twine round each other, the obliteration of the ventricular cavities is readily effected.

An important inference to be deduced from the spiral nature of the ventricular fibres and ventricular cavities and *the undoubted spiral action of the auriculo-ventricular valves*, is the effect produced on the blood as it leaves the ventricles, that fluid being projected by a wringing or twisting movement, which communicates to it *a gliding spiral motion*. This view is favoured by the spiral ·inclination of the sinuses of Valsalva to each other, these structures—as has been already explained —gradually introducing the blood so projected into the vessels. The phrase 'wringing the heart's blood' is consequently true in fact. It is not a little curious that other hollow viscera besides the heart, as the bladder and uterus, also expel their contents spirally.

The Mechanical and Vital Theories of the Action of the Mitral and Tricuspid Valves considered.—That the theory which attributes the closure of the auriculo-ventricular valves to the mechanical floating up of the segments from beneath by the blood, forced by the auricles[1] into the ventricles, distending equally in all directions[2], is of itself inadequate to explain all the phenomena, is, I think, probable from analogy and the nature of things; for if a merely mechanical arrangement of parts was sufficient for the closure of the auriculo-ventricular orifices, then it may be asked, why were these apertures in birds and mammals not furnished with sigmoid or semilunar valves similar in all respects to those met with in the veins and arteries? The answer to this question is no doubt to be found in the nature of the structures in which the valves are situated, as well as in the circulation itself. In the veins, as is well known, the movements of the blood are sluggish—the closure of the vessels being feeble, and not consequently calculated to interfere to any great extent with the closing of the valves. In the arteries, where the circulation is more vigorous, and the closure of the vessels more decided, the valves are surrounded by dense fibrous rings, which protect them from the opening and closing alike of the ventricles and vessels. No such fibrous rings occur in the bulbus arteriosus of fishes, and as a consequence the valves are exposed to the influence of muscular movements. To

---

[1] According to Harvey, Lower, Senac, Haller, and others, the auricles contract with a very considerable degree of energy.

[2] 'In a quantity of fluid submitted to compression, the whole mass is equally affected and similarly in all directions.'—*Hydrostatic Law*. Dr. George Britton Halford attributes the closure of the auriculo-ventricular valves entirely to the pressure exercised by the auricles on the blood forced by them into the ventricles. That however this is not the sole cause, will be shown further on.

obviate this difficulty *the segments of the valves are not only increased in number, but chordae tendineae*, in the shape of tendinous bands, *begin to make their appearance.* In the auriculo-ventricular valves of fishes and reptiles, *chordae tendineae in various stages of development are discovered*, these being attached to the interior of the ventricle *to more or less fully developed musculi papillares.* The musculi papillares in fishes and reptiles are in no instance so well marked as in birds and mammals. As we rise in the scale of being, and the requirements of the circulation become greater, it will be observed *that the relation of the segments to actively moving structures* becomes more and more defined. In the ventricle of the fish, as I pointed out, the fibres proceed in wavy lines from base to apex, and from apex to base, from without inwards and circularly; so that the organ closes and opens very much *as one would shut and open the hand.* In the reptilia the external and internal fibres pursue a slightly spiral direction—*the ventricles rotating more or less when in action.* In the cold-blooded animals moreover, as every one is aware, the circulation is languid or slow, so that an arrangement of valves similar in some respects, though more complex than that which exists in the veins and venous sinuses and in the arteries, amply suffices. In the hearts however of the warm-blooded animals, where the ventricles are composed entirely of spiral fibres, and where the circulation, on account *of the sudden twisting and untwisting of the fibres, is rapid*, a system of valves which will act with greater alacrity and precision is absolutely necessary. But functional precision implies structural excellence; and hence that exquisite arrangement of parts in the auriculo-ventricular valves of mammals, whereby every portion of every segment (by reason of the ever-varying length and strength of the chordae tendineae) bears a graduated relation to the musculi papillares and carneae columnae. Although the partial closing of the valves during the diastole is occasioned by the uniform expansion of the blood owing to the force exercised upon it by the closure of the auricles, still it must be evident to all who reflect, that this cause is not of itself adequate to the complete closure, and for a very obvious reason. The blood which is the expanding force, enters the ventricular cavities by the auriculo-ventricular orifices. Once in the ventricles, however, the blood has no inherent expansive power by which it can of its own accord entirely shut off or close the apertures by which it entered. This act requires for its consummation the force exercised by the closure of the ventricles at the commencement of the systole. Admitting however that the expansion of the blood was adequate to the closure of the auriculo-ventricular valves at one period,—say at the end of the ventricular diastole, when the ventricles are full of blood and the auriculo-ventricular orifices widest,—it is scarcely possible that it could keep them closed towards the end of the systole, when the auriculo-ventricular orifices are greatly diminished in size and the blood itself all but ejected. A regulating and motor power therefore, in addition to the blood, for adapting the different portions of the segments of the valves to the varying conditions of the auriculo-ventricular orifices and cavities during the systole, seems requisite. Such a power, in my opinion, resides in the conical-shaped spiral musculi papillares with their proper tendons, the chordae tendineae.

That the theory which ascribes the closing of the auriculo-ventricular valves entirely 'to the contraction of the musculi papillares,' is likewise of itself insufficient, appears for the following reasons :—

1st, If the valves which, at the commencement of the ventricular diastole, are floated mechanically upwards, and have their edges approximated by the blood towards the termination of the diastole, were dragged upon at the beginning of the systole from above downwards, or in an opposite direction to that in which the force by which they were brought together acts, the segments of the valves, instead of being further approximated, would inevitably be drawn asunder, and regurgitation to a fatal extent supervene.

2nd, By such an arrangement as Dr. Halford has satisfactorily shown, the cavities of the ventricles would not only be materially diminished at a very inconvenient time[1], but a

---

[1] Dr. Halford states his belief, 'that the segments of the valves are forced even beyond the level of the auriculo-ventricular orifices, and in this way become convex towards the auricles, and deeply concave towards the ventricles.'—*On the Time and Manner of Closure of the Auriculo-ventricular Valves.* Churchill, London, 1861. In his zeal for the enlarged accommodation of the ventricles, Dr. Halford forgets

certain amount of the force required for the expulsion of the blood from the ventricular cavities would be expended in closing the valves.

The auriculo-ventricular valves are so constructed and so placed that they equally obey the impulses communicated by the blood and by the musculi papillares. Thus, as the blood finds its way into the ventricular cavities, the segments of the valves are floated upwards upon its surface like the leaves of water-plants. This floating upwards brings the delicate margins of the segments into such accurate apposition, that they are closed the instant the ventricles begin to contract, an arrangement which effectually prevents regurgitation. The sudden closure of the ventricles upon their contained blood has the effect of momentarily forcing the valves in an upward direction into the auricular cavities—a movement limited by the chordae tendineae, which effectually prevent eversion. The upward movement is gradually checked as the systole advances and the musculi papillares shorten; the valves being made to descend upon the blood rapidly disappearing from the ventricular cavities. In this movement the valves form depending cones, the sides of which fit accurately into the conical spaces formed at the base of the heart by the slanting heads of the musculi papillares. The ventricular cavities are diminished towards the base of the heart by the depending position of the segments of the mitral and tricuspid valves towards the end of the systole. If to this be added the fact that, at this particular period, the musculi papillares twine into and around each other so as to become strongly embraced, and the ventricles are greatly diminished from below upwards and from without inwards, it will not be difficult to understand how the ventricular cavities are drained of blood during the systole.

that the auricles are equally entitled to consideration, and that it is unfair to give to the one and take from the other; for if, as he argues, the segments of the valves form convex partitions, whose convexities throughout the entire systole of the ventricles point in the direction of the auricles, the space beyond the level of the auriculo-ventricular orifices is appropriated from the auricles without compensation. As, however, such an arrangement could not fail materially to inconvenience the auricles when *they are fullest* of blood, we naturally turn to the ventricles for redress. The additional space required is, as I have already shown, supplied by the descent of the segments of the bicuspid and tricuspid valves towards the end of the systole, when the ventricles are almost drained of blood.

It therefore appears to me that the auriculo-ventricular valves are alternately active and passive, there being a brief period when they are neither the one nor the other. The passive state corresponds to the diastole or opening of the ventricles; the active state, to the systole or closing; and the neutral or intermediate state, to that short interval which embraces the termination of the diastole and the commencement of the systole. In speaking of the closure of the valves, it is of great importance to remember that the action, although very rapid, is a strictly progressive one, and necessarily consists of stages. In this however, as in many other vital acts, it is often very difficult, if not indeed impossible, to say precisely where the one stage terminates and the other begins. As the action of the valves is, to a certain extent, dependent upon and induced by the action of the auricles and ventricles, the following slight differences as regards time are to be noted. The passive state of the valves corresponds to that period in which *their segments are floated mechanically upwards, and their margins partially approximated* by the blood forced by the auricles into the ventricles; the neutral state, to that almost inappreciable interval which succeeds the sudden closure of the ventricles, in which the blood set in motion is arranged in spiral columns, and acts in such a way as not only instantly closes the valves, but *screws and wedges the segments thereof into each other*[1], *in an upward spiral direction.* The active state corresponds to the period occupied by the progressive closing of the ventricles. During this period *the valves are dragged forcibly downwards by the shortening of the musculi papillares, in an opposite direction to that by which they ascended; and are twisted into or round each other to form spiral dependent cones.* In the active stage, as in the neutral, the blood acts from beneath, and keeps the delicate margins and apices of the segments of the valves in accurate contact. The appearances presented are represented at Figs. 141—144, p. 281.

---

[1] This act takes place just before the blood finds its way into the aorta and pulmonary artery, the amount of pressure required for shutting and screwing home the auriculo-ventricular valves being less than that required for raising the semilunar ones.

That the foregoing is the true explanation of the gradual approximation and continued closure of the auriculo-ventricular valves, there can, I think, be little doubt, both from the disposition and structure of the·parts, and from experi-

Fig. 141.   Fig. 142.

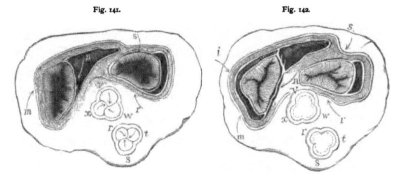

Figs. 141, 142 and 143 show the mitral (*r s*) and tricuspid (*m i n*) valves in action (human): how the segments, acted upon by the spiral columns of blood, *roll up* from beneath towards the end of the diastole (Fig. 141); how, at the beginning of the systole, they are wedged and twisted into each other, on a level with the auriculo-ventricular orifices (Fig. 142); and how, if the pressure exerted be great, they project into the auricular cavities (Fig. 143). When the mitral and tricuspid valves (Fig. 141 *r s, m n*) are open, the aortic and pulmonic semilunar valves (*v w x, r s t*) are closed. When, on the other hand, the mitral and tricuspid valves are closed (Figs. 142, 143, and 144, *r s, m i n*), the aortic and pulmonic semilunar ones (*v w x, r s t*) are open. To this there is no exception.—*Original.*

Fig. 143.   Fig. 144

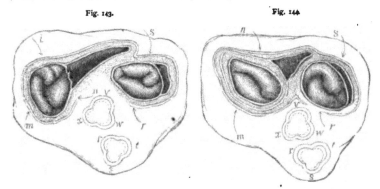

Fig. 144 shows a human heart with a true mitral valve in both ventricles as seen in action at the commencement of the systole. The letters are the same as in Figs. 141, 142, 143.—*Original.*
Note.—The spiral downward movement of the mitral and tricuspid valves (Fig. 141) has only been partly shown, from the difficulty experienced in representing spiral cavities.

ment. If, *e.g.*, the coagula be carefully removed from perfectly fresh ventricles, and two tubes of appropriate calibre ' be cautiously introduced past the semilunar valves, and securely fixed in the aorta and pulmonary artery[1], and the

___
[1] Strictly speaking, the tubes should be introduced into the auriculo-ventricular orifices, as it is through these apertures that the blood passes during the dilatation .

preparation be sunk in water until the ventricular cavities fill, it will be found, when one of the tubes[1], say that fixed in the aorta, is carefully blown into, that the segments of the bicuspid valve roll up from beneath in a spiral direction (Fig. 141, *r s*, p. 281), in a progressive and gradual manner ; each of the two larger or major segments, by folding upon itself, more or less completely, in a direction from within outwards, forming itself into a provisional or temporary cone, the apex of which is directed towards the apex of the left ventricle (*first stage in which the crescentic margins and apices of the segments are slowly approximated by the uniform expansion of the blood forced into the ventricle by the auricle*). As the pressure exerted by the air is gradually increased, and the action of the valve is further evolved, the segments, folded upon themselves as described, *are gradually elevated, until they are on the same plane with the auriculo-ventricular fibrous ring*, where they are found to be wedged and screwed into each other, and present a level surface above (Fig. 142, *r s*, p. 281).

At this, the second stage of the closure, the crescentic margins of the segments are observed to be accurately applied to each other, *to form two perpendicular crescentic walls*, which accord in a wonderful manner with similar walls formed by the union of the semilunar valves (Fig. 133 C, *b*, p. 252) ; in fact the manner of closure is, to a certain extent, the same in both ; the segments in either case being folded upon themselves by the blood, and presenting delicate crescentic margins, which are flattened against each other in proportion to the amount of pressure employed. When the crescentic margins of the segments are so accurately applied to each other as to become perfectly unyielding, and the distending process is carried beyond a certain point, the bodies or central portions of the segments bulge in an upward or downward direction respectively, the segments of the mitral valve protruding into the auricle (Fig. 143, *r s*, p. 281) ; those of

---

of the ventricles. As, however, the insertion of tubes, however small, into the auriculo-ventricular openings would necessarily prevent the complete closure of the valves, that is one good reason for adopting the plan recommended in the text.

[1] Thin metallic tubes with unyielding parietes are best adapted for this purpose, as they can be readily fixed in the vessels, and the amount of pressure exercised by the breath on the valves easily ascertained.

the semilunar ones into the ventricle (Fig. 134, p. 253, and Fig. 141, *v w x, r s t,* p. 281). Compare Figs. 85 and 86, p. 174.

This completes the first and second stages of the process by which the mitral or bicuspid valve is closed; but the more important, as being the more active and difficult, is yet to come. *This consists in adapting the segments of the valve to the gradually diminishing auriculo-ventricular orifice; and in dragging them down into the left ventricular cavity,* to diminish the ventricle towards the base. By this act, the segments, as has been shown, are made to form a spiral dependent cone, an arrangement which renders the obliteration of the left ventricular cavity towards the base a matter of certainty.

The third stage of the closure of the mitral valve entirely differs from the first and second stages, inasmuch as the chordae tendineae, when the musculi papillares shorten, drag the segments in a downward direction, to adapt them to the altered conditions of the auriculo-ventricular orifice and ventricular cavity. That this downward movement actually takes place, is proved as follows:—If a portion of the fluid be withdrawn by applying the mouth to the tube in the aorta, so as to create a certain amount of suction, the segments of the bicuspid valve are found gradually to descend in a spiral direction (Fig. 141, *m, n,* p. 281), forming as they do so a spiral cone, whose apex becomes more and more defined in proportion as the suction is increased; the water in the interior keeping the margins of the segments- accurately in apposition, and thereby preserving the symmetry of the cone. If, again, the musculi papillares be cut out of the ventricular walls and made to act in the direction of their fibres, *i. e.* in a spiral direction from left to right downwards, they will be found, in virtue of being connected by the chordae tendineae more or less diagonally to either segment of the bicuspid valve, to act simultaneously on that side of the segment which is next to them; the anterior musculus papillaris acting spirally on the margin and apex of the larger or anterior segment; the posterior musculus papillaris acting spirally on the margin and apex of the smaller or posterior segment, in a precisely opposite direction. The effect of these apparently incongruous movements on the segments is very striking.

The space which naturally exists between the segments is gradually but surely diminished, and the segments twisted into or round each other to form the spiral dependent cone referred to.

This arrangement, I may observe, while it facilitates the spiral movement, absolutely forbids any other.

The closure is rendered perfect by the pressure exercised on the delicate margins of the segments by the spiral columns of blood, as already explained.

By the time the blood is ejected from the left ventricle, and the segments of the mitral valve have formed the spiral dependent cone, the left auricle is distended; and due advantage being taken of the extra space afforded by the descent of the mitral valve, the blood assumes a spiral wedge-shaped form, which is the best possible for pushing the segments of the mitral valve in an outward direction, these being in the most favourable position for falling away from the ventricular axis towards the ventricular walls. The same phenomena are repeated, with unerring regularity, with each succeeding action of the heart. What has been said of the manner of closure of the mitral or bicuspid valve applies, I need scarcely add, with slight modifications to the tricuspid.

The Sounds of the Heart; to what owing.—With regard to the sounds of the heart and their mode of production, there is much discrepancy of opinion. Harvey was aware of their existence, and compared them to the sounds produced by the passage of fluids along the oesophagus of the horse when drinking. Laennec was the first strongly to direct attention to them. He described their character, the order of their succession, and showed how a knowledge of them would enable us to detect many cardiac lesions. He has therefore laid the profession under lasting obligations. The sounds have been divided for convenience into two, a first and second sound. The first sound is dull, deep, and prolonged; and the second, which follows immediately after the first, is quick, sharp, and more superficial[1]. The second

---

[1] These sounds have also been called inferior and superior, long and short, dull and sharp, systolic and diastolic.

sound was compared by Laennec to the flapping of a valve or the lapping of a dog; the first and second sounds being likened by Dr. Williams to the syllables 'lupp, dupp.' The first sound immediately precedes the radial pulse, and corresponds with the impulse of the heart against the thorax, the closure and susurrus of the ventricles, the rush of the blood through the aortic and pulmonic valves, and the closing and tightening of the auriculo-ventricular valves and chordae tendineae. The second sound coincides with the closure and susurrus of the auricles, the rush of the blood through the auriculo-ventricular orifices into the ventricular cavities, the opening of the auriculo-ventricular valves, and the closing of the aortic and pulmonic valves. As the different substances set in motion by the action of the heart, such as the blood, valves, muscular fibres, etc., are all capable of causing sound, it is reasonable to conclude that the several structures and substances moving at the time the sound is heard are one and all concerned in its production. It is this circumstance, combined with the fact that sound once propagated repeats itself or echoes—sounds of different intensity running into each other—which makes it so exceedingly difficult to determine what actually produces the sounds under consideration. What I mean will be understood when I state, that at the same instant the ventricles are closing and striking the chest, and while they are forcing their blood through the pulmonary artery and aorta, opening the aortic and pulmonic valves, and closing the mitral and tricuspid ones—at this same instant the heart is rolling within the pericardium, and the venae cavae and the pulmonic veins are closing, and forcing their blood into the auricles, which are actively dilating to receive it. The sounds produced by the latter movements are therefore, on our part, unconsciously mixed up with the sounds produced by the former movements, and must be added to them. When again the auricles are closing and forcing their blood into the ventricular cavities, when the auriculo-ventricular valves are being pushed aside and opened, and the aortic and pulmonic valves closed, at that same instant the ventricles, the venae cavae, and pulmonic veins are actively dilating. The sounds which one hears are consequently numerous and of a mixed character, as regards intensity and duration; and to make matters worse, they run into each other by insensible gradations, sometimes slowly, sometimes suddenly. The sounds in fact merge into each other precisely in the same way that the movements of the different parts of the heart merge into each other. They have their points of maximum and minimum intensity, and it is upon these the physiologist and physician fixes when he attempts to define their nature and duration. Such definitions I need scarcely add are more or less arbitrary. The first and second sounds are followed by apparent pauses—the pauses corresponding to the brief intervals which follow the closing of the ventricles and auricles respectively. Thus the dull, deep, prolonged, or first sound is followed by a short pause, while the sharp, short, or second sound is followed by another and longer pause. The sounds and the pauses which occur between them follow in regular order, and when taken in connexion with the closing and opening of the different parts of the heart to which they owe their origin, constitute the rhythm of the heart. They occasionally vary in duration, just as the pulse varies in frequency, and in certain cardiac affections the sounds are increased in number, while the pauses are decreased in duration. When the movements and sounds of the heart are very irregular, the condition is expressed by the term 'tumultuous.' Various attempts have been made to represent the duration of the sounds and pauses in figures. Thus some authors state that if the number 9 be made to represent one complete pulsation, the first sound occupies a third; the short pause a sixth, the second sound a sixth, and the long pause a third. Others aver that if we divide one entire action of the heart into four parts, the two first will be occupied by the first sound, the third by the second sound, and the fourth by the pause; all which proves very conclusively that the sounds and pauses run into each other and cannot be separated with any degree of accuracy. When so many causes exist it is exceedingly difficult, perhaps dangerous, to particularise. There are however many circumstances which induce me to believe that the susurrus, or sound produced by the opening and closing of the auricles. and ventricles, and the rushing of the fluid blood against the valves and into the cavities and vessels of the heart, constitute the major factors, the opening and closing of the valves the minor.

The Dublin committee, appointed to investigate this matter, concluded that the first sound is produced either by the rapid passage of the blood over the irregular internal surface of the ventricles on its way towards the mouth of the arteries, or by the *bruit musculaire* (susurrus) of the ventricles, or probably by both of these causes. The London committee, appointed for a like purpose, came to similar conclusions. It found that the sound produced by the contraction (shortening) of the abdominal muscles, as heard through a flexible tube, resembles the systolic sound, and that the impulse of the heart against the chest in certain positions of the body intensified this sound. M. Marc D'Espine maintained that both the first and second sounds depend on muscular movements—the first sound upon the systole and the second upon the diastole of the ventricles. D'Espine, it will be observed, attributes sound both to the diastole or opening of the ventricles, and to the systole or closing of them, and in this I think he is perfectly correct—the opening and closing of the different parts of the heart, as I have endeavoured to show, being equally vital movements. That muscle invariably produces sound during its action is well known ; and that a powerful compound muscle like the heart, with fibres interlacing in every direction, should, when closing and opening in hollow cavities such as the pericardium and thorax, produce audible and characteristic sounds, is what we would *a priori* expect. That sound may be produced by the impinging of fluids against animal tissues, or by the trituration of the particles of the fluid itself, can be proved by direct experiment. Valentin, *e.g.*, showed that if a portion of a horse's intestine be tied at one end, and moderately distended with water without any admixture of air, and a syringe containing water be fixed into the other end, by pressing the piston of the syringe down, and forcing in more water, the first sound is exactly imitated. When, on the other hand, the aortic or pulmonic valves are diseased, their surfaces roughened, and the apertures which they guard diminished, the character of the first sound is altered.

Laennec and Dr. C. J. B. Williams regard the susurrus or noise produced by the contracting (closing) ventricles as the exclusive cause of the first sound; and the latter endeavoured to prove the point by cutting away the aorta and pulmonic vessels, and by placing the fingers in the auriculo-ventricular orifices, so as to exclude the blood. He found under these circumstances that the sound was still produced. I cannot however agree with Laennec and Dr. Williams when they state that the contraction (closure) of the ventricles is the sole cause; for, in cases of hypertrophy of the heart, the intensity of the first sound, instead of being increased, which it would be if solely due to the closing of the ventricles, is diminished. An attempt has been made to clear away this difficulty by saying that in such cases the susurrus of the superficial fibres alone is heard. That the first sound is in part due to the ventricular susurrus must, I think, be conceded, but that it is also due to the attrition of the blood against the great vessels and valves seems proved, 1st, by the experiment of Valentin with the piece of intestine already quoted; 2nd, by cases of anaemia, where the character of the sound is changed, although the valves and vessels are healthy; and 3rd, by cases of diseased valves and vessels where the character of the sound is altered, the blood being normal. Rouanet, Billing, and Bryan referred the first sound to the rapid approximation of the auriculo-ventricular valves during the contraction (closure) of the ventricles. This however cannot be the sole cause; for, as I pointed out when explaining the action of these valves, their movements are not sudden but gradual and progressive. The auriculo-ventricular valves, in fact, move up and down like diaphragms as the systole proceeds. Thus they are elevated at the beginning of the systole, and drawn down or lowered towards the end of it. Bouillaud attributes the first sound partly to the closing of the auriculo-ventricular valves, and partly to the sudden opening of the pulmonic and aortic valves; while Mr. Carlisle refers it to the rush of blood along the pulmonary artery and aorta, occasioned by the contraction (closure) of the ventricles. The first sound, there are good grounds for believing, is referable, 1st, to the ventricular susurrus; 2nd, to the impinging of the blood against the auriculo-ventricular and semilunar valves; 3rd, to the closing of the auriculo-ventricular valves and the opening of the semilunar ones; 4th, to the impulse of the heart; 5th, to the flow of blood into the auricles, caused by the closing of the cavae and pulmonic veins; and 6th, to the rolling of the heart within the pericardium.

As Laennec attributed the first sound to the contraction (closure) of the ventricles, so in like manner he referred the second sound to the contraction (closure) of the auricles. The susurrus of the auricles no doubt contributes to this result, but the walls of the auricles are so thin that the share they take in the production of the sound must be trifling.

M. Rouanet, Billing, Bryan, Carlisle, Bouillaud, and Dr. Elliot have attributed the second sound principally to the regurgitation of the blood in the aorta and pulmonary artery, and the flapping together, closure, and tightening of the semilunar valves [1].

Dr. C. J. B. Williams endeavoured to prove this by actual experiment on the ass. He passed a common dissecting hook through a segment of the pulmonic valve, with the effect of weakening the normal sound and producing a hissing one. He then passed a curved shoemaker's awl through a segment of the aortic valve, and the second sound ceased, a hissing sound being substituted. This author states that the second sound is loudest over the great vessels, and that it is suspended if these are artificially occluded and the auricles laid open. It must be admitted that the experiments referred to are not of a delicate or exact character. By opening the auricles those structures lose the power they possess of injecting the blood into the ventricular cavities: the characteristic sounds produced by the impinging of the blood against the auriculo-ventricular valves, chordae tendineae, carneae columnae, and musculi papillares being removed. By occluding the great vessels the sound resulting from the flow or oscillation of the blood within them, as apart from the effect produced on the valves, is destroyed. In healthy semilunar valves there is little, if any, regurgitation,

---

[1] These valves are closed with considerable energy, partly because of the elasticity of the great vessels, and partly because of the sucking action exerted by the ventricles during the diastole.

U

the segments, from their being more or less in contact at
the end of the systole, being closed by the slightest reflux,
and with almost no noise. By transfixing by hooks two of
the six segments composing the aortic and pulmonic semilunar valves, an abnormal element is introduced which renders
the experiment of little value. The substitution of one sound
for another proves nothing, and if the second sound is destroyed there is some fallacy, as only two of the six segments
which were supposed to produce it were restrained. I am
therefore disposed to put a different construction on the
results obtained by Dr. Williams, and to attribute the second
sound partly to the closure and susurrus of the auricles, but
mainly to the rush of blood into the ventricular cavities, and
against the auriculo-ventricular valves, chordae tendineae,
carneae columnae, and musculi papillares. To this is to be
added the flapping together of the semilunar valves, a slight
degree of regurgitation, and the susurrus produced by the
dilatation of the ventricles, venae cavae, and pulmonic veins.

As an illustration of the extreme difficulty experienced by
investigators in determining the precise nature of the movements and sounds of the heart, I may cite the case of M.
Groux, who exhibited in his person an almost unique example
of congenital fissure of the sternum. Here we had the parts
in the vicinity of the heart opened up as it were for inspection.
M. Groux visited the principal schools on the Continent, in
America, Russia, and Britain, and was examined by upwards
of 2000 physicians, many of them eminently distinguished.
The discrepancy of opinion is quite remarkable. In M.
Groux's case, the fissure extended the whole length of the
sternum, and presented a **V**-shaped appearance. In natural
respiration, the fissure was depressed to variable depths, and
had a transverse measurement at its upper boundary of one
inch and a quarter; this increasing at the central part on a
level with the third and fourth ribs to an inch and a half,
and decreasing at the lower boundary of the fissure to a
quarter of an inch. Through the action of the pectoral
muscles, the hands being joined and pulling upon each
other, the fissure could be dilated to the width of about
two and a half inches. The fissure could be increased
by forced expiration and decreased by forced inspiration.

About the middle of the fissure, on a level with the fourth rib, a large pulsating tumour could be seen and felt. In a vertical line with the principal tumour were two smaller ones, the one above, which could be felt; the other below, which could, like the large one, be seen and felt. I examined the pulsating tumours with others interested in the heart when M. Groux was in Edinburgh, and at first sight it appeared as if no great difficulty would be experienced in determining which parts of the heart produced the pulsations and sounds. A closer examination however revealed innumerable difficulties, all traceable to the circumstances already adverted to—viz. that the movements and sounds of the heart merge into each other by slow and sudden transitions. This case, simple as it appeared, has baffled the most expert physiologists and stethoscopists in all countries, so that instead of a few valuable facts we have a mass of conflicting evidence of comparatively little value. By some the large tumour has been supposed to be the aorta, by others the right auricle, by others the right ventricle, by others the infundibulum or conus arteriosus, and by others the arteria innominata. I have taken the pains to tabulate some of those opinions. Professor Hamernjck (Prague), Dr. Wilhelm Reil (Halle), Professor Baumgärtner (Friburg), Professor Forget (Strasburg), M. Jules Biclard, M. Aran, M. Piorry, M. Pouchet (Rouen), Dr. Ernst (Zurich), Dr. F. W. Pavy (London), Dr. C. Radcliffe Hall (Torquay), and Dr. Robert D. Lyons (Dublin), thought the pulsating tumour was the right auricle; Sir James Paget, Dr. George Burrows, Dr. William Baly (London), and Dr. Traube (Berlin), that it was the right ventricle; Dr. Lionel S. Beale (London), Dr. John Hughes Bennett (Edinburgh), and Dr. Charles C. King (Galway), that it was the right auricle and ventricle; Dr. Lombard (Liège), and Dr. Francis Sibson (London), that it was the aorta and right auricle; M. Boillaud and M. Marc d'Espine (Geneva), that it was the aorta; Professor Virchow, that it was the right ventricle and conus arteriosus; Dr. Carlisle (Belfast), that it was the ascending aorta and pulmonary artery; Dr. P. Redfern (Aberdeen), that it was the aorta, right auricle, and ventricle; Professor W. T. Gairdner (Glasgow), that it was the right auricular appendage, aorta, and right ventricle; and Dr. C. J. B. Williams (London), that it was the right auricle, ventricle, pulmonary artery, and aorta.

The account given by Drs. Pavy and Williams of M. Groux's pulsating tumour are very interesting. Dr. Pavy, who believed it to be the right auricle, states that it rises rapidly and suddenly, and. instantaneously after falls with that peculiar thrill, wave, or vermicular movement, proceeding from above to below, which he pointed out as, at this period of the heart's action, running through the parietes of the auricle of the dog. Dr. Pavy, it will be observed, character- ises the action of the auricle as progressive,—the auricle contracting (closing) with a peculiar thrill, wave, or vermicular movement, proceeding from above to below. Dr. Williams, who thought the pulsation corresponded with the right auricle, states that the closing of the auricle immediately precedes the closing of the ventricle; the wave of motion, in slow pulsations, beginning with the auricle, and rapidly passing downwards to the ventricle.

In quick pulsations the closing of the auricle and the closing of the ventricle appear synchronous (mark how the auricular and ventricular movements glide into each other, and with what rapidity). Dr. Williams goes on to say that, by the aid of a small flexible ear-tube, with a narrow pectoral end, he heard *a distinct sound accompanying* the commence- ment of the auricular contraction or closure. It is faint, short, or flapping, and ends in the less abrupt and more distinct sound of the ventricular contraction or closure. When the stethoscope is placed over the ventricle the flapping sound of the auricle is not heard, but the vessel swells or rolls out its peculiar sound, till it ends with the sharp clack of the diastolic or valvular sound. Dr. Williams concludes from this that each movement of the heart has its proper sound, and that the reason why the auricular sound is not usually heard is, that it is too faint to pass through the intervening lung. Dr. Radcliffe Hall thought there were three distinct degrees of distance of sound, indicating as many distinct sources ; the sound in the presumed auricle being far more superficial and bell-like than that produced by the aorta above, or the right ventricle below. Dr. Williams thought he made out two distinct valvular sounds. By placing the stethoscope over the aorta, he detected a simple sound (lubb-dup); but when he placed it partly over the aorta, and partly over the pulmonary artery, he obtained a double sound (lubb-darrup) from the valves not closing at exactly the same instant. This want of synchronism in the action of the aortic and pulmonic valves occurs principally in disease; but it is also found in health, and tends to show that the closure of the right and left ventricles is progressive, which is just what we would expect when we remember that muscular movements originate in the sarcous elements and diffuse themselves.

The nerves of the heart, from the influence they exert upon its movements, come next to be considered.

The Ganglia and Nerves of the Heart, and their connexion with the Cerebro-spinal and Sympathetic Systems in Mammalia.

The movements of the heart and the circulation generally are directly and indirectly influenced by the nervous system. This is sufficiently proved by the division and irritation of such nerves as send filaments to the organ; these experiments being attended in some cases with a *slowing* of the heart's action, and in others by *quickening*. Similar results are obtained by the administration of certain active substances, some of which paralyse and others stimulate the nerves conducting to and from the heart. The movements of the heart, as is well known, cannot be controlled by efforts of the will; they are nevertheless influenced by certain mental conditions, sudden joy being calculated to render the movements of the organ tumultuous; and protracted grief and watching to impede rather than quicken them. The intimate connexion between the head and heart induced the ancients to regard the heart as the seat of the affections—a view which is adopted in popular discourse.

The nerves of the heart are derived from two sources, viz. the pneumogastric (nervus vagus, par vagum) and the sympathetic (nerve of organic life, Bichat).

The pneumogastric and sympathetic nerves are compound in their nature; *i.e.* they contain afferent or sensory and efferent or motor nerve-filaments.

The pneumogastric nerve has its origin within the cranium, while the sympathetic lies outside the spinal chord. Both however are connected by nerve-filaments to each other and to the cranial and spinal nerves, an arrangement which in part accounts for the involuntary rhythmic movements of the heart, ánd for the influence exerted upon those movements by certain mental states. · Considerable difference of opinion exists as to the exact nature of the so-called *sympathetic* and *cerebro-spinal nerves*. Thefe are two leading views:—'According to the one, which is of old date, but which has lately been revived and ably advocated by Valentin, the sympathetic nerve is a mere dependency, offset, or embranchment of the cerebro-spinal system of nerves, containing no fibres but such as centre in the brain and cord, although it is held that these fibres are modified· in their· motor and sensory ·properties, in passing through the ganglia in their way to and from the viscera and involuntary organs. According to the other, the sympathetic nerve (commonly so called) not only contains fibres derived from the brain and cord, but also proper or intrinsic fibres which take their rise in the ganglia ; and in its communications with the spinal and cranial nerves, not only receives from these nerves cerebro-spinal fibres, but imparts to them a share of its own proper ganglionic fibres, to be incorporated in their branches and· distributed peripherally with them. Therefore, according to this latter view, the sympathetic nerve, commonly so called, though not a mere offset of the cerebro-spinal nerves, yet receiving as it does a share of their fibres, is not wholly independent, and for a like reason the cerebro-spinal nerves (as commonly understood) cannot be considered as constituted ·independently of the sympathetic ; in short, both the cerebro-spinal and sympathetic are mixed nerves ; that is, the branches of either system consist of two sets of fibres of different and independent ·origin, one connected· centrally with the brain and cord, the other with the ganglia.'

In order to comprehend the relation existing between the heart and the cerebro-spinal and sympathetic systems of nerves, it will be necessary to speak first of the pneumogastric and those branches which it sends to the heart ; second, of such parts of the sympathetic as supply filaments to the organ; and third, of those nervous extensions which connect the pneumogastric, sympathetic, and cerebro-spinal nerves together. This done, we shall then be in a position to describe the meshes or plexuses formed by the splitting up and mingling of the several nerves referred to at the base of the heart, their distribution on the surface and in the substance of the organ, and the nature of the ganglionic enlargements which characterise the cardiac nerve reticulations.

In man the pneumogastric nerve springs from that part of the cerebro-spinal axis known as the *medulla oblongata*. It issues from the jugular foramen, an aperture at the base of the skull, and courses down the neck and chest to supply filaments to the organs of voice, respiration, the alimentary canal as far as the stomach, and to the heart. It is the longest of the cranial nerves, and displays two ganglionic enlargements or swellings, the one designated the *ganglion of the root* of the pneumogastric, situated within the jugular foramen; the other the *ganglion of the trunk* of the pneumogastric, situated half an inch or so below that opening.

The upper ganglion, viz. that of the root, is somewhat spherical in shape, two lines in diameter, and of a grayish colour; the lower ganglion, viz. that of the trunk, being of a flattened cylindrical form, ten lines in length, two in breadth, and reddish in colour. In the neck the ganglion of the root (upper ganglion) is connected by nerve-filaments with the facial, the glosso-pharyngeal, spinal-accessory, and sympathetic nerves; the ganglion of the trunk (lower ganglion) being connected in the same region with the hypo-glossal, spinal, and sympathetic nerves.

In the thorax the branches of the right and left pneumogastric nerves pursue somewhat different courses: the recurrent laryngeal branch on the right side curving backwards and upwards round the first part of the right subclavian artery, the recurrent laryngeal branch on the left side curving backwards and upwards round the arch of the aorta. The recurrent nerves send branches to the so-called deep cardiac plexus, placed behind the pulmonary artery and aorta. The pneumogastric nerves (right and left) supply branches to the ear, pharynx, larynx, lungs, the œsophagus, stomach, spleen, liver, and other organs. They also furnish two sets of nerves to the heart—a cervical and thoracic set: with these alone we have to deal in the present instance.

The cervical cardiac-branches are given off by the pneumo-gastric at the upper and lower portions of the neck. The upper branches unite with the cardiac nerves of the sympa-thetic, are few in number, and small. There is only one lower branch. This, in the left side, crosses the arch of the aorta, and terminates in what is called the superficial cardiac plexus, situated in front of the pulmonary artery and aorta. On the right side it unites with one of the cardiac nerves and takes part in the formation of the deep cardiac plexus, located, as explained, behind the pulmonary artery and aorta. The nerves constituting the superficial and deep cardiac plexuses are continuous with each other, and completely envelop the great vessels (pulmonary artery and aorta) at their origins.

The thoracic cardiac branches on the right side proceed from the first part of the right recurrent laryngeal nerve, and the trunk of the right pneumogastric nerve, where it is in contact with the trachea; those on the left side proceeding from the left recurrent laryngeal nerve. The thoracic branches assist in the formation of the deep cardiac plexus. The pneumogastric nerves, as will be seen from the foregoing account, are con-nected with the cranial nerves issuing from the head, with the spinal nerves issuing from the spinal cord, and with the sympathetic nerves lying in front of the spinal cord.

The sympathetic system supplies the major portion of the nerves to the heart. It also sends branches to the lungs and stomach, the upper part of the alimentary canal, the bladder, uterus, and the coats of the blood-vessels.

The nerves of the sympathetic system consist of a com-plicated series of ganglia, cords, and plexuses; the ganglia and the cords which extend between them being arranged in a double row on either side of the spine, and corresponding for the most part in situation with the bodies of the cervical, dorsal, and lumbar vertebrae. There are, however, only three ganglionic enlargements in the neck in man to seven verte-brae, there being even fewer in some of the lower animals. This state of matters is probably due to the ganglia in the neck having at some period approximated and coalesced.

The sympathetic cervical ganglia in man are designated superior, middle, and inferior, from their respective positions; one being placed at the base of the skull, a second at the root of the neck, and the third above the head of the first rib. They are united to the spinal nerves in their immediate vicinity by short cords composed of white and gray matter; the white matter, it is believed, proceeding from the spinal nerves to the ganglia, the gray matter from the ganglia to the spinal nerves. The cords extending between the ganglia are similarly constituted.

The superior cervical ganglia are connected with certain of the cranial nerves as well as with the spinal nerves. Thus small twigs unite the superior cervical ganglion with the first four spinal nerves, with the first and second ganglia of the pneumogastric, with the ninth cranial nerve, and with the petrosal ganglion of the glosso-pharyngeal nerve. Besides the branches which it gives off to the spinal and cranial nerves, the superior cervical ganglion supplies branches to the pharynx, blood-vessels, and heart.

The middle and inferior cervical ganglia likewise supply branches to the heart.

The branches given off by the three cervical ganglia of the sympathetic are named respectively the *superior, middle,* and *inferior cardiac branches.*

The cardiac branches vary in size, and also in their distribution on the right and left sides.

The upper cardiac nerve of the right side proceeds from two or more branches of the superior cervical ganglion, with occasionally a branch from the main cord which connects the superior and middle cervical ganglia. In its passage down the neck it is joined by filaments from the external laryngeal and the trunk of the pneumogastric, and as it enters the chest it unites with the recurrent laryngeal. It contributes to the formation of the deep cardiac plexus. On the left side the upper cardiac nerve runs parallel with the left carotid artery until it reaches the arch of the aorta, where it breaks up to assist in forming the superficial or deep cardiac plexus according as it passes in front of or behind that vessel.

The middle cardiac nerve on the right side communicates with the upper cardiac nerve and the recurrent branch of the pneumogastric. It sends filaments to the deep cardiac plexus. The middle cardiac nerve on the left side also sends branches to the deep plexus.

The inferior cardiac nerve on the right side communicates with the middle cardiac and recurrent laryngeal nerves, and terminates in the cardiac plexus at the arch of the aorta. On the left side it unites with the middle cardiac nerve and ends in the deep cardiac plexus.

The superficial and deep cardiac plexuses, as already stated, are continuous with each other. They receive filaments from the recurrent, lower cervical, and thoracic branches of the right and left pneumogastric trunks; and from the superior, middle, and inferior cardiac nerves of the right and left sympathetic trunks. They envelop the origins of the pulmonary artery and aorta in a meshwork, after which they resolve themselves on the anterior and posterior surfaces of the heart.

Thus the superficial cardiac plexus sends branches to the anterior and right coronary arteries, and to the anterior portions of the right and left auricles and ventricles; the deep cardiac plexus sending branches to the coronary sinus and left coronary artery, and the posterior surface of the right and left auricles and ventricles. A few of the branches forming the superficial cardiac plexus pass backwards and appear on the posterior surface of the heart; a certain number of the branches from the deep cardiac plexus passing forwards to appear on the anterior surface of the heart. It is quite correct to say that the surface and substance of the auricles and ventricles are enveloped in a more or less uniform plexus. The superficial and deep cardiac plexuses and their prolongations on the surface and in the substance of the heart display numerous ganglionic enlargements, to be described presently.

The branches supplied by the pneumogastric and sympathetic nerves to the heart on the right side of the human subject are represented at Fig. 145. This figure also shows the interlacing of the nervous filaments which forms the various plexuses described, as well as the ganglionic enlargements, which are a distinguishing feature of the plexuses.

In the lower animals the relations of the pneumogastric and sympathetic nerves are less complicated than in man, and if time had permitted it would have been interesting to trace

Fig. 145.

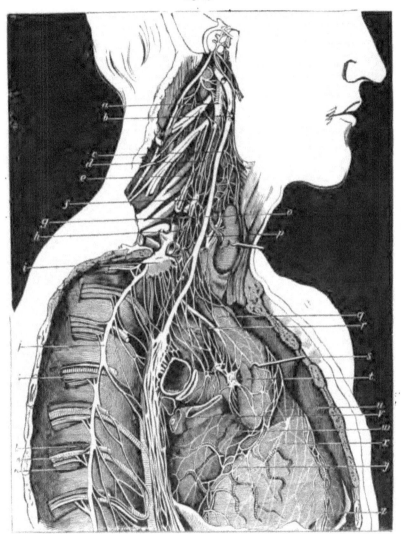

Fig. 145 shows the nerve-filaments supplied to the heart by the pneumogastric and sympathetic nerves on the right side in man (after Hirschfeld and Leveillé). c, trunk of right pneumogastric nerve in neck. b, ganglion of trunk of right pneumogastric nerve. d trunk of great sympathetic nerve in neck. h, ditto at root of neck. f, ditto in thorax. a, superior cervical ganglion of sympathetic nerve. f, middle cervical ganglion of sympathetic. i, inferior cervical ganglion of sympathetic. e, superior cardiac nerve. g, middle cardiac nerve. o, nerve from middle cervical ganglion of sympathetic proceeding to right recurrent laryngeal nerve (p). k, intercostal nerves. l, intercostal vein. m, intercostal artery furnished with nerve from ganglion of sympathetic. n, intercostal nerve receiving branch from trunk of sympathetic. q, innominate artery. r, trachea with nerves proceeding to deep cardiac plexus. s, arch of aorta with nerve-plexus, dragged forward by a hook. t, posterior or deep cardiac plexus with ganglion. u, pulmonary artery with nerve-plexus. v, superior cava cut across. w, right auricle with nerve-plexus. x, right ventricle with nerve-plexus. y, plexus of nerves investing the vessels occupying the horizontal, or right auriculo-ventricular groove. z, a similar plexus investing the vessels occupying the vertical ventricular groove anteriorly.

the gradations through which the nerves furnished to the heart by the pneumogastric and sympathetic in some of the lower animals pass. I have dissected them in the cat, rabbit, and calf, and find that, while the branches supplied by the pneumogastric nerves are tolerably constant, those furnished by the ganglia of the sympathetic and the ganglia themselves vary. Thus, in the cat, according to my dissections, only four

Fig. 146.　　　　　　　　　　　　　　　Fig. 147.

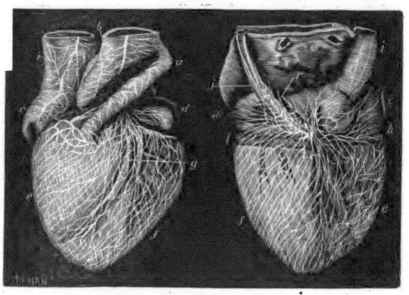

Fig. 146.—Nerves and ganglia on anterior surface of calf's heart. *a*, *b*, pulmonary artery and aorta with nerve-plexuses and ganglia. *t*, descending cava with nerve-plexus and ganglia. *c*, right auricle. *d*, left auricle. *e*, Nerves and ganglia distributed on right side of heart. *f*, ditto on left side. *g*, anterior coronary vessels covered with nerve-plexuses and gang i .—*Original.*

Fig. 147.—Nerves and ganglia on posterior surface of calf's heart. *t*, descending cava. *c*, nerves and ganglia on right auricle. *d*, ditto on left. *g*, nerves and ganglia on right ventricle. *f*, ditto on left. *j*, great nerve-plexus and ganglia covering coronary sinus (*r*) and extending itself on the right (*h*), left (*i*), and posterior coronary vessels, and the right (*e*) and left (*f*) ventricles generally. The ganglia in this case are very numerous, particularly on the coronary sinus (*r*).—*Original.*

ganglia (two on the right side and two on the left) send branches to the heart; whereas in the rabbit, the ganglia supplying branches are increased to six, and in the calf to eight. The number of nerves found on the surface and in the substance of the calf's heart is greater than in any heart which I have examined,—a circumstance which has induced me to select it for description[1].

[1] My cardiac nerve dissections, fifty in number, are deposited in the Anatomical Museum of the University of Edinburgh, where they may be consulted. They

Plexuses formed on the Roots of the Pulmonary Artery and Aorta in the Calf.—These plexuses are virtually three in number.

First, That found on the ascending aorta (Fig. 146 *b*, p. 300) and superior cava (*i*), composed of branches from the superior or first dorsal ganglion of either side, and from the pneumogastric of the right side.

Secondly, That situated on the pulmonary artery (*a*), and between that vessel and the left auricle (*d*), composed of branches from the first dorsal ganglion of the left side, left pneumogastric, and left recurrent laryngeal.

Thirdly, That formed on the coronary sinus (Fig. 147, *j, r,* p. 300), composed almost exclusively of branches from the second and third dorsal ganglia of the sympathetic of the left side. The aortic plexus supplies branches to that surface of the right auricle (Fig. 146 *c*, p. 300) directed towards the aorta, and likewise to the right ventricle (*e*) and right coronary vessels (Fig. 149 *k*, p. 304). These plexuses, as well as the distribution of the nerves on the anterior and posterior surfaces of the heart generally, are seen at Figs. 146 and 147, p. 300.

Plexus formed on the Anterior Coronary Vessels of the Calf.—Those branches of the first dorsal ganglion which do not expend themselves on the ascending aorta, descend behind the pulmonary artery to supply branches to the anterior aspect of the left auricle (Fig. 146 *d*, p. 300). They then appear between the left auricle and pulmonary artery, and form an elaborate plexus on the anterior coronary vessels (*g*) and the anterior surface of the ventricles generally (*e, f*). This plexus is well seen in the human heart (Fig. 145, p. 299) and that of the horse (Fig. 148 A, *a, b, c, d, e,* p. 302), and if the nerves composing it be carefully examined they will be found to display a great number of ganglionic enlargements and spindle-shaped swellings, particularly where they cross vessels, and where they split up to change their direction and enter the substance of the heart. Some of these ganglia are of large size, and communicate with as many as four, six, and eight nerve-filaments.

embrace specimens of the cardiac nerves of man, the horse, calf, sheep, cat, rabbit, etc. For descriptions of the dissections *vide* Gold-Medal Inaugural Dissertation 'On the Ganglia and Nerves of the Heart,' deposited in the Library of the University of Edinburgh in 1861.

Plexus formed on the Coronary Sinus of the Calf.—This
plexus, which is either altogether omitted or very imperfectly
represented in works on the nerves of the heart, is composed
almost exclusively of branches from the ·second and third
dorsal ganglia of the sympathetic on the left side (Fig. 147, *j, r*,
p. 300, and Fig. 148 C, *j, r*). It affords the chief supply to
the left ventricle, which it occasionally envelops in a beautiful

Fig. 148.

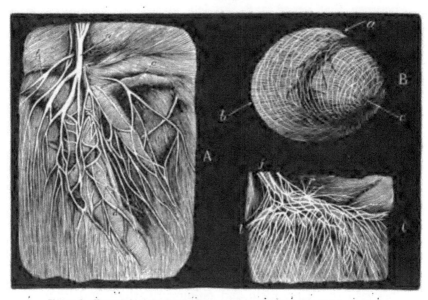

Fig. 148, A.—Nerves and ganglia on horse's heart. *a*, large quadrangular ganglion communicating
with five ,branches. Three of these branches form ampullae or spindle-shaped swellings where they
cross the coronary artery. Similar swellings are observed where the nerves cross the vessels occupying
the anterior ventricular groove (*d, c*).—*Original.*
    B.—Apex of left ventricle of calf's heart. Shows that the muscular fibres of the ventricle pursue a
spiral direction from left to right downwards (*b*); the nerves pursuing a spiral direction from right to
left downwards (*a*), and always crossing the muscular fibres at nearly right angles. Several ganglia are
to be observed on the nerves as they approach the apex (*c*).—*Original.*
    C.—Nerve-plexus and ganglia on coronary sinus (*j*) and base of left ventricle (*l*) of calf's heart. The
ganglia (*r*) in this situation are for the most part quadrangular and triangular in shape, and stand boldly
out. They consist of a superficial and a deep set.—*Original.*

network of delicate nerves, as shown at *f* of Figs. 147, p. 300,
and 150, p. 304. The nerves forming the coronary plexus are in
many cases so fragile that it is impossible to preserve them. In
one specimen, which I showed Professor Goodsir, the sinus was
completely covered with nerve-filaments, so that it would
have been difficult to insert the head of a pin between them.
In other specimens (Fig. 147, *r*, p. 300; Fig. 148 C, *r*) the nerves
are stronger and not so plentiful, the meshes or spaces between

the nerve-filaments being somewhat greater. In every case the nerves on the coronary sinus and posterior surface of the heart display a vast number of ganglionic enlargements and spindle-shaped swellings, some of them so large as readily to be detected by the naked eye; others requiring the aid of a pocket lens and a good light. The ganglia vary in shape as well as size. Thus in one of my dissections a stellate-shaped ganglion with seven branches is found on the coronary sinus; another with five branches is seen in a second dissection on the left coronary artery posteriorly; a large triangular mass, with numerous nerve-filaments, is detected in a third, where the coronary sinus receives the left coronary vein. In a fourth, several irregularly-shaped ganglionic masses of large size occupy the coronary sinus. In a fifth, a triangular-shaped ganglion is found on the left coronary artery below the sinus; while in a sixth a well-marked ganglionic enlargement, situated on the sinus and having five branches, is readily recognised.

The cardiac plexuses have been more or less accurately represented by Scarpa, Remak, Swan, Lee, and others.

Distribution of the Nerves on the Surface and in the Substance of the Auricles of the Calf.—The nerves supplied to the right auricle are as a rule very delicate, and proceed from the right pneumogastric, from the first dorsal ganglion of the sympathetic on the right side, and from the coronary plexus.

Those supplied to the left auricle are derived principally from the coronary plexus, some offsets being sent from the left pneumogastric, and the first dorsal ganglion of the sympathetic on the left side. The nerves, on reaching the surface of the auricles, break up and spread out to form a nervous reticulation or network. Ganglia may be detected in numbers where the nerves split up, where they encounter vessels, and where they dip into the substance of the auricles. Of the nerves which enter the substance of the auricles not a few pass through the auricular walls. The nerves supplied to the auricles are not quite so numerous as those supplied to the ventricles.

Distribution of the Nerves on the Surface and in the Substance of the Ventricles of the Calf.—The nerves on the surface of the ventricles, if allowance be made for their breaking up slightly to form meshes, follow a common course; *i. e.* they run in spiral lines from right to left downwards. The direction pursued by the nerves is precisely the opposite of that pursued by the muscular fibres; in other words, the muscular fibres form left-handed spirals, whereas the nerves form right-handed spirals. I mention this, because although it has been noted that the nerves cross the muscular fibres

Fig. 149.   Fig. 150.

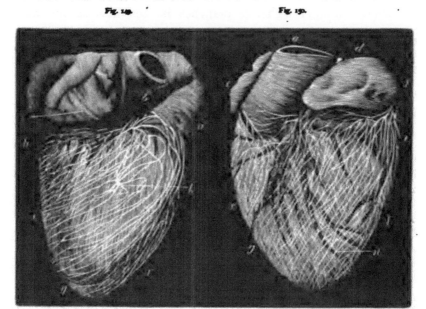

Fig. 149.—Nerves and ganglia on right ventricle of calf's heart. *a,* pulmonary artery. *b,* aorta. *c,* right auricle. *b,* plexus of nerves on right coronary vessels. *a,* nerves and ganglia on right ventricle. *f,* left ventricle. *g,* anterior coronary vessels. *h,* large ganglion with numerous nerves proceeding to and from it. A large number of similar but smaller and more delicate ganglia are seen on a close examination.—*Original.*

Fig. 150.—Nerves and ganglia on left ventricle of calf's heart. *a,* pulmonary artery. *c,* right auricle. *d,* left ditto. *e,* ganglia and nerves on right ventricle. *f,* ditto on left. *j,* ganglia and nerves on coronary sinus, which extends to left coronary vessel (*i*) and left ventricle (*f*), both of which it envelops in a beautiful network of nerves and ganglia. The ganglia are well seen on the left coronary artery (*i*) and one of the branches (*n*) of the anterior coronary artery. The swellings or enlargements of the nerves as they cross the vessels are represented more especially at *n*, but they are observed wherever vessels occur.—*Original.*

obliquely from base to apex, no allusion is made to the complete spirals formed by them, particularly as they near the apex. These points are illustrated at Figs. 146, 147, p. 300, 148 B, p. 302, 149 and 150.

The nerves, from the fact of their crossing the muscular fibres and blood-vessels at a great many different points, are in a position to stimulate or intercept stimulus, so that one can readily understand how the nerves regulate not only the movements but also the nourishment of the ventricles. The blood-vessels, as is well known, occupy the anterior and posterior coronary grooves; *i.e.* the vertical *sulci* or furrows which separate the right and left ventricles from each other. They also occupy the transverse or horizontal grooves which separate the right and left auricles from the right and left ventricles. As the manner in which the coronary vessels break up to nourish the heart is not well understood, I may state that the branches are given off from the main trunks very obliquely, and in such a manner that their course corresponds exactly with that of the muscular fibres. When they have proceeded a certain distance they dip into the substance of the ventricles and branch or bifurcate; the smallest branches penetrating the muscular walls in a direction from without inwards. The anterior and posterior coronary vessels consequently have the same direction as the nerves; whereas the branches of those vessels have the same direction as the muscular fibres, and a contrary direction to that of the nerves (Figs. 146, 147 and 150, pp. 300, 304). The smallest vessels, as stated, penetrate the substance of the ventricles from without inwards. From this it follows that the nerves intersect the larger branches of the coronary vessels and muscular fibres always at nearly right angles. That the nerves bear an important relation to the blood-vessels will appear from this. The nerves invariably form plexuses on the vessels, and the ganglionic enlargements and spindle-shaped swellings are always most numerous where the nerves come in contact with or cross them (Fig. 146 *g*, p. 300; Fig. 147 *j*, *r*, *l*, *h*, p. 300; Fig. 148 A, *a*, *b*, *c*, *d*, *e*; C, *j*, *r*, *l*, p. 302; Fig. 149 *h*, *g*, p. 304; and Fig. 150 *j*, *i*, *n*, *g*, p. 304). The nerves occasionally even swerve from their original course to intersect and accompany certain vessels. They likewise form nervous rings or loops on such vessels as are embedded in the substance of the ventricles but accidentally rise to the surface. In a word, the nerves not only constantly intersect the vessels, but they in many instances send off fine filaments to run in the direction of the length of the vessels, a triangular enlargement or ganglion being found where the nerves divide. As a rule the nerves are thickened and flattened where they cross

X

the vessels, the nerves at these points presenting a spindle-shaped characteristic appearance (Fig. 148 A, *a, b, c, d, e,* p. 302 ; and Fig. 150 *n*, p. 304). These ampullae or swellings on the nerves where they cross the vessels were described by Lee as ganglia, although on what grounds he does not state. He is quite correct in so regarding them, as I find they contain numerous unipolar with a few bipolar nerve-cells. Similar remarks may be made regarding the stellate-shaped ganglionic enlargements everywhere perceptible on the surface of the heart (Figs. 146, 147, 148, A, B, C, 149 and 150, pp. 300, 302, 304). To these allusion is made further on.

Distribution of the Nerves on the Right Ventricle.—As a proof that some purpose is served by the spiral distribution of the nerves on the ventricles, I may refer to the arrangement on the right ventricle (Fig. 149, p. 304). This ventricle, it will be remembered, is supplied by the nerve-plexus formed on the aorta, and between that vessel and the pulmonary artery (*b*). As, however, the plexus in question is situated behind the pulmonary artery and the *infundibulum* or *conus arteriosus*[1], it follows that if the nerves were at once to proceed on their downward course, not only would the *infundibulum* be left destitute of nerves, but their direction would nearly correspond with that of the muscular fibres. In order, therefore, to enable the nerves to run in a contrary direction to that of the muscular fibres, they at first proceed in a forward direction so as to cross the *infundibulum* and supply the vessels thereon, after which (and mark this) they suddenly bend upon themselves at nearly right angles in order fairly to intersect the muscular fibres in spiral lines in a direction from left to right downwards.

The points to be more particularly attended to in the distribution of the nerves on the right ventricle are the following :—They are derived from the plexus which invests the aorta, and extends between that vessel and the pulmonary artery. They receive, as was formerly stated, a few branches from the plexus on the anterior coronary vessels. They run in a spiral direction from before backwards and downwards ; a course the opposite of that pursued by the muscular fibres

---

[1] The *conus arteriosus* corresponds to the conical-shaped portion of the right ventricle from which the pulmonary artery springs.

and the branches of the cardiac vessels. Generally, they split up from time to time, the branches maintaining a certain parallelism and becoming finer and finer as they reach the posterior of the ventricle (Fig. 149 *e*, p. 304). Occasionally the nerves coalesce or run together, and under these circumstances there is a marked increase of nerve-substance at the point of junction. This is particularly the case in the large ganglion represented at *k* of Fig. 149, p. 304. When the nerves reach the posterior surface of the ventricle (*e*), they unite with others from the plexus on the coronary sinus to form stellate-shaped expansions or ganglia—well seen at *e* of Fig. 147, p. 300. The expansions referred to display, on microscopic examination, numerous unipolar and bipolar nerve-cells. The plexus formed on the right coronary artery (Fig. 149 *h*, p. 304), when examined with a lens in a good light, is found to be very complex. The nerves on the right ventricle (Figs. 147 and 149 *e*, pp. 300, 304) are fewer in number than those on the left ventricle (Fig. 150 *f*, p. 304). Posteriorly, there is usually a part of the right ventricle comparatively unprovided for, where the terminal nerve-filaments of the right ventricle unite with similar terminal nerve-filaments from the plexus on the coronary sinus.

Distribution of the Nerves on the Left Ventricle.—This ventricle derives its nervous supply almost exclusively from the plexus situated on the coronary sinus (Fig. 147 *j*, *r*, p. 300 ; Fig. 148 C, *j*, *r*, p. 302 ; Fig. 150 *j*, p. 304). It exhibits still more clearly than the right the spiral course pursued by the nerves. As a rule, the nerves on the posterior surface of the left ventricle proceed in almost parallel lines (Fig. 147 *f*, p. 300), subdividing and becoming more attenuated as they near the apex. On the lateral and anterior aspect of the ventricle the arrangement is more irregular, *i.e.* it assumes to a certain extent the plexiform character (Fig. 150 *f*, *g*, p. 304). In one of my dissections it is altogether plexiform, and the nerves, by alternately dividing, subdividing, and reuniting, produce a beautiful network of nerves which envelops the ventricle from base to apex. In examining this network I find that sometimes as many as three branches unite when crossing a vessel, after which they separate and reunite when another vessel is to be crossed (*n*). The plexus formed on the left coronary vessels (Fig. 147 *l*, p. 300) is an extension of that formed on the sinus (*j*, *r*). It is very intricate, and when patiently examined with a lens in a good light numerous ganglia and spindle-shaped enlargements are discovered (Fig. 148 C, p. 302). The spindle-shaped enlargements occurring on the general surface of the left ventricle are usually met with where the nerves cross the vessels, as was correctly described and figured by Lee. Lee, however, it appears to me, has slightly exaggerated the number and size of the enlargements, as well as the number of branches with which they communicate. The enlargements in many cases are apparently produced by a mere flattening of the nerves on the projecting rounded surface of the vessels (Fig. 150 *n*, p. 304). The appearance of the enlargements (they are spindle-shaped) suggests this idea. I am, however, satisfied that there is an actual increase of nerve-substance ; a view favoured by the fact that they contain a large number of nerve-cells, and not a few of them give off one or more delicate nerve-filaments to the vessels they cross. In this respect they resemble the typical stellate-shaped ganglia found on the coronary sinus (Fig. 147 *j*, *r*, p. 300 ; and Fig. 148 C, *j*, *r*, p. 302). In the heart of a camel which I had the good fortune to obtain through the kindness of Professor Goodsir, the increase of nerve-substance was very marked, the enlargements in this instance having a somewhat quadrangular shape, and sending branches to the vessels and other nerves.

The number of nerves which dip into the substance of the left ventricle is considerable. Large and small branches disappear separately or together without apparently following any order. Generally speaking, they take advantage of a vessel entering the substance and accompany it, or they seek one of the openings occurring between the muscular fasciculi. In a dissection which I made of the horse's heart, three branches were observed to enter the posterior wall of the left ventricle within a few lines of each other. The distribution of the nerves in the substance of the right ventricle is similar in all respects to that described in the left. The arrangement of the nerves in the substance of the heart is essentially the same as on its surface. Thus, the nerves run slantingly, and so come in contact with the vessels and muscular fibres.

Ganglia are found on the deep nerves as on the more superficial ones, although not to the same extent.

Distribution of the Nerves in the Human Heart.—The
number of nerves is slightly fewer in the human heart than in
that of the calf and some of the lower animals (Fig. 145, p. 299).
The nerves are also more delicate, the aggregate of the nerve-
filaments as compared with the aggregate of the muscular
fibres being less. The distribution and arrangement are as
nearly as may be identical with that described in the calf.
It is somewhat difficult to get a good view of the nerves of
the human heart, partly from the greatly thickened condition
of the exocardium or outer covering of the heart, and partly
from the excessive quantity of fat which usually invests it,
particularly in the vertical and horizontal coronary grooves.
By a diligent search extending over several years, I have
secured some very fine specimens, the best of which have
been obtained from young or emaciated patients, or those
who died from dropsy, in which case an excess of pericardial
fluid had softened and rendered the exocardium more or less
transparent. The nervous supply to the posterior surface of
the human heart is, comparatively speaking, very scanty; a
deficiency observed in the hearts of many of the lower
animals, though not to the same extent. As regards the
actual number of nerves on the ventricles of the human heart,
authorities differ. According to Scarpa and what I myself
have seen, the nerves are fewer and more delicate than in the
lower animals. Of this I think there can be little doubt,
as I have examined some hundreds of human hearts more or
less carefully. Lee nevertheless affirms that the nerves of
the human heart are quite as numerous as those of the heart
of the heifer. He corroborates his statement by drawings
of the nerves as seen on the heart of a child nine years of age,
and on the adult human heart hypertrophied[1]. Lee's preparations are deposited in the Museum of St. George's
Hospital, London, and I am disposed to believe, from an
inspection of them, that he has to some extent been misled
by his not having injected the minute cardiac vessels, and by
his manner of dissection (he teases the nerves out by the aid

[1] Dr. Robert Lee 'On the Ganglia and Nerves of the Heart,' Plates 1 and 5.
Phil. Trans. 1849.)

of needles—a procedure which displaces the nerves, and causes shreds of the exocardium or fibrous membrane investing the heart greatly to resemble nerves). In my own dissections, deposited in the Anatomical Museum of the University of Edinburgh, I have endeavoured to avoid this source of error by careful injections of the cardiac arteries. and veins with two colours, and from dissecting everything away from the nerves, without dragging or pulling upon the nerves themselves. The nerves in my dissections are consequently all *in situ*, and their relations to the cardiac vessels and muscular fibres undisturbed. The ganglionic enlargements found on the nerves of the human heart have been partially figured by Scarpa and more fully by Lee. I have shown them at Fig. 145, p. 299. They are not so distinct as those found on the nerves of the heart of the calf, neither are they so numerous; nevertheless, they are sufficiently numerous and well-marked to attract attention.

The arrangement of the nerves in the heart of the camel, alpaca, panther, seal, and all the other mammals which I have examined, is in every respect similar to that already described in the calf.

Microscopic Appearances presented by the Ganglia found on the Coronary Sinus and Cardiac Vessels.

The ganglia of the heart, as already explained, vary greatly in size, some being so minute that a pocket lens or microscope is required to detect them; others being so large as to be readily recognised by the unaided eye even at a distance. In every case they are characterised by an increase of nerve-substance, the aggregate of any one ganglion being greater than the aggregate of the nerves which enter and leave it. The increase in bulk is due for the most part to the presence of an infinite number of unipolar nerve-cells mixed with a few bipolar ones[1]. The ganglia also vary in form. Thus some, as has been stated, are stellate-shaped, others quadrangular, others oblong, others triangular, and others spindle-shaped.

---

[1] Similar ganglia are found in the stomach, intestines, bladder, uterus, and certain of the blood-vessels; and it is worthy of remark, that the structures here enumerated are endowed with more or less typical rhythmical movements.

The form depends in a great measure on the number of nerve-filaments which conduct to and from the ganglion. Thus, if a ganglion is connected with eight nerve-filaments, it is stellate-shaped; if with four, quadrangular or oblong; if with three, triangular; and if with only two, spindle-shaped. The spindle-shaped ganglia are found where the nerves cross the smaller vessels; the others on the coronary sinus and larger vessels, and on the surface, and in the substance of the heart generally, particularly where the nerves bifurcate and break up with a view to changing their direction. The ganglia consist for the most part of irregular aggregations of nerve-cells, with nerve-filaments proceeding to and from them (Fig. 151 C, p. 312). This is the character of the irregular-shaped ganglia found on the coronary sinus. In other cases, the aggregation of nerve-cells assume an oval form, the nerves proceeding to and from the cells being arranged in two sets, as witness the spindle-shaped ganglia found on the nerves as they cross the smaller vessels (Fig. 151 B, p. 312). In other cases the nerve-cells are disposed in the form of a bulb, the nerves conducting to and from the nerve-cells being arranged in a fasciculus; the ganglion with its leash of nerves resembling a hyacinth bulb with its leaves (Fig. 151 A, p. 312). Wherever a large terminal ganglion is found, one or more smaller ones, apparently in process of formation, may be detected. The following is the arrangement as ascertained by me in 1861 :—
' The bundles of nerve-filaments on entering the clump (terminal ganglion) resolve themselves into their component nerve-fibres, and each fibre selects and becomes connected with a nerve-cell[1].'

In order to see the nerve-cells to advantage, the best plan is to take a fresh heart and remove one of the ganglia from its surface in such a manner as not to injure or compress it in any way. This done, the ganglion is placed in an ammoniacal solution of carmine for a short time. The unequal staining produced by this pigment differentiates the nerve-cells and nerve-filaments. The ganglion is then transferred to a glass slide and a little glycerine added with a view to examination with a low power. A cursory examination at once reveals

[1] Inaugural Dissertation by the Author, ' On the Ganglia and Nerves of the Heart,' p. 36. University of Edinburgh Library, 1861.

the dark central mass of the nerve-centre and the lighter nerve-filaments in connexion therewith. A keen eye may also detect traces of the nerve-cells, which appear as dark rounded masses. To see the nerve-cells properly, the ganglion, if large, must be broken up with needles; if small, a thin covering-glass should be employed, and pressure applied with a view to flattening and even squashing it. A microscope,

Fig. 151.

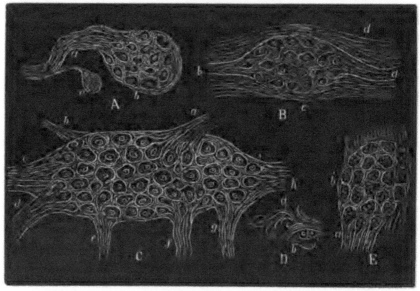

Fig. 151 A.—Large and small terminal ganglia with nerve-cells and nerve-fibres proceeding to and from them. *a*, bundle of nerve-filaments in connexion with large ganglion (*b*). A similar bundle is connected with small ganglion (*c*).—*Original.*

B. Ganglionic enlargement or swelling of nerve as it crosses a vessel. *a, b*, nerve-filaments proceeding to and from the ganglion and nerve-cells (*c*). *d*, nerve-substance surrounding and investing ganglion (*c*). —*Original.*

C. Large ganglion crowded with nerve-cells from coronary sinus of calf. *a, b, c, d, e, f, g, h*, nerve-filaments proceeding to and from the ganglion and nerve-cells. The nerve-cells contain a nucleus and one or more nucleoli. They are for the most part unipolar in character. A few bipolar nerve-cells are also found.—*Original.*

D. Unipolar (*a*) and bipolar (*b*) nerve-cells from cardiac ganglion, displaying nucleus and nucleolus.— *Original.*

E. Terminal ganglion or aggregation of cells in a nerve as it crosses a vessel. *a*, nerve-filaments proceeding to and from the nerve-cells of the terminal ganglion (*b*).—*Original.*

magnifying from 300 to 400 diameters, will reveal the nerve-cells as represented at Fig. 151 A, B, C, D, E. These figures are copied from my Inaugural Dissertation, deposited in the Library of the University of Edinburgh in 1861, and it will be observed that they remarkably accord with analogous figures representing the ganglia and nerve-cells in the heart of the frog, published by Dr. Beale in 1863.

The cells, as has been already pointed out, are for the most part unipolar, with a sprinkling of bipolar ones (Fig. 151 D, p. 312). They contain a nucleus and one or more nucleoli (A, B, C, D). In some cases and under certain conditions they present a granular appearance (E). Analogy inclines me to believe that the ganglia and nerve-cells just described are to be regarded as nerve-centres or diminutive brains. In this I agree with Winslow, Winterl, Johnstone, Unger, Lecat, and Peffingers. They assist in regulating and co-ordinating the movements of the heart, and preside over its nutrition. This view, if taken in connexion with the vital properties inhering in involuntary muscles, in part accounts for the rhythmic movements of the heart when the organ is cut out of the body, when it is severed from its nervous connexions, and when it is deprived of blood, unless such as is found within its walls. It is the blood within the muscular parietes of the heart which keeps it alive and enables it to move rhythmically.

Why does the Heart act Rhythmically?

To this question no satisfactory reply can be given in the present state of science. The older observers attributed the phenomenon to various and extraordinary causes. Stahl, e.g. declared the movements of the heart to be under the guidance of the *anima* or soul. Sylvius, the head of the chemical sect, traced them to an effervescence caused by a mixture of the old and alkaline blood with the acid chyle and acid pancreatic juice; while Descartes referred them to a succession of explosions occurring within the heart due to a generation of steam. Willis, with a greater show of reason, attributed the movements of the heart to the cerebellum and the eighth pair of nerves. To these Boerhaave added two additional causes, viz. the action of the blood of the arteries on its fibres, and of the venous blood on the surface of its cavities. The hypothesis of Willis explained how the heart is subject to the storm of the passions, but it did not explain how the heart beat in the *anencephalous* foetus (foetus devoid of brain and spinal cord), or in animals whose brain and spinal cord were crushed or removed. Still less did it explain how the heart moved with a regular rhythm, when cut out of the body, deprived of its blood, and placed in an exhausted receiver with a view to excluding the air which was supposed to act as an irritant. This difficulty induced Haller to deny that the heart owed its movements to its nerves, and led him ultimately to declare that the movements of the heart are due to irritability inhering in the muscular fibres (*vis insita*) as apart from its nerves. Haller's theory failed to account for the presence of nerves on the surface and in the substance of the heart, and for the connexion which is known to exist between that organ and the head. Some of his followers, Soemmering and Behrends for instance, endeavoured to evade this difficulty by supposing that the cardiac nerves were distributed only to the vessels of the heart; a view which, in the present state of the subject, is untenable. Stannius, in recent times, has made experiments to show that the rhythm of the heart is referrible to its ganglia, which he regards as automatic nerve-centres; and Sir James Paget has argued with much ability to the effect that it is due to rhythmic nutrition. There are no sufficient grounds for believing that the nerves actually produce the movements of the heart. These in all probability originate in the sarcous elements composing the muscular fibres of the heart, as is partially demonstrated by the following experiment :—When the nerves proceeding to a muscle are poisoned by certain substances, such as woorara, so that stimulation of the nerves fails to produce shortening or contraction of the muscle, the muscle may nevertheless be made to shorten by applying the stimulus to its fibres directly. Furthermore, Bowman asserts from observation, that a muscular fibre destitute of nerves may be made to contract. The heart acts rhythmically for protracted periods after it is cut out of the body and its nerves divided [1],—a circumstance which compels us to conclude either that the rhythmic movements inhere in the muscular substance or are referrible to the ganglia which are found in great numbers on the surface and in the substance of the heart generally. But, as has been stated, the nerves may be poisoned, and still the heart contract under stimulation. The

[1] The heart of the frog, if supplied with fresh *serum*, will pulsate for several days after removal.

will exercises no influence upon the movements of the heart under ordinary circumstances, and the brain and spinal cord may be crushed without interfering with them even in a remote degree. In the *anencephalous* foetus, where the brain and spinal cord are absent, the heart acts rhythmically and regularly. On the other hand, it is well known that certain mental states (joy, grief, etc.) affect the heart, and that division of the pneumogastric nerves is followed by a quickening of the heart's action, while irritation of the cut ends of these nerves is accompanied by slowing of the heart's action. Division of the nerves tends to prove the regulating influence of the nervous system ; the cause of the rhythm of the heart remaining still unexplained. Sir James Paget, whose philosophic utterances have necessarily great weight, is disposed, as already stated, to attribute the rhythm of the heart to rhythmic nutrition. This however cannot be accepted as the final explanation ; for one naturally inquires, Why should the nutrition of the heart be rhythmic, seeing it is only a muscle, and there are innumerable other muscles equally well nourished whose movements are not rhythmic ?

There is a further difficulty as to whether nutrition is to be accredited with the movements, for cilia vibrate rhythmically when removed from the body, and even when on the verge of putrefaction. Granting however that the rhythmic nutrition of the heart produces its rhythmic movements, the question still remains (and it is equally hard of solution), What causes the rhythmic nutrition? The rhythmic nutrition hypothesis only removes the difficulty one step further back ; it cannot be accepted as a final explanation. All nutrition is not rhythmic, and when it is, there must be laws to regulate it. Those laws are as yet undiscovered, and are probably only to be recognised by their effects. For reasons to be stated presently I am disposed to believe that the rhythm of the adult heart is due partly to a healthy nutrition, partly to the inherent vitality or power of moving residing in muscles, and partly to the influence exerted on the cardiac movements by the ganglia and nerves situated on the surface and in the substance of the heart and other parts of the body. There can be no doubt that the nervous system presides over the nutrition of the circulatory apparatus as a whole, and it is equally evident that the movements of the heart and blood-vessels, and the degree of vascular tension or pressure, are modified by the condition of certain nerves and nerve-centres. With a view to simplifying our comprehension of this very involved but highly interesting problem, I propose to arrange existing materials under two heads :—

I. Proofs that the heart can move independently of the nerves.

II. Proofs that the movements of the heart are regulated and co-ordinated by the nerves.

Proofs that the Heart may act independently of the Nerves.— Analogy favours this view.

(*a.*) Certain plants when vigorous and exposed to a bright light, such as the Hedysarum (*Desmodium gyrans*), exhibit rhythmical movements.

(*b.*) Professor Busk showed that at a certain period of the development of the *Volvox globator* (a very simple vegetable organism), there appear in each zoospore, or in the bands of protoplasm with which the zoospores are connected, vacuoles, spaces or cavities, of about $\frac{1}{8000}$ of an inch in diameter, which contract with regular rhythm at intervals of from 38 to 41 seconds, quickly contracting and then more slowly dilating again, as in the heart.

(*c.*) Similar phenomena were observed by Cohn to occur in *Gonium pectorale* and *Chlamydomonas*, the vacuoles or water vesicles contracting regularly at intervals of from 40 to 45 seconds. Here, of course, neither nerve nor muscle, nor blood, nor any kind of stimulus, or anything in the shape of irritation, is present. Sir James Paget attributes the rhythmic movements in plants to rhythmic nutrition. This, however, can only be accepted as a partial explanation. All nutrition is not rhythmic. Only certain plants exhibit rhythmic movements, but all plants are equally nourished.

(*d.*) Rhythmic movements occur in cilia, these, so far as known at present, not being supplied with nerves. That ciliary movements, at least, are not due to rhythmic nutrition appears from this, that cilia vibrate rhythmically when removed from the body, and even when on the verge of putrefaction.

(*e.*) The amoeba, which consists of an undifferentiated mass equally devoid of nerve and muscle, can change shape in every direction, and can open and close any part of its body to produce a temporary stomach.

(*f.*) The heart pulsates while yet a mass of nucleated cells, *i. e.* before it is furnished with either muscular fibres, nerves, or blood.

(*g.*) Bowman showed that a muscular fibrilla on or in which no nerve can be detected may be made to contract artificially.

(*h.*) The brain and spinal cord may be gradually crushed without in the slightest disturbing the movements of the heart (Marshall Hall).

(*i.*) The branches of the pneumogastric nerves which supply filaments to the heart have little or no sensibility, and the filaments supplied to the organ by the sympathetic trunks only act upon it after being stimulated a short time previously.

(*j.*) The great sympathetic nerves which furnish the principal nervous supply to the heart in the mammal are particularly sluggish in their action, and when stimulated affect the movements of the heart only after a considerable interval; the effect produced not ceasing when the stimulation is discontinued.

(*k.*) When woorara poison has been administered to an animal, it completely paralyses the motor nerves, leaving the sensory nerves and muscular irritability intact. Under these circumstances the muscular fibres may be made to contract by the direct application of a stimulus, showing that movement inheres in the sarcous elements of the muscular fibres of the heart. This power of moving on the application of a stimulus which inheres in muscle was designated by Haller the *vis insita.*

(*l.*) When an animal is poisoned by woorara, and the rhythm of the heart maintained by artificial respiration, the galvanisation of both pneumogastric nerves does not affect its movements. If the pneumogastrics be powerfully galvanised the heart is stopped for a short period, but resumes its functions as soon as the motor filaments are temporarily exhausted and deprived of what is termed their inhibitory or slowing power (Bernard).

(*m.*) In birds, according to Bernard, galvanisation of the pneumogastric nerves does not affect the heart.

(*n.*) The heart may be cut out of the body and deprived of blood, and still beat regularly. This experiment shows either that the movements of the heart are independent of the nerves as a whole, or are referrible to the nerves and ganglia situated on its surface and in its substance; but, as has been already explained, the nerves of the heart may be paralysed by woorara poison in such a manner that they do not respond to stimuli; the muscular fibres, on the other hand, responding to the stimuli as if no poison had been administered. The latter fact inclines to the belief that the motor power of the heart resides in its muscular fibres.

(*o.*) Many physiologists maintain that the rhythmical movements of the heart continue not only in the heart as a whole when its cerebro-spinal and sympathetic connexions are severed, and when it is removed from the body and deprived of blood, but also in fragments of the muscular substance in which no ganglia or nerve-centres can be discovered. Those who oppose this view aver that nerve-cells can, as a rule, be detected in the pulsating shreds, whereas they are absent in the non-pulsating shreds. This, however, does not always hold true.

Proofs that the Movements of the Heart are Regulated and Co-ordinated by the Nerves.

(*a.*) That the movements of the heart are regulated and co-ordinated by the nerves, is proved indirectly by their presence on the organ and by the fact that the nerves exercise a marked influence on the movements of voluntary muscles; the voluntary muscles, as has been shown, being a differentiation and development of the involuntary.

(*b.*) Mental excitement arising from sudden joy, etc., quickens the movements of the heart.

(*c.*) The heart may be stopped indirectly by a voluntary effort. This is effected, first, by distending the lungs, stopping the mouth and nose, and making a strong *expiratory* effort; and, second, by partially emptying the lungs, stopping the mouth and nose, and making a strong *inspiratory* effort. These are dangerous experiments.

(*d.*) The direct action of the pneumogastric nerves upon the heart is through their motor filaments, as shown by division of the nerves in the neck. Galvanisation of their central ends does not affect the heart, while stimulation of their peripheral ends stops it. Some experimenters, however, aver that if the nerves be divided and their peripheral ends feebly stimulated by galvanism, the action of the heart is *quickened*. These contradictory statements show that the division and irritation of nerves may yield fallacious results.

(*e.*) The motor filaments of the pneumogastric nerves which act directly on the heart are derived from the communicating branch of the spinal accessory (Waller).

(*f.*) When one of the pneumogastric nerves is divided in the neck of the dog, the number of pulsations is slightly increased, and the cardiac pressure, as indicated by the cardiometer fixed in the carotid artery, slightly diminished. When both pneumogastrics are divided, the beats of the heart are doubled in frequency, but are weak and tremulous. A similar result is produced if the afferent nerves of the sympathetic which are united to the pneumogastrics are divided. The acceleration in the latter case is produced by a reflex act.

(*g.*) When the pneumogastric nerves in the neck are galvanised the action of the heart is *slowed*, and if the galvanism be sufficiently powerful it is *arrested* (The brothers Weber). The action of the pneumogastrics is therefore supposed to be inhibitory.

(*h.*) The heart may be stopped for a few moments by pressure on the right pneumogastric at a certain point in the neck (Czermak).

(*i.*) If the action of the heart is arrested by galvanisation of the medulla oblongata, the action is resumed if both pneumogastrics be divided (Longet).

(*j.*) If the pneumogastric nerves be divided in the neck, galvanism of their central ends modifies the movements of the heart, by modifying the respirations, the latter being diminished in frequency (Traube and Bernard).

(*k.*) If the central extremities of the divided depressor nerves [1] be galvanised, the heart is *slowed*, and the arterial

---

[1] The depressor nerve in the rabbit arises in the neck by two roots, one connected with the trunk of the pneumogastric, the other with the superior laryngeal branch. It passes down the neck, and when it reaches the chest receives filaments from the sympathetic. The nerve thus augmented passes by numerous short

pressure in the arteries *diminished* by a reflex action. The diminution of arterial pressure is not due to the slowing of the heart, for it occurs even when both pneumogastrics are divided in the neck and the action of the heart quickened (Cyon and Ludwig). These experiments are calculated to show that the depressor nerves exert a twofold influence; viz. on the heart and on the blood-vessels.

(*l.*) If the spinal cord be divided immediately below the medulla oblongata and the. cord stimulated by electricity, the arterial pressure is increased and the movements of the heart quickened (Ludwig and Thiry). The nerves by the instrumentality of which those changes are produced, pass through the lower cervical ganglion, and are known as the '*accelerator nerves.*' They are regarded as the antagonists of the pneumogastric nerves, whose function, as stated, is supposed to be '*inhibitory.*'

(*m.*) The filaments of the sympathetic nerves everywhere invest the heart and blood-vessels. These they supply with innumerable nerve-plexuses and ganglia, the nerves to the smaller vessels being in some cases excessively minute.

(*n.*) Division of the sympathetic produces *vascular congestion and widening of the vessels* supplied by the portion of the sympathetic divided. The congestion is removed by irritating by electricity the portion of the nerve supplied to the tissues (Bernard).

(*o.*) Excitation of the spinal cord of the frog by electricity causes *contraction or narrowing of the arteries* of the web of the frog's foot, and if the excitement is kept up, the circulation in the arteries is stopped.

(*p.*) Direct excitation of a vaso-motor nerve causes *contraction of the arteries* to which it sends nerve-filaments. Division of a vaso-motor nerve, on the other hand, produces *dilatation.*

(*q.*) Division of the sympathetic in the neck of the rabbit, causes dilatation of the central artery of the ear; but if the peripheral end of the nerve be excited, the artery contracts (Brown-Sequard).

(*r.*) If one of the splanchnic nerves be divided in the rabbit,

---

branches to the heart between the origins of the great vessels (pulmonary artery and aorta). Cyon finds the homologue of the depressor nerves of the rabbit in the horse.—(*Brit. and For. Med.-Chir. Rev.* Lond. 1871. No xcvi. p. 540.

the arterial pressure is reduced; but if the divided nerve be
stimulated by electricity, *it is increased.*

(*s.*) If a portion of the base of a frog's heart be removed
with a sharp knife or scissors, it acts rhythmically ; whereas a
portion removed from the apex does not, as a rule, act rhythmically. This does not always hold true, but when it does,
it is supposed to be due to an increase in the ganglia and
nerves at the base of the heart as compared with the apex.

(*t.*) If a ligature be adjusted so as to enclose or map off
the sinus venosus of the frog's heart, it is found that when
the ligature is tightened the sinus continues to pulsate,
whereas the ventricle after a few beats is arrested in diastole.
After a short interval the ventricle also begins to pulsate,
but the pulsations of the sinus venosus and ventricle are no
longer synchronous (Stannius). This experiment is supposed
to prove that the sinus venosus contains an automatic nerve-
centre, *i.e.* a ganglion in which nerve energy is accumulated
and discharged at stated intervals or rhythmically. As, however, the automatic motor centre has not been demonstrated
to exist anatomically, the statement must be received with
caution. Admitting, however, that the automatic motor
centre really exists, the rhythm of the heart is still unexplained. The mystery of the movement confronts us as
before. The question, then, comes to be, What causes the
automatic motor centre to act rhythmically? The answer
to this question will probably bring us face to face with the
hidden springs of life itself; and the why and the wherefore
of existence, there is reason to believe, will for ever remain
a sealed book.

*The theory of Irritability as bearing on the Action of the
Heart, considered.* — The voluntary muscles, according to
Haller, are alone under the influence of the nerves ; the
hollow muscles, such as the heart, stomach, bladder, and
uterus, not being stimulated by their nerves but by their
contents. In Haller's opinion, the blood is the stimulus to
the heart. Dr. John Reid also adopted this view. He says,
'The ordinary and natural stimulus of the heart is the blood
which is constantly flowing into its cavities. The greater
irritability of the inner surface over the outer is evidently
connected with the manner in which the stimulus is habitually

applied. When the blood is forced on more rapidly towards the heart, as in exercise, its contractions become proportionally more frequent; and when the current moves on more slowly, as in a state of rest, its frequency becomes proportionally diminished. If the contractions of the heart were not dependent upon the blood, and their number regulated by the quantity flowing into its cavities, very serious and inevitably fatal disturbances in the circulation would soon take place.' If, however, the impinging of the blood against the inside of the heart is the cause of the heart's movements, it is natural to suppose the heart would close the instant the blood enters its cavities, without waiting until those cavities are full. If exception be taken to this statement, and it is asserted that the blood only becomes a stimulus when a certain quantity has been collected, then we are equally entitled to assume that the heart has become accustomed to the stimulus up to a certain point. But if so, seeing the heart is always receiving blood, why does it not become altogether accustomed to the presence of blood, and the blood cease to act as a stimulus? I will go further, and ask, how can the blood possibly act as a stimulus to the dilating ventricles? When the ventricles have closed, every drop of blood is literally wrung out of them. The ventricles, in fact, at the end of the systole, form a solid mass; the auricles have no power to force blood into a solid mass; and, if the blood be not present, it cannot act as a stimulus. The heart, moreover, closes and opens when removed from the body and placed in an exhausted receiver, and when neither blood nor air are present. I have on many occasions made transverse sections of the human and other hearts when in the contracted state, and have satisfied myself that the ventricles can completely obliterate their cavities [1].

---

[1] The ventricles of the heart obliterate their cavities in the following manner:—
Towards the ends of the systole, the walls of the ventricle thicken to a marked extent; the ventricles become shorter; the musculi papillares shorten and twist and plait into each other, and the auriculo-ventricular valves are dragged down into the ventricular cavities to form two dependent twisted cones, The thickening of the ventricular walls from without inwards, aided by the shortening of the more oblique spiral fibres, tends to diminish the ventricular cavities from side to side; while the shortening of the more longitudinal spiral fibres and spiral musculi

That no blood is contained in the ventricular cavities at the termination of the systole, is proved by the fact that in animals bled to death the ventricular cavities are, for the most part, completely obliterated. This arises from the surfaces of the ventricular walls, which are directed towards the axes of the cavities, being closely and accurately applied to each other throughout.

In the frog and other animals with semi-transparent hearts, the ventricle is blanched at the end of the systole—an appearance due, not, as was thought, to the absence of blood in its walls, but in its interior. The impinging of the blood against the endocardium cannot therefore be regarded as the prime mover of the heart. As well might we say that the presence of the pericardial fluid and the impinging of the exocardium or outer surface of the heart against the pericardium was the source of its activity. This would be an equally if not a more satisfactory explanation, the more especially as there is, as has been shown, a superabundant supply of nerves and ganglia on the external surface of the heart.

That the doctrine of irritability has elements of fallacy in it is, I think, proved by the movements in plants, cilia, the worm, the tentacles of the snail, sea anemone, and allied structures, already described. It seems also proved by the movements of the hollow viscera as a class. If the contents of the hollow viscera acted as stimuli to them, these organs could not consistently be employed as receptacles either for living or dead matter. If the blood formed the stimulus for the heart, the food for the stomach, the urine for the

papillares, aided by the descent of the auriculo-ventricular valves, diminishes the cavities from above downwards. The apices of the ventricles are closed by the shortening and thickening of the spiral fibres in those regions; the spiral fibres, particularly of the left apex, forming a whorl or vortex of great beauty. The spiral fibres, by their shortening and thickening, press the walls of the apices forcibly together, in a direction from without inwards and from below upwards, and so convert them into a solid mass. This is necessary, because the apices are the weakest portions of the ventricular walls—the left apex of even the horse's heart being something like 1-8th of an inch in thickness; that of the human heart being little over 1-16th of an inch. The tenuity of the ventricular walls at the apices enables the several orders of spiral fibres to coil and uncoil with great facility during the systole and diastole, when the fibres of the heart screw home and then unscrew.

bladder, the faeces for the rectum, and the foetus for the uterus, these organs would eject their contents, not at stated intervals, but whenever the stimulus was applied to them. It would be impossible, I apprehend, to apply the stimulus of electricity to any one of them, without producing violent closure of their muscular walls; nor would this state of matters be improved by keeping up the electricity with a view to familiarising them with it, as this would result in paralysis. The hollow viscera are living muscles; they open out, to receive the substances prepared for them, and when they have received the full measure thereof, they close and expel them according to fixed laws, and independently of irritation. If the closing of the hollow viscera was due simply to irritation, our bodies would be much more uncomfortable habitations than they are. I am disposed to believe that a living organism has the power in all its parts of avoiding or rejecting and selecting and appropriating whatever it chooses. It is this power which makes it superior to the outer world in which it lives, moves, and has a being. It is more rational to suppose that a living creature, or a part thereof, controls or avoids the inanimate matter by which it is surrounded, than that the inanimate matter inaugurates and controls its movements. For my own part, I cannot for a moment imagine that the presence of the urine and the faeces in the bladder and rectum act as irritating stimuli. I can still less believe that the blood and foetus act as such to the heart and uterus. This view will no doubt be met by the old objection, viz. that we may have an irritable stomach, bladder, or rectum, and that under these circumstances the viscera close as soon as anything is placed within them. If this argument proves anything, it proves that, in a normal or healthy condition, the contents of the hollow viscera do not act as irritants. I am aware that those who hold the doctrine of irritability in its entirety, assert that, when a call is made to pass faeces or urine, and the call is not attended to, the uneasy feeling passes away, because the viscus becomes accustomed to the irritant which is stimulating it. Would, let me ask, the viscus become accustomed to the presence of a coil of wire in its interior conveying electricity? The fact that the uneasy feelings do pass away when the call is not attended to, proves conclu-

sively that the contained matter is not an irritant in the
ordinary acceptation of the term. It is very difficult, I
believe impossible, to reconcile the theory of irritability with
vital manifestations in a healthy organism. The effects produced by artificial stimuli are, I strongly suspect, calculated
to mislead. Even the amoeba, which is a mere protoplasmic
jelly-like mass, has the power of taking in, containing, and
ejecting at will, the dead or living matter on which it depends for support; and it will take no great stretch of the
imagination to believe that the hollow viscera are provided
with a like power, the more especially as they are abundantly supplied with blood, and provided with innumerable
nerve-plexuses and ganglia. The oesophagus seizes and
transmits the food intended for the stomach, the muscular
walls of this tube closing or contracting behind the bolus,
and expanding or dilating in front of it—a fact inconsistent
with the doctrine of irritability; for in that case the oesophagus would close before the bolus, and not behind it.
The stomach, when it has received the food which constitutes a meal, immediately sets to work upon it, and causes
it to travel in certain determinate directions in its interior,
until, in conjunction with the gastric and other secretions,
it reduces it to a pulp. This done, it opens its pyloric valve,
and causes the more fluid portions of the mass to pass into
the duodenum. The pyloric valve is then closed, and the contents of the stomach rolled about as before. The pyloric valve
is a second time opened, and the more pultaceous portions of
the digesting mass ejected. The pyloric valve is a second
time closed, and the contents of the stomach again rolled
about and manipulated as by an intelligent agent. The
pyloric valve is opened a third time, and the entire contents
of the stomach ejected [1]. Now, it will be observed that it
cannot be the irritation produced by the food which causes
the movements of the stomach; for in that case, the food
would be expelled immediately it came in contact with the
lining membrane of the stomach, which it is not. If moreover, the food be regarded as the irritant which causes the
body of the stomach to close or contract, it cannot con-

---

[1] In the case of Alexis St. Martin, who had the anterior portion of his stomach
removed by a gunshot wound, these movements could be seen.

sistently be regarded as the irritant which causes the pyloric valve or sphincter of the stomach to open, as these are opposite acts, and the sphincter lies beyond the source of the irritation. What is said of the stomach applies equally to the heart, the bladder, the rectum, and the uterus. All these have a common structure and a common nervous supply, and their movements are, strictly speaking, rhythmic in character. The heart acts rhythmically when deprived of blood, both before and after it is removed from the body, and M. Chauveau has introduced caoutchouc bags into the ventricles of the heart, when full of blood and acting normally, without in the slightest degree disturbing their action.

The bladder in a healthy subject acts from four to six times in the twenty-four hours, *i. e.* it contains a fluid for six hours at a time, without causing the slightest inconvenience to the patient. During that period the urine certainly does not act as an irritant in the common acceptation of the term, yet this same fluid at the end of the sixth hour is said to occasion its own expulsiòn. It could only do so by being suddenly transformed into a highly irritating fluid, which its presence in the bladder for six hours proves it not to be. But granting that the irritating nature of the fluid at the sixth hour caused the body of the bladder to contract, it could not cause the sphincter of the bladder to open, as this is an opposite act, and the sphincter is placed beyond the reach of the irritating medium. If I am here met by the argument, that it is the irritation produced by the increased pressure of the urine at the sixth hour, I reply that this cause cannot operate in the case of the stomach—the stomach and bladder, as has been pointed out, having a common structure and a common nervous supply. Similar remarks may be made of the rectum and its sphincters. The rectum in a condition of health receives faeces for twenty-four hours, at the expiry of which period it closes by a rhythmic movement and expels its contents. The closing of the body of the rectum is accompanied by the opening of its sphincters, but the former act does not produce the latter, both being equally vital in their nature. The uterus in the human subject retains its contents for nine months. During this long period (and the term is greatly exceeded in the case of the elephant), the foetus, notwithstanding its vigorous movements and ever-varying position, occasions little or no inconvenience to the mother. It is assuredly not to be regarded as an irritant. After a few incipient contractions of the uterus (the false pains of obstetricians), occurring at intervals during the period of gestation, and a few vigorous contractions (the true pains of obstetricians), towards the full term, the foetus is thrown off or expelled. While the body of the uterus is contracting or closing, the sphincter of the uterus is expanding or opening. These acts are independent and separate, and constitute the rhythm of the organ.

But to return to the heart.

The heart beats, because its elementary particles—*i. e.* its ultimate or sarcous elements—live. If a potent poison is introduced into the substance of the heart, the particles die, and the heart ceases to act both within and without the body. If, moreover, the nerve-plexuses of the heart be suddenly destroyed, and the nutrition of the heart impaired, the action of the organ becomes irregular, or altogether ceases. The blood within the substance of the heart, and not within its cavities, is the cause of its movements, and these movements are not due to irritation, but to a healthy nutrition and assimilation, which go on so long as the body lives and the heart beats. That the movements of the heart are not due to the blood which it contains in its several cavities acting as a stimulus is, I think, apparent from Reid's own writings. In his admirable paper on the 'Heart,' he states that in extensive injuries to the central organs of the nervous system, such as concussion of the brain, severe mechanical injuries, the shock after operations, extensive burns, peritonitis, etc., the quantity of the blood entering the heart is reduced, the action of the heart quickened[1], and its contractility lessened. If, however, the blood contained within the cavities of the heart stimulate the organ to contract, how, it may reasonably be asked, are the contractions more frequent when the supply

---

[1] The frequency of the heart's action in man varies at different periods of life. Thus, in the human foetus, the heart beats 140 times per minute; at birth, 130; second year after birth, 100; third year, 90; fourteenth year, 80; middle age, 70; old age, 60, or even less. The variations in the frequency of the beat of the heart in the lower animals is still more remarkable.

of blood is reduced, and the contractile power of the organ diminished? The heart, as I have already pointed out, does not, in a state of health, contract the instant the blood touches its interior; on the contrary, its several parts do not begin contracting until they have received all the blood they are capable of containing. If, however, the heart, under certain circumstances, contracts more frequently when it contains a small quantity of blood and its irritability is diminished, than when there is a full supply of blood and its irritability is greatest, then we are, I think, entitled to conclude the blood contained within the cavities is not the cause of the movements of the heart. Furthermore, it is known that arterial tension or fulness retards rather than increases the heart's action; the pulsations being fewest when the blood is as it were dammed up in the heart. If, e.g. the aorta is compressed, the pulse rate is at once diminished. The injuries to which Reid alludes most probably change the character of the heart's action by paralysing or otherwise impairing the function of the nerves which regulate its nutrition. The rapid feeble pulse in the cases referred to is rather to be attributed to the fact that the vitality of the heart is temporarily lowered, and that it only admits a minimum quantity of blood as it has not the power to expel the maximum quantity. In the same way, in certain chest complaints, the respiratory efforts are increased in frequency—the inspiratory and expiratory acts being decreased in duration. Dr. Kay furnishes a direct proof that the presence of blood within the cavities of the heart is not the cause of the movements of the heart. In his experiments on asphyxia, he describes how the left side of the heart dies. He says, 'A smaller quantity of blood is received into its cavities and expelled vigorously into the arteries. The ventricle, meanwhile, diminishes in size as the quantity of blood supplied becomes less, until at length, although spontaneous contractions still occur in its fibres, no blood issues from the divided artery, and the ventricle, by contraction, has obliterated its cavity.' As a further proof that the heart does not depend for its movements on the blood it contains, the following experiment may be cited :—If a frog be slightly curarized and its spinal cord destroyed, it is found on .

exposing the heart that the sinus venosus, vena cava inferior, the auricles and ventricle, are quite destitute of blood, and yet the organ beats normally and with the utmost regularity. The heart also beats normally when cut out of the body, *deprived of blood,* and placed under a bell-jar. Furthermore, the interior of the heart, as M. Chauveau has shown, is almost devoid of sensibility. He proved this by introducing small caoutchouc bags (cardiac sounds) into the cavities of the ventricles of the horse, without causing the animal either pain or inconvenience.

Concluding Remarks.

In bringing the present lectures to a close, I have to express my gratitude for the kindly spirit in which they have been received. I am no stranger to their defects, but, like others discharging a variety of duties, have to plead 'Time stolen by snatches.' To the more advanced, some of the lectures may savour of redundancy; while to the novice they may even appear fragmentary. My having had to address a mixed audience affords an explanation of this circumstance. I have aimed at producing a comprehensive view of the circulation as it exists in the lowest vegetable and highest animal forms; and in carrying out this design have been compelled to expunge much that is old and introduce much that is new. How far I have been right in doing so, time and an advanced Physiology will determine. I will not attempt a recapitulation; suffice it to say, I have endeavoured to prove by a variety of arguments that the circulation, whenever and wherever found, differs less in kind than in degree; that fluids may move in living tissues with or without vessels and hearts; that the circulation in an aggregation of vegetable cells is essentially the same as that which occurs in the tissues of our own bodies. As a chain is composed of links, all of which are formed on a common type and fit into each other, so the circulation in the lowest vegetables and animals gradually develops into that of the higher, until we reach man himself; the circulation in the one being relatively as perfect as in the other.

OXFORD:

E. PICKARD HALL AND J. H. STACY,
PRINTERS TO THE UNIVERSITY.

MESSRS. MACMILLAN AND CO.'S

MEDICAL WORKS.

HUMPHRY.—Works by G. M. HUMPHRY, M.D., F.R.S., Professor of Anatomy in the University of Cambridge.

THE HUMAN SKELETON (including the joints). With 260 Illustrations, drawn from nature. Medium 8vo. 28s.

OBSERVATIONS IN MYOLOGY. 8vo. 6s.

MACPHERSON.—Works by JOHN MACPHERSON, M.D.

THE BATHS AND WELLS OF EUROPE: their Action and Uses. With Notices of Climatic Resorts and Diet Cures. With Map. Second Edition enlarged. Extra fcap. 8vo. 6s. 6d.

OUR BATHS AND WELLS. The Mineral Waters of the British Islands ; with a list of Sea Bathing Places. Extra fcap. 8vo. 3s. 6d.

RADCLIFFE.—DYNAMICS OF NERVE AND MUSCLE. By CHARLES BLAND RADCLIFFE, M.D., F.R.C.P., Physician to the Westminster Hospital, and to the National Hospital for the Paralysed and Epileptic. Crown 8vo. 8s. 6d.

REYNOLDS (J. R.)—A SYSTEM OF MEDICINE. Edited by J. RUSSELL REYNOLDS, M.D., F.R.S. London. Vol. I. Second Edition. 8vo. 25s.

Part I. General Diseases, or Affections of the Whole System. § I.—Those determined by agents operating from without, such as the exanthemata, malarial diseases, and their allies. § II.—Those determined by conditions existing within the body, such as Gout, Rheumatism, Rickets, etc. Part II. Local Diseases, or Affections of particular Systems. § I.—Diseases of the Skin.

A SYSTEM OF MEDICINE. Vol. II. Second Edition. 8vo. 25s.

Part II. Local Diseases (continued). § I.—Diseases of the Nervous System. A. General Nervous Diseases. B. Partial Diseases of the Nervous System. 1. Diseases of the Head. 2. Diseases of the Spinal Column. 3. Diseases of the Nerves. § II.—Diseases of the Digestive System. A. Diseases of the Stomach.

A SYSTEM OF MEDICINE. Vol. III. 8vo. 25s.

Part II. Local Diseases (continued). § II. Diseases of the Digestive System (continued). B. Diseases of the Mouth. C. Diseases of the Fauces, Pharynx, and Œsophagus. D. Diseases of the Intestines. E. Diseases of the Peritoneum. F. Diseases of the Liver. G. Diseases of the Pancreas. § III.—Diseases of the Respiratory System. A. Diseases of the Larynx. B. Diseases of the Thoracic Organs.

Volume IV. *in the Press.*

REYNOLDS (O.)—SEWER GAS, AND HOW TO KEEP IT OUT OF HOUSES. A Handbook on House Drainage. By OSBORN REYNOLDS, M.A., Professor of Engineering at Owens College, Manchester, Fellow of Queens' College, Cambridge. Second Edition. Crown 8vo. cloth. 1s. 6d.

SEATON.—A HANDBOOK OF VACCINATION. By EDWARD C. SEATON, M.D., Medical Inspector to the Privy Council. Extra fcap. 8vo. 8s. 6d.

MACMILLAN AND CO.

29 AND 30, BEDFORD STREET, STRAND, LONDON, W.C.

BEDFORD STREET, COVENT GARDEN, LONDON,

October 1873.

MACMILLAN & CO.'S CATALOGUE of WORKS in MATHEMATICS and PHYSICAL SCIENCE; including PURE and APPLIED MATHEMATICS; PHYSICS, ASTRONOMY, GEOLOGY, CHEMISTRY, ZOOLOGY, BOTANY; PHYSIOLOGY, ANATOMY, and MEDICAL WORKS generally; and of WORKS in MENTAL and MORAL PHILOSOPHY and Allied Subjects.

MATHEMATICS.

Airy.— Works by Sir G. B. AIRY, K.C.B., Astronomer Royal :—

ELEMENTARY TREATISE ON PARTIAL DIFFERENTIAL EQUATIONS. Designed for the Use òf Students in the Universities. With Diagrams. Crown 8vo. cloth. 5*s*, 6*d*.

It is hoped that the methods of solution here explained, and the instances exhibited, will be found sufficient for application to nearly all the important problems of Physical Science, which require for their complete investigation the aid of Partial Differential Equations.

ON THE ALGEBRAICAL AND NUMERICAL THEORY OF ERRORS OF OBSERVATIONS AND THE COMBINATION OF OBSERVATIONS. Crown 8vo. cloth. 6*s*. 6*d*.

In order to spare astronomers and observers in natural philosophy the confusion and loss of time which are produced by referring to the ordinary treatises embracing both branches of probabilities (the first

Airy (G. B.)—*continued.*

relating to chances which can be altered only by the changes of entire units or integral multiples of units in the fundamental conditions of the problem ; the other concerning those chances which have respect to insensible gradations in the value of the element measured), this volume has been drawn up. It relates only to errors of observation, and to the rules, derivable from the consideration of these errors, for the combination of the results of observations.

UNDULATORY THEORY OF OPTICS. Designed for the Use of Students in the University. New Edition. Crown 8vo. cloth. 6s. 6d.

The undulatory theory of optics is presented to the reader as having the same claims to his attention as the theory of gravitation,—namely, that it is certainly true, and that, by mathematical operations of general elegance, it leads to results of great interest. This theory explains with accuracy a vast variety of phenomena of the most complicated kind. The plan of this tract has been to include those phenomena only which admit of calculation, and the investigations are applied only to phenomena which actually have been observed.

ON SOUND AND ATMOSPHERIC VIBRATIONS. With the Mathematical Elements of Music. Designed for the Use of Students of the University. Second Edition, revised and enlarged. Crown 8vo. 9s.

This volume consists of sections, which again are divided into numbered articles, on the following topics:—General recognition of the air as the medium which conveys sound ; Properties of the air on which the formation and transmission of sound depend ; Theory of undulations as applied to sound, etc.; Investigation of the motion of a wave of air through the atmosphere; Transmission of waves of soniferous vibrations through different gases, solids, and fluids; Experiments on the velocity of sound, etc.; On musical sounds, and the manner of producing them; On the elements of musical harmony and melody, and of simple musical composition; On instrumental music; On the human organs of speech and hearing.

A TREATISE ON MAGNETISM. Designed for the Use of Students in the University. Crown 8vo. 9s. 6d.

As the laws of Magnetic Force have been experimentally examined, with philosophical accuracy, only in its connection with iron and steel, and in the influence excited by the earth as a whole, the accurate portions of this work are confined to the investigations connected with these metals and the earth. The latter part of the work, however, treats in a more general way of the laws of the connection between Magnetism on the one hand and Galvanism and Thermo-Electricity on the other. The work is divided into Twelve Sections, and each section into numbered articles, each of which states concisely and clearly the subject of the following paragraphs.

Ball (R. S., A.M.)—EXPERIMENTAL MECHANICS. A Course of Lectures delivered at the Royal College of Science for Ireland. By ROBERT STAWELL BALL, A.M., Professor of Applied Mathematics and Mechanics in the Royal College of Science for Ireland (Science and Art Department). Royal 8vo. 16s.

The author's aim in these twenty Lectures has been to create in the mind of the student physical ideas corresponding to theoretical laws, and thus to produce a work which may be regarded either as a supplement or an introduction to manuals of theoretic mechanics. To realize this design, the copious use of experimental illustrations was necessary. The apparatus used in the Lectures and figured in the volume has been principally built up from Professor Willis's most admirable system. In the selection of the subjects, the question of practical utility has in many cases been regarded as the one of paramount importance, and it is believed that the mode of treatment which is adopted is more or less original. This is especially the case in the Lectures relating to friction, to the mechanical powers, to the strength of timber and structures, to the laws of motion, and to the pendulum. The illustrations, drawn from the apparatus, are nearly all original and are beautifully executed. "In our reading we have not met with any book of the sort in English."—Mechanics' Magazine.

Bayma.—THE ELEMENTS OF MOLECULAR MECHANICS. By JOSEPH BAYMA, S.J., Professor of Philosophy, Stonyhurst College. Demy 8vo. cloth. 10s. 6d.

Of the twelve Books into which this treatise is divided, the first and second give the demonstration of the principles which bear directly on the constitution and the properties of matter. The next three books contain a series of theorems and of problems on the laws of motion of elementary substances. In the sixth and seventh, the mechanical constitution of molecules is investigated and determined: and by it the general properties of bodies are explained. The eighth book treats of luminiferous ether. The ninth explains some special properties of bodies. The tenth and eleventh contain a radical and lengthy investigation of chemical principles and relations, which may lead to practical results of high importance. The twelfth and last book treats of molecular masses, distances, and powers.

Boole.—Works by G. BOOLE, D.C.L, F.R.S., Professor of Mathematics in the Queen's University, Ireland :—

A TREATISE ON DIFFERENTIAL EQUATIONS. Third Edition. Edited by I. TODHUNTER. Crown 8vo. cloth. 14s.

Professor Boole has endeavoured in this treatise to convey as complete an account of the present state of knowledge on the subject of Differential Equations, as was consistent with the idea of a work intended, primarily, for elementary instruction. The earlier sections of each chapter contain that kind of matter which has usually been thought suitable for the beginner, while the latter ones are devoted either to an account of recent discovery, or the discussion of such deeper questions of principle as are likely to present themselves to the reflective student in connection with the methods and processes of his previous course. "A treatise incomparably superior to any other elementary book on the subject with which we are acquainted."— Philosophical Magazine.

A TREATISE ON DIFFERENTIAL EQUATIONS. Supplementary Volume. Edited by I. TODHUNTER. Crown 8vo. cloth. 8s. 6d.

This volume contains all that Professor Boole wrote for the purpose of enlarging his treatise on Differential Equations.

THE CALCULUS OF FINITE DIFFERENCES. Crown 8vo. cloth. 10s. 6d. New Edition revised.

In this exposition of the Calculus of Finite Differences, particular attention has been paid to the connection of its methods with those of the Differential Calculus —a connection which in some instances involves far more than a merely formal analogy. The work is in some measure designed as a sequel to Professor Boole's Treatise on Differential Equations.

Brook-Smith (J.)—ARITHMETIC IN THEORY AND PRACTICE. By J. BROOK-SMITH, M.A., LL.B., St. John's College, Cambridge; Barrister-at-Law ; one of the Masters of Cheltenham College. Crown 8vo. 4*s.* 6*d.*

Writers on Arithmetic at the present day feel the necessity of explaining the principles on which the rules of the subject are based, but few as yet feel the necessity of making these explanations strict and complete ; or, failing that, of distinctly pointing out their defective character. If the science of Arithmetic is to be made an effective instrument in developing and strengthening the mental powers, it ought to be worked out rationally and conclusively ; and in this work the author has endeavoured to reason out in a clear and accurate manner the leading propositions of the science, and to illustrate and apply those propositions in practice. In the practical part of the subject he has advanced somewhat beyond the majority of preceding writers; particularly in Division, in Greatest Common Measure, in Cube Root, in the chapters on Decimal Money and the Metric System, and more especially in the application of Decimals to Percentages and cognate subjects. Copious examples, original and selected, are given.

Cambridge Senate-House Problems and Riders, WITH SOLUTIONS :—

1848-1851.—PROBLEMS. By FERRERS and JACKSON. 8vo. cloth. 15*s.* 6*d.*

1848-1851.—RIDERS. By JAMESON. 8vo. cloth. 7*s.* 6*d.*

1854.—PROBLEMS AND RIDERS. By WALTON and MACKENZIE. 8vo. cloth. 10*s.* 6*d.*

1857.—PROBLEMS AND RIDERS. By CAMPION and WALTON. 8vo. cloth. 8*s.* 6*d.*

1860.—PROBLEMS AND RIDERS. By WATSON and ROUTH. Crown 8vo. cloth. 7*s.* 6*d.*

1864.—PROBLEMS AND RIDERS. By WALTON and WILKINSON. 8vo. cloth. 10*s.* 6*d.*

These volumes will be found of great value to Teachers and Students, as indicating the style and range of mathematical study in the University of Cambridge.

Cambridge and Dublin Mathematical Journal. The-Complete Work, in Nine Vols. 8vo. cloth. 10*l.* 10*s.*

Only a few copies remain on hand. Among contributors to this work will be found Sir W. Thomson, Stokes, Adams, Boole, Sir W. R. Hamilton, De Morgan, Cayley, Sylvester, Jellet, and other distinguished mathematicians.

Cheyne.—Works by C. H. H. CHEYNE, M.A., F.R.A.S.:—

AN ELEMENTARY TREATISE ON THE PLANETARY THEORY. With a Collection of Problems. Second Edition. Crown 8vo. cloth. 6s. 6d.

In this volume, an attempt has been made to produce a treatise on the Planetary theory, which, being elementary in character, should be so far complete as to contain all that is usually required by students in the University of Cambridge. This Edition has been carefully revised. The stability of the Planetary System has been more fully treated, and an elegant geometrical explanation of the formulæ for the secular variation of the node and inclination has been introduced.

THE EARTH'S MOTION OF ROTATION. Crown 8vo. 3s. 6d.

The first part of this work consists of an application of the method of the variation of elements to the general problem of rotation. In the second part the general rotation formulæ are applied to the particular case of the earth.

Childe.—THE SINGULAR PROPERTIES OF THE ELLIPSOID AND ASSOCIATED SURFACES OF THE NTH DEGREE. By the Rev. G. F. CHILDE, M.A., Author of "Ray Surfaces," "Related Caustics," &c. 8vo. 10s. 6d.

The object of this volume is to develop peculiarities in the Ellipsoid ; and, further, to establish analogous properties in the unlimited congeneric series of which this remarkable surface is a constituent.

Dodgson.—AN ELEMENTARY TREATISE ON DETERMINANTS, with their Application to Simultaneous Linear Equations and Algebraical Geometry. By CHARLES L. DODGSON, M.A., Student and Mathematical Lecturer of Christ Church, Oxford. Small 4to. cloth. 10s. 6d.

The object of the author is to present the subject as a continuous chain of argument, separated from all accessories of explanation or illustration. All such explanation and illustration as seemed necessary for a beginner are introduced either in the form of foot-notes, or, where that would have occupied too much room, of Appendices.

Earnshaw (S., M.A.)—PARTIAL DIFFERENTIAL EQUATIONS. An Essay towards an entirely New Method of Integrating them. By S. EARNSHAW, M.A., of St. John's College, Cambridge. Crown 8vo. 5s.

The peculiarity of the system expounded in this work is, that in every equation, whatever be the number of original independent variables, the work of integration is at once reduced to the use of one independent variable only. The author's object is merely to render his method thoroughly intelligible. The various steps of the investigation are all obedient to one general principle: and though in some degree novel, are not really difficult, but on the contrary, easy when the eye has become accustomed to the novelties of the notation. Many of the results of the integrations are far more general than they were in the shape in which they appeared in former Treatises, and many Equations will be found in this Essay integrated with ease in finite terms, which were never so integrated before.

Ferrers.—AN ELEMENTARY TREATISE ON TRILINEAR CO-ORDINATES, the Method of Reciprocal Polars, and the Theory of Projectors. By the Rev. N. M. FERRERS, M.A., Fellow and Tutor of Gonville and Caius College, Cambridge. Second Edition. Crown 8vo. 6s. 6d.

The object of the author in writing on this subject has mainly been to place it on a basis altogether independent of the ordinary Cartesian system, instead of regarding it as only a special form of Abridged Notation. A short chapter on Determinants has been introduced.

Frost.—Works by PERCIVAL FROST, M.A., late Fellow of St. John's College, Mathematical Lecturer of King's College, Cambridge :—

THE FIRST THREE SECTIONS OF NEWTON'S PRINCIPIA. With Notes and Illustrations. Also a Collection of Problems, principally intended as Examples of Newton's Methods. Second Edition. 8vo. cloth. 10s. 6d.

Frost—*continued.*

The author's principal intention is to explain difficulties which may be encountered by the student on first reading the Principia, *and to illustrate the advantages of a careful study of the methods employed by Newton, by showing the extent to which they may be applied in the solution of problems ; he has also endeavoured to give assistance to the student who is engaged in the study of the higher branches of mathematics, by representing in a geometrical form several of the processes employed in the Differential and Integral Calculus, and in the analytical investigations of Dynamics.*

AN ELEMENTARY TREATISE ON CURVE TRACING. 8vo. 12s.

The author has written this book under the conviction that the skill and power of the young mathematical student, in order to be thoroughly available afterwards, ought to be developed in all possible directions.   The subject which he has chosen presents so many faces, pointing in directions towards which the mind of the intended mathematician has to radiate, that it would be difficult to find another which, with a very limited extent of reading, combines, to the same extent, so many valuable hints of methods of calculations to be employed hereafter, with so much pleasure in its present use. In order to understand the work it is not necessary to have much knowledge of what is called Higher Algebra, nor of Algebraical Geometry of a higher kind than that which simply relates to the Conic Sections.   From the study of a work like this, it is believed that the student will derive many advantages.   Especially he will become skilled in making correct approximations to the values of quantities, which cannot be found exactly, to any degree of accuracy which may be required.

Frost and Wolstenholme.—A TREATISE ON SOLID GEOMETRY. By PERCIVAL FROST, M.A., and the Rev. J. WOLSTENHOLME, M.A., Fellow and Assistant Tutor of Christ's College. 8vo. cloth. 18s.

Intending to make the subject accessible, at least in the earlier portions, to all classes of students, the authors have endeavoured to explain completely all the processes which are most useful in dealing with ordinary theorems and problems, thus directing the student to the selection of methods which are best adapted to the exigencies of each problem: In the more difficult portions of the subject, they have considered themselves to be addressing a higher class of students ;

and they have there tried to lay a good foundation on which to build, if any reader should wish to pursue the science beyond the limits to which the work extends.

Godfray.—Works by HUGH GODFRAY, M.A., Mathematical Lecturer at Pembroke College, Cambridge :—

A TREATISE ON ASTRONOMY, for the Use of Colleges and Schools. 8vo. cloth. 12s. 6d.

This book embraces all those branches of Astronomy which have, from time to time, been recommended by the Cambridge Board of Mathematical Studies: but by far the larger and easier portion, adapted to the first three days of the Examination for Honours, may be read by the more advanced pupils in many of our schools. The author's aim has been to convey clear and distinct ideas of the celestial phenomena. "It is a working book," says the Guardian, "taking Astronomy in its proper place in the Mathematical Sciences. . . . It is a book which is not likely to be got up unintelligently."

AN ELEMENTARY TREATISE ON THE LUNAR THEORY, with a Brief Sketch of the Problem up to the time of Newton. Second Edition, revised. Crown 8vo. cloth. 5s. 6d.

*These pages will, it is hoped, form an introduction to more recondite works. Difficulties have been discussed at considerable length. The selection of the method followed with regard to analytical solutions, which is the same as that of Airy, Herschel, etc., was made on account of its simplicity ; it is, moreover, the method which has obtained in the University of Cambridge. "As an elementary treatise and introduction to the subject, we think it may justly claim to supersede all former ones."—*London, Edinburgh, and Dublin Phil. Magazine.

Green (George).—MATHEMATICAL PAPERS OF THE LATE GEORGE GREEN, Fellow of Gonville and Caius College, Cambridge. Edited by N. M. FERRERS, M.A., Fellow and Tutor of Gonville and Caius College. 8vo. 15s.

The publication of this book may be opportune at present, as several of the subjects with which they are directly or indirectly concerned have recently been introduced into the course of mathematical study at Cambridge. They have also an interest as being the work of an almost entirely self-taught mathematical genius. The Papers *comprise the following:—An Essay on the application of Mathematical Analysis to the Theories of Electricity and Magnetism— On the Laws of the Equilibrium of Fluids analogous to the Electric Fluid—On the Determination of the Attractions of Ellipsoids of variable Densities—On the Motion of Waves in a variable Canal of small depth and width—On the Reflection and Refraction of Sound—On the Reflection and Refraction of Light at the Common Surface of two Non-Crystallized Media—On the Propagation of Light in Crystallized Media—Researches on the Vibrations of Pendulums in Fluid Media. " It has been for some time recognized that Green's writings are amongst the most valuable mathematical productions we possess."—*Athenæum.

Hemming.—AN ELEMENTARY TREATISE ON THE DIFFERENTIAL AND INTEGRAL CALCULUS. For the Use of Colleges and Schools. By G. W. HEMMING, M.A., Fellow of St. John's College, Cambridge. Second Edition, with Corrections and Additions. 8vo. cloth. 9s.

*" There is no book in common use from which so clear and exact a knowledge of the principles of the Calculus can be so readily obtained."—*Literary Gazette.

Jackson.—GEOMETRICAL CONIC SECTIONS. An Elementary Treatise in which the Conic Sections are defined as the Plane Sections of a Cone, and treated by the Method of Projections. By J. STUART JACKSON, M.A., late Fellow of Gonville and Caius College. Crown 8vo. 4s. 6d.

This work has been written with a view to give the student the benefit of the Method of Projections as applied to the Ellipse and Hyperbola. When this method is admitted into the treatment of Conic Sections there are many reasons why they should be defined, not with reference to the focus and directrix, but according to the original definition from which they have their name, as Plane Sections of a Cone. This method is calculated to produce a material simplification in the treatment of these curves and to make the proof of their properties more easily understood in the first instance and more easily remembered. It is also a powerful instrument in the solution of a large class of problems relating to these curves.

Morgan.—A COLLECTION OF PROBLEMS AND EXAMPLES IN MATHEMATICS. With Answers. By H. A. MORGAN, M.A., Sadlerian and Mathematical Lecturer of Jesus College, Cambridge. Crown 8vo. cloth. 6s. 6d.

This book contains a number of problems, chiefly elementary, in the Mathematical subjects usually read at Cambridge. They have been selected from the Papers set during late years at Jesus College. Very few of them are to be met with in other collections, and by far the larger number are due to some of the most distinguished Mathematicians in the University.

Newton's Principia.—4to. cloth. 31s. 6d.

It is a sufficient guarantee of the reliability of this complete edition of Newton's Principia that it has been printed for and under the care of Professor Sir William Thomson and Professor Blackburn, of Glasgow University. The following notice is prefixed:—"Finding that all the editions of the Principia are now out of print, we have been induced to reprint Newton's last edition [of 1726] without note or comment, only introducing the 'Corrigenda' of the old copy and correcting typographical errors." The book is of a handsome size, with large type, fine thick paper, and cleanly-cut figures, and is the only recent edition containing the whole of Newton's great work.

Parkinson.—Works by S. PARKINSON, D.D., F.R.S., Fellow and Tutor of St. John's College, Cambridge :—

AN ELEMENTARY TREATISE ON MECHANICS. For the Use of the Junior Classes at the University and the Higher Classes in Schools. With a Collection of Examples. Fourth Edition, revised. Crown 8vo. cloth. 9s. 6d.

In preparing a fourth edition of this work the author has kept the same object in view as he had in the former editions—namely, to include in it such portions of Theoretical Mechanics as can be conveniently investigated without the use of the Differential Calculus, and so render it suitable as a manual for the junior classes in the University and the higher classes in Schools. With one or two short exceptions, the student is not presumed to require a knowledge of any

Parkinson—*continued.*

branches of Mathematics beyond the elements of Algebra, Geometry, and Trigonometry.   Several additional propositions have been incorporated in the work for the purpose of rendering it more complete, and the collection of Examples and Problems has been largely increased.

A TREATISE ON OPTICS. Third Edition, revised and enlarged.   Crown 8vo. cloth.   10s. 6d.

A collection of Examples and Problems has been appended to this work, which are sufficiently numerous and varied in character to afford useful exercise for the student.   For the greater part of them, recourse has been had to the Examination Papers set in the University and the several Colleges during the last twenty years.

Phear.—ELEMENTARY HYDROSTATICS.   With Numerous Examples.   By J. B. PHEAR, M.A., Fellow and late Assistant Tutor of Clare College, Cambridge.   Fourth Edition.   Crown 8vo. cloth.   5s. 6d.

This edition has been carefully revised throughout, and many new Illustrations and Examples added, which it is hoped will increase its usefulness to students at the Universities and in Schools.   In accordance with suggestions from many engaged in tuition, answers to all the Examples have been given at the end of the book.

Pratt.—A TREATISE ON ATTRACTIONS, LAPLACE'S FUNCTIONS, AND THE FIGURE OF THE EARTH.   By JOHN H. PRATT, M.A., Archdeacon of Calcutta, Author of "The Mathematical Principles of Mechanical Philosophy."   Fourth Edition.   Crown 8vo. cloth.   6s. 6d.

The author's chief design in this treatise is to give an answer to the question, "Has the Earth acquired its present form from being originally in a fluid state?"   This edition is a complete revision of the former ones.

Puckle.—AN ELEMENTARY TREATISE ON CONIC SECTIONS AND ALGEBRAIC GEOMETRY.   With numerous

Examples and Hints for their Solution ; especially designed for the Use of Beginners. By G. H. PUCKLE, M.A. New Edition, revised and enlarged. Crown 8vo. cloth. 7*s*. 6*d*.

This work is recommended by the Syndicate of the Cambridge Local Examinations. The Athenæum *says the author "displays an intimate acquaintance with the difficulties likely to be felt, together with a singular aptitude in removing them."*

Routh.—AN ELEMENTARY TREATISE ON THE DYNA- MICS OF THE SYSTEM OF RIGID BODIES. With numerous Examples. By EDWARD JOHN ROUTH, M.A., late Fellow and Assistant Tutor of St. Peter's College, Cambridge ; Examiner in the University of London. Second Edition, enlarged. Crown 8vo. cloth. 14*s*.

In this edition the author has made several additions to each chapter: he has tried, even at the risk of some little repetition, to make each chapter, as far as possible, complete in itself, so that all that relates to any one part of the subject may be found in the same place. This arrangement will enable every student to select his own order in which to read the subject. The Examples which will be found at the end of each chapter have been chiefly selected from the Examina- tion Papers which have been set in the University and the Colleges in the last few years.

Smith's (Barnard) Works.—See EDUCATIONAL CATA- LOGUE.

Snowball.—THE ELEMENTS OF PLANE AND SPHERI- CAL TRIGONOMETRY ; with the Construction and Use of Tables of Logarithms. By J. C. SNOWBALL, M.A. Tenth Edition. Crown 8vo. cloth. 7*s*. 6*d*.

In preparing the present edition for the press, the text has been sub- jected to a careful revision ; the proofs of some of the more import- ant propositions have been rendered more strict and general ; and a considerable addition of more than two hundred examples, taken principally from the questions set of late years in the public exami- nations of the University and of individual Colleges, has been made to the collection of Examples and Problems for practice.

Tait and Steele.—DYNAMICS OF A PARTICLE. With numerous Examples. By Professor TAIT and Mr. STEELE. New Edition. Crown 8vo. cloth. 10s. 6d.

In this treatise will be found all the ordinary propositions, connected with the Dynamics of Particles, which can be conveniently deduced without the use of D'Alembert's Principle. Throughout the book will be found a number of illustrative examples introduced in the text, and for the most part completely worked out ; others with occasional solutions or hints to assist the student are appended to each chapter. For by far the greater portion of these, the Cambridge Senate-House and College Examination Papers have been applied to.

Taylor.—GEOMETRICAL CONICS; including An harmonic Ratio and Projection, with numerous Examples. By C. TAYLOR, B.A., Scholar of St. John's College, Cambridge. Crown 8vo. cloth. 7s. 6d.

This work contains elementary proofs of the principal properties of Conic Sections, together with chapters on Projection and Anharmonic Ratio.

Todhunter.—Works by I. TODHUNTER, M.A., F.R.S., of St. John's College, Cambridge :—

"Perspicuous language, vigorous investigations, scrutiny of difficulties, and methodical treatment, characterize Mr. Todhunter's works."— Civil Engineer.

THE ELEMENTS OF EUCLID; MENSURATION FOR BEGINNERS; ALGEBRA FOR BEGINNERS; TRIGONOMETRY FOR BEGINNERS; MECHANICS FOR BEGINNERS.—See EDUCATIONAL CATALOGUE.

ALGEBRA. For the Use of Colleges and Schools. Sixth Edition. Crown 8vo. cloth. 7s. 6d.

This work contains all the propositions which are usually included in elementary treatises on Algebra, and a large number of Examples for Exercise. The author has sought to render the work easily intelligible to students, without impairing the accuracy of the demonstrations, or contracting the limits of the subject. The Examples, about Sixteen hundred and fifty in number, have been selected with

Todhunter (I.)—*continued.*

a view to illustrate every part of the subject. The work will be found peculiarly adapted to the wants of students who are without the aid of a teacher. The Answers to the Examples, with hints for the solution of some in which assistance may be needed, are given at the end of the book. In the present edition two New Chapters and Three hundred *miscellaneous Examples have been added. "It has merits which unquestionably place it first in the class to which it belongs."*—Educator.

KEY TO ALGEBRA FOR THE USE OF COLLEGES AND SCHOOLS. Crown 8vo. 10s. 6d.

AN ELEMENTARY TREATISE ON THE THEORY OF EQUATIONS. Second Edition, revised. Crown 8vo. cloth. 7s. 6d.

This treatise contains all the propositions which are usually included in elementary treatises on the theory of Equations, together with Examples for exercise. These have been selected from the College and University Examination Papers, and the results have been given when it appeared necessary. In order to exhibit a comprehensive view of the subject, the treatise includes investigations which are not found in all the preceding elementary treatises, and also some investigations which are not to be found in any of them. For the second edition the work has been revised and some additions have been made, the most important being an account of the Researches of Professor Sylvester respecting Newton's Rule. "A thoroughly trustworthy, complete, and yet not too elaborate treatise."
—Philosophical Magazine.

PLANE TRIGONOMETRY. For Schools and Colleges. Fourth Edition. Crown 8vo. cloth. 5s.

The design of this work has been to render the subject intelligible to beginners, and at the same time to afford the student the opportunity of obtaining all the information which he will require on this branch of Mathematics. Each chapter is followed by a set of Examples: those which are entitled Miscellaneous Examples, *together with a few in some of the other sets, may be advantageously reserved by the student for exercise after he has made some progress in the subject. In the Second Edition the hints for the solution of the Examples have been considerably increased.*

Todhunter (I.)—continued.

A TREATISE ON SPHERICAL TRIGONOMETRY. Third Edition, enlarged. Crown 8vo. cloth. 4s. 6d.

The present work is constructed on the same plan as the treatise on Plane Trigonometry, to which it is intended as a sequel. In the account of Napier's Rules of circular parts, an explanation has been given of a method of proof devised by Napier, which seems to have been overlooked by most modern writers on the subject. Considerable labour has been bestowed on the text in order to render it comprehensive and accurate, and the Examples (selected chiefly from College Examination Papers) have all been carefully verified. "For educational purposes this work seems to be superior to any others on the subject."—Critic.

PLANE CO-ORDINATE GEOMETRY, as applied to the Straight Line and the Conic Sections. With numerous Examples. Fourth Edition, revised and enlarged. Crown 8vo. cloth. 7s. 6d.

The author has here endeavoured to exhibit the subject in a simple manner for the benefit of beginners, and at the same time to include in one volume all that students usually require. In addition, therefore, to the propositions which have always appeared in such treatises, he has introduced the methods of abridged notation, which are of more recent origin: these methods, which are of a less elementary character than the rest of the work, are placed in separate chapters, and may be omitted by the student at first.

A TREATISE ON THE DIFFERENTIAL CALCULUS. With numerous Examples. Sixth Edition. Crown 8vo. cloth. 10s. 6d.

The author has endeavoured in the present work to exhibit a comprehensive view of the Differential Calculus on the method of limits. In the more elementary portions he has entered into considerable detail in the explanations, with the hope that a reader who is without the assistance of a tutor may be enabled to acquire a competent acquaintance with the subject. The method adopted is that of Differential Coefficients. To the different chapters are appended Examples sufficiently numerous to render another book unnecessary; these Examples being mostly selected from College Examination Papers. This and the following work have been translated into

Todhunter (I.)—*continued.*

*Italian by Professor Battaglini, who in his Preface speaks thus :—
" In publishing this translation of the Differential and Integral
Calculus of Mr. Todhunter, we have had no other object than to
add to the books which are in the hands of the students of our Universities, a work remarkable for the clearness of the exposition, the
rigour of the demonstrations, the just proportion in the parts, and
the rich store of examples which offer a large field for useful
exercise."*

A TREATISE ON THE INTEGRAL CALCULUS AND ITS
APPLICATIONS. With numerous Examples. Third Edition,
revised and enlarged. Crown 8vo. cloth. 10s. 6d.

*This is designed as a work at once elementary and complete, adapted
for the use of beginners, and sufficient for the wants of advanced
students. In the selection of the propositions, and in the mode of
establishing them, it has been sought to exhibit the principles clearly,
and to illustrate all their most important results. The process of
summation has been repeatedly brought forward, with the view
of securing the attention of the student to the notions which form the
true foundation of the Calculus itself, as well as of its most
valuable applications. Every attempt has been made to explain those
difficulties which usually perplex beginners, especially with reference
to the limits of integrations. A new method has been adopted in
regard to the transformation of multiple integrals. The last chapter
deals with the Calculus of Variations. A large collection of Exercises, selected from College Examination Papers, has been appended
to the several chapters.*

EXAMPLES OF ANALYTICAL GEOMETRY OF THREE
DIMENSIONS. Third Edition, revised. Crown 8vo. cloth. 4s.

A TREATISE ON ANALYTICAL STATICS. With numerous
Examples. Third Edition, revised and enlarged. Crown 8vo.
cloth. 10s. 6d.

*In this work on Statics (treating of the laws of the equilibrium of
bodies) will be found all the propositions which usually appear in
treatises on Theoretical Statics. To the different chapters Examples
are appended, which have been principally selected from University
Examination Papers. In the Third Edition many additions have
been made, in order to illustrate the application of the principles of
the subject to the solution of problems.*

B

Todhunter (I.)—*continued.*

A HISTORY OF THE MATHEMATICAL THEORY OF
PROBABILITY, from the Time of Pascal to that of Laplace.
8vo.   18*s.*

*The subject of this work has high claims to consideration on account
of the subtle problems which it involves, the valuable contributions
to analysis which it has produced, its important practical applications, and the eminence of those who have cultivated it ; nearly
every great mathematician within the range of a century and
a half comes under consideration in the course of the history.   The
author has endeavoured to be quite accurate in his statements, and
to reproduce the essential elements of the original works which he
has analysed.   Besides being a history, the work may claim the title
of a comprehensive treatise on the Theory of Probability, for it
assumes in the reader only so much knowledge as can be gained from
an elementary book on Algebra, and introduces him to almost every
process and every special problem which the literature of the subject
can furnish.*

RESEARCHES IN THE CALCULUS OF VARIATIONS,
Principally on the Theory of Discontinuous Solutions: An Essay
to which the Adams' Prize was awarded in the University of
Cambridge in 1871.   8vo.   6*s.*

*The subject of this Essay was prescribed in the following terms by the
Examiners :—" A determination of the circumstances under which
discontinuity of any kind presents itself in the solution of a problem
of maximum or minimum in the Calculus of Variations, and
applications to particular instances.   It is expected that the discussion of the instances should be exemplified as far as possible geo-
metrically, and that attention be especially directed to cases of real or
supposed failure of the Calculus."   While the Essay is thus mainly
devoted to the consideration of discontinuous solutions, various
other questions in the Calculus of Variations are examined and
elucidated ; and the author hopes he has definitely contributed to the
extension and improvement of our knowledge of this refined department of analysis.*

A HISTORY OF THE MATHEMATICAL THEORIES OF
ATTRACTION, and the Figure of the Earth, from the time of
Newton to that of Laplace.   Two vols. 8vo.   24*s.*

Wilson (W. P.)—A TREATISE ON DYNAMICS. By
W. P. WILSON, M.A., Fellow of St. John's College, Cambridge,
and Professor of Mathematics in Queen's College, Belfast. 8vo.
9*s.* 6*d.*

Wolstenholme.—A BOOK OF MATHEMATICAL
PROBLEMS, on Subjects included in the Cambridge Course.
By JOSEPH WOLSTENHOLME, Fellow of Christ's College, some
time Fellow of St. John's College, and lately Lecturer in Mathematics at Christ's College. Crown 8vo. cloth. 8*s.* 6*d.*

CONTENTS :—*Geometry (Euclid)—Algebra—Plane Trigonometry—
Geometrical Conic Sections—Analytical Conic Sections—Theory of
Equations—Differential Calculus—Integral Calculus—Solid Geo-
metry—Statics—Elementary Dynamics—Newton—Dynamics of a
Point—Dynamics of a Rigid Body—Hydrostatics—Geometrical
Optics—Spherical Trigonometry and Plane Astronomy. In some
cases the author has prefixed to certain classes of problems frag-
mentary notes on the mathematical subjects to which they relate.*
" *Judicious, symmetrical, and well arranged.*"—Guardian.

PHYSICAL SCIENCE.

Airy (G. B.)—POPULAR ASTRONOMY. With Illustrations. By Sir G. B. AIRY, K.C.B., Astronomer Royal. Seventh and cheaper Edition. 18mo. cloth. 4s. 6d.

This work consists of Six Lectures, which are intended "to explain to intelligent persons the principles on which the instruments of an Observatory are constructed (omitting all details, so far as they are merely subsidiary), and the principles on which the observations made with these instruments are treated for deduction of the distances and weights of the bodies of the Solar System, and of a few stars, omitting all minutiæ of formulæ, and all troublesome details of calculation." The speciality of this volume is the direct reference of every step to the Observatory, and the full description of the methods and instruments of observation.

Bastian.—Works by H. CHARLTON BASTIAN, M.D., F.R.S., Professor of Pathological Anatomy in University College, London, etc. :—

THE MODES OF ORIGIN OF LOWEST ORGANISMS: Including a Discussion of the Experiments of M. Pasteur, and a Reply to some Statements by Professors Huxley and Tyndall. Crown 8vo. 4s. 6d.

The present volume contains a fragment of the evidence which will be embodied in a much larger work—now almost completed—relating to the nature and origin of living matter, and in favour of what is termed the Physical Doctrine of Life. "It is a work worthy of the highest respect, and places its author in the very first class of scientific physicians. . . . It would be difficult to name an instance in which skill, knowledge, perseverance, and great reasoning power have been more happily applied to the investigation of a complex biological problem."—British Medical Journal.

Bastian (H. C.)—*continued.*

THE BEGINNINGS OF LIFE: Being some Account of the Nature, Modes of Origin, and Transformations of Lower Organisms. In Two Volumes. With upwards of 100 Illustrations, Crown 8vo. 28*s*.

These volumes contain the results of several years' investigation on the Origin of Life, and it was only after the author had proceeded some length with his observations and experiments that he was compelled to change the opinions he started with for those announced in the present work—the most important of which is that in favour of " spontaneous generation "—the theory that life has never ceased to be actually originated. The First Part of the work is intended to show the general reader, more especially, that the logical consequences of the now commonly accepted doctrines concerning the " Conservation of Energy " and the " Correlation of the Vital and Physical Forces " are wholly favourable to the possibility of the independent origin of "living" matter. It also contains a view of the " Cellular Theory of Organisation." In the Second Part of the work, under the head " Archebiosis," the question as to the present occurrence or non-occurrence of " spontaneous generation " is considered. " It is a book that cannot be ignored, and must inevitably lead to renewed discussions and repeated observations, and through these to the establishment of truth."—A. R. WALLACE in Nature.

Birks (T. R.)—ON MATTER AND ETHER ; or, The Secret Laws of Physical Change. By THOMAS RAWSON BIRKS, M.A., Professor of Moral Philosophy in the University of Cambridge. Crown 8vo. 5*s*. 6*d*.

The author believes that the hypothesis of the existence of, besides matter, a luminous ether, of immense elastic force, supplies the true and sufficient key to the remaining secrets of inorganic matter, of the phenomena of light, electricity, etc. In this treatise the author endeavours first to form a clear and definite conception with regard to the real nature both of matter and ether, and the laws of mutual action which must be supposed to exist between them. He then endeavours to trace out the main consequences of the fundamental hypothesis, and their correspondence with the known phenomena of physical change.

Blanford (W. T.)—GEOLOGY AND ZOOLOGY OF ABYSSINIA. By W. T. BLANFORD. 8vo. 21s.

This work contains an account of the Geological and Zoological Obser-vations made by the author in Abyssinia, when accompanying the British Army on its march to Magdala and back in 1868, and during a short journey in Northern Abyssinia, after the departure of the troops. Part I. Personal Narrative; Part II. Geology; Part III. Zoology. With Coloured Illustrations and Geological Map. "The result of his labours," the Academy *says, "is an important contribution to the natural history of the country."*

Clodd.—THE CHILDHOOD OF THE WORLD: a Simple Account of Man in Early Times. By EDWARD CLODD, F.R.A.S. Second Edition. Globe 8vo. 3s.

"Likely, we think, to prove acceptable to a large and growing class of readers."—Pall Mall Gazette.

PROFESSOR MAX MULLER, *in a letter to the Author, says: "I read your book with great pleasure. I have no doubt it will do good, and I hope you will continue your work. Nothing spoils our temper so much as having to unlearn in youth, manhood, and even old age, so many things which we were taught as children. A book like yours will prepare a far better soil in the child's mind, and I was delighted to have it to read to my children."*

Cooke (Josiah P., Jun.)—FIRST PRINCIPLES OF CHEMICAL PHILOSOPHY. By JOSIAH P. COOKE, Jun., Ervine Professor of Chemistry and Mineralogy in Harvard College. Crown 8vo. 12s.

The object of the author in this book is to present the philosophy of Chemistry in such a form that it can be made with profit the subject of College recitations, and furnish the teacher with the means of testing the student's faithfulness and ability. With this view the subject has been developed in a logical order, and the principles of the science are taught independently of the experimental evidence on which they rest.

Cooke (M. C.)—HANDBOOK OF BRITISH FUNGI, with full descriptions of all the Species, and Illustrations of the Genera. By M. C. COOKE, M.A. Two vols. crown 8vo. 24s.

During the thirty-five years that have elapsed since the appearance of the last complete Mycologic Flora no attempt has been made to revise it, to incorporate species since discovered, and to bring it up to the standard of modern science. No apology, therefore, is necessary for the present effort, since all will admit that the want of such a manual has long been felt, and this work makes its appearance under the advantage that it seeks to occupy a place which has long been vacant. No effort has been spared to make the work worthy of confidence, and, by the publication of an occasional supplement, it is hoped to maintain it for many years as the "Handbook" for every student of British Fungi. Appended is a complete alphabetical Index of all the divisions and subdivisions of the Fungi noticed in the text. The book contains 400 figures. "Will maintain its place as the standard English book, on the subject of which it treats, for many years to come."—Standard.

Dawkins,—CAVE-HUNTING : Researches on the Evidence of Caves respecting the Early Inhabitants of Europe. By W. BOYD DAWKINS, F.R.S. Illustrated. 8vo. [*In the Press.*]

Dawson (J. W.)—ACADIAN GEOLOGY. The Geologic Structure, Organic Remains, and Mineral Resources of Nova Scotia, New Brunswick, and Prince Edward Island. By JOHN WILLIAM DAWSON, M.A., LL.D., F.R.S., F.G.S., Principal and Vice-Chancellor of M'Gill College and University, Montreal, &c. Second Edition, revised and enlarged. With a Geological Map and numerous Illustrations. 8vo. 18*s.*

The object of the first edition of this work was to place within the reach of the people of the districts to which it relates, a popular account of the more recent discoveries in the geology and mineral resources of their country, and at the same time to give to geologists in other countries a connected view of the structure of a very interesting portion of the American Continent, in its relation to general and theoretical Geology. In the present edition, it is hoped this design is still more completely fulfilled, with reference to the present more advanced condition of knowledge. The author has endeavoured to convey a knowledge of the structure and fossils of the region in such a manner as to be intelligible to ordinary readers, and has devoted much attention to all questions relating to the nature and present or prospective value of deposits of useful minerals.

Besides a large coloured Geological Map of the district, the work is illustrated by upwards of 260 cuts of sections, fossils, animals, etc. "The book will doubtless find a place in the library, not only of the scientific geologist, but also of all who are desirous of the industrial progress and commercial prosperity of the Acadian provinces."—Mining Journal. *"A style at once popular and scientific. . . . A valuable addition to our store of geological knowledge."*—Guardian.

Flower (W. H.)—AN INTRODUCTION TO THE OSTE-OLOGY OF THE MAMMALIA. Being the substance of the Course of Lectures delivered at the Royal College of Surgeons of England in 1870. By W. H. FLOWER, F.R.S., F.R.C.S., Hunterian Professor of Comparative Anatomy and Physiology. With numerous Illustrations. Globe 8vo. 7s. 6d.

Although the present work contains the substance of a Course of Lectures, the form has been changed, so as the better to adapt it as a handbook for students. Theoretical views have been almost entirely excluded: and while it is impossible in a scientific treatise to avoid the employment of technical terms, it has been the author's endeavour to use no more than absolutely necessary, and to exercise due care in selecting only those that seem most appropriate, or which have received the sanction of general adoption. With a very few exceptions the illustrations have been drawn expressly for this work from specimens in the Museum of the Royal College of Surgeons.

Galton.—Works by FRANCIS GALTON, F.R.S. :—

METEOROGRAPHICA, or Methods of Mapping the Weather. Illustrated by upwards of 600 Printed Lithographic Diagrams. 4to. 9s.

As Mr. Galton entertains strong views on the necessity of Meteorological Charts and Maps, he determined, as a practical proof of what could be done, to chart the entire area of Europe, so far as meteorological stations extend, during one month, viz. the month of December, 1861. Mr. Galton got his data from authorities in every part of Britain and the Continent, and on the basis of these has here drawn up nearly a hundred different Maps and Charts, showing the state of the weather all over Europe during the above period. "If the various Governments and scientific bodies would perform for the

Galton—*continued.*

*whole world for two or three years what, at a great cost and labour,
Mr. Galton has done for a part of Europe for one month, Meteoro-
logy would soon cease to be made a joke of.*"—Spectator.

HEREDITARY GENIUS: An Inquiry into its Laws and Consequences. Demy 8vo. 12s.

"*I propose,*" *the author says, "to show in this book that a man's
natural abilities are derived by inheritance, under exactly the same
limitations as are the form and physical features of the whole organic
world. I shall show that social agencies of an ordinary character,
whose influences are little suspected, are at this moment working
towards the degradation of human nature, and that others are
working towards its improvement. The general plan of my argument is to show that high reputation is a pretty accurate test of high
ability; next, to discuss the relationships of a large body of fairly
eminent men, and to obtain from these a general survey of the laws
of heredity in respect of genius. Then will follow a short chapter,
by way of comparison, on the hereditary transmission of physical
gifts, as deduced from the relationships of certain classes of oarsmen
and wrestlers. Lastly, I shall collate my results and draw conclusions.*" *The* Times *calls it "a most able and most interesting
book;" and* Mr. Darwin, *in his "Descent of Man" (vol.* i. *p.* 111*),
says, "We know, through the admirable labours of Mr. Galton,
that Genius tends to be inherited.*"

Geikie (A.)—SCENERY OF SCOTLAND, Viewed in Connection with its Physical Geography. With Illustrations and a new
Geological Map. By ARCHIBALD GEIKIE, Professor of Geology
in the University of Edinburgh. Crown 8vo. 10s. 6d.

"*We can confidently recommend Mr. Geikie's work to those who wish
to look below the surface and read the physical history of the Scenery
of Scotland by the light of modern science.*"—Saturday Review.
"*Amusing, picturesque, and instructive.*"—Times.

Guillemin.—THE FORCES OF NATURE: A Popular Intro-
duction to the Study of Physical Phenomena. By AMÉDÉE
GUILLEMIN. Translated from the French by MRS. NORMAN
LOCKYER; and Edited, with Additions and Notes, by J. NORMAN

LOCKYER, F.R.S.   Illustrated by 11 Coloured Plates and 455
Woodcuts.   Second Edition.   Imperial 8vo. cloth, extra gilt.
31s. 6d.

*M. Guillemin is already well known in this country as a most success-
ful populariser of the results of accurate scientific research, his
works, while eloquent, intelligible, and interesting to the general
reader, being thoroughly trustworthy and up to date.   The present
work consists of Seven Books, each divided into a number . of
Chapters, the Books treating respectively of Gravity, Sound,
Light, Heat, Magnetism, Electricity, and Atmospheric Meteors.
The programme of the work has not been confined to a simple
explanation of the facts: but an attempt has been made to grasp
their relative bearings, or, in other words, their laws, and that
too without taking for granted that the reader is acquainted
with mathematics.   " The author's aim has been to smooth the way
for those who desire to extend their studies, and likewise to present
to general readers a sufficiently exact and just idea of this branch of
science."—Daily News.   " Translator and Editor have done
justice to their trust.   The text has all the force and flow of original
writing, combining faithfulness to the author's meaning with
purity and independence in regard to idiom ; while the historical
precision and accuracy pervading the work throughout, speak of the
watchful editorial supervision which has been given to every scientific
detail.   Nothing can well exceed the clearness and delicacy of the
illustrative woodcuts, borrowed from the French edition, or the
purity and chromatic truth of the coloured plates.   Altogether, the
work may be said to have no parallel, either in point of fulness or
attraction, as a popular manual of physical science.   . . . .
What we feel, however, bound to say, and what we say with
pleasure, is, that among works of its class no publication can stand
comparison either in literary completeness or in artistic grace with
it."—Saturday Review.*

Henslow.—THE THEORY OF EVOLUTION OF LIVING
THINGS, and the Principles of Evolution applied to Religion
considered as Illustrative of the Wisdom and Beneficence of the
Almighty.   By the Rev. GEORGE HENSLOW, M.A., F.R.S.
Crown 8vo.   6s.

Hooker (Dr.)—THE STUDENT'S FLORA OF THE
BRITISH ISLANDS. By J. D. HOOKER, C.B., F.R.S.,
M.D., D.C.L., Director of the Royal Gardens, Kew. Globe 8vo.
10s. 6d.

*The object of this work is to supply students and field-botanists with a
fuller account of the Plants of the British Islands than the manuals
hitherto in use aim at giving. The Ordinal, Generic, and Specific
characters have been re-written, and are to a great extent original,
and drawn from living or dried specimens, or both.* " *Cannot fail to
perfectly fulfil the purpose for which it is intended.*"—Land and
Water. " *Containing the fullest and most accurate manual of the
kind that has yet appeared.*"—Pall Mall Gazette.

Huxley (Professor).—LAY SERMONS, ADDRESSES,
AND REVIEWS. By T. H. HUXLEY, LL.D., F.R.S. New
and Cheaper Edition. Crown 8vo. 7s. 6d.

Fourteen Discourses on the following subjects:—(1) *On the Advisable-
ness of Improving Natural Knowledge:*—(2) *Emancipation—
Black and White :*—(3) *A Liberal Education, and where to find
it :*—(4) *Scientific Education:*—(5) *On the Educational Value of
the Natural History Sciences:*—(6) *On the Study of Zoology:*—
(7) *On the Physical Basis of Life:*—(8) *The Scientific Aspects of
Positivism:*—(9) *On a Piece of Chalk:*—(10) *Geological Contem-
poraneity and Persistent Types of Life:*—(11) *Geological Reform:*—
(12) *The Origin of Species:*—(13) *Criticisms on the " Origin of
Species:"*—(14) *On Descartes' " Discourse touching the Method of
using One's Reason rightly and of seeking Scientific Truth." The
momentous influence exercised by Mr. Huxley's writings on physical,
mental, and social science is universally acknowledged: his works
must be studied by all who would comprehend the various drifts of
modern thought.*

ESSAYS SELECTED FROM LAY SERMONS, ADDRESSES,
AND REVIEWS. Crown 8vo. 1s.

This volume includes Numbers 1, 3, 4, 7, 8, and 14, of the above.

CRITIQUES AND ADDRESSES. 8vo. 10s. 6d.

*These " Critiques and Addresses," like the " Lay Sermons," etc., pub-
lished three years ago, deal chiefly with educational, scientific, and*

Huxley (Professor)—*continued.*

philosophical subjects; and, in fact, as the author says, "indicate the high-water mark of the various tides of occupation by which I have been carried along since the beginning of the year 1870." The following is the list of Contents:—1. Administrative Nihilism. 2. The School Boards: what they can do, and what they may do. 3. On Medical Education. 4. Yeast. 5. On the Formation of Coal. 6. On Coral and Coral Reefs. 7. On the Methods and Results of Ethnology. 8. On some Fixed Points in British Ethnology. 9. Palæontology and the Doctrine of Evolution. 10. Biogenesis and Abiogenesis. 11. Mr. Darwin's Critics. 12. The Genealogy of Animals. 13. Bishop Berkely on the Metaphysics of Sensation.

LESSONS IN ELEMENTARY PHYSIOLOGY. With numerous Illustrations. New Edition. 18mo. cloth. 4s. 6d.

This book describes and explains, in a series of graduated lessons, the principles of Human Physiology, or the Structure and Functions of the Human Body. The first lesson supplies a general view of the subject. This is followed by sections on the Vascular or Venous System, and the Circulation; the Blood and the Lymph; Respiration: Sources of Loss and of Gain to the Blood; the Function of Alimentation; Motion and Locomotion; Sensations and Sensory Organs; the Organ of Sight; the Coalescence of Sensations with one another and with other States of Consciousness; the Nervous System and Innervation; Histology, or the Minute Structure of the Tissues. A Table of Anatomical and Physiological Constants is appended. The lessons are fully illustrated by numerous engravings. The new edition has been thoroughly revised, and a considerable number of new illustrations added: several of these have been taken from the Rabbit, the Sheep, the Dog, and the Frog, in order to aid those who attempt to make their knowledge real, by acquiring some practical acquaintance with the facts of Anatomy and Physiology. " Pure gold throughout."—Guardian. " Unquestionably the clearest and most complete elementary treatise on this subject that we possess in any language."—Westminster Review.

Jellet (John H., B.D.) — A TREATISE ON THE THEORY OF FRICTION. By JOHN H. JELLET, B.D.,

Senior Fellow of Trinity College, Dublin ; President of the Royal Irish Academy. _8vo. 8s. 6d.

The Theory of Friction, considered as a part of Rational Mechanics, has not, the author thinks, received the attention which it deserves. On this account many students have been probably led to regard the discussion of this force as scarcely belonging to Rational Mechanics at all ; whereas the theory of friction is as truly a part of that subject as the theory of gravitation. The force with which this theory is concerned is subject to laws as definite, and as fully susceptible of mathematical expression, as the force of gravity. This book is taken up with a special investigation of the laws of friction ; and some of the principles contained in it are believed to be here enunciated for the first time. The work consists of eight Chapters as follows :—I. Definitions and Principles. II. Equilibrium with Frictions. III. Extreme Positions of Equilibrium. IV. Movement of a Particle or System of Particles. V. Motion of a Solid Body. VI. Necessary and Possible Equilibrium. VII. Determination of the Actual Value of the Acting Force of Friction. VIII. Miscellaneous Problems—1. Problem of the Top. 2. Friction Wheels and Locomotives. 3. Questions for Exercise. " The book supplies a want which has hitherto existed in the science of pure mechanics."—Engineer.

Jones.—THE OWENS COLLEGE JUNIOR COURSE OF PRACTICAL CHEMISTRY. By FRANCIS JONES, Chemical Master in the Grammar School, Manchester. With Preface by Professor ROSCOE. 18mo. with Illustrations. 2s. 6d.

Kingsley.—GLAUCUS : OR, THE WONDERS OF THE SHORE. By CHARLES KINGSLEY, Canon of Westminster. New Edition, revised and corrected, with numerous Coloured Plates. Crown 8vo. 5s.

Kirchhoff (G.)—RESEARCHES ON THE SOLAR SPECTRUM, and the Spectra of the Chemical Elements. By G. KIRCHHOFF, Professor of Physics in the University of Heidelberg. Second Part. Translated, with the Author's Sanction, from the Transactions of the Berlin Academy for 1862, by HENRY R. ROSCOE, B.A., Ph.D., F.R.S., Professor of Chemistry in Owens College, Manchester. Part II. 4to. 5s.

"It is to Kirchhoff we are indebted for by far the best and most accurate observations of these phenomena."—Edin. Review. *" This memoir seems almost indispensable to every Spectrum observer."*—Philosophical Magazine.

Lockyer (J. N.)—Works by J. NORMAN LOCKYER, F.R.S.—
ELEMENTARY LESSONS IN ASTRONOMY. With numerous Illustrations. New Edition. 18mo. 5*s.* 6*d.*

The author has here aimed to give a connected view of the whole subject, and to supply facts, and ideas founded on the facts, to serve as a basis for subsequent study and discussion. The chapters treat of the Stars and Nebulæ; the Sun; the Solar System; Apparent Movements of the Heavenly Bodies; the Measurement of Time; Light; the Telescope and Spectroscope; Apparent Places of the Heavenly Bodies; the Real Distances and Dimensions; Universal Gravitation. The most recent Astronomical Discoveries are incorporated. Mr. Lockyer's work supplements that of the Astronomer Royal. " The book is full, clear, sound, and worthy of attention, not only as a popular exposition, but as a scientific 'Index.'"—Athenæum. *" The most fascinating of elementary books on the Sciences."*— Nonconformist.

THE SPECTROSCOPE AND ITS APPLICATIONS. By J. NORMAN LOCKYER, F.R.S. With Coloured Plate and numerous Illustrations. Second Edition. Crown 8vo. 3*s.* 6*d.*

*This forms Volume One of "*Nature Series*," a series of popular Scientific Works now in course of publication, consisting of popular and instructive works, on particular scientific subjects—Scientific Discovery, Applications, History, Biography—by some of the most eminent scientific men of the day. They will be so written as to be interesting and intelligible even to non-scientific readers. Mr. Lockyer's work in Spectrum Analysis is widely known. In the present short treatise will be found an exposition of the principles on which Spectrum Analysis rests, a description of the various kinds of Spectroscopes, and an account of what has already been done with the instrument, as well as of what may yet be done both in science and in the industrial art.*

CONTRIBUTIONS TO SOLAR PHYSICS. With numerous Illustrations. Royal 8vo., uniform with Roscoe's " Spectrum Analysis," Thompson's " Depths of the Sea," and Ball's " Mechanics." 31*s.* 6*d.*

Macmillan (Rev. Hugh).—For other Works by the same Author, see THEOLOGICAL CATALOGUE.

HOLIDAYS ON HIGH LANDS; or, Rambles and Incidents in search of Alpine Plants. Crown 8vo. cloth. 6s.

The aim of this book is to impart a general idea of the origin, character, and distribution of those rare and beautiful Alpine plants which occur on the British hills, and which are found almost everywhere on the lofty mountain chains of Europe, Asia, Africa, and America. In the first three chapters the peculiar vegetation of the Highland mountains is fully described; while in the remaining chapters this vegetation is traced to its northern cradle in the mountains of Norway, and to its southern European termination in the Alps of Switzerland. The information the author has to give is conveyed in a setting of personal adventure. "One of the most charming books of its kind ever written."—Literary Churchman. *" Mr. M.'s glowing pictures of Scandinavian scenery."*—Saturday Review.

FOOT-NOTES FROM THE PAGE OF NATURE. With numerous Illustrations. Fcap. 8vo. 5s.

" Those who have derived pleasure and profit from the study of flowers and ferns—subjects, it is pleasing to find, now everywhere popular —by descending lower into the arcana of the vegetable kingdom, will find a still more interesting and delightful field of research in the objects brought under review in the following pages."—Preface. *" The naturalist and the botanist will delight in this volume, and those who understand little of the scientific parts of the work will linger over the mysterious page of nature here unfolded to their view."*—John Bull.

Mansfield (C. B.)—A THEORY OF SALTS. A Treatise on the Constitution of Bipolar (two-membered) Chemical Compounds. By the late CHARLES BLACHFORD MANSFIELD. Crown 8vo. 14s.

" Mansfield," says the editor, " wrote this book to defend the principle that the fact of voltaic decomposition afforded the true indication, if properly interpreted, of the nature of the saline structure, and of the atomicity of the elements that built it up. No chemist

will peruse this book without feeling that he is in the presence of an original thinker, whose pages are continually suggestive, even though their general argument may not be entirely concurrent in direction with that of modern chemical thought."

Miller.—THE ROMANCE OF ASTRONOMY. By R. KALLEY MILLER, M.A., Fellow and Assistant Tutor of St. Peter's College, Cambridge. Crown 8vo. 3s. 6d.

" On the whole, the information contained is of a trustworthy character, and we cordially recommend it to the perusal of those who, without being in possession of the knowledge requisite for discussing astronomical theories, or the means by which they are arrived at, are yet desirous of becoming acquainted with some of the most interesting of astronomical conclusions."—Athenæum.

Mivart (St. George).—Works by ST. GEORGE MIVART, F.R.S. etc., Lecturer in Comparative Anatomy at St. Mary's Hospital:—

ON THE GENESIS OF SPECIES. Crown 8vo. Second Edition, to which notes have been added in reference and reply to Darwin's "Descent of Man." With numerous Illustrations. pp. xv. 296. 9s.

*The aim of the author is to support the doctrine that the various species have been evolved by ordinary natural laws (for the most part unknown) controlled by the subordinate action of "natural selection," and at the same time to remind some that there is and can be absolutely nothing in physical science which forbids them to regard those natural laws as acting with the Divine concurrence, and in obedience to a creative fiat originally imposed on the primeval cosmos, " in the beginning," by its Creator, its Upholder, and its Lord. Nearly fifty woodcuts illustrate the letter-press, and a complete index makes all references extremely easy. Canon Kingsley, in his address to the "Devonshire Association," says, "Let me recommend earnestly to you, as a specimen of what can be said on the other side, the ' Genesis of Species,' by Mr. St. George Mivart, F.R.S., a book which I am happy to say has been received elsewhere as it has deserved, and, I trust, will be received so among you."
" In no work in the English language has this great controversy been treated at once with the same broad and vigorous grasp of facts, and the same liberal and candid temper."*—Saturday Review.

Mivart (St. George)—*continued.*

LESSONS IN ELEMENTARY ANATOMY. With upwards of
400 Illustrations. 18mo. 6s. 6d.

*This volume is intended to form one of the series of Elementary Class-
Books of Science, and the Lessons are intended in the first place for
teachers and for earnest students of both sexes, not already acquainted
with human anatomy. The author has endeavoured, secondly, by
certain additions and by the mode of treatment, to fit them for
students in medicine, and generally for those acquainted with
human anatomy, but desirous of learning its more significant relations to the structure of other animals: the author therefore hopes
his volume may serve as a hand-book of Human Morphology. The
book is amply illustrated with carefully drawn woodcuts.*

Murphy.—Works by JOSEPH JOHN MURPHY :—

HABIT AND INTELLIGENCE, in Connection with the Laws of
Matter and Force : A Series of Scientific Essays. Two Vols.
8vo. 16s.

*The author's chief purpose in this work has been to state and to dis-
cuss what he regards as the special and characteristic principles of
life. The most important part of the work treats of those vital
principles which belong to the inner domain of life itself, as distinguished from the principles which belong to the border-land
where life comes into contact with inorganic matter and force. In
the inner domain of life we find two principles, which are, the
author believes, coextensive with life and peculiar to it : these are
Habit and Intelligence. He has made as full a statement as
possible of the laws under which habits form, disappear, alter under
altered circumstances, and vary spontaneously. He discusses that
most important of all questions, whether intelligence is an ultimate
fact, incapable of being resolved into any other, or only a resultant
from the laws of habit. The latter part of the first volume is
occupied with the discussion of the question of the Origin of Species.
The first part of the second volume is occupied with an inquiry
into the process of mental growth and development, and the nature
of mental intelligence. In the chapter that follows, the author discusses the science of history, and the three concluding chapters
contain some ideas on the classification, the history, and the logic, of
the sciences. The author's aim has been to make the subjects treated
of intelligible to any ordinary intelligent man. " We are pleased*

C

Murphy—*continued.*

to listen," says the Saturday Review, "*to a writer who has so firm a foothold upon the ground within the scope of his immediate survey, and who can enunciate with so much clearness and force propositions which come within his grasp."*

THE SCIENTIFIC BASES OF FAITH. 8vo. 14*s.*

Nature.—A WEEKLY ILLUSTRATED JOURNAL OF SCIENCE. Published every Thursday. Price 4*d.* Monthly Parts, 1*s.* 4*d.* and 1*s.* 8*d.* ; Half-yearly Volumes, 10*s.* 6*d.* Cases for binding Vols. 1*s.* 6*d.*

"*Backed by many of the best names among English philosophers, and by a few equally valuable supporters in America and on the Continent of Europe."*—Saturday Review. "*This able and well-edited Journal, which posts up the science of the day promptly, and promises to be of signal service to students and savants."*—British Quarterly Review.

Oliver.—Works by DANIEL OLIVER, F.R.S., F.L.S., Professor of Botany in University College, London, and Keeper of the Herbarium and Library of the Royal Gardens, Kew :—

LESSONS IN ELEMENTARY BOTANY. With nearly Two Hundred Illustrations. New Edition. 18mo cloth. 4*s.* 6*d.*

This book is designed to teach the elements of Botany on Professor Henslow's plan of selected Types and by the use of Schedules. The earlier chapters, embracing the elements of Structural and Physiological Botany, introduce us to the methodical study of the Ordinal Types. The concluding chapters are entitled, "How to Dry Plants" and "How to Describe Plants." A valuable Glossary is appended to the volume. In the preparation of this work free use has been made of the manuscript materials of the late Professor Henslow.

FIRST BOOK OF INDIAN BOTANY. With numerous Illustrations. Extra fcap. 8vo. 6*s.* 6*d.*

This manual is, in substance, the author's "Lessons in Elementary Botany," adapted for use in India. In preparing it he has had in view the want, often felt, of some handy résumé *of Indian Botany, which might be serviceable not only to residents of India, but also to anyone about to proceed thither, desirous of getting some preliminary idea of the botany of the country. It contains a well-digested summary of all essential knowledge pertaining to Indian Botany, wrought out in accordance with the best principles of scientific arrangement."*—Allen's Indian Mail.

Penrose (F. C.)—ON A METHOD OF PREDICTING BY GRAPHICAL CONSTRUCTION, OCCULTATIONS OF STARS BY THE MOON, AND SOLAR ECLIPSES FOR ANY GIVEN PLACE. Together with more rigorous methods for the Accurate Calculation of Longitude. By F. C. PENROSE, F.R.A.S. With Charts, Tables, etc. 4to. 12s.

The author believes that if, by a graphic method, the prediction of occultations can be rendered more inviting, as well as more expeditious, than by the method of calculation, it may prove acceptable to the nautical profession as well as to scientific travellers or amateurs. The author has endeavoured to make the whole process as intelligible as possible, so that the beginner, instead of merely having to follow directions imperfectly understood, may readily comprehend the meaning of each step, and be able to illustrate the practice by the theory. Besides all necessary charts and tables, the work contains a large number of skeleton forms for working out cases in practice.

Roscoe.—Works by HENRY E. ROSCOE, F.R.S., Professor o Chemistry in Owens College, Manchester :—

LESSONS IN ELEMENTARY CHEMISTRY, INORGANIC AND ORGANIC. With numerous Illustrations and Chromolitho of the Solar Spectrum, and of the Alkalies and Alkaline Earths. New Edition. 18mo. cloth. 4s. 6d.

It has been the endeavour of the author to arrange the most important facts and principles of Modern Chemistry in a plain but concise and scientific form, suited to the present requirements of elementary instruction. For the purpose of facilitating the attainment of exactitude in the knowledge of the subject, a series of exercises and questions upon the lessons have been added. The metric system of weights and measures, and the centigrade thermometric scale, are

Roscoe—*continued.*

used throughout this work. The new edition, besides new wood-cuts, contains many additions and improvements, and includes the most important of the latest discoveries. "We unhesitatingly pronounce it the best of all our elementary treatises on Chemistry."— Medical Times.

SPECTRUM ANALYSIS. Six Lectures, with Appendices, Engravings, Maps, and Chromolithographs. Royal 8vo. 21*s.*

*A Third Edition of these popular Lectures, containing all the most recent discoveries and several additional illustrations. "In six lectures he has given the history of the discovery and set forth the facts relating to the analysis of light in such a way that any reader of ordinary intelligence and information will be able to understand what 'Spectrum Analysis' is, and what are its claims to rank among the most signal triumphs of science."—*Nonconformist. *"The lectures themselves furnish a most admirable elementary treatise on the subject, whilst by the insertion in appendices to each lecture of extracts from the most important published memoirs, the author has rendered it equally valuable as a text-book for advanced students."—*Westminster Review.

Stewart (B.)—LESSONS IN ELEMENTARY PHYSICS. By BALFOUR STEWART, F.R.S., Professor of Natural Philosophy in Owens College, Manchester. With numerous Illustrations and Chromolithos of the Spectra of the Sun, Stars, and Nebulæ. New Edition. 18mo. 4*s.* 6*d.*

A description, in an elementary manner, of the most important of those laws which regulate the phenomena of nature. The active agents, heat,' light, electricity, etc., are regarded as varieties of energy, and the work is so arranged that their relation to one another, looked at in this light, and the paramount importance of the laws of energy, are clearly brought out. The volume contains all the necessary illustrations. The Educational Times *calls this "the beau-ideal of a scientific text-book, clear, accurate, and thorough."*

Taylor.—SOUND AND MUSIC: A Non-Mathematical Treatise cn the Physical Constitution of Musical Sounds and Harmony,

including the Chief Acoustical Discoveries of Professor Helmholtz. By SEDLEY TAYLOR, M.A., late Fellow of Trinity Col-
ledge, Cambridge. Large crown 8vo. 8*s.* 6*d.*

*This treatise aims at placing before persons unacquainted with
Mathematics an intelligible and succinct account of that part of
the Theory of Sound which constitutes the physical basis of the
Art of Music. No preliminary knowledge, save of Arithmetic
and of the musical notation in common use, is assumed to be possessed by the reader. The importance of combining theoretical and
experimental modes of treatment has been kept steadily in view
throughout. Though the author has incorporated the·chief acoustical discoveries of Professor Helmholtz, the present volume is not a
mere epitome of his work, but the result of independent study.*

Thomson.—THE DEPTHS OF THE SEA : An Account of the
General Results of the Dredging Cruises of H.M.SS. "Porcupine"
and "Lightning" during the Summers of 1868-69 and 70, under
the scientific direction of Dr. Carpenter, F.R.S., J. Gwyn Jeffreys,
F.R.S,, and Dr. Wyville Thomson, F.R.S. By Dr. WYVILLE
THOMSON, Director of the Scientific Staff of the "Challenger."
Expedition. With nearly 100 Illustrations and 8 coloured Maps
and Plans. Second Edition. Royal 8vo. cloth, gilt. 31*s.* 6*d.*

*It was the important and interesting results recorded in this volume
that induced the Government to send out the great Expedition now
launched under the scientific guidance of Dr. Wyville Thomson.
The Athenæum says, "Professor {Thomson's book is full of interesting matter, and is written by a master of the art of popular
exposition. It is excellently illustrated, both coloured maps and
woodcuts possessing high merit. Those who have already become
interested in dredging operations will of course make a point of
reading this work ; those who wish to be pleasantly introduced to the
subject, and rightly to appreciate the news which arrives from time
to time from the " Challenger," should not fail to seek instruction
from Professor Thomson."*

Thornton.—OLD-FASHIONED ETHICS, AND COMMON-
SENSE METAPHYSICS, with some of their Applications. By
WILLIAM THOMAS THORNTON, Author of "A Treatise on Labour."
8vo. 10*s.* 6*d.*

The present volume deals with problems which are agitating the minds of all thoughtful men. The following are the Contents:— I. Ante-Utilitarianism. II. History's Scientific Pretensions. III. David Hume as a Metaphysician. IV. Huxleyism. V. Recent Phases of Scientific Atheism. VI. Limits of Demonstrable Theism.

Thudichum and Dupré.—A TREATISE ON THE ORIGIN, NATURE, AND VARIETIES OF WINE.

Being a Complete Manual of Viticulture and Œnology. By J. L. W. THUDICHUM, M.D., and AUGUST DUPRÉ, Ph.D., Lecturer on Chemistry at Westminster Hospital. Medium 8vo. cloth gilt. 25s.

*In this elaborate work the subject of the manufacture of wine is treated scientifically in minute detail, from every point of view. A chapter is devoted to the Origin and Physiology of Vines, two to the Principles of Viticulture; while other chapters treat of Vintage and Vinification, the Chemistry of Alcohol, the Acids, Ether, Sugars, and other matters occurring in wine. This introductory matter occupies the first nine chapters, the remaining seventeen chapters being occupied with a detailed account of the Viticulture and the Wines of the various countries of Europe, of the Atlantic Islands, of Asia, of Africa, of America, and of Australia. Besides a number of Analytical and Statistical Tables, the work is enriched with eighty-five illustrative woodcuts. "A treatise almost unique for its usefulness either to the wine-grower, the vendor, or the consumer of wine. The analyses of wine are the most complete we have yet seen, exhibiting at a glance the constituent principles of nearly all the wines known in this country."—*Wine Trade Review.

Wallace (A. R.)—CONTRIBUTIONS TO THE THEORY OF NATURAL SELECTION. A Series of Essays. By

ALFRED RUSSEL WALLACE, Author of "The Malay Archipelago," etc. Second Edition, with Corrections and Additions. Crown 8vo. 8s. 6d. (For other Works by the same Author, see CATALOGUE OF HISTORY AND TRAVELS.)

Mr. Wallace has good claims to be considered as an independent originator of the theory of natural selection. Dr. Hooker, in his address to the British Association, spoke thus of the author: "Of Mr. Wallace and his many contributions to philosophical biology it is not easy to speak without enthusiasm; for, putting *aside their great merits, he, throughout his writings, with a modesty as rare as I believe it to be unconscious, forgets his own unquestioned claim to the honour of having originated independently of Mr. Darwin, the theories which he so ably defends."* The Saturday Review *says: "He has combined an abundance of fresh and original facts with a liveliness and sagacity of reasoning which are not often displayed so effectively on so small a scale."* The Essays in this volume are:—I. "On the Law which has regulated the introduction of New Species." II. "On the Tendencies of Varieties to depart indefinitely from the Original Type." III. "Mimicry, and other Protective Resemblances among Animals." IV. "The Malayan Papilionidæ, as illustrative of the Theory of Natural Selection." V. "On Instinct in Man and Animals." VI. "The Philosophy of Birds' Nests." VII. "A Theory of Birds' Nests." VIII. "Creation by Law." IX. "The Development of Human Races under the Law of Natural Selection." X. "The Limits of Natural Selection as applied to Man."*

Warington.—THE WEEK OF CREATION; OR, THE COSMOGONY OF GENESIS CONSIDERED IN ITS RELATION TO MODERN SCIENCE. By GEORGE WARINGTON, Author of "The Historic Character of the Pentateuch Vindicated." Crown 8vo. 4s. 6d.

The greater part of this work is taken up with the teaching of the Cosmogony. Its purpose is also investigated, and a chapter is devoted to the consideration of the passage in which the difficulties occur. "A very able vindication of the Mosaic Cosmogony, by a writer who unites the advantages of a critical knowledge of the Hebrew text and of distinguished scientific attainments."— Spectator.

Wilson.—Works by the late GEORGE WILSON, M.D., F.R.S.E., Regius Professor of Technology in the University of Edinburgh :—

RELIGIO CHEMICI. With a Vignette beautifully engraved after a design by Sir NOEL PATON. Crown 8vo. 8s. 6d.

"George Wilson," says the Preface to this volume, "had it in his heart for many years to write a book corresponding to the Religio Medici *of Sir Thomas Browne, with the title* Religio Chemici. *Several of the Essays in this volume were intended to form chapters of it.*

Wilson—*continued.*

> *These fragments being in most cases like finished gems waiting to be set, some of them are now given in a collected form to his friends and the public. In living remembrance of his purpose, the name chosen by himself has been adopted, although the original design can be but very faintly represented." The Contents of the volume are:—"Chemistry and Natural Theology." "The Chemistry of the Stars; an Argument touching the Stars and their Inhabitants." "Chemical Final Causes; as illustrated by the presence of Phosphorus, Nitrogen, and Iron in the Higher Sentient Organisms." "Robert Boyle." "Wollaston." "Life and Discoveries of Dalton." "Thoughts on the Resurrection; an Address to Medical Students." "A more fascinating volume," the* Spectator *says, " has seldom fallen into our hands." The* Freeman *says: "These papers are all valuable and deeply interesting. The production of a profound thinker, a suggestive and eloquent writer, and a man whose piety and genius went hand in hand."*

THE PROGRESS OF THE TELEGRAPH. Fcap. 8vo. 1s.

> *" While a complete view of the progress of the greatest of human inventions is obtained, all its suggestions are brought out with a rare thoughtfulness, a genial humour, and an exceeding beauty of utterance."*—Nonconformist.

Wilson (Daniel.)—CALIBAN : THE MISSING LINK. By DANIEL WILSON, LL.D., Professor of History and English Literature in University College, Toronto. 8vo. 10s. 6d.

> *In the present state of the controversy as to the Origin of Man, this work of a competent scholar and critic, in which the Monster Caliban is studied from various points of view, will be of considerable interest. Besides " Caliban," the work treats of various other matters of Shakespearian interest, as " The Supernatural," " Ghosts and Witches," " Fairy Folk-Lore," " The Commentators," " The Folios." The two last chapters contain notes on " The Tempest," and " A Midsummer Night's Dream."*

Winslow.—FORCE AND NATURE : ATTRACTION AND REPULSION. The Radical Principles of Energy graphically

discussed in their Relations to Physical and Morphological Development. By C. F. WINSLOW, M.D. 8vo. 14*s.*

The author having for long investigated Nature in many directions, has ever felt unsatisfied with the physical foundations upon which some branches of science have been so long compelled to rest. The question, he believes, must have occurred to many astronomers and physicists whether some subtle principle antagonistic to attraction does not also exist as an all-pervading element in nature, and so operate as in some way to disturb the action of what is generally considered by the scientific world a unique force. The aim of the present work is to set forth this subject in its broadest aspects, and in such a manner as to invite thereto the attention of the learned. The subjects of the eleven chapters are:—I. "Space." II. "Matter." III. "Inertia, Force, and Mind." IV. "Molecules." V. "Molecular Force." VI. "Union and Inseparability of Matter and Force." VII. and VIII. "Nature and Action of Force—Attraction—Repulsion." IX. "Cosmical Repulsion." X. "Mechanical Force." XI. "Central Forces and Celestial Physics." "Deserves thoughtful and conscientious study."—Saturday Review.

Wurtz.—A HISTORY OF CHEMICAL THEORY, from the Age of Lavoisier down to the present time. By AD. WURTZ. Translated by HENRY WATTS, F.R.S. Crown 8vo. 6*s.*

" The discourse, as a résumé of chemical theory and research, unites singular luminousness and grasp. A few judicious notes are added by the translator."—Pall Mall Gazette. *" The treatment of the subject is admirable, and the translator has evidently done his duty most efficiently."*—Westminster Review.

Young.—SIMPLE PRACTICAL METHODS OF CALCULATING STRAINS ON GIRDERS, ARCHES, AND TRUSSES ; with a Supplementary Essay on Economy in Suspension Bridges. By E. W. YOUNG, Member of the Institution of Civil Engineers. 8vo. 7*s.* 6*d.*

received by the profession is a gratifying sign that Mr. Barwell's principles have made their value and their weight felt. Many pages and a number of woodcuts have been added to the Second Edition.

Corfield (Professor W. H.)—A DIGEST OF FACTS RELATING TO THE TREATMENT AND UTILIZATION OF SEWAGE. By W. H. CORFIELD, M.A., B.A., Professor of Hygiene and Public Health at University College, London. 8vo. 10s. 6d. Second Edition, corrected and enlarged.

The author in the Second Edition has revised and corrected the entire work, and made many important additions. The headings of the eleven chapters are as follow:—I. "Early Systems: Midden-Heaps and Cesspools." II. "Filth and Disease — Cause and Effect." III. "Improved Midden-Pits and Cesspools; Midden-Closets, Pail-Closets, etc." IV. "The Dry-Closet Systems." V. "Water-Closets." VI. "Sewerage." VII. "Sanitary Aspects of the Water-Carrying System." VIII. "Value of Sewage; Injury to Rivers." IX. "Town Sewage; Attempts at Utilisation." X. "Filtration and Irrigation." XI. "Influence of Sewage Farming on the Public Health." An abridged account of the more recently published researches on the subject will be found in the Appendices, while the Summary contains a concise statement of the views which the author himself has been led to adopt: references have been inserted throughout to show from what sources the numerous quotations have been derived, and an Index has been added. "Mr. Corfield's work is entitled to rank as a standard authority, no less than a convenient handbook, in all matters relating to sewage."—Athenæum.

Elam (C.)—A PHYSICIAN'S PROBLEMS. By CHARLES ELAM, M.D., M.R.C.P. Crown 8vo. 9s.

CONTENTS :—" *Natural Heritage." " On Degeneration in Man." " On Moral and Criminal Epidemics." "Body v. Mind." "Illusions and Hallucinations." "On Somnambulism." "Reverie and Abstraction." These Essays are intended as a contribution to the Natural History of those outlying regions of Thought and Action whose domain is the debatable ground of Brain, Nerve, and Mind. They are designed also to indicate the origin and mode of perpetuation of those varieties of organization, intelligence, and general tendencies towards vice or virtue, which seem to be so*

*capriciously developed among mankind. They also point to causes
for the infinitely varied forms of disorder of nerve and brain—
organic and functional—far deeper and more recondite than those
generally believed in. " The book is one which all statesmen,
magistrates, clergymen, medical men, and parents should study and
inwardly digest."—*Examiner.

Fox.—Works by WILSON FOX, M.D. Lond., F.R.C.P., F.R.S.,
Holme Professor of Clinical Medicine, University College, London,
Physician Extraordinary to her Majesty the Queen, etc. :—

DISEASES OF THE STOMACH : being a new and revised
Edition of "THE DIAGNOSIS AND TREATMENT OF THE
VARIETIES OF DYSPEPSIA." 8vo. 8s. 6d.

ON THE ARTIFICIAL PRODUCTION OF TUBERCLE IN
THE LOWER ANIMALS. With Coloured Plates. 4to. 5s. 6d.

*In this Lecture Dr. Fox describes in minute detail a large number of
experiments made by him on guinea-pigs and rabbits for the purpose of inquiring into the origin of Tubercle by the agency of direct
irritation or by septic matters. The work is illustrated by three
plates, containing a number of coloured illustrations from nature.*

ON THE TREATMENT OF HYPERPYREXIA, as Illustrated
in Acute Articular Rheumatism by means of the External Application of Cold. 8vo. 2s. 6d.

*The object of this work is to show that the class of cases included under
the title, and which have hitherto been invariably fatal, may, by
the use of the cold bath, be brought to a favourable termination.
Details are given of the successful treatment by this method of two
patients by the author, followed by a Commentary on the cases, in
which the merits of this mode of treatment are discussed and compared with those of other methods. Appended are tables of the
observations made on the temperature during the treatment; a table
showing the effect of the immersion of the patients in the baths employed, in order to exhibit the rate at which the temperature was
lowered in each case; a table of the chief details of twenty-two
cases of this class recently published, and which are referred to in
various parts of the Commentary. Two Charts are also introduced,*

giving a connected view of the progress of the two successful cases, and a series of sphygmographic tracings of the pulses of the two patients. "*A clinical study of rare value. Should be read by everyone.*"—Medical Press and Circular.

Galton (D.)—AN ADDRESS ON THE GENERAL PRIN-CIPLES WHICH SHOULD BE OBSERVED IN THE CONSTRUCTION OF HOSPITALS. Delivered to the British Medical Association at Leeds, July 1869. By DOUGLAS GALTON, C.B., F.R.S. Crown 8vo. 3s. 6d.

In this Address the author endeavours to enunciate what are those principles which seem to him to form the starting-point from which all architects should proceed in the construction of hospitals. Besides Mr. Galton's paper the book contains the opinions expressed in the subsequent discussion by several eminent medical men, such as Dr. Kennedy, Sir James Y. Simpson, Dr. Hughes Bennet, and others. The work is illustrated by a number of plans, sections, and other cuts. "*An admirable exposition of those conditions of structure which most conduce to cleanliness, economy, and convenience.*" —Times.

Harley (J.)—THE OLD VEGETABLE NEUROTICS, Hemlock, Opium, Belladonna, and Henbane; their Physiological Action and Therapeutical Use, alone and in combination. Being the Gulstonian Lectures of 1868 extended, and including a Complete Examination of the Active Constituents of Opium. By JOHN HARLEY, M.D. Lond., F.R.C.P., F.L.S., etc. 8vo. 12s.

The author's object throughout the investigations and experiments on which this volume is founded has been to ascertain, clearly and definitely, the action of the drugs employed on the healthy body in medicinal doses, from the smallest to the largest; to deduce simple practical conclusions from the facts observed; and then to apply the drug to the relief of the particular conditions to which its action appeared suited. Many experiments have been made by the author both on men and the lower animals; and the author's endeavour has been to present to the mind, as far as words may do, impressions of the actual condition of the individual subjected to the drug.

Hood (Wharton).—ON BONE-SETTING (so called), and its Relation to the Treatment of Joints Crippled by Injury, Rheumatism, Inflammation, etc. etc. By WHARTON P. HOOD, M.D., M.R.C.S. Crown 8vo. 4s. 6d.

The author for a period attended the London practice of the late Mr. Hutton, the famous and successful bone-setter, by whom he was initiated into the mystery of the art and practice. Thus he is amply qualified to write on the subject from the practical point of view, while his professional education enables him to consider it in its scientific and surgical bearings. In the present work he gives a brief account of the salient features of a bone-setter's method of procedure in the treatment of damaged joints, of the results of that treatment, and of the class of cases in which he has seen it prove successful. The author's aim is to give the rationale of the bone-setter's practice, to reduce it to something like a scientific method, to show when force should be resorted to and when it should not, and to initiate surgeons into the secret of Mr. Hutton's successful manipulation. Throughout the work a great number of authentic instances of successful treatment are given, with the details of the method of cure; and the Chapters on Manipulations and Affections of the Spine are illustrated by a number of appropriate cuts.

Humphry.—Works by G. M. HUMPHRY, M.D., F.R.S., Professor of Anatomy in the University of Cambridge, and Honorary Fellow of Downing College :—

THE HUMAN SKELETON (including the Joints). With 260 Illustrations, drawn from nature. Medium 8vo. 28s.

In lecturing on the Skeleton it has been the author's practice, instead of giving a detailed account of the several parts, to request his students to get up the descriptive anatomy of certain bones, with the aid of some work on osteology. He afterwards tested their acquirements by examination, endeavouring to supply deficiencies and correct errors, adding also such information—physical, physiological, pathological, and practical—as he had gathered from his own observation and researches, and which was likely to be useful and excite an interest in the subject. This additional information forms, in great part, the material of this volume, which is intended to be supplementary to existing works on anatomy. Considerable space has been devoted to the description of the joints, because it is less fully given in other works, and because an accurate knowledge

Humphry—*continued.*

of the structure and peculiar form of the joints is essential to a correct knowledge of their movements. The numerous illustrations were all drawn upon stone from nature; and in most instances from specimens prepared for the purpose by the author himself.

OBSERVATIONS IN MYOLOGY. 8vo. 6s.

This work includes the Myology of Cryptobranch, Lepidosiren, Dog-Fish, Ceratodus, and Pseudopus Pallasii, with the Nerves of Cryptobranch and Lepidosiren and the Disposition of Muscles in Vertebrate Animals. The volume contains a large number of illustrations.

Huxley's Physiology.—See p. 27, preceding.

Journal of Anatomy and Physiology.

Conducted by Professors HUMPHRY and NEWTON, and Mr. CLARK of Cambridge, Professor TURNER of Edinburgh, and Dr. WRIGHT of Dublin. Published twice a year. Old Series, Parts I. and II., price 7s. 6d. each. Vol. I. containing Parts I. and II., Royal 8vo., 16s. New Series, Parts I. to IX. 6s. each, or yearly Vols. 12s. 6d. each.

Leishman.—A SYSTEM OF MIDWIFERY, including the Diseases of Pregnancy and the Puerperal State. By WILLIAM LEISHMAN, M.D., Regius Professor of Midwifery in the University of Glasgow; Physician to the University Lying-in Hospital; Fellow and late Vice-President of the Obstetrical Society of London, etc. etc. 8vo. Illustrated. 30s.

The author's object in this work has been to furnish to students and practitioners a complete system of the Midwifery of the present day. There exists no text-book in English which can be compared with those of Cazeaux and Scauzoni; this want the author has endeavoured to supply by the publication of the present work, in writing which he has availed himself of all the most recent researches. The work is profusely illustrated.

Lankester.—COMPARATIVE LONGEVITY IN MAN AND THE LOWER ANIMALS. By E. RAY LANKESTER, B.A. Crown 8vo. 4s. 6d.

This Essay gained the prize offered by the University of Oxford for the best Paper on the subject of which it treats. This interesting subject is here treated in a thorough manner, both scientifically and statistically.

Maclaren.—TRAINING, IN THEORY AND PRACTICE.

By ARCHIBALD MACLAREN, the Gymnasium, Oxford. 8vo. Handsomely bound in cloth, 7s. 6d.

The ordinary agents of health are Exercise, Diet, Sleep, Air, Bathing, and Clothing. In this work the author examines each of these agents in detail, and from two different points of view. First, as to the manner in which it is, or should be, administered under ordinary circumstances : and secondly, in what manner and to what extent this mode of administration is, or should be, altered for purposes of training ; the object of "training," according to the author, being " to put the body, with extreme and exceptional care, under the influence of all the agents which promote its health and strength, in order to enable it to meet extreme and exceptional demands upon its energies." Appended are various diagrams and tables relating to boat-racing, and tables connected with diet and training. " The philosophy of human health has seldom received so apt an exposition."—Globe. "After all the nonsense that has been written about training, it is a comfort to get hold of a thoroughly sensible book at last."—John Bull.

Macpherson.—Works by JOHN MACPHERSON, M.D. :—

THE BATHS AND WELLS OF EUROPE ; Their Action and Uses. With Notices of Climatic Resorts and Diet Cures. With a Map. New Edition, revised and enlarged. Extra fcap. 8vo. 6s. 6d.

This work is intended to supply information which will afford aid in the selection of such Spas as are suited for particular cases. It exhibits a sketch of the present condition of our knowledge on the subject of the operation of mineral waters, gathered from the author's personal observation, and from every other available source of information. It is divided into four books, and each book into several chapters :—Book I. Elements of Treatment, in which, among other matters, the external and internal uses of water are treated of. II. Bathing, treating of the various kinds of baths. III. Wells, treating of the various kinds of mineral waters.

Macpherson (J.)—*continued.*

IV. Diet Cures, in which various vegetable, milk, and other "cures" are discussed. Appended is an Index of Diseases noticed, and one of places named. Prefixed is a sketch map of the principal baths and places of health-resort in Europe. "Dr. Macpherson has given the kind of information which every medical practitioner ought to possess."—The Lancet. *" Whoever wants to know the real character of any health-resort must read Dr. Macpherson's book."*—Medical Times.

OUR BATHS AND WELLS : The Mineral Waters of the British Islands, with a List of Sea-bathing Places. Extra fcap. 8vo. pp. xv. 205. 3*s*. 6*d*.

Dr. Macpherson has divided his work into five parts. He begins by a few introductory observations on bath life, its circumstances, uses, and pleasures ; he then explains in detail the composition of the various mineral waters, and points out the special curative properties of each class. A chapter on "The History of British Wells" from the earliest period to the present time forms the natural transition to the second part of this volume, which treats of the different kinds of mineral waters in England, whether pure, thermal and earthy, saline, chalybeate, or sulphur. Wales, Scotland, and Ireland supply the materials for distinct sections. An Index of mineral waters, one of sea-bathing places, and a third of wells of pure or nearly pure water, terminate the book. "This little volume forms a very available handbook for a large class of invalids."—Nonconformist.

Maudsley.—Works by HENRY MAUDSLEY, M.D., Professor of Medical Jurisprudence in University College, London :—

BODY AND MIND : An Inquiry into their Connection and Mutual Influence, specially in reference to Mental Disorders ; being the Gulstonian Lectures for 1870. Delivered before the Royal College of Physicians. Crown 8vo. 5*s*. New Edition, with Psychological Essays added. Crown 8vo. 6*s*. 6*d*.

The volume consists of three Lectures and two long Appendices, the general plan of the whole being to bring Man, both in his physical and mental relations, as much as possible under the scope of scientific inquiry. The first Lecture is devoted to an exposition of the physical

Maudsley (H.)—*continued.*

conditions of mental function in health. In the second Lecture are sketched the features of some forms of degeneracy of mind, as exhibited in morbid varieties of the human kind, with the purpose of bringing prominently into notice the operation of physical causes from generation to generation, and the relationship of mental to other diseases of the nervous system. In the third Lecture are displayed the relations of morbid states of the body and disordered mental function. Appendix I. is a criticism of the Archbishop of York's address on "The Limits of Philosophical Inquiry." Appendix II. deals with the "Theory of Vitality," in which the author endeavours to set forth the reflections which facts seem to warrant.

THE PHYSIOLOGY AND PATHOLOGY OF MIND. Second Edition, Revised. 8vo. 16s.

This work is the result of an endeavour on the author's part to arrive at some definite conviction with regard to the physical conditions of mental function, and the relation of the phenomena of sound and unsound mind. The author's aim throughout has been twofold : I. To treat of mental phenomena from a physiological rather than from a metaphysical point of view. II. To bring the manifold instructive instances presented by the unsound mind to bear upon the interpretation of the obscure problems of mental science.

Morgan.—UNIVERSITY OARS : Being a Critical Enquiry into the After-health of the Men who rowed in the Oxford and Cambridge Boat-Race, from the year 1829 to 1869, based upon the personal experience of the Rowers themselves. By JOHN E. MORGAN, M.D., M.A. Oxon., F.R.C.P., late Captain of the John + (Coll. Univ.), Physician to the Manchester Royal Infirmary, author of " The Deterioration of Races," etc. Crown 8vo. 10s. 6d.

" *Dr. Morgan's book presents in a most admirable manner full and accurate statistics of the duration of life, and of the causes of death, of all the men who have rowed in Oxford and Cambridge boats from 1829 to 1869, and also gives letters addressed to the author by nearly every individual of the number.*"—Daily News.

Practitioner (The).—A Monthly Journal of Therapeutics
and Public Health. Edited by FRANCIS E. ANSTIE, M.D.
8vo. Price 1s. 6d. Half-yearly vols., 8vo. cloth. 10s. 6d. each.

Radcliffe.—DYNAMICS OF NERVE AND MUSCLE. By
CHARLES BLAND RADCLIFFE, M.D., F.R.C.P., Physician to the
Westminster Hospital, and to the National Hospital for the
Paralysed and Epileptic. Crown 8vo. 8s. 6d.

> *This work contains the result of the author's long investigations into
> the Dynamics of Nerve and Muscle, as connected with Animal Elec-
> tricity. He endeavours to show from these researches that the state
> of action in nerve and muscle, instead of being a manifestation of
> vitality, must be brought under the domain of physical law in order
> to be intelligible, and that a different meaning, also based upon pure
> physics, must be attached to the state of rest.*

Reynolds (J. R.)—A SYSTEM OF MEDICINE. Vol. I.
Edited by J. RUSSELL REYNOLDS, M.D., F.R.C.P. London.
Second Edition. 8vo. 25s.

> *" It is the best Cyclopædia of medicine of the time."*—Medical Press.
>
> *Part I. General Diseases, or Affections of the Whole System.
> § I.—Those determined by agents operating from without, such as
> the exanthemata, malarial diseases, and their allies. § II.—Those
> determined by conditions existing within the body, such as Gout,
> Rheumatism, Rickets, etc. Part II. Local Diseases, or Affections
> of particular Systems. § I.—Diseases of the Skin.*

A SYSTEM OF MEDICINE. Vol. II. Second Edition. 8vo.
25s.

> *Part II. Local Diseases (continued). § I.—Diseases of the Nervous
> System. A. General Nervous Diseases. B. Partial Diseases of
> the Nervous System. 1. Diseases of the Head. 2. Diseases of the
> Spinal Column. 3. Diseases of the Nerves. § II.—Diseases of
> the Digestive System. A. Diseases of the Stomach.*

A SYSTEM OF MEDICINE. Vol. III. 8vo. 25s.

> *Part II. Local Diseases (continued). § II. Diseases of the Digestive
> System (continued). B. Diseases of the Mouth. C. Diseases of*

the Fauces, Pharynx, and Œsophagus. D. Diseases of the In-
testines. E. Diseases of the Peritoneum. F. Diseases of the
Liver. G. Diseases of the Pancreas. § III.—Diseases of the
Respiratory System. A. Diseases of the Larynx. B. Diseases of
the Thoracic Organs.

Reynolds (O.)—SEWER GAS, AND HOW TO KEEP IT
OUT OF HOUSES. A Handbook on House Drainage. By
OSBORNE REYNOLDS, M.A., Professor of Engineering at Owens
College, Manchester, Fellow of Queen's College, Cambridge.
Second Edition. Crown 8vo. cloth. 1s. 6d.

The author's chief object in writing on this subject is to suggest a plan
for preventing the evil which has been causing so much alarm since
the recent illness of the Prince of Wales—viz. the back-flow of gas
into our houses. Of the plan he here suggests, he has now had
four years' experience, and has, without exception, found it to answer
perfectly. He applied it to his own house, a house of the ordinary
type drained into a foul sewer, at a cost of about fifty shillings.
Before the introduction of the new plan it was never free from smells;
while since, there has been no annoyance of the kind, nor have the
drains required any attention whatever. The plan is very simple
and can be applied to any house without requiring the inside drains
to be disturbed. Besides fully explaining the plan and showing its
application by means of illustrations, the author throws out sug-
gestions with regard to drainage generally which many will find
to be very valuable. "Professor Reynolds' admirable pamphlet will
a thousand times over repay its cost and the reader's most attentive
perusal."—Mechanics' Magazine.

Rolleston.—THE HARVEIAN ORATION, 1873. By GEORGE
ROLLESTON, M.D., F.R.S., Linacre Professor of Anatomy and
Physiology, and Fellow of Merton College, in the University of
Oxford. Crown 8vo. 2s. 6d.

In this Lecture the author expounds certain advances recently made
in our knowledge of the anatomy and physiology of the circulatory
organs, and gives the as yet unrecorded history of one of the many
attempts to rob Harvey of the glory of the great discovery.

Seaton.—A HANDBOOK OF VACCINATION. By EDWARD C. SEATON, M.D., Medical Inspector to the Privy Council. Extra fcap. 8vo. 8s. 6d.

The author's object in putting forth this work is twofold: First, to provide a text-book on the science and practice of Vaccination for the use of younger practitioners and of medical students ; secondly, to give what assistance he could to those engaged in the administration of the system of Public Vaccination established in England. For many years past, from the nature of his office, Dr. Seaton has had constant intercourse in reference to the subject of Vaccination, with medical men who are interested in it, and especially with that large part of the profession who are engaged as Public Vaccinators. All the varieties of pocks, both in men and the lower animals, are treated of in detail, and much valuable information given on all points connected with lymph, and minute instructions as to the niceties and cautions which so greatly influence success in Vaccination. The administrative sections of the work will be of interest and value, not only to medical practitioners, but to many others to whom a right understanding of the principles on which a system of Public Vaccination should be based is indispensable.

Symonds (J. A., M.D.)—MISCELLANIES. By JOHN ADDINGTON SYMONDS, M.D. Selected and Edited, with an Introductory Memoir, by his Son. 8vo. 7s. 6d.

*The late Dr. Symonds of Bristol was a man of a singularly versatile and elegant as well as powerful and scientific intellect. In order to make this selection from his many works generally interesting, the editor has confined himself to works of pure literature, and to such scientific studies as had a general philosophical or social interest. Among the general subjects are articles on "the Principles of Beauty," on "Knowledge," and a "Life of Dr. Prichard ;" among the Scientific Studies are papers on "Sleep and Dreams," "Apparitions," "the Relations between Mind and Muscle," "Habit," etc.; there are several papers on "the Social and Political Aspects of Medicine ;" and a few Poems and Translations selected from a great number of equal merit. "A collection of graceful essays on general and scientific subjects, by a very accomplished physician."—*Graphic.

WORKS ON MENTAL AND MORAL PHILOSOPHY, AND ALLIED SUBJECTS.

Aristotle.—AN INTRODUCTION TO ARISTOTLE'S RHETORIC. With Analysis, Notes, and Appendices. By E. M. COPE, Trinity College, Cambridge. 8vo. 14s.

This work is introductory to an edition of the Greek Text of Aristotle's Rhetoric, which is in course of preparation. Its object is to render that treatise thoroughly intelligible. The author has aimed to illustrate, as preparatory to the detailed explanation of the work, the general bearings and relations of the Art of Rhetoric in itself, as well as the special mode of treating it adopted by Aristotle in his peculiar system. The evidence upon obscure or doubtful questions connected with the subject is examined; and the relations which Rhetoric bears, in Aristotle's view, to the kindred art of Logic are fully considered. A connected Analysis of the work is given, and a few important matters are separately discussed in Appendices. There is added, as a general Appendix, by way of specimen of the antagonistic system of Isocrates and others, a complete analysis of the treatise called 'Ρητορικὴ πρὸς 'Αλέξανδρον, with a discussion of its authorship and of the probable results of its teaching.

ARISTOTLE ON FALLACIES; OR, THE SOPHISTICI ELENCHI. With a Translation and Notes by EDWARD POSTE, M.A., Fellow of Oriel College, Oxford. 8vo. 8s. 6d.

Besides the doctrine of Fallacies, Aristotle offers, either in this treatise or in other passages quoted in the Commentary, various glances over the world of science and opinion, various suggestions or pro- blems which are still agitated, and a vivid picture of the ancient system of dialectics, which it is hoped may be found both interesting and instructive. "*It will be an assistance to genuine students of Aristotle.*"—Guardian. "*It is indeed a work of great skill.*"—Saturday Review.

Birks.—FIRST PRINCIPLES OF MORAL SCIENCE; Or, a First Course of Lectures delivered in the University of Cambridge. By the Rev. T. R. BIRKS, Professor of Moral Philosophy. Crown 8vo. 8s. 6d.

Boole. — AN INVESTIGATION OF THE LAWS OF THOUGHT, ON WHICH ARE FOUNDED THE MATHEMATICAL THEORIES OF LOGIC AND PROBABILITIES. By GEORGE BOOLE, LL.D., Professor of Mathematics in the Queen's University, Ireland, &c. 8vo. 14s.

The design of this treatise is to investigate the fundamental laws of those operations of the mind by which reasoning is performed; to give expression to them in the symbolical language of a Calculus, and upon this foundation to establish the science of Logic and construct its method; to make that method itself the basis of a general method for the application of the mathematical doctrine of Probabilities; and, finally, to collect from the various elements of truth brought to view in the course of these inquiries some probable intimations concerning the nature and construction of the human mind. The problem is one of the highest interest, and no one is better able than Professor Boole to treat of this side of it at any rate.

Butler (W. A.), Late Professor of Moral Philosophy in the University of Dublin:—

LECTURES ON THE HISTORY OF ANCIENT PHILOSOPHY. Edited from the Author's MSS., with Notes, by WILLIAM HEPWORTH THOMPSON, M.A., Master of Trinity College, and Regius Professor of Greek in the University of Cambridge. Two Volumes. 8vo. 1l. 5s.

These Lectures consist of an Introductory Series on the Science of Mind generally, and five other Series on Ancient Philosophy, the greater part of which treat of Plato and the Platonists, the Fifth Series being an unfinished course on the Psychology of Aristotle, containing an able Analysis of the well known though by no means well

Butler (W. A.)—*continued.*

understood Treatise, περὶ ψυχῆς. *These Lectures are the result of patient and conscientious examination of the original documents, and may be considered as a perfectly independent contribution to our knowledge of the great master of Grecian wisdom. The author's intimate familiarity with the metaphysical writings of the last century, and especially with the English and Scotch School of Psychologists, has enabled him to illustrate the subtle speculations of which he treats in a manner calculated to render them more intelligible to the English mind than they can be by writers trained solely in the technicalities of modern German schools. The editor has verified all the references, and added valuable Notes, in which he points out sources of more complete information. The Lectures constitute a History of the Platonic Philosophy—its seed-time, maturity, and decay.*

SERMONS AND LETTERS ON ROMANISM.—See THEO-
LOGICAL CATALOGUE.

Calderwood.—Works by the Rev. HENRY CALDERWOOD, M.A., LL.D., Professor of Moral Philosophy in the University of Edinburgh :—

PHILOSOPHY OF THE INFINITE: A Treatise on Man's Knowledge of the Infinite Being, in answer to Sir W. Hamilton and Dr. Mansel. Cheaper Edition. 8vo. 7s. 6d.

The purpose of this volume is, by a careful analysis of consciousness, to prove, in opposition to Sir W. Hamilton and Mr. Mansel, that man possesses a notion of an Infinite Being, and to ascertain the peculiar nature of the conception and the particular relations in which it is found to arise. The province of Faith as related to that of Knowledge, and the characteristics of Knowledge and Thought as bearing on this subject, are examined; and separate chapters are devoted to the consideration of our knowledge of the Infinite as First Cause, as Moral Governor, and as the Object of Worship. "*A book of great ability . . . . written in a clear style, and may be easily understood by even those who are not versed in such discussions.*"—British Quarterly Review.

A HANDBOOK OF MORAL PHILOSOPHY. Second Edition. Crown 8vo. 6s.

" It is, we feel convinced, the best handbook on the subject, intellectually and morally, and does infinite credit to its author."—Standard.

Elam.—A PHYSICIAN'S PROBLEMS. — See MEDICAL CATALOGUE, preceding.

Galton (Francis).—HEREDITARY GENIUS : An Inquiry into its Laws and Consequences. See PHYSICAL SCIENCE CATALOGUE, preceding.

Green (J. H.)—SPIRITUAL PHILOSOPHY : Founded on the Teaching of the late SAMUEL TAYLOR COLERIDGE. By the late JOSEPH HENRY GREEN, F.R.S., D.C.L. Edited, with a Memoir of the Author's Life, by JOHN SIMON, F.R.S., Medical Officer of Her Majesty's Privy Council, and Surgeon to St. Thomas's Hospital. Two Vols. 8vo. 25s.

The late Mr. Green, the eminent surgeon, was for many years the intimate friend and disciple of Coleridge, and an ardent student of philosophy. The language of Coleridge's will imposed on Mr. Green the obligation of devoting, so far as necessary, the remainder of his life to the one task of systematising, developing, and establishing the doctrines of the Coleridgian philosophy. With the assistance of Coleridge's manuscripts, but especially from the knowledge he possessed of Coleridge's doctrines, and independent study of at least the basal principles and metaphysics of the sciences and of all the phenomena of human life, he proceeded logically to work out a system of universal philosophy such as he deemed would in the main accord with his master's aspirations. After many years of preparatory labour he resolved to complete in a compendious form a work which should give in system the doctrines most distinctly Coleridgian. The result is these two volumes. The first volume is devoted to the general principles of philosophy; the second aims at vindicating à priori (on principles for which the first volume has contended) the essential doctrines of Christianity. The work is divided into four parts: I. "On the Intellectual Faculties and processes which are concerned in the Investigation of Truth." II. "Of First Principles in Philosophy." III. "Truths of Religion." IV. "The Idea of Christianity in relation to Controversial Philosophy."

Huxley (Professor.)—LAY SERMONS, ADDRESSES, AND REVIEWS. See PHYSICAL SCIENCE CATALOGUE, preceding.

Jevons.—Works by W. STANLEY JEVONS, M.A., Professor of Logic in Owens College, Manchester :—

THE SUBSTITUTION OF SIMILARS, the True Principle of Reasoning. Derived from a Modification of Aristotle's Dictum. Fcap. 8vo. 2s. 6d.

"All acts of reasoning," the author says, " seem to me to be different cases of one uniform process, which may perhaps be best described as the substitution of similars. This phrase clearly expresses that familiar mode in which we continually argue by analogy from like to like, and take one thing as a representative of another. The chief difficulty consists in showing that all the forms of the old logic, as well as the fundamental rules of mathematical reasoning, may be explained upon the same principle; and it is to this difficult task I have devoted the most attention. Should my notion be true, a vast mass of technicalities may be swept from our logical text-books and yet the small remaining part of logical doctrine will prove far more useful than all the learning of the Schoolmen." Prefixed is a plan of a new reasoning machine, the Logical Abacus, *the construction and working of which is fully explained in the text and Appendix. " Mr. Jevons' book is very clear and intelligible, and quite worth consulting."*—Guardian.

Maccoll.—THE GREEK SCEPTICS, from Pyrrho to Sextus. An Essay which obtained the Hare Prize in the year 1868. By NORMAN MACCOLL, B.A., Scholar of Downing College, Cambridge. . Crown 8vo. 3s. 6d.

This Essay consists of five parts: I. "Introduction." II. "Pyrrho and Timon." III. "The New Academy." IV. "The Later Sceptics." V. " The Pyrrhoneans and New Academy contrasted."—" Mr. Maccoll has produced a monograph which merits the gratitude of all students of philosophy. His style is clear and vigorous; he has mastered the authorities, and criticises them in a modest but independent spirit."—Pall Mall Gazette.

M'Cosh.—Works by JAMES M'COSH, LL.D., President of Princeton College, New Jersey, U.S.

> "*He certainly shows himself skilful in that application of logic to psychology, in that inductive science of the human mind which is the fine side of English philosophy. His philosophy as a whole is worthy of attention.*"—Revue de Deux Mondes.

THE METHOD OF THE DIVINE GOVERNMENT, Physical and Moral. Tenth Edition. 8vo. 10*s.* 6*d.*

> *This work is divided into four books. The first presents a general view of the Divine Government as fitted to throw light on the character of God; the second deals with the method of the Divine Government in the physical world; the third treats of the principles of the human mind through which God governs mankind; and the fourth is on Pastoral and Revealed Religion, and the Restoration of Man. An Appendix, consisting of seven articles, investigates the fundamental principles which underlie the speculations of the treatise.* "*This work is distinguished from other similar ones by its being based upon a thorough study of physical science, and an accurate knowledge of its present condition, and by its entering in a deeper and more unfettered manner than its predecessors upon the discussion of the appropriate psychological, ethical, and theological questions. The author keeps aloof at once from the* à priori *idealism and dreaminess of German speculation since Schelling, and from the onesidedness and narrowness of the empiricism and positivism which have so prevailed in England.*"—Dr. Ulrici, in "Zeitschrift für Philosophie."

THE INTUITIONS OF THE MIND. A New Edition. 8vo. cloth. 10*s.* 6*d.*

> *The object of this treatise is to determine the true nature of Intuition, and to investigate its laws. It starts with a general view of intuitive convictions, their character and the method in which they are employed, and passes on to a more detailed examination of them, treating them under the various heads of "Primitive Cognitions," "Primitive Beliefs," "Primitive Judgments," and "Moral Convictions." Their relations to the various sciences, mental and physical, are then examined. Collateral criticisms are thrown into preliminary and supplementary chapters and sections.* "*The undertaking to adjust the claims of the sensational and intuitional*

M'Cosh (J.)—*continued.*

·*philosophies, and of the* à posteriori *and* à priori *methods, is accomplished in this work with a great amount of success.*"— Westminster Review. "*I value it for its large acquaintance with English Philosophy, which has not led him to neglect the great German works. I admire the moderation and clearness, as well as comprehensiveness, of the author's views.*"—Dr. Dörner, of Berlin.

AN EXAMINATION OF MR. J. S. MILL'S PHILOSOPHY: Being a Defence of Fundamental Truth. Crown 8vo. 7*s*. 6*d*.

This volume is not put forth by its author as a special reply to Mr. Mill's "Examination of Sir William Hamilton's Philosophy." In that work Mr. Mill has furnished the means of thoroughly estimating his theory of mind, of which he had only given hints and glimpses in his logical treatise. It is this theory which Dr. M'Cosh professes to examine in this volume; his aim is simply to defend a portion of primary truth which has been assailed by an acute thinker who has extensive influence in England. "In such points as Mr. Mill's notions of intuitions and necessity, he will have the voice of mankind with him."—Athenæum. "*Such a work greatly needed to be done, and the author was the man to do it. This volume is important, not merely in reference to the views of Mr. Mill, but of the whole school of writers, past and present, British and Continental, he so ably represents.*"—Princeton Review.

THE LAWS OF DISCURSIVE THOUGHT: Being a Text-book of Formal Logic. Crown 8vo. 5*s*.

The main feature of this Logical Treatise is to be found in the more thorough investigation of the nature of the notion, in regard to which the views of the school of Locke and Whately are regarded by the author as very defective, and the views of the school of Kant and Hamilton altogether erroneous. The author believes that errors spring far more frequently from obscure, inadequate, indistinct, and confused Notions, and from not placing the Notions in their proper relation in judgment, than from Ratiocination. In this treatise, therefore, the Notion (with the term, and the Relation of Thought to Language) will be found to occupy a larger relative place than in any logical work written since the time of the famous

M'Cosh (J.)—*continued.*

Art of Thinking. "*The amount of summarised information which it contains is very great; and it is the only work on the very important subject with which it deals. Never was such a work so much needed as in the present day.*"—London Quarterly Review.

CHRISTIANITY AND POSITIVISM : A Series of Lectures to the Times on Natural Theology and Apologetics. Crown 8vo. 7s. 6d.

These Lectures were delivered in New York, by appointment, in the beginning of 1871, as the second course on the foundation of the Union Theological Seminary. There are ten Lectures in all, divided into three series :—I. "Christianity and Physical Science" (three lectures). II. "Christianity and Mental Science" (four lectures). III. "Christianity and Historical Investigation" (three lectures). The Appendix contains articles on "Gaps in the Theory of Development;" "Darwin's Descent of Man ;" "Principles of Herbert Spencer's Philosophy." In the course of the Lectures Dr. M'Cosh discusses all the most important scientific problems which are supposed to affect Christianity.

Masson.—RECENT BRITISH PHILOSOPHY : A Review, with Criticisms ; including some Comments on Mr. Mill's Answer to Sir William Hamilton. By DAVID MASSON, M.A., Professor of Rhetoric and English Literature in the University of Edinburgh. Crown 8vo. 6s.

The author, in his usual graphic and forcible manner, reviews in considerable detail, and points out the drifts of the philosophical speculations of the previous thirty years, bringing under notice the work of all the principal philosophers who have been at work during that period on the highest problems which concern humanity. The four chapters are thus titled :—I. "A Survey of Thirty Years." II. "The Traditional Differences : how repeated in Carlyle, Hamilton, and Mill." III. "Effects of Recent Scientific Conceptions on Philosophy." IV. "Latest Drifts and Groupings." The last seventy-six pages are devoted to a Review of Mr. Mill's criticism of Sir William Hamilton's Philosophy. "We can nowhere point to a work which gives so clear an exposition of

*the course of philosophical speculation in Britain during the past
century, or which indicates so instructively the mutual influences of
philosophic and scientific thought."*—Fortnightly Review.

Maurice.—Works by the Rev. FREDERICK DENISON MAURICE,
M.A., Professor of Moral Philosophy in the University of Cam-
bridge. (For other Works by the same Author, see THEOLOGICAL
CATALOGUE.)

SOCIAL MORALITY. Twenty-one Lectures delivered in the
University of Cambridge. New and Cheaper Edition. Crown 8vo.
10s. 6d.

*In this series of Lectures, Professor Maurice considers, historically
and critically, Social Morality in its three main aspects : I. "The
Relations which spring from the Family—Domestic Morality."
II. "The Relations which subsist among the various constituents
of a Nation—National Morality." III. "As it concerns Universal Humanity—Universal Morality." Appended to each series
is a chapter on "Worship:" first, "Family Worship;" second,
"National Worship;" third, "Universal Worship." "Whilst
reading it we are charmed by the freedom from exclusiveness and
prejudice, the large charity, the loftiness of thought, the eagerness to
recognize and appreciate whatever there is of real worth extant in
the world, which animates it from one end to the other. We gain
new thoughts and new ways of viewing things, even more, perhaps,
from being brought for a time under the influence of so noble and
spiritual a mind."*—Athenæum.

THE CONSCIENCE : Lectures on Casuistry, delivered in the
University of Cambridge. New and Cheaper Edition. Crown
8vo. 5s.

*In this series of nine Lectures, Professor Maurice, with his wonted
force and breadth and freshness, endeavours to settle what is meant
by the word "Conscience," and discusses the most important
questions immediately connected with the subject. Taking "Casuistry" in its old sense as being the "study of cases of Conscience,"
he endeavours to show in what way it may be brought to bear at
the present day upon the acts and thoughts of our ordinary
existence. He shows that Conscience asks for laws, not rules ;
for freedom, not chains ; for education, not suppression. He*

Maurice (F. D.)—*continued.*

has abstained from the use of philosophical terms, and has touched on philosophical systems only when he fancied "they were inter-fering with the rights and duties of wayfarers." The Saturday Review *says: "We rise from them with detestation of all that is selfish and mean, and with a living impression that there is such a thing as goodness after all."*

MORAL AND METAPHYSICAL PHILOSOPHY. New Edition and Preface. Vol. I. Ancient Philosophy and the First to the Thirteenth Centuries ; Vol. II. the Fourteenth Century and the French Revolution, with a glimpse into the Nineteenth Century. New Edition. 2 Vols. 8vo. 25*s.*

This is an Edition in two volumes of Professor Maurice's History of Philosophy from the earliest period to the present time. It was formerly scattered throughout a number of separate volumes, and it is believed that all admirers of the author and all students of philosophy will welcome this compact Edition. The subject is one of the highest importance, and it is treated here with fulness and candour, and in a clear and interesting manner. In a long intro-duction to this Edition, in the form of a dialogue, Professor Maurice justifies some of his own peculiar views, and touches upon some of the most important topics of the time.

Murphy.—THE SCIENTIFIC BASES OF FAITH. By JOSEPH JOHN MURPHY, Author of " Habit and Intelligence." 8vo. 14*s.*

" The book is not without substantial value ; the writer continues the work of the best apologists of the last century, it may be with less force and clearness, but still with commendable persuasiveness and tact ; and with an intelligent feeling for the changed conditions of the problem."—Academy.

Picton.—THE MYSTERY OF MATTER AND OTHER ESSAYS. By J. ALLANSON PICTON, Author of " New Theories and the Old Faith." Crown 8vo. 10*s.* 6*d.*

CONTENTS :— *The Mystery of Matter—The Philosophy of Igno-rance—The Antithesis of Faith and Sight—The Essential Nature of Religion—Christian Pantheism.*

Thring (E., M.A.)—THOUGHTS ON LIFE-SCIENCE. By EDWARD THRING, M.A. (Benjamin Place), Head Master of Uppingham School. New Edition, enlarged and revised. Crown 8vo. 7s. 6d.

In this volume are discussed in a familiar manner some of the most interesting problems between Science and Religion, Reason and Feeling. "Learning and Science," says the author, "are claiming the right of building up and pulling down everything, especially the latter. It has seemed to me no useless task to look steadily at what has happened, to take stock as it were of men's gains, and to endeavour amidst new circumstances to arrive at some rational estimate of the bearings of things, so that the limits of what is possible at all events may be clearly marked out for ordinary readers. . . . . This book is an endeavour to bring out some of the main facts of the world."

Venn.—THE LOGIC OF CHANCE: An Essay on the Foundations and Province of the Theory of Probability, with especial reference to its application to Moral and Social Science. By JOHN VENN, M.A., Fellow of Gonville and Caius College, Cambridge. Fcap. 8vo. 7s. 6d.

This Essay is in no sense mathematical. Probability, the author thinks, may be considered to be a portion of the province of Logic regarded from the material point of view. The principal objects of this Essay are to ascertain how great a portion it comprises, where we are to draw the boundary between it and the contiguous branches of the general science of evidence, what are the ultimate foundations upon which its rules rest, what the nature of the evidence they are capable of affording, and to what class of subjects they may most fitly be applied. The general design of the Essay, as a special treatise on Probability, is quite original, the author believing that erroneous notions as to the real nature of the subject are disastrously prevalent. "Exceedingly well thought and well written," says the Westminster Review. *The* Nonconformist *calls it a "masterly book."*

LONDON : R. CLAY, SONS, AND TAYLOR, PRINTERS, BREAD STREET HILL.

Milton Keynes UK
Ingram Content Group UK Ltd.
UKHW010635220124
436466UK00008B/424